Magnolia Square

Margaret Pemberton

CORGI BOOKS

MAGNOLIA SQUARE
A CORGI BOOK : 0 552 14124 0

First publication in Great Britain

PRINTING HISTORY
Corgi edition published 1996

Set in 10pt Linotype Plantin by
County Typesetters, Margate, Kent

Corgi Books are published by Transworld Publishers Ltd,
61–63 Uxbridge Road, London W5 5SA,
in Australia by Transworld Publishers (Australia) Pty Ltd,
15–25 Helles Avenue, Moorebank, NSW 2170,
and in New Zealand by Transworld Publishers (NZ) Ltd,
3 William Pickering Drive, Albany, Auckland.

Reproduced, printed and bound in Great Britain by
Cox & Wyman Ltd, Reading, Berks.

For my daughter, Polly.

*A gypsy at heart, but a world-travelling
gypsy, who always returns to the green and
grassy corner of south-east London
which is home*

Chapter One

'Blimey,' Carrie Collins, *née* Jennings, said graphically to her best friend Kate Voigt as they escaped from the exuberant street party, paper Union Jacks on sticks still in their hands, 'have you ever known a day like it?'

'Never!' With her eyes shining, her face radiant, Kate led the way into her sun-filled kitchen, making straight for the stove and the kettle that sat on the top of it. 'The war is over, Carrie! *Over!*'

As Carrie plumped her Junoesque figure exhaustedly into the rocking-chair that sat on top of a gaily coloured rag rug, Kate carried the kettle over to the sink. 'Or it's nearly over,' she amended, turning on the tap, 'because the war in the Far East can't go on for much longer, surely?'

Outside, in the Square, the VE party was going at full throttle with 'Land of Hope and Glory' being sung with gusto by all their friends and neighbours. Carrie beat time with her Union Jack, saying with unabashed frankness, 'Bugger the Far East, Kate. All that matters to me is that no-one we know or love is still fighting. My Danny and your Leon are already home, thank God. And what's more, they're *staying* home!' The muffled strains of 'Land of Hope and Glory' merged into 'We'll Meet

Again', and she put her Union Jack down on the nearby kitchen table, the sunlight glinting on her wedding ring as she did so.

Kate sat the kettle on the gas hob and then, leaning her slender weight against the stone sink, said musingly, 'But what are they going to do for jobs, now they're home? I know your Danny's been working at the biscuit factory, but I don't suppose he wants to stay there for ever. And I'm not sure Leon will be able to go back to working on the river. Every demobbed mechant seaman in London will be looking for work as a Thames lighterman.'

Carrie didn't know what the chances were of Leon being able to return to his pre-war job, but she did know what she felt about Danny's future work prospects. 'I don't care what Danny does as long as we can be together,' she said fiercely, the radiant vivacity in her sea-green eyes replaced by passionate intensity. 'I don't want us to live like we did before the war, when he was a professional soldier and always away at Catterick or somewhere even further north, and me and Rose were at home with my mum and dad and gran. This time, whatever he does and wherever he goes, me and Rose go too.'

Kate's eyes widened in alarm. 'But you won't be going anywhere, will you, Carrie? Even if Danny gets a better job, it will be a local job, won't it?' The thought of Carrie moving away from the Square they'd both been born and brought up in, horrified her. What would she do without being able to rely on her daily chats and giggles with Carrie? Ever since she could remember, Carrie's noisy, boisterous, laughter-filled home at the bottom end of Magnolia Square had been a second home to her.

Her own home had always been happy, but it had been

quiet. Her widowed, German-born father was intellectual by inclination and introspective by nature, and in contrast to her own sedate home life, Carrie's part-Jewish, market-trader family had been a revelation to her. Leah, Carrie's gran, cooked like a dream and thrived on histrionics, indulging in them with relish. Bonzo, her dog, seemed to think barking and howling was a way of justifying his existence. Carrie's big-hearted *goy* father, Albert, was so used to hollering out his wares down Lewisham Market that he no longer seemed to know what a normal speaking voice was. 'Speak up a little louder, why don't yer,' Carrie's mother, Miriam, was always saying to him in loving sarcasm after he had bellowed some comment to her, 'they can't 'ear yer in Purfleet!'

'I don't know,' Carrie said starkly. 'Danny'll just have to take what he can get, and it might mean moving north of the river.'

Despite her alarm at the thought of Carrie moving out of the Square, a smile twitched the corners of Kate's generously shaped mouth. Like all south-east Londoners, Carrie spoke of the Thames as if it was a divide as great as the English Channel.

Kate's waist-length, wheat-gold braid of hair had fallen over her shoulder and she flicked it back, saying, 'I can imagine a lot of things, but I can't imagine living anywhere but in Magnolia Square. Where else in London is so near to both the river and high, open heathland?'

Carrie, who much preferred the hustle and bustle of Lewisham's High Street and market, to Blackheath's nearby, gorse-covered Heath, said a little indifferently, 'Nowhere, I s'pose. Are you going to brew that tea today, Kate, or wait until next week?'

With a grin, Kate returned her attention to the kettle, lifting it off the hob and scalding out the waiting teapot. She was wearing a pre-war, ice-blue cotton dress which she had frugally renovated, but the original cap sleeves and full gathered skirt made her look more like a young girl fresh from the schoolroom than a woman in her mid-twenties: a woman who, though still unmarried, was mother to three young children.

Amusement gleamed in Carrie's eyes. As a child, she'd always been the careless, harum-scarum one, the one most likely to find herself in trouble. Yet it had been quiet, well-brought-up, well-spoken Kate who had found herself literally 'in trouble' within a couple of years of leaving school.

As Kate put three caddy spoonfuls of tea into the warmed teapot, Carrie's eyes flicked to the photograph propped high on the kitchen dresser against a little-used cream-jug. Toby Harvey had been handsome – and brave. Only twenty-three, he had died engaging his Spitfire in combat with a Messerschmitt above the bloody beaches of Dunkirk. The heroic circumstances of his death had protected Kate from too much censure when Matthew had been born eight months later, and there was certainly no censure when, the Blitz at its height, she had given a home to bombed-out, orphaned, lovable little Daisy. Carrie's wry amusement deepened. No, it hadn't been Matthew's illegitimacy or her un-official fostering of Daisy that had set the cat among Magnolia Square's pigeons. It had been Kate's sub-sequent love affair with Leon Emmerson that had sent shock-waves vibrating far and wide.

'Do you want a ginger biscuit with your cup of tea, or

have you stuffed yourself to sickness point on VE party jellies and cakes?' Kate asked, breaking in on Carrie's thoughts.

'I only had *one* helping of jelly,' Carrie said defensively, 'and I never got near the cakes. Your kids and Rose and our Billy and Beryl saw to that!'

Billy and Beryl Lomax were her niece and nephew and, because her happy-go-lucky, pleasure-loving older sister hardly ever bothered to reprimand them, or keep an eye on them, they were a constant source of despair to Carrie. She said now, helping herself to a biscuit as Kate set a tin in the middle of the scrubbed wooden table, 'I don't suppose you've seen Billy's latest acquisition to his personal ammunition dump, have you? He only dragged it home this morning. God knows where he found it. It's at least four feet long and has fins on it. One of these days he's going to pilfer something that's live and the whole bloomin' Square will go up in the biggest bang since the Germans bombed the oil refineries down at Woolwich.'

Laughter bubbled up in Kate's throat. She had a soft spot for the Square's acknowledged tearaway, and whenever he embarked on one of his escapades he often did so provisioned with her home-made scones and buns.

'It's all right you laughing,' Carrie said darkly, dunking a ginger biscuit into her steaming cup of tea. 'You don't live next door to him. You'd think, now that he's thirteen, he'd be starting to show a bit more sense, but instead he's fast on the road to becoming an out and out hooligan, and it's all Mavis's fault. As a mum, that sister of mine'd make a perishin' good bus driver . . .'

'Hallooo! Anyone 'ome?' a familiar voice carolled out

in carrying tones from the front of the house and the open doorway.

Carrie raised her eyes to heaven. She loved her mother dearly, but the tart repartee they so happily indulged in was based on the mutual pretence that they drove each other to distraction.

Without bothering to wait for an answer, Miriam Jennings barrelled through into the kitchen. 'What the bleedin' 'ell are you two doin' hidin' away in 'ere when the biggest party of the century's takin' place in the Square?' she demanded cheerily, her hair still in metal curlers even though the party was at its height, a gaily patterned wraparound pinafore tied securely around her ample figure. 'Our Mavis is just about to let rip singin' a bit o' Boogie-Woogie an' she wants all the audience she can get.' She eyed the teapot with enthusiasm. 'And is that tea fresh, because if it is I'll 'ave a cuppa.'

'Yes, it is, and no, I'm not coming out to watch Mavis make an exhibition of herself,' Carrie said crossly as her mother pulled out a kitchen chair and plonked herself down on it.

As Kate obligingly took another cup and saucer down from the dresser, Miriam looked around her. Satisfying herself that no-one else was in the kitchen, she said a trifle exasperatedly, 'I thought I might have found Christina 'ere. Gawd knows where she's 'ared off to. There's been no sight or sign of 'er for the past hour.'

'Christina's a grown woman, Mum.' Carrie's hand hovered over the biscuit tin as she wondered whether, with her ever-expanding hips, she should treat herself to another biscuit. 'And she's never liked crowded get-togethers,' she continued, deciding that one more

12

couldn't possibly make much difference. 'She's probably gone off for a walk and taken Bonzo with her.'

'She ain't taken Bonzo 'cos yer dad's just 'ad to throw a bucket o' water over 'im to stop him doing rudies to Charlie Robson's Alsatian bitch.'

Kate made a choking noise. Carrie said disbelievingly, ''Ow the hell could Bonzo try to copulate with Queenie? He's only a whippet, for God's sake!'

''E might be only a whippet, but 'e's a game little bugger.' Miriam heaved her bosoms up over the edge of the table so that she could reach the biscuit tin more easily. 'An' 'owever much Christina 'ates knees-ups, you'd think she'd be the 'eart and soul of this one, wouldn't yer? She is both German *and* Jewish after all. If she doesn't want to celebrate the Nazis being thrashed into surrenderin', wot will she ever want to bloomin' celebrate?'

Neither Kate or Carrie attempted to answer her. Though they were each other's best friend, Christina was their closest other friend and, despite being their close friend, she was an enigma neither of them truly understood.

Miriam, aware that she had drawn a blank where Christina was concerned, blew on her tea to cool it, saying grudgingly, 'It's nice to 'ave five minutes' peace and quiet after all the ruckus that's goin' on outside. I told the Vicar the church bells nearly deafened me when 'e rang 'em when peace was declared and that 'e'd no need to ring 'em again, but 'e said as 'ow as St Mark's stood in the middle o' the Square, it was only right St Mark's bells should ring when the Square was 'avin' its VE party.'

One of Carrie's two tortoiseshell combs had come adrift and she pushed an unruly mass of near-black hair away from her face, re-anchoring it. 'Your eldest daughter will be doing her Billie Holiday impression by now,' she said meaningfully as she did so, 'and you did say she wanted all the audience she could get.'

'Mebbe she does, but I'm comfy now.' Miriam folded her beefy arms and rested them on the table. 'There's beer and shandy and lemonade runnin' like rivers outside, but there ain't no decent tea, not since the Vicar's lady-friend accidentally dropped a washing-up cloth into the urn.'

Carrie giggled. Her mother always knew just who had done what, when.

'And Nellie Miller from number fifteen isn't as 'appy as she could be,' Miriam continued, getting into her stride. 'She says it's all right every bugger that's been fighting in Europe and the Middle East coming 'ome, but her nephew 'Arold is a prisoner of the Japs, and she doesn't know when the 'ell 'e'll be on his way 'ome.' She crunched into a ginger biscuit. 'The Red Cross did tell 'er just after 'e was first captured that 'e was 'elping to build a railway. It always seemed rum to me.' She flicked ginger biscuit crumbs from her chest, adding in explanation, ''Arold was a milkman before he was conscripted, an' apart from going on an annual train ride to Margate, 'e knows nothin' about railways, and certainly wouldn't know 'ow to go about building one!'

Kate felt a pang of guilt. She'd been so ecstatic about Leon's release as a POW, and his return home, that she'd forgotten Nellie Miller wouldn't be similarly celebrating. 'Let's go and have a word with her,' she said to Carrie. 'It can't be very nice for her, everyone celebrating, when Harold's still a POW.'

Carrie, well aware that, if they didn't return to the street party, they'd have her mother with them for the duration, rose to her feet. 'You have a word with her. I need to make sure Danny's still keeping an eye on Rose. He seems to think that now she's started school she doesn't need watching so much, but given half a chance she'll be down by the river with Billy and getting into goodness knows what kinds of trouble.'

'Rose never gets into trouble,' Miriam said, staunchly defending her favourite grandchild. She heaved herself reluctantly to her feet. 'The trouble with you, Carrie, is that yer like to keep tabs on everyone a little too much. It wouldn't 'ave done Danny any 'arm to 'ave stayed in the Army an—'

'Can you pass me that basket, Miriam, please,' Kate interrupted hurriedly. 'I expect all the party sandwiches are gone by now and I might as well begin gathering up all the plates I loaned.'

With a full-scale shenanigans between Carrie and her mother avoided, Kate hurried them out of the house and into the flag-and-balloon-bedecked Square. Trestle tables graced the front of St Mark's. The church stood on a grassy island in the centre of the Square and both the island and the narrow road that encompassed it were thick with partying Magnolia Square residents.

A piano belonging to Carrie's mother-in-law, Hettie Collins, had been trundled out on to the pavement. Carrie's sister, Mavis Lomax, was seated on top of it, belting out a rip-roaring version of 'Boogie Woogie Bugle Boy'. Her peroxide-blonde hair piled high, Betty Grable fashion, her silk-clad, provocatively crossed legs showing an indecent amount of stocking-top.

Nellie Miller, whose enormous bulk would have made two of the ample Miriam, was sitting in the front of Mavis's appreciative audience, wedged in an armchair that had been specially wheeled out of the vicarage for her. In one hand she held a piece of string which was attached to a buoyantly floating red balloon. In the other was a slab of home-made mint and currant pasty. Ignoring the discomfort to her elephantine legs, she was tapping a foot up and down in time to Hettie's exuberant piano playing.

With not much more than crumbs and an occasional cake left on the crêpe-paper-covered trestle tables, children were no longer seated at them but running and shrieking everywhere. There was no sign of Rose, however, or Danny.

'If he's sloped off for a quiet game of billiards and taken Rose with him I'll blooming kill him!' Carrie said, fending off a big black Labrador that had bounded up to greet them.

The Labrador was Kate's and she said admonishingly as he threatened to knock both her and Carrie off their feet, 'Down, Hector! Down!'

Hector obediently sat and as he did so Kate caught sight of Leon. He was talking to Daniel Collins, Carrie's father-in-law. Their little son, Luke, was laughingly straddling his broad shoulders and clutching on to his tight, crinkly hair. Matthew was clinging to one of his hands and chattering away to him ten to the dozen, while Daisy was holding tightly on to his other hand. Kate felt her heart turn over in her chest. God, but she loved him!

16

For nearly three years he had been a prisoner of the Germans, transported to a prison camp deep in captured Russian territory after his ship had been torpedoed and sunk in Arctic waters. Unlike Nellie where Harold was concerned, she had never had any communication from either the War Office or the Red Cross, informing her that he was alive and a POW. All she had had was deep, sure, unswerving inner certainty. And what if she had been wrong? The very thought made her dizzy with horror. How would she have been able to face life if Leon had not returned to her? How would she have been able to wake and face each new day without Leon's cheery good humour; his compassion and tolerance; his tender, passionate love-making?

As if sensing the intensity of her thoughts, Leon turned his head slightly, looking directly towards her, his gold-flecked, amber-brown eyes meeting hers, his vivid, loving smile splitting his chocolate-dark face. She knew that people would be eyeing them with covert, prurient curiosity, because people always did. 'Nice' girls didn't consort with black sailors, and they certainly didn't have babies with them. Radiantly she smiled back at him, her eyes ablaze with love. Soon the street party would be over; soon the children would be bathed and in bed; soon they would be alone together and in each other's arms, loving each other as they had burned to do all through the long, lonely years of their separation.

'So who's going to be married first?' Nellie Miller called out to her. 'You an' Leon or the Vicar an' his lady-friend?'

With agonizing reluctance Kate broke eye contact with

17

the man she loved with all her heart. 'Me and Leon,' she said without a second's hesitation.

Nellie grinned, displaying a mouthful of appallingly crooked and broken teeth. 'I'm glad to 'ear it. It's about time at least one of your whipper-snappers was made legit.'

Kate crossed over to Nellie's shabby armchair and perched on the arm. 'They're both going to be legitimized,' she said as Hettie began playing a conga, and the throng around them exuberantly pushed and pulled themselves into a long conga line. 'The minute we're married, Leon's going to adopt Matthew and we're both going to apply to adopt Daisy. With a little luck, by the end of the year we'll be an ordinary family.'

Nellie looked across to where Leon was again talking to Daniel Collins, the children swarming around him like a band of boisterous monkeys. Daisy's hair was dark and straight and fine, her blue eyes and magnolia-pale skin indicating she had more than a little Irishness in her blood. Luke was as dark-skinned as his father and, though his mop of curls wasn't yet as tight and wiry as Leon's, it would be when he was older. As for Matthew . . . Toby Harvey had been fair-haired and, as Kate's hair was the colour of ripe wheat, Matthew's colouring was as Nordic as a little Viking's.

Nellie chuckled. Whatever else the about-to-be-formed Emmerson family might be, it was certainly never going to be ordinary! 'An' who's going to be matron-of-honour?' she asked as the conga line noisily encircled her chair. 'Yer can't have both Carrie *an'* Christina.'

'Why not?'

18

Nellie clicked her tongue. 'Because though you can 'ave as many bridesmaids as yer want, you're only supposed to 'ave one married friend as a matron-of-honour. So who's it going to be? Carrie or Christina?'

'Then it will have to be Carrie. After all, we've been best friends ever since we were toddlers. I've only known Christina since she came here as a refugee.'

As the conga line danced its way down to the bottom end of the Square, she saw that Carrie had run Danny and Rose to earth, for they were walking hand in hand, with Rose skipping along in front of them, to where Leon and Danny's father were still deep in conversation.

'It's 'ard to think of 'er as a refugee, ain't it?' Nellie said ruminatively. 'I mean, it's not as if she speaks like a foreigner, is it? There's Ukrainians and Poles down in Woolwich can't speak a word of the King's English, poor bleeders. Gawd knows 'ow they manage, I don't. Christina speaks it like a nob.'

'Her gran was English,' Kate said, remembering that her intention had been to sympathize with Nellie about her nephew's continuing imprisonment by the Japanese, and that she hadn't yet done so. 'She was born and brought up in Bermondsey and went to school with Carrie's gran. That's why, when Christina came to England, she moved in with Carrie's family.'

'Well, she's English enough now she's married Charlie Robson's son,' Nellie said, who didn't much understand why Christina's Bermondsey-born grandmother should have wanted to go off and marry a Hun, even if it had been before the First World War when she'd done so. 'Though it might be some time before Jack's demobbed. Fighting in Greece last time anyone 'eard, wasn't 'e?

19

Commandos don't 'alf get about. 'E'll find Civvie Street pretty boring after rampaging all over Greece with knives stuck down his boots, and grenades 'angin' from his belt.'

'I came to sympathize with you about your nephew,' Kate said, eager to accomplish her mission so that she could join Leon. 'It can't be much fun, everyone celebrating the end of the war in Europe, when he's still being held by the Japanese.'

'No, it ain't,' Nellie said frankly as Hector slumped at her swollen feet, patiently waiting for Kate to make a move. 'But the Yanks'll soon 'ave the Japs on the run and old 'Irohito'll get his just desserts just like old 'Itler did. An' when we 'ave a Victory over Japan party, I'll be conga-ing with the best of 'em, bad feet or no bad feet. I can't understand why Christina ain't 'ere, you'd think she'd be dancin' 'er 'eart out, wouldn't yer?'

Christina Robson had never felt less like dancing in her life. She stood on the far, north-west corner of the Heath, looking out over a superb view of Greenwich and the River Thames and, a little more distantly, the City and the glittering dome of St Paul's Cathedral. London. It was the city that had given her refuge, and for that reason alone she would be grateful to it for as long as she lived. But she wasn't merely grateful to it, she loved it. She loved its tree-shaded squares, its unexpected patches of green, its noise and its bustle and its friendliness. It had become her home, and she wanted no other. Why, then, did she continue to feel so dispossessed? Why did she feel as if she were never, ever, going to become a Londoner herself? She was, after all, married to a south-Londoner.

All her friends were south-Londoners. All her neighbours. Surely, by now, she should feel she was a south-Londoner by adoption?

Despite the heat of the sun, she hugged her arms. She certainly hadn't done so when Magnolia Square's street party had been at its height. She had felt like the biblical Ruth amid the alien corn. Everyone else, with the exception of Nellie Miller, had been celebrating reunions or pending reunions. Though a general demob was still weeks, and possibly months, away, brothers and fathers, boy-friends and husbands, would soon be returning home *en masse*. Danny Collins, who had been a prisoner of the Italians, and Leon Emmerson, who had been freed by the Russians from a German prison camp, were both already home.

Had it been the realization of all those reunions that had brought the past hurtling back to engulf her so cruelly? Or had it been the talk of weddings? The Vicar's wedding to his rather surprisingly young, but extremely pleasant, lady-friend. Leon and Kate's imminent wedding. Both weddings would take place in St Mark's, as had her own wedding to Jack – and St Mark's was an Anglican church, and she was Jewish.

While her friends and neighbours had gossiped around her, she had stood with her back to one of the magnolia trees the Square had been named after, staring up at St Mark's glittering spire, wondering what her father would have said, what her mother and grandmother would say – and it had been then, as, for the first time in ten years, she thought of her mother and grandmother in the present tense, that mental and emotional pain had sliced cripplingly through her. How could she possibly have

21

thought of them as if they were still alive? How, after all that had happened in her homeland over the last decade, could she subconsciously have thought of them in the present tense, betraying vain hope that they had survived, that a reunion was still a possibility?

Leon Emmerson might have walked jauntily into the Square after an absence of information indicating he hadn't drowned over three years ago, but German-born Jews, Jacoba Berger and Eva Frank, dragged from their Heidelberg home and incarcerated in a concentration camp even before the war had begun, weren't likely to be so lucky.

Distantly, on the light summer breeze, came the sound of piano playing and discordant but exuberant singing. Magnolia Square's street party was still going at full throttle. In a nearby shrub, two sparrows wrangled noisily. A butterfly alighted briefly on one of the shaking leaves and then flew off, the sun glinting on the scarlet markings of its wings. Christina's fingers dug deeper into the flesh of her arms. Ever since she had escaped from Germany, she had schooled herself to accept that her mother and grandmother were dead. Why now, after all this time, had doubt begun to return? Certainly the news reports of the last few weeks had given no cause for hope. The first Allied troops into the camps had found horrors beyond imagining, and the estimate of the number of Jews who had died in them now ran into the millions. To entertain any hope that two women who had been imprisoned as long ago as 1936 could have survived was not only vain, it was ridiculous.

Or was it?

The sparrows flew off, still wrangling. A bee began to

circle the bush, looking for flowers and pollen. Slowly, as she stood there, the hope she had suppressed for so many years began to take fierce hold. All over Europe displaced people would be struggling to make their way back to their homes. All over Europe, reunions similar to Leon and Kate's would be taking place. What if her mother and grandmother hadn't died in the concentration camp they had been taken to? What if, by some miracle, they, like Leon, had survived?

'Hello there!' a middle-aged woman she knew only by sight called out to her cheerily, a mongrel skittering at her heels. 'I've just been told your vicar's thinking of marrying again. Lovely woman Bob Giles's first wife was. I remember the day she was killed. The first air-raid of the war, it was. Such a shame, and her only a young woman too. Still, it's nice he's found happiness again.'

With great effort Christina dragged her thoughts away from a ravaged Europe and the thousands upon thousands of displaced persons trailing the rutted road, their pathetically few belongings piled high in old prams and handcarts. 'Yes,' she agreed, smiling politely. 'It is.'

The woman would have liked to stay for a longer chat, but there was something about Christina Robson that was definitely not encouraging. She was polite enough, of course, but she wasn't a friendly, jolly south-London girl, like her friends Kate Voigt and Carrie Collins. She was too reserved. Too deep. Which all came of her being a foreigner of course, and Jewish into the bargain.

'Toodle-oo,' she said amiably, making allowances for what the poor girl couldn't help, adding as an afterthought, 'Your hubby will be demobbed soon I expect, or he will be if he doesn't decide to make a career of commando-ing. I've seen newsreels of Commando attacks. The Commandos were all guyed up in balaclava helmets with muck on the bits that show so they'd merge into the background, and they were bristling with knives and pistols. Should suit your Jack a treat. He always was on the wild side.'

Christina made no comment. She didn't want to think about Jack yet for a bit. Thinking about Jack was too unsettling, too intimidating. She would think about her mother and grandmother instead. She would think of ways she could try to discover what had happened to them, if they were alive or dead and, if they were dead, where they had died, and how. And if they were alive? Her throat was so tight she could hardly breathe. If they were alive she would find them. She would find them if it was the very last thing she ever did.

Kate sidestepped a running toddler and joined Leon as he continued to chat with Carrie and Danny and Danny's dad, Daniel.

'. . . that kid should've bin a requisitions officer,' Danny was saying, quite obviously referring to Billy and his private ammunition dump. ''E's got a natural-born talent for scroungin'.'

Kate slid her arm around Leon's waist. The street party seemed to be going on for ever. When on earth would it come to an end? When would they be able to escape and have some privacy?

His hand cupped her far shoulder as he hugged her close, his thoughts exactly the same as hers. As she leant her head against his shoulder, he looked down at her in

24

utter love, his throat tightening in emotion. Christ, but she was beautiful! No woman he had ever seen had hair of such a rich, glorious gold colour. Or hair so long and lustrous. And she had waited for him. For over three years she hadn't known whether he was dead or alive, but she had given birth to his son and had waited faithfully in fierce hope.

'I love you,' he whispered in her ear as their son continued to ride high on his shoulders, and Daisy and Matthew engaged in a giggling game of tag with Rose. 'When the devil can we escape and be alone together?'

Before she could make a response, Daniel Collins said genially to her, 'Have you heard that you and the Vicar aren't the only ones having weddings this month? Charlie Robson has just announced he's going to marry your next-door neighbour. Funny old couple they'll make, her a retired headmistress and a spinster and him a widower with a criminal past, barely able to read and write.'

'They've been friends for a long time,' Carrie said, wondering what Christina would think of her father-in-law's rather surprising wedding plans.

Danny ran a hand through his spiky, mahogany-red hair in baffled bemusement. 'Wasn't 'Arriet Godfrey Jack's old 'eadmistress? And didn't she once say Jack was more suited to a Borstal than 'er junior school? I wonder what 'e's goin' to think when 'e comes 'ome and finds she's about to become 'is stepmother!'

They all roared with laughter, not noticing Mavis's approach. 'Is it a private joke or can anyone join in?' she asked, strolling up to them on perilously high, peep-toed, wedge-heeled sandals, her toenails a vivid scarlet beneath her sheer silk stockings.

Carrie sighed, her laughter subsiding. Her older sister was a constant source of irritation to her. Where, in these days of deprivation, had the silk stockings come from, for instance? Wherever it was, the supply would have to stop when Ted was demobbed. He'd been upset enough about her long-standing flirtatious relationship with Jack Robson, and he knew Jack well. He certainly wouldn't countenance a similarly dubious relationship with a stranger, and the stockings must have come from a stranger because Jack hadn't swaggered into Magnolia Square on leave since the weekend he'd been home and married Christina.

'We were just anticipating Jack's surprise when he comes home and finds his dad has married Harriet Godfrey,' Kate said, flashing Mavis a wide, warm smile. 'She used to be his headmistress when he was in junior school. I can't imagine he's going to find it easy calling her Mother, can you?'

At the very thought, Mavis spluttered into throaty laughter, and even Carrie began to giggle again. 'Well, we'll all be finding out how he's going to manage soon enough,' Mavis said when her laughter finally subsided. 'I had a letter from him this morning. He says he thinks he'll be home by the end of next month, and demobbed soon after.'

'When he does come home, you just make sure you give him a wide berth,' Carrie said, suddenly serious. 'He's married now, and no matter how much you and he might protest that your horse-play is innocent, Christina mightn't think it innocent. And she's been hurt enough in the past, losing all her family the way she has done, without being hurt by your shenanigans.'

Mavis put a hand on an aquamarine-skirted, curvaceous hip, and tapped a foot up and down. 'Why the hell can't you keep your useless opinions to yourself, Carrie?' she demanded witheringly, uncaring of their embarrassed audience. 'Me and Jack are mates. Always 'ave been. Always will be. And 'is 'avin' married Christina isn't going to make a ha'p'orth's difference to that friendship, so don't you go 'opin' it will. And as Christina is 'eading this way at this very moment,' she added, her eyes no longer holding Carrie's but looking over Carrie's shoulder, 'I suggest we put the kibosh on this conversation, don't you?'

Before Carrie could make any response, they all heard Nellie boom out from the depths of her sagging armchair, 'Where the 'ell 'ave you been, Christina? You've been missing all the fun!'

'I've not been far,' Christina said, smiling at Nellie with affectionate warmth. 'I just wanted to be on my own for a little while.'

'Well, you chose a rum day for it, dearie!' Nellie's red balloon still bobbed jauntily on the end of its string. 'Still, it takes all sorts and I 'spect you wanted to enjoy the news about your Jack coming 'ome and 'opin' to be demobbed soon. It's grand news, ain't it?'

Christina stared at her. 'I'm sorry,' she said, utterly bewildered. 'I don't understand. How do you know Jack's going to be home soon?'

'Mavis told me,' Nellie said blithely. 'She 'ad a letter from 'im this mornin'. I expect her Ted will be 'ome soon as well. I 'aven't 'ad news about 'Arold, but that's only to be expected . . .'

Christina was no longer listening to her. She was

27

looking across at Mavis, her face so white it looked as if it were carved from marble.

'Bloody *hell*,' Mavis said graphically to the world at large, 'that's torn it. How was I to know Jack hadn't written her with the news yet?'

'Well, you know now,' Danny said dryly as his father began prudently edging away from what was obviously going to be the centre of a very unpleasant explosion.

'And if I were you, Mavis, I'd start thinking what to do about it,' Carrie added, grim-faced. 'And I'd start thinking fast. Very fast indeed!'

Chapter Two

Of all four girls, Christina was the most petite. Though Kate was ethereally slender, she was tall. Carrie was curvaceously heavy-bosomed and broad-hipped, far too much so for her own liking. Mavis was narrow-waisted and buxom, and happily emphasized the fact. Christina was small-boned, and there was an air of fragility about her that brought out fierce protectiveness in some people and irritation in others. In Mavis, well aware that beneath Christina's apparently wand-like fragility lay true steel, it brought out irritation. It brought it out in bucket-loads.

Christina's true steel was blazingly apparent now. It flamed out of her eyes, turning their beautiful amethyst colour near black. 'Nellie says my husband has written to you, telling you he's coming home on leave and hopes to be demobbed soon. Is that true?' She faced Mavis full square, not putting her hands on her hips in confrontational south-London fashion, but with her hands clenched at her sides, every nerve and muscle as taut as a coiled spring.

Mavis sighed. For all her noisy exuberance, she didn't like scenes and she had no particular desire to spoil Magnolia Square's street party by pitching into a

29

full-scale brawl with the Jewish refugee it had collectively taken under its wing. 'Yes,' she said, keeping her voice as pleasant as her patience would allow. 'It was a general sort of letter. A letter to the family. If you haven't heard from him yet it must mean his letter to you is snarled up somewhere. You can't expect Forces post to be normal these days, can you?'

'No,' Carrie said, hurriedly agreeing with her and trying to defuse the situation. 'Whenever Danny wrote to me and his mum he always posted the letters off together and they never arrived together. That's true, isn't it, Danny?' She looked towards him for support.

Danny dutifully nodded, his freckled face struggling for an effect of earnest sincerity. 'Absolutely. Carrie would receive her letter weeks before Mum did, or Mum would get 'ers and Carrie's wouldn't even arrive!'

Christina was not remotely interested in the vagaries of Danny's mail. 'I would like to see the letter,' she said tautly to Mavis, her lips nearly as white as her face. 'I would like to read Jack's comments for myself.'

The conga procession had begun making its way back up the Square, with Albert Jennings spiritedly leading it. His two daughters and Kate and Christina were oblivious of him.

Mavis eyed Christina thoughtfully, the tension almost unbearable. 'I don't think I can 'elp you out there,' she said at last as Leon cleared his throat uncomfortably and Danny shifted his feet. 'Letters are private things. Sorry, Christina.'

Christina sucked in her breath, furious with herself for having asked anything of Mavis; furious with Mavis for so laconically refusing her request; furious

30

with Jack for having written the letter to Mavis in the first place.

'Aiya, aiya . . . *conga*,' Albert bellowed, kicking his left leg out at a jaunty angle as he led his tipsy conga line towards them. 'Come on, Mavis! Show a leg there! Aiya, aiya *conga*! Churchill is a *hero* . . . !'

Mavis grinned and accepted her dad's invitation with relief. The local young scoutmaster, who had long wanted to get his arms around her, seized his opportunity and latched on behind her and away they all went, conga-ing rumbustiously towards the Blackheath end of the Square.

Carrie looked across at Christina unhappily. Christina was trembling, though what the emotion was that was causing her to tremble, Carrie wasn't sure. It could have been distress or it could have been anger. She tried to imagine how she would feel if Danny had written to a young married woman telling her when he expected to be home, and she hadn't received a letter with such news herself. She couldn't. Firstly, because Danny hated putting pen to paper to such an extent that even if Betty Grable asked him to be her pen-friend he'd refuse on the grounds that the task was too arduous. And secondly, because it was simply something Danny would never do. Not in a million years.

'Christina, I . . .' she began awkwardly.

'It doesn't matter,' Christina said quickly, not wanting her to see how deeply hurt she was. 'I'm on my way into the house to make a cup of fresh tea. 'Bye.' Speedily she took her leave of them, not wanting to see the embarass-ment in their eyes. Or the pity. What on earth had she been thinking of to have reacted to Nellie's news in such a public manner? Why hadn't she simply pretended Jack had written to her also with the news that he was coming home soon, and that he was hoping for an early demob? Why had she allowed Mavis the satisfaction of knowing how intensely she resented the long-standing, disturbingly free and easy relationship between her and Jack?

She turned in at the Jennings's gateway. There was no gate. Billy's constant swinging on it had broken its hinges years ago. The front door was ajar, but that didn't necessarily mean that anyone was home. In Magnolia Square doors were often left ajar, and a locked door was unheard of. Wearily she pushed the door open and stepped into the sanctuary of the cluttered hallway.

'Is that you, *bubbeleh*?' Leah Singer called out from the kitchen.

A slight smile touched Christina's still tense mouth. Leah's greeting would do for any female member of the family who wandered in: Miriam, Carrie, Mavis, Carrie's daughter, Rose; Mavis's daughter, Beryl.

Mavis. Her smile died. Unlike the rest of the Jennings family, Mavis alone had not welcomed her with effusive affection when she had arrived in Magnolia Square, numbed from the horrors taking place in her homeland, vastly relieved to have been able to move on from the Swiss *Auffanglager* where she had first been given shelter after her escape from Germany.

Mavis hadn't been hostile or openly unwelcoming, merely indifferent. At the time it was an indifference Christina had merely shrugged away. Now, however, she couldn't help wondering if Mavis's lack of interest had been occasioned by the fact that, from the first moment she, Christina, had stepped into Magnolia Square, Jack

Robson had expressed fierce romantic interest in her, pursuing her with relentless persistence.

'It's me, Leah!' she called out in answer to Leah's greeting, negotiating her way around a heavily laden clothes-horse that took up most of the room in the hall-way.

Had Mavis regarded Jack as her own property even then, way back in 1936? Had it been sixth sense on Mavis's part that had prompted her to keep her distance when everyone else in the Square had been so wonder-fully welcoming? Had Mavis instantly sensed that Jack, notoriously heart-whole after breaking nearly every female heart in south London, was finally going to have his affections seriously engaged?

'There's some soup on the stove,' Leah said, her sleeves rolled up to her elbows, an apron tied around her comfortably thick waist as she pounded strudel dough on a floured board. 'Beans and barley, and made with decent beef bones for once.'

'Thanks, but no.' Christina kissed Leah affectionately on her wrinkled cheek. 'I need a cup of tea, not food.'

Leah turned to look at her, saw the expression in her eyes and the strain around her mouth and immediately pushed the strudel dough to one side of the board and dusted her hands. 'Sit down and I'll make the tea,' she said, well aware that there was far more wrong with Christina than tiredness caused by over-celebrating. Not that Germany's defeat *could* be over-celebrated. She'd been giving thanks for it herself non-stop ever since she'd heard the news. And so should Christina have been, not looking instead as if she'd all the troubles in the world on her shoulders. 'So, what's the *tummel*?' she asked when

33

she had put the kettle on to boil. 'Today's a joyous occasion. Why you look so troubled?'

Christina sat at the kitchen table that, over the years, had been scrubbed until the wood was almost white, and pushed a fall of soft dark hair away from her face. Surely, with Leah, she could share her mental burdens? Leah had been her grandmother's girlhood friend. Leah, like herself, was Jewish. If anyone would understand how, for her, the war was not yet over, Leah would. Perhaps it was the reason Leah wasn't with the rest of their neighbours, conga-ing the length and breadth of Magnolia Square in euphoric celebration. Perhaps Leah, too, was thinking of Jacoba Berger and her daughter Eva, and was wondering what their fates had been; was wondering if they could possibly be still alive.

As for her other anguish – Leah had known Jack since he was a baby, and Mavis was her granddaughter. If anyone could enlighten her about the true nature of the relationship between the two of them, Leah probably could. 'I've been thinking about *Mutti* and *Grossmutti*,' she said at last, her voice unsteady. 'I've been wondering what happened to them after they were taken away in the trucks.'

'You know what happened, *faygeleh*,' Leah said gently, sitting down beside her. 'They were taken to a concentration camp. And they died.' Her gnarled hand took hold of Christina's. What more could be said? How could such horrors ever be put into words, without the words cheapening the suffering? And how ironic it was that Jacoba, born and bred in south London, should have been one of the first of Hitler's victims, her German-Jewish son-in-law's shop burned to the ground, he and his son shot in the street, and herself and her middle-aged daughter taken off to a camp.

Leah's hand tightened on Christina's. A camp. They had never known which camp, though in those early days of 1936, when the camps were being described to the foreign press as 'mild reform centres for Germans who have not yet seen the light', the most likely was the new women's concentration camp at Lichtenburg.

'But what if they didn't die?' Christina said urgently, putting her newly-born hope into words for the first time. 'What if they were released after I had left Heidelberg? They wouldn't have known where to look for me. They wouldn't have known I had escaped to Switzerland, or that I had applied for asylum in England.'

'They would have guessed,' Leah protested, shocked. 'Jacoba would have written me—'

'Would she?' Christina's amethyst eyes burned with fierce intensity. 'The two of you hadn't been in contact with each other for years and years. It was only when Red Cross officials questioned me as to whether my family had any relatives or friends, however distant, in Britain or America or Canada, that I remembered *Grossmutti*'s girlhood friendship with you.'

Leah was silent, remembering far distant schooldays in Bermondsey. They had used slates to write on and, if she closed her eyes, she could still conjure up the smell of chalk and the rank smell of poverty that had filled the crowded schoolroom. Jacoba had sat at the desk next to hers. 'Be kind to Jacoba,' their teacher had said, 'her father's been killed at Majuba, fighting the nasty Boers.' And so she had been kind to Jacoba, and Jacoba had become her friend. They had been together when the

35

second Boer War had broken out eight years later, and when the country had celebrated Queen Victoria's Jubilee, and when London had received the news that General Gordon had been killed in Khartoum.

And then Jacoba had met Anton Berger, a German-Jewish medical student studying in London, and she had married him and accompanied him back to his home town of Heidelberg. There had been letters, of course. A lot at first, reducing to a trickle as the years passed, and then drying up entirely when Europe plunged into the darkness of the 1914–18 war. Afterwards, there had been an occasional card. Enough for Leah to know that Jacoba had been widowed and that her daughter Eva was now married and had given birth to a daughter. And then, some time during the twenties, all communication had ceased. Had it been her fault, or had it been Jacoba's? Or had it simply been that their lives had grown so far apart that, even on paper, they had become strangers to each other?

Leah gave a deep sigh. '*Oy veh*,' she said, tears winding their way down her cheeks, '*Oy veh, oy veh*. So much trouble. So much misery.'

'But do you agree with me, Leah?' Christina persisted, not allowing Leah to avoid her question. 'It might never have occurred to *Grossmutti* that I would get in touch with you. And if she and *Mutti* became separated . . .' she faltered slightly, 'if she and *Mutti* became separated,' she said again, her voice raw with pain, 'I doubt if the possibility would even have entered *Mutti*'s head.'

The possibility that her old schoolfriend and her daughter were still alive had certainly never entered Leah's head, not even way back in 1936. Why should it have done? Jews had already been banned from German public life. They were merely 'subjects' without rights. And as Christina's father and brother had been dragged from their burning home and shot before her eyes, why should any hopes have been entertained that Jacoba and Eva would emerge alive from wherever it was they had been taken to? That after all these years Christina was expressing the hope they may have survived, disturbed her deeply. It meant that, though everyone had assumed Christina had come to terms with her family tragedy, she had, in fact, never done so. It meant she was still conjuring up horrors that her mother and grandmother might be enduring. And it meant she was living in hope. A hope Leah was certain would never come to fruition.

'They're dead, *faygeleh*,' she said again, very gently. 'Haven't we said *Kaddish* for them? Don't we know in our hearts they're at peace now?'

Until a little while ago, Christina would have been in reluctant agreement with her. She was so no longer. Hadn't many people given Leon Emmerson up for dead, and wasn't Leon very much alive? And there would be hundreds, perhaps thousands, of other people who had also been given up for dead who would prove to be alive.

'I'll brew the tea,' she said, rising to her feet, knowing that if she continued the conversation Leah would only grow even more distressed. Instead she would speak to Kate about the possibility that her mother and grandmother were alive. Kate was always very positive and optimistic. And Carl Voigt, Kate's German-born father, might very well know how she should go about beginning her search.

* * *

37

'Blimey!' Danny said as he and Carrie and Kate and Leon watched Christina walk away from them. 'That was a bit of a show-down and no mistake.'

'Do you think I should go after her?' Carrie asked, frowning. 'I've never seen Christina so upset before. She usually keeps everything bottled up inside, or I presume she does, because she certainly doesn't give vent to much. I've always had my suspicions that Mavis's friendship with Jack distressed her, but that's the first time she's ever *shown* it distressed her.'

Kate, too, was frowning slightly. 'It's a shame, isn't it?' she said, disturbed at the thought of Christina being so unhappy on such a wonderful day. 'I'd stake my life that Mavis and Jack's friendship is completely innocent.'

Carrie gave a rude snort, and Leon said mildly, 'I'm sure you're right, love. They've grown up living next door to each other, haven't they? They're bound to be pretty close in a brother and sisterly kind of way.'

Carrie raised her eyes to heaven. Leon had only spent a few short months in Magnolia Square when, recovering from war wounds, he had moved into Kate's home as a lodger and then, after being declared fit for active service again, a short leave. After that leave his ship had been sunk and he had been taken prisoner. The time he'd spent in the Square had been long enough for him to have fallen irrevocably in love with Kate, but had quite obviously not been enough for him to get Mavis's measure.

'Are the fireworks over?' Daniel asked, ambling back up to them now it looked safe to do so, a rolled newspaper tucked beneath his arm. 'Dear oh dear, but I thought for a minute we were going to be in for a bit of scratching and biting and hair-pulling!'

Danny grinned at his dad affectionately. 'Keepin'' out of the danger area as usual, were you? No wonder Mum always complains you're never around when she wants to 'ave a barney!'

'No-one with any sense would be,' Daniel retorted, deep feeling in his voice. 'There ain't a more frightening sight in the world than my Hettie brandishing a rolling-pin!'

The little rejoinder lifted the troubled atmosphere. Danny caught hold of his six-year-old daughter as she dashed by, chased by Daisy and Matthew. ''Ow about calming dahn a bit?' he said lovingly. 'I can't 'ear myself fink for your shrieking, and Maffew's dad is just goin' to tell me who liberated him, the Russkies or the Yanks.'

Leon and Kate exchanged hopeless, frustrated glances; were they never, ever, going to be able to slip away on their own?

Carrie, seeing the look and interpreting it correctly, said to her nearest and dearest, 'Why don't you leave chin-wagging with Leon about your mutual POW experience till you're both in The Swan with a couple of pints in your hands? In the meantime you can take Rose, Daisy, Matthew and Luke down to the river to see the tugs.'

As he stared at her in incredulity, Leon and Kate seized their chance. 'Matthew!' Kate called. 'Daisy! Come over here! Rose's daddy is going to take you down to the river.'

Matthew hurtled up to her, pretending to be an aeroplane, his arms going like windmills. 'Don't want to go with Rose's daddy,' he panted breathlessly, 'want to stay with you and Leon.'

Kate bent down to him, saying with gentle firmness, '*I* want you to go with him. It will be nice for Luke to see the tugs, they'll be all decked out in flags and bunting, and he won't go if you don't.'

This was true, and Matthew knew it. His little brother wouldn't go anywhere unless he went too. The desire to be a good boy and do what was being asked of him, and the desire to stay close to Leon's side, fought for supremacy. Leon was going to be his daddy – and no-one else he knew, no-one else at all, had a daddy who looked so excitingly different, a daddy who was chocolate-coloured!

Seeing his disappointment, Leon squatted down on his haunches in front of him. 'If you go with Luke down to the river today, with Rose's daddy, I'll take you down there tomorrow on your own. We might even see the boat I used to work the river in and, with a bit of luck, go aboard her.'

Matthew beamed at him sunnily, his eyes shining. His new daddy-Leon had been a Thames Waterman before he'd gone away to fight, and when he grew up, he was going to be a Thames Waterman too. 'All right,' he said, only too happy now to indulge his mother's wish, 'I'll go with Rose's daddy.'

'That's a good boy, pet lamb.' Kate ruffled his blond hair lovingly, hardly able to believe that Danny was going to take *all* her children off her hands for her.

As Leon swung Luke down from his shoulders, his gratitude to Carrie knowing no bounds, Danny said plaintively, 'Blimey, Carrie. Yer don't 'alf drop a fella in it! I'm goin' to be like the Pied Piper of bloomin' Hamelin with this little lot!'

40

'You'll enjoy it,' Carrie said placidly, knowing he would do no such thing, 'and it's a way of keeping Matthew, Daisy and Luke out of Kate and Leon's hair for a little while.'

'Out of their 'air?' He was looking at her with incredulity, his own mahogany-red hair standing up in tousled tufts. 'Out of their 'air?' he said again as Leon and Kate, their arms tightly around each other's waists, began walking speedily away from them, Hector lolloping at their heels. 'Lord 'ave mercy, Carrie! Leon's only been 'ome a shake of a donkey's tail. Why the 'ell would 'e already be wantin' the kids out of 'is 'air?'

Carrie looked at him pityingly. She loved him with all her heart, but it had to be admitted that there were moments when he was as thick as two short planks. 'For the simple reason that he's not been home the length of time you have! Do use your head, Danny! They want to be on their own together for a bit of lovey-dovey.'

'Well, they won't get much lovey-dovey sharin' a 'ouse with 'er dad,' Danny said, a wealth of feeling in his voice. 'We don't get much bloomin' lovey-dovey living with your mam and dad, do we? And I don't suppose even you can talk Carl Voigt into troopin' dahn the river for the rest of the arternoon!'

'I'll have no need to,' Carrie said with the serenity of certain knowledge. 'Like the Vicar and Charlie, he's got himself a lady-friend. She lives in Greenwich and that's where he is now. Would you like to take Bonzo down the river with you? He could do with a walk.'

'No, I blinkin' wouldn't!' Indignantly he swung Luke high up on to his shoulders, took Rose's hand in his, and said to Daisy and Matthew, 'Come on, let's be goin' before we end up lookin' like a circus with every dog in the bloomin' Square 'angin' on our 'eels!'

Nellie, who never missed a trick, watched from the depths of her armchair as Danny led his little troupe out of the Square in the direction of the river. Carrie wasn't going with them, which meant she was probably going to go after Christina and have a comforting word with her. It had certainly looked to be a fair old argy-bargy between Christina and Mavis. She grunted, uncomfortably aware that she'd been unintentionally responsible for it.

On the far side of the Square the front door of number four slammed hastily shut behind Kate and Leon and then, seconds later, a bedroom window was slammed down on the noise of the party and the curtains hurriedly closed. Nellie's currant-black eyes gleamed. What with Charlie Robson popping the question to Harriet Godfrey, and the Vicar deciding to re-marry, and Kate and Leon so obviously making up for all the years they'd been apart, passion was certainly alive and kicking in Magnolia Square. The question was, when was any of it going to come her way? She cackled at the very thought. It would take a strong man – a very strong man indeed! Happily content at the thought of all the weddings that were to come, she let go of her balloon, watching as it gaily sailed high over the rooftops in the direction of the Thames.

Chapter Three

'Where we goin' to live when we're married, 'Arriet?' Charlie Robson, Christina's father-in-law, asked Harriet Godfrey, Queenie padding at his heels. 'Your 'ouse or mine?'

Magnolia Square's street party had come to a happy, exhausted conclusion. Hettie Collins's piano had been trundled back into her parlour. Bob Giles, the Vicar, had scrupulously picked up all the litter that had drifted on to St Mark's grassy island. Mavis had helped her mother and Hettie clear the trestle tables, and Daniel Collins and Albert Jennings had moved them away, stacking them in the church hall.

Charlie and Harriet were now walking hand in hand over the Heath towards Blackheath Village and Charlie's next-to-favourite pub, The Princess of Wales. The Swan, tucked tidily away at the bottom end of Magnolia Hill, was his favourite pub, but The Swan was a no-nonsense workmen's pub and not the kind of watering-hole into which he could happily take Harriet, an ex-headmistress.

Charlie's question was one Harriet had been mulling over for several months, long before Charlie had even plucked up the courage to ask her to marry him. Her house, at the top end of Magnolia Square, was immaculate.

No children had ever scuffed the furniture or frayed the carpets. Original watercolours hung in narrow gilt frames on cream-papered walls. A walnut drawleaf table that had been her mother's graced the dining-room, smelling pleasantly of beeswax. A marquetry display cabinet that had been her grandmother's held pride of place in her sitting-room. Her bedroom furniture was carved mahogany, her bed-linen and bedspread a pristine, lace-edged white.

Charlie's home, in the bottom, less salubrious half of the Square, was nearly as battered as the Lomaxes who lived next-door-but-one to him. The dining-room was home to Charlie's bicycle and the array of tools needed to keep it roadworthy. The sitting-room possessed a moquette-covered three-piece suite with sagging springs, a framed picture of King George and Queen Elizabeth in their coronation robes, and a wireless. The kitchen was the heart of the house, with its black-leaded fire and oven, its deal table, well-worn rag rugs and thick, blue-and-white striped crockery. Charlie, however, loved his home dearly, just as she loved hers. And Harriet knew that Charlie would find it as hard to feel at home living in her house as she would do living in his.

'It's a problem, isn't it?' she said, slowing her naturally-inclined strides down so that she didn't out-pace him. A big man, Charlie never strode. He ambled. He never looked pin-neat either, as she did, though over the years she had managed to persuade him to wear his trouser belt through the loops provided for it, and to occasionally fasten a collar to his collar-stud. She looked across at him lovingly. She didn't give tuppence about his shambolic appearance. He was generous-hearted, compassionate and kind, and she thought herself the luckiest woman in all the world that, having lived all her life as a spinster and after being retired for more years than she cared to remember, she was now on the verge of becoming his wife.

'My house is too formal for you to feel comfortable in, and your house is too casual for me to feel comfortable in.'

Charlie nodded agreement. Harriet had a wonderful way of summing things up. It came of her being educated.

'And so we'll just have to compromise,' Harriet said, choosing her words carefully. 'If I come to live with you, you'll have to let me make a few changes. I wouldn't want your bicycle in the dining-room for instance, and I'd want to re-decorate the sitting-room. And if you come and live with me I'll put all my bone-china away and we can use your blue-and-white-crockery and—'

'But where'd I put my bicycle, 'Arriet?' Charlie asked as they skirted one of the Heath's gorse-covered gravel-pits, and Queenie raced down one side of it and up the other. 'I can't put it in the shed. My pigeons are in the shed. And I can't leave it propped in the back garden 'cos Billy Lomax will have his 'ands on it if I do.'

'That's true,' Harriet said thoughtfully, her tweed skirt flapping a few inches above her sensibly brogued feet, a pearl necklace adding a touch of elegance to her raspberry-coloured twin-set. 'And there's another snag, Charlie.'

Charlie looked alarmed. It wasn't like Harriet to admit there were snags. Harriet didn't hold with snags. Snags were something she always speedily sorted out. 'What's that, petal?' he asked nervously. 'It's not the pigeons, is it? I wouldn't want to part with my pigeons.'

'Of course it isn't the pigeons,' Harriet said truthfully. 'It's something a little more awkward than that.' She hesitated and then said gently, 'It's your Jack.'

'Jack?' Charlie's craggy face was pathetically bewildered. 'But Jack ain't 'ome, 'Arriet. 'E's in the Commandos!'

'But he's *coming* home, Charlie.' Harriet steered him across the road flanking the Heath and towards the pub. 'And soon he won't just be home on leave. He'll be demobbed and home for good. And if he comes home to find I've moved in he might not like it.'

It was an understatement and Charlie knew it.

'And then there's Christina,' Harriet said adroitly, moving in for the *coup de grâce*. 'She and Jack will want to be setting up home together and they can't do so at the Jenningses. Their house is packed to the rafters as it is.'

'Jack wouldn't live at the Jenningses!' Charlie said, indignant at the very thought. 'Why should 'e when 'e's got a 'ome of 'is own?'

This was exactly the conclusion Harriet had been steering him towards. As she seated herself at their favourite table near the door, and Queenie lay docilely down at her feet, she said reasonably, 'And so Christina will be moving in with you and Jack, and if I move in as well, we're going to be nearly as crowded as the Jenningses.' She tucked a straying strand of hair back into her bun, saying tentatively, 'And so it might be best if you moved in with me and let Christina and Jack have the house to themselves. I know they'd appreciate that, Charlie. And I would make my house as comfy as possible for you. After all, if we share the house it will be

46

yours just as much as mine. And it's always been a lonely house. With you in it, it won't be lonely any longer.'

Charlie looked down at her, a lump in his throat. Lonely? Had his Harriet really been lonely before she met him? It was hard for him to credit. She was so organized, always sitting on committees and such like. And yet it was he who had transformed her life. Him. Charlie Robson, ex-illiterate and ex-criminal. Well, thanks to her patient teaching he was illiterate no longer. And he wasn't a criminal any longer, either.

'You're right, 'Arriet,' he said, happy to bow to her superior judgement. 'Jack and Christina need to set up 'ouse together, and though the government's promised 'omes in plenty for men being demobbed, there's precious few 'omes for 'eroes being built yet. And I reckon me and Queenie could settle anywhere just as long as I 'ave a pint mug for my char and Queenie has a bed that ain't in a draught.'

At his mention of Queenie, and at the thought of dog hairs on her Turkish carpets, a spasm almost of pain crossed Harriet's face. It was quickly vanquished. Queenie was a well-behaved animal and she had known, right from the beginning of her friendship with Charlie, that where he went, Queenie went too. Making the ultimate sacrifice, she said, 'Queenie can have her basket in the kitchen, next to the Aga. And now I think I'd like a dry sherry, Charlie. It's been quite a day, hasn't it? And the best bit was seeing Kate and Leon so happy together. It did my heart good just looking at them.'

'It was wonderful to see Kate and Leon together,' Kate's father's middle-aged lady-friend said as they sat drinking mugs of hot cocoa in her little terraced house in Greenwich. 'I expect there'll be a wedding now, just as soon as one can be arranged.'

Carl Voigt nodded, his rimless spectacle lenses glinting in the light of the small gas-lamp she had lit when dusk had fallen. 'Though it won't be a white wedding,' he said with a small, sad smile.

Ellen Pierce's eyes widened slightly. Carl had never spoken to her of Leon's West Indian blood, and it was totally unlike him to make a dry joke of it, especially when the joke hung on the hook of his daughter's wedding.

'Does it matter so much to you?' she asked in deep concern. 'Because if it does, you must remember that it could have been far worse. Leon might have been a black American serviceman, not a black British serviceman, and then where would you have been? He would have taken Kate to America, and she and the children would be living in Pennsylvania or Virginia or Alabama—' She broke off, aware that he was staring at her in blank perplexity. 'It *was* Leon's skin colour you were referring to, wasn't it?' she asked, suddenly unsure and feeling desperately awkward.

'His skin colour?' Carl frowned, trying to remember exactly what it was he had said. 'Why should that have any bearing on Kate being unable to wear white on her wedding day? I was thinking about the fact that she's already a mother. A mother twice over.'

Ellen flushed deeply. Carl was a quiet, cultivated, sensitive man to whom any sort of coarseness was anathema. 'It hasn't any bearing on it,' she said hurriedly, hoping he wouldn't realize in what way she

48

had misunderstood him, 'and you're quite right, it *is* a pity that a girl as young as Kate should be unable to have a white wedding with all the trimmings.' She put her mug of cocoa down on the tiled hearth of the fireplace. 'That is, it's a pity if it really *is* impossible. Under the circumstances, Matthew's father being killed before he even knew Kate was having a baby, and Leon being a prisoner from before Luke was born, I don't think Mr Giles would mind too much. I mean, I don't think he would refuse to marry Kate if she decided she wanted to wear white.'

'Probably not,' Carl said, doubt in his voice, 'but even if Bob Giles didn't object, the local matrons would have plenty to say! It would be asking for unkind comments, and there may be enough of those, from people who don't know Leon well.'

Ellen remained silent, not knowing quite what to say. She knew that this time he really *was* referring to Leon's skin colour and was nervous that anything she said might sound wrong. If she said Leon's skin colour didn't matter, Carl might take the view she wasn't being aware enough of the difficulties Kate and Leon would undoubtedly face in the years ahead of them. If she agreed there would be unkind comment, Carl might assume she not only thought such comments to be expected, but that she had a glimmer of sympathy with them.

She clasped her hands tightly in her lap, torn by an agony of indecision. Why, oh why did she constantly feel so apprehensive of what was the proper thing to say or do? Was it Carl's natural reticence that made conversational intimacy between them so difficult? Or was it just her own deep-seated sense of insecurity? And *why* was she so insecure? She was forty-two for goodness sake! She had a good job, good health, and owned her own home. And she was terrified of losing Carl Voigt's affection. Terrified that he would one day realize she wasn't his intellectual equal.

'Whatever Kate wears, she's going to be a beautiful bride,' she said, knowing with relief that this statement at least was utterly true, and utterly safe. 'It's going to be a joyous wedding. The most joyous Magnolia Square has ever had.'

It was late afternoon the next day when Christina walked up the Voigts' garden path and the short flight of shallow steps that led to their immaculate, primrose-painted front door. She knew she wouldn't be intruding on Kate and Leon because she had seen Leon striding down the Square towards Magnolia Hill, Luke astride his shoulders, Matthew and Daisy skipping along at either side of him. Even from inside number eighteen she had heard the children's happy laughter. Wherever Leon was, there was always happiness and laughter.

As she let the polished bronze knocker fall in a light tap against the door, she felt a spasm of envy. Kate and Leon were such an *uncomplicated* couple. There were no hidden depths to either of them, or none that she had ever been able to discern. It was impossible to think of Kate tormenting herself because Leon was, in ways she couldn't quite define, a stranger to her. And it was impossible to think of Leon causing Kate jealousy.

She gave a slight, almost Gallic shrug of her shoulders. What on earth was the point of feeling envious? Even if she could have Leon as a husband she wouldn't want

50

him. Likeable as he was he could never, in a million years, set her heart racing and her pulse pounding as the mere thought of Jack did. And once Jack was home for good, he would no longer seem like a stranger to her. And she would make utterly, utterly sure that she had no cause for jealousy. None at all.

'Come in!' Kate called out, from what Christina judged to be the kitchen, 'the door's on the latch.'

She opened the door to be nearly bowled over by Hector. 'Down!' she commanded, fending off his friendly overtures, wondering why it was the British thought no house a home unless it contained a dog. Leah had a whippet. Her father-in-law had an Alsatian. Ellen Pierce, Kate's father's lady-friend, had *three* dogs, all of which she had taken in as bombed-out strays.

'I'm making some fairy cakes for the children's tea,' Kate said, greeting her with a wide, sunny smile. 'Hettie's given me the icing sugar left over from the cake she made for the street party. She must have had the packet since before the war – it was so lumpy I had to take a rolling-pin to it!'

Christina's anwering smile was unintentionally as enigmatic as the Mona Lisa's.

'Why can't Christina smile properly?' Hettie Collins had once demanded of Jack Robson. 'Why can't she show her teeth like other people do?'

'Because she isn't other people,' Jack had said irritably. 'She's beautiful, and beautiful women don't grin. They have pussy-cat smiles instead.'

She said now, clasping her hands together on top of the table, 'There's something I want to talk to you about, Kate. Something important.'

51

Kate iced the last fairy cake, dropped the knife into a sink of soapy water and turned to look at her, her eyes apprehensive. Was it about Mavis and Jack? Was Christina going to admit that it was a relationship deeply troubling her? 'What is it?' she asked, hoping fervently that her guess wasn't going to be proved correct.

Christina waited until Kate had seated herself at the table opposite her and then said thickly, 'It's about my family, Kate. I can't stop thinking about them. I can't help wondering if, by some miracle, they might still be alive.'

Kate's eyes widened. In all the years she had known Christina, she had never discussed her family with her. She said hesitantly, 'Have you any reason to think it a possibility? I always understood your brother and father had been shot, and that your mother and grandmother had been taken to a concentration camp.'

Christina's beautiful face was pale, and there were faint blue shadows beneath her eyes. Revealing her feelings and emotions had never been easy for her, and even now, after nine years, she was totally unable to speak of the deaths of her brother and father. She said instead, 'My mother and grandmother could still be alive. I never knew which camp they were taken to, or even if they were taken to a camp. I only knew that the Nazis regarded our family as being an enemy of the state and were intent on stamping it out.'

Kate blinked. She had always assumed Christina's family had been murdered and hounded simply because they were Jews. Was there more to it, then? Had they been actively plotting against Hitler and his government at a time when the British government was still trying to read pacific intentions into Hitler's aggressive actions? In 1936, Nazi troops had occupied the Rhineland. British politicians had expressed the view that Hitler was 'only re-occupying his own back yard.' Later in the year, Hitler had signed a pact with Mussolini. Though it was obvious to anyone who had eyes to see, that the two dictators would now terrorize and hunt as a pack, the British Ambassador in Berlin had been a guest at the ceremony.

She said cautiously, knowing she was on very sensitive ground, 'Did the Nazis regard your family as being an enemy of the state because of its Jewishness?'

Christina remained silent, her eyes fixed on her clasped hands, smoke-dark wings of hair falling softly forward on either side of her delicately etched face. She had known how difficult it would be to confide in anyone, but she had forgotten how bizarre it would be, confiding in someone with a German surname. Someone whose father was an Aryan German. She took a deep, steadying breath. Carl Voigt hadn't lived in Germany since the outbreak of World War I. He had never, in even the minutest way, been an admirer of Hitler. But he was German. The country he had grown up in was the country she had grown up in. They shared a mutual language, though neither of them ever, apart from an occasional expletive or endearment, lapsed into it. He understood the German way of doing things, the German love of bureaucracy. And if anyone would be able to help her through the nightmare of finding out what had happened to her mother and grandmother, he would be able to do so.

'My father was printing anti-Nazi leaflets in the

53

basement of his chemist's shop,' she said, looking up from her clasped hands and meeting Kate's eyes. 'Heinrich was distributing them.'

It was the first time Kate had even known Christina's brother's Christian name. She drew in a deep, unsteady breath. Through the open window came the sound of Daniel Collins mowing his lawn; Nellie Miller chatting to Harriet Godfrey; the clip-clop and rattle of the horse-drawn hearse that Albert Jennings used as a fruit and vegetable cart; the chime of St Mark's Church clock. It seemed so strange, listening to these familiar sounds and hearing Christina talk at first-hand experience of the horrors of being Jewish in Hitler's Germany.

'Your father and brother must have been very brave,' she said at last, awkwardly.

Christina clasped her hands even tighter, the knuckles showing white. 'My father's friend, who helped him with the printing, told me I mustn't wait to see if my mother and grandmother would return.' Her voice trembled. 'He told me they would never return and that if I wanted to avoid being arrested and never being seen again, I had to leave Germany immediately. He knew of a route into Switzerland; people who would help me.' Tears glittered on her eyelashes. 'He was going to come with me, but on the night we were to leave he was arrested. And so I left alone.' Her voice had become barely audible. 'And I feel so guilty, Kate. I feel so guilty for having escaped and for living so cosily in Magnolia Square when . . . when . . .' She couldn't go on. Tears were spilling down her cheeks. She had said it. She had admitted to the guilt that was so heavy she sometimes thought she wouldn't be able to breathe for it. She was alive and her father and Heini were dead. All through the war years she had lived in the relative safety of London, in the bosom of a loving, noisy family, and her mother and grandmother had been – where? Lichtenburg? Dachau? It didn't bear thinking about. To think about it would be to lose her reason, and so for years she had told herself that her mother and grandmother had died almost immediately after their arrest, that they were no longer suffering, that they were at peace. And the guilt of her own survival had been almost more than she could bear.

Kate reached across the table and covered Christina's clasped hands with her own. 'There's no need to feel guilty, Christina. It's the very last thing your father and brother would have wanted. As for your mother and grandmother . . .' Her throat tightened. She didn't want to encourage Christina to hope if all hope was futile. And certainly it must be nearly futile. How could two Jewish women, one middle-aged and the other elderly, possibly have survived the war years in Germany, especially when it was known without doubt that they had been arrested as long ago as 1936? Yet there were people who had believed that Leon had died in 1942. She had never believed it. She had *known* he was still alive. But Christina had no such sixth sense about her mother and grandmother, for if she had, she would have expressed the belief years ago.

She said carefully, 'If they have survived the war, then I'm sure that now it's over they will contact Leah. And if they don't . . .' Her words hung heavily in the bright, sunny kitchen. 'If they don't, then you will just have to accept that they are dead, Christina. That they have been dead for a long, long time.'

The brass knocker tapped against the front door, and before Christina could make any kind of a response the door was opened. 'Cooee!' Hettie Collins called out cheerily. 'Anyone in?'

Kate held Christina's eyes for a long, agonized moment. There was no way their conversation could be continued now. Giving Christina's hands a comforting squeeze, Kate called back, 'I'm in the kitchen, Hettie! Christina's with me!'

Hettie bustled down the hallway leading from the front of the house to the back. 'I've just come from doing the flowers at the church,' she announced as she burst into the kitchen. 'Albert gave me some lovely delphiniums. They look a treat at either side of the aisle.' She looked across to the table and the lack of any sign of a teapot or cups. 'Shall I put the kettle on?' she asked, already reaching for it. 'I'm gasping for a cuppa.' She turned on the tap, running water into the kettle, saying as she did so, 'In the old days, Constance Giles always invited me into the vicarage for a cuppa when I'd finished doing the flowers. 'Course, I don't expect the Vicar to invite me in for a cuppa, but I miss it all the same.' The kettle was banged down on top of the oven's gas hob, and the imitation cherries on her black straw hat shuddered and bobbed. 'And when he marries again,' Hettie continued without pausing for breath, 'which, being a man, he's going to do, I don't expect I'll be offered tea. I expect his new, slip-of-a-girl missus will think herself far too lah-di-dah for that.'

Both Kate and Christina remained silent. Both of them knew and liked Ruth Fairbairn, Bob Giles's fiancée, but at the present moment neither of them had the heart to enter the lists on her behalf. For one thing, they both knew nothing they could say would change Hettie's attitude towards Ruth, and for another, their thoughts were still firmly on the conversation Hettie had interrupted.

'And so I wondered what flowers you'd be wanting in church for your wedding,' Hettie continued, slapping cups on to saucers as if the kitchen was her own. 'If the wedding's going to be this week or next week there won't be many roses out. There's some Canary Bird rioting all over the local bomb-site, but Canary Bird's a little on the tiny side to go well with fern, and I can't remember the last time I saw a bride with yellow roses. You want red for a wedding. Carrie had red roses when she married our Danny, and if I say so myself her bouquet was a sight for sore eyes.'

'I think I'd rather like a bouquet of Canary Bird,' Kate said, aware that verbal response to her unwanted visitor was long overdue. 'It would be both pretty and unusual.'

Hettie sniffed. Flowers from a bomb-site weren't her idea of wedding flowers, even if they were roses. Next thing she knew, Kate would be asking her to arrange stepmother blossom and rose-bay willow-herb all the way down the aisle!

'The kettle is boiling,' Christina said, as steam began to puff upwards.

Hettie sniffed again. She didn't need a foreigner to tell her when a kettle was boiling. Pointedly leaving it for another few seconds she poured milk into the cups. She'd never overly taken to Christina. Other people had suffered in the war, as well as the Jews. What about Constance Giles, the Vicar's wife? A nicer lady had never lived. She'd never had a bad word for anyone. Never hurt a fly. It was typical that, when she'd been blasted to kingdom come in the first air-raid of the war, she'd been making a visit to one of her husband's sick parishioners.

Using a kettle-holder Kate had made years ago, when she had been a Girl Guide, she poured some boiling water into the teapot, swirled it round and poured it out and then spooned tea into the warmed pot. To her mind, Christina was a hard little piece, and she didn't know what Jack Robson saw in her. He'd have been better off marrying a south-London girl. He'd have known where he stood then. She poured boiling water on to the tea-leaves. She and Daniel only had one son, Danny, and he, thank goodness, had had the good sense to marry a proper south-London girl. Everyone knew where they were with Carrie. She was always bright and cheery and straight as a die. Whereas Christina . . . Her mouth tightened as she waited for the tea to brew. In her opinion, Jack Robson would never know where he stood with Christina. Still waters ran deep, and there were none stiller than Christina.

'One sugar or two?' she said to her now, miffed that she had been cheated of her heart-to-heart with Kate, adding acerbically, 'Or have you given it up to help the Jenningses with their rationing?'

Chapter Four

'And now the war is over, you'll never go away again?' Matthew was asking Leon anxiously as they squelched over the mud flats below Greenwich.

'No,' Leon said, holding on to Luke's chubby hands as he straddled his neck.

Luke. He still couldn't get over the wonderment of his son. Or the name Kate had given him. It wasn't a very West Indian name. It wasn't even a very common English name, or at least it wasn't common in south London. He grinned to himself. First Matthew. Now Luke. If they had another two sons would Kate insist on christening them Mark and John?

'And we'll be a proper family now, won't we?' Daisy said, walking as close to him as was humanly possible. 'We'll be just like other people, won't we?'

'We're going to be a grand family,' Leon said, flashing her his sunlit smile. Though she was still only seven, Daisy remembered him from when he had been home on his last leave; the leave Luke had been conceived. Matthew had been only a baby then. Matthew had no memories of him, though it was hard to believe from the proprietorial way he dogged his every step.

'Want to throw stones,' Luke announced. 'Want to throw stones in the river.'

Leon swung him down from his shoulders, and Luke's wellington boots made a satisfyingly squelchy sound as they made contact with the mud.

'We're going to look for treasure,' Matthew said, speaking for Daisy as well as himself. 'Pirate ships used to anchor here and there's *lots* of buried treasure!'

A paddle-steamer on the way to Southend trawled down-river, its wash causing small waves to ripple outwards towards the banks. Luke screamed with delight as his wellingtons received a soaking. Daisy and Matthew hastily scampered out of range. Leon watched his little tribe indulgently. All kids loved playing about near the water's edge. His own childhood had been spent further down the river, at Chatham, and he had spent many happy hours searching for plunder amongst the flotsam and jetsam swept up by the tide.

Very few people ever believed him when he told them he hadn't only lived in Chatham as a child, but had been born there. 'Don't be daft,' even his closest friends had said, '''ow could you 'ave bin, when you're a darkie? Yer must 'ave bin born in Africa. Darkies come from Africa.' That had been before the war, of course; before black American servicemen stationed in England had startled, and often shocked, the local populace.

'My father came from Barbados,' he had said patiently, time and time again. 'My mother was English. Kent born and bred.' It had never made any difference. His skin was dark and Darkie had become his nickname, and no-one ever believed he was as British as they were.

'We've found some money!' Matthew shouted gleefully.

'A threepenny-bit. And Daisy's found a mouth-organ. It doesn't work, but it might do when it's dried out!'

A seaman on a tug ploughing up river recognized Leon's naval jersey and gave him a friendly wave. Leon waved back. He'd met with very little racial prejudice at sea, thank goodness, and ever since he had saved young Billy Lomax from being injured or killed in a runaway lorry, he had met with none at all in Magnolia Square. What he would do when he met with it in his children's presence, he didn't yet know. It was an ugliness he didn't want any of them exposed to, and yet they *would* be exposed to it, it was impossible they wouldn't be. And they would be exposed to it directly, as well as on his behalf.

For Luke, it would come in a different form to the remarks Matthew and Daisy would have to contend with. For all three of them it would be difficult. And somehow, he and Kate had to prepare them for the jokes that would hurt, the jibes that would be meant to hurt.

'Can we spend the threepenny-bit at Mr Jennings's fruit stall, Daddy-Leon?' Matthew asked, looking up at him, his little face shining with happiness. 'Can we have a picnic on the Heath?'

'Of course we can,' he ruffled Matthew's blond hair lovingly, 'and I'll tell you what else we can do. We can go to the pond at the top end of the village and see if anyone is sailing boats. And tonight I'll start building you a boat of your own. A boat with sails and masts and a flag.'

'Miss Radcynska is a displaced person,' Bob Giles said a few days later to his two churchwardens. 'The Church of England charity seeking to help victims of the war have

61

asked me if a home can be provided for her in St Mark's parish.' He paused, toying with a pencil on his desk, wondering just how to continue. Did he tell Daniel Collins and Wilfred Sharkey all he knew of Miss Radcynska's history, or would doing so be counter-productive? He looked across his cluttered desk at them both: Daniel, stolid and dependable and with a heart as big as Asia; Wilfred, austere, ascetic, and with rigid convictions no force on earth could sway. 'Miss Radcynska has suffered greatly,' he continued, choosing his words with care, deciding not to disclose for the moment just how stupefyingly horrific Anna Radcynska's suffering had been – and still was. 'She isn't well enough to live a completely independent life . . . and this gives rise to difficulties.'

Daniel waited patiently for the difficulties to be explained. When they were, whatever they were, he would set his mind to overcoming them. Wilfred frowned. He didn't like difficulties. They upset the tenor of a well-organized existence, and a well-organized existence was an existence that was centred in Christ.

'As I'm a widower, it isn't possible for Miss Radcynska to move temporarily into the vicarage,' Bob Giles continued, a shadow darkening his eyes as it always did whenever he spoke of the loss of his wife, however obliquely. 'But number eight is church property, and the bombed-out East End family we rehoused in the lower half of the house are moving out and moving back to the other side of the water.' Though he wasn't London-born and bred, Bob Giles had lived so long in south London that he spoke of the Thames as his friends and neighbours did, as if it were a cultural divide there was no overcoming.

'Then there's no problem,' Daniel said cheerily. 'With the Tillotsons living above her and Wilfred and his family living next door to her, Miss Radcynska will be as snug as a bug in a rug.'

Wilfred cleared his throat. It was all very well for Daniel to be so magnanimous. He wasn't the one who would be living next door to Miss whatever-her-name-was. 'Perhaps we shouldn't be too hasty,' he said, an air of condescension in his voice. Daniel was a boiler-maker and Wilfred, a draughtsman, felt by far his social superior. 'There are, after all, lots of *British*-born homeless people who would be only too happy to tenant number eight. How do we know how the Tillotsons will feel about Miss . . . Miss . . .' rather than risk mispronouncing the name he didn't attempt it, 'about a foreigner moving in beneath them? How do we know that the young woman in question can speak English?'

'As far as the Tillotsons are concerned, there isn't an immediate problem,' Bob Giles said, disappointed, as always, by Wilfred's ungenerous spirit. 'It could well be the beginning of next year before Major Tillotson is demobbed, and Mrs Tillotson is, as you know, in Scotland with her mother. As to your other question, Wilfred, the answer is, I'm afraid, that I don't know.'

'Well, if she can't speak English, all the more reason why she should be living among people who will only be too happy to help her learn it,' Daniel said, impatient at such nit-picking. 'Christina's as much at home now in south London as if she'd been born here, and Miss Radcynska soon will be as well.'

'Let's hope so, Daniel,' Bob Giles said, speedily taking the matter as having been settled. 'And now I think we'd better be heading over to the church. I've a wedding to conduct in twenty minutes unless I'm very much mistaken.'

'Weddings!' Hettie Collins said to Miriam, as they sat in one of the right-hand pews. 'This one's all right, but what Harriet Godfrey thinks she's doing, marrying for the first time at her age, I don't know. You'd think an educated woman like her would have something better to do with her time. As for the Vicar . . .' The bunch of imitation cherries on the plum straw hat, which replaced her workaday black one, wobbled with the force of her indignation. 'You'd think if he was going to marry again, he'd at least have married someone near his dead wife's age, not a young woman still in her twenties. He could have married a widow. There's plenty of 'em about these days, poor devils.'

'I know what you mean,' Miriam said sagely, nodding a head of iron-grey hair, for once not encased in hair curlers. 'It's almost as if he's *'appy* to be marryin' again. I wouldn't want my Albert to be 'appy to be marryin' again. I'd be revolvin' in my grave at the very thought!'

'And I thought Kate said she was only 'avin' a small weddin'.' Hettie continued, looking around the nearly full church. 'There couldn't be more people in 'ere if she'd invited all of Lewisham!'

'They've not all been invited,' Miriam said knowledgably. 'Word's spread and they're just noseyin'.'

'Well, I 'spect they've somethin' to nosey at,' Hettie conceded, her eyes on the groom.

In his naval uniform, and in the stark white and polished wood interior of St Mark's, Leon didn't look merely chocolate-coloured. He looked as black as the ace of spades.

'They'll do all right together,' Miriam said generously, knowing exactly what it was that Hettie, with unusual tact, hadn't put into words. 'An' it isn't as if 'er mother's alive to be upset, is it?'

Hettie grunted agreement, grateful that she hadn't any daughters who could run off marrying black sailors. She folded her arms across her matronly chest, saying in a voice that settled the matter, 'What's she going to wear though? She can't very well wear white, can she? Not with two of her nippers in the front pew. Your Carrie looked lovely in her wedding dress when she married our Danny. Say what you like, you can't beat a white wedding. Is that Doris Sharkey over there? Why has she got her hat pulled half over her face? She looks as if she's attending a funeral, not a blooming wedding!'

'You look beautiful, *Liebling*,' Carl Voigt said to Kate, a lump in his throat. 'Your mother would have been so proud of you!'

Kate looked towards the mantel where a photograph of her mother had stood for sixteen years, ever since her untimely death. From the silver frame loving, laughing eyes met hers. Would her mother have been proud of her? She hoped so. She hoped so with all her heart. There had been times, when first Matthew had been born illegitimately and then Luke had followed him, that she had often wondered what her mother's reaction to their births would have been. She stood silently for a few moments, the blue silk dress she had made with Carrie's help falling sleekly to her ankles, her eyes moving from

65

her mother's photograph to the photograph standing next to it.

Toby had been twenty-three when the photograph was taken. In a fleece-lined RAF flying jacket, he stood nonchalantly beside his Spitfire, a lock of Nordic-blond hair falling low across his forehead. Two weeks after the photograph was taken he had been killed, piloting his Spitfire over the Dunkirk beaches, engaging in battle with the Heinkels and Messerschmitts strafing the retreating British Army.

She had loved Toby. In a way that Leon completely understood, she still did love him. But her love hadn't been forged in maturity as her love for Leon was forged. She was bound to Leon with hoops of steel. Because of his mixed-blood parentage, Leon had always been a social misfit and, when they had first met in the dark, seemingly hopeless days of the war, she too, because of her father's German nationality, had also been a misfit, reviled and ostracized, and unbearably lonely. Her tummy muscles tightened at the mere memory. People had long ago resumed normal, friendly relations with her, but for an unforgettable period of time she and Leon had faced a hostile world together, and it was an experience that had welded them together as no other experience could have done. She knew the indignities Leon often suffered on account of his racial difference, for she had suffered very similar indignities. She knew the stoicism and hurt that lay beneath his apparent indifference to those indignities for she, too, had erected a similar false front. And now, at last, they were going to be married.

She turned away from the photographs and picked up

her wedding bouquet of yellow Canary Bird roses. 'I'm ready, Dad,' she said, slipping her free arm through his. 'I've never been more ready in all my life.'

There were murmurs of appreciation from her friends as she stepped inside the church on her father's arm, to the measured strains of 'The Wedding March'. Her dress was blue, not white: a deep lavender blue that emphasized the blue of her wide-spaced, thick-lashed eyes. She was wearing a hat, not a veil. With a shallow crown and large picture brim, dyed to the exact same shade as her dress and decorated with a tiny posy of Canary Bird roses, it looked both stylish and seductive.

Carrie, as matron-of-honour, was dressed in a simple blue floral summer dress, her bouquet a smaller version of Kate's. Daisy, who was Kate's only small bridesmaid, was dressed similarly in a dress that was blue and white and summery, though, where Carrie's dress was prudently unadorned, Daisy's was as flounced and ruffled as a princess's. She wore a large white satin ribbon in her straight dark hair, and another white satin ribbon decorated her posy of Canary Bird bud roses.

As Kate reached Leon's side, and as the sound of Ruth Fairbairn's organ playing faded away, Bob Giles looked at them both and smiled. It was the first wedding in Magnolia Square since the German surrender. Soon it would be followed by Charlie and Harriet's wedding, and then by his own wedding to Ruth. Soon too, pray God, the war still being fought in the Far East and the islands of the Pacific would also come to an end. Life was again full of hope. And for the young couple standing before him it was full of deep, abiding joy.

'Dearly beloved,' he said, lifting his eyes from their radiant faces, looking out over his abnormally large congregation, 'we are gathered together here in the sight of God, to join together this Man and this Woman in holy Matrimony . . .'

Ellen Pierce clasped her net-gloved hands tightly together. Kate looked beautiful. With her long, heavy braid of wheat-gold hair coiled into an elegant knot in the nape of her neck, she looked more than beautiful. She looked regal. A spasm almost of pain flared through Ellen's eyes. Kate's looks hadn't been inherited from Carl who, with his thinning hair and rimless spectacles, was pleasingly intellectual-looking but far from handsome, but from her mother. Was that why Carl had still not asked her to marry him? Because he couldn't bear the thought of settling, in middle age, for a plain, socially awkward woman, when he had once been married to a woman who, if her photograph was anything to go by, had looked like a happy Greta Garbo?

'Thirdly,' Bob Giles was saying, 'it was ordained for the mutual society, help, and comfort, that the one ought to have of the other, both in prosperity and adversity. Into which holy estate these two persons present come now to be joined. Therefore if any man can show any just cause, why they may not lawfully be joined together, let him now speak, or else hereafter for ever hold his peace.'

There was a silence in which a pin could have been heard dropping. It was broken by Wilfred Sharkey clearing his throat in what was interpreted, by many people, to be a disapproving manner. Ellen was oblivious of Wilfred's contribution to the proceedings. 'Mutual society, help, and comfort.' The words rang in her head.

That was what she wanted to share with Carl. He had been on his own for a long time and he wasn't a gregarious man. If he had been, she would never have had the temerity to offer him her friendship in the first place.

'I require and charge you both,' Bob Giles was now saying solemnly to both Kate and Leon, 'as ye will answer at the dreadful day of judgement when the secrets of all hearts shall be disclosed, that if either of you know any impediment, why ye may not be lawfully joined together in Matrimony, ye do now confess it . . .'

Of course, offering Carl friendship way back in early 1940 had been an easy thing to do. Kate had been a secretary at Harvey's Builders where she, Ellen, was Personnel Manageress. When Kate had disclosed to her that her father had been interned, she had shyly begun a correspondence with him to help him combat the loneliness and boredom she was sure he was experiencing. There had been many times since his release from internment when she had wondered if their pen-pal friendship hadn't been easier, and more rewarding, than the personal relationship which had succeeded it.

'Wilt thou have this Woman to thy wedded wife,' Bob Giles was now saying to Leon, 'to live together after God's ordinance in the holy estate of Matrimony? Wilt thou love her, comfort her, honour, and keep her in sickness and in health; and, forsaking all other, keep thee only unto her, so long as ye both shall live?'

Christina sat in one of the left-hand pews. It was the first time she had listened to the words of the Anglican wedding service since they had been spoken at her own wedding. After the ceremony, and the obligatory

69

reception held in the church hall, she and Jack had driven into Kent. Their wedding night had been spent in a small, lattice-windowed room above the White Bear Inn, in Brasted. That was all the time they had had together. The next morning he had returned to his unit and he had had no leave since. And at the end of the month, according to Mavis, he was going to be home again. Soon he would be coming home for good, and their married life together could truly start.

Leon had made his response in his distinctive, honey-dark voice. It was now Kate's turn to make hers.

'I will,' she said quietly, and without the least sign of nervousness.

Christina twisted her wedding ring round and round on her finger. Why hadn't Jack written to her with such important news? Had he, perhaps, done so, and had the letter gone astray in the mail, as Carrie insisted so many of Danny's letters had done? And even if he *had* written to her with the news, why had he written to Mavis at all? Mavis was a married woman, for goodness sake. Jealousy flared through her. Was he still continuing his gossip-arousing relationship with Mavis because of what had happened, or rather what had not happened, on their wedding night?

She felt sick with apprehension and regret. Why hadn't Jack been more understanding? Why hadn't he realized how traumatic the day had been for her, marrying in an Anglican church? Marrying without one member of her family being there as a witness. Marrying with her heart and mind full of thoughts of her dead and missing loved ones.

'Forasmuch as Katherine and Leon have consented

together in holy wedlock,' Bob Giles was saying sonorously, 'and have witnessed the same before God and this company, and thereto have given and pledged their troth either to other, and have declared the same by giving and receiving of a Ring, and by joining of hands; I pronounce that they be Man and Wife together, In the Name of the Father, and of the Son, and of the Holy Ghost. Amen.'

Christina became aware that an elderly neighbour, Emily Helliwell, was watching the way she was twisting her wedding ring round and round. Quickly she dropped her hands to her sides. Emily was Magnolia Square's local palm-reader and clairvoyant, and Christina knew that it wouldn't take much to alert her to the fact that things between her and Jack weren't quite as they should be.

'Almighty God,' began Bob Giles, embarking on his final blessing of the happy couple, 'who at the beginning did create our first parents, Adam and Eve, and did sanctify and join them together in marriage; Pour upon you the riches of His grace . . .'

As she stood behind Kate at the altar, tears stung Carrie's eyes. She, more than anyone else in the church, knew just how much Kate deserved her present happiness. There had been the anguish she had suffered when, at the outbreak of war, her father had been interned. Then there had been Toby Harvey's death at Dunkirk. And lastly, but by no means least, there had been the traumatic years after Leon had been reported missing and she had not known if he had been taken prisoner, or if he had died.

'. . . sanctify and bless you, that ye may please Him

71

both in body and soul, and live together in holy love unto your lives' end. Amen.'

And now Kate and Leon were married. And unlike most newly married couples, they already had a family of three children. With every fibre of her being, Carrie wished them well. She had been married long enough herself to know that marriage wasn't the fairy tale they had believed it to be when they were schoolgirls. When a house had to be shared with parents, and care had to be taken that neither love-making nor arguments were overheard, it was hard work. And it was even harder work when a man accustomed to wielding authority as a sergeant had to acclimatize himself to being just another factory employee.

Lines of tension etched her mouth. Ever since Danny had been eighteen, he had been a professional soldier. Or he had been until the last few months when, liberated in poor health from his Italian prison camp, he had been given the opportunity of opting for a Sick Discharge. He hadn't wanted to take it. He had wanted to return to non-active service – and she had persuaded him otherwise.

Ruth Fairbairn began to play the organ again. The hymn was 'All Things Bright and Beautiful', chosen by Kate because it was her children's favourite. Carrie sang the familiar words, her thoughts far away from them. Though she hadn't admitted it to anyone yet, not even Kate, she knew now that she had made a grave mistake. Danny had been happy in the Army. He had known respect and responsibility, and was Sergeant Collins, *sir*. In Civvie Street, working at the biscuit factory, he was just another debilitated returnee with no authority whatsoever. And he wasn't happy. He wasn't happy at all.

With a heavy heart, she wondered just how long it would be before he began laying the blame at her door, and what on earth the two of them would do when he did so.

'Doesn't Kate look *elegant*!' Harriet Godfrey said to Nellie Miller as, the hymn having come to an end, the bride and groom began to walk back down the aisle to joyful organ music.

'She looks the bee's knees,' Nellie said, hoisting herself to her feet with difficulty. The pew seat was very narrow, and as her posterior was very large, the last twenty minutes or so had been exceedingly uncomfortable. 'I wonder who Kate is going to throw 'er bouquet to?' she said as they filed out of the pew and into the aisle in the wake of Kate and Leon.

'Prudence Sharkey is young and single,' Harriet said musingly. 'Perhaps she'll throw it to Prudence.'

Nellie made a disparaging noise that turned several heads. Harriet lifted her eyebrows slightly. Nellie was unrepentant. 'Don't go givin' me none of your 'eadmistressy looks, 'Arriet,' she said, looking across to where Wilfred Sharkey was saying something to his wife, a frown pulling his eyebrows together. 'With Wilfred for a father, that young lady stands *no* chance of becoming a bride.'

It was Harriet's turn to frown slightly. She prided herself on being an excellent judge of character and had always regarded Wilfred Sharkey as being a pillar of Magnolia Square's little community. 'I don't quite understand,' she said as they stepped out of the church into the blazing summer sunshine. 'Wilfred's manner can be a little severe, but—'

73

'Severe?' Nellie looked as if she were going to explode. ''E's more than severe, 'Arriet, 'e's a proper misery, and 'e makes 'is family's life a misery too. There's no popping into The Swan for a drink and a bit of a knees-up for Doris. Oh dear me, no. Wilfred don't approve of drink and 'e don't approve of a good time either. Poor Prudence isn't allowed any boyfriends. The only thing in pants allowed over Wilfred's doorstep is the insurance man, and 'e must be eighty if 'e's a day!'

'Come on, ladies,' Albert Jennings exhorted, a box of pre-war confetti at the ready. 'Stop the chatter and pay the bride and groom some attention.'

Harriet, aware it was a miracle they hadn't been overheard, was only too happy to do as he suggested. As an ex-headmistress, she felt obliged to set a certain standard of behaviour, and gossiping at a wedding about a fellow wedding guest and neighbour was not the way to do it.

'I want the bride and groom on their own for the first photograph,' Daniel was saying authoritatively, a box Brownie camera hung importantly around his neck. 'In front of the church porch will be lovely, if the children can be lifted out of the way.'

Carrie scooped up a bewildered Luke and removed him from the field of Daniel's vision. Charlie ambled forward and lifted a protesting Matthew high into his arms.

'Only *one* photograph without the children,' Kate said to her photographer, radiant with happiness and not wanting that happiness to be flawed by her children's displeasure at being removed so unceremoniously from her side.

'I must have a little room,' Daniel protested as he was jostled by the happy couple's friends and neighbours. 'Will someone get that dog out of the way, please?'

'Oh, do get a move on, Daniel!' Miriam Jennings called out in exasperation. 'You're takin' a wedding photograph, not paintin' the bloomin' Sistine Chapel!'

Daniel took the photograph. Charlie swung Matthew down to the ground, and Carrie released her hold on Luke. With Matthew grasping tight hold of Leon's hand, Luke holding on to Kate's, Daisy in front of them and Carrie to one side of them, another photograph was laboriously taken. Then Daniel wanted to take a photograph of Kate and her father. And then one of Kate and Carrie and Daisy.

'Hey up,' Charlie said in a whispered aside to Harriet, his eyes not on the happy couple but on the exceedingly flash car he had just spied parked at the top end of the Square, and on the elderly, bulldog-jawed, expensively-suited figure standing beside it, 'but I fink Kate's got trouble, 'Arriet.'

Harriet turned her head, saw what he had seen, and sucked her breath in sharply.

'Do you fink I should 'ave a word with 'im?' Charlie asked, deeply troubled. 'Do you fink I should tell 'im it will spoil 'er day if she sees him standin' there, watchin'?'

Harriet immediately laid a restraining hand on his arm. 'No, Charlie. It would only make matters worse. With a little luck, he'll have gone by the time Daniel has finished taking photographs.'

Charlie looked towards the menacing figure of old Joss Harvey, of Harvey Construction Ltd, the man who was little Matthew's paternal great-grandfather, and hoped she was right. And if she wasn't? What could he, or anyone else, do about it? Old man Harvey was little Matthew's great-grandfather. He had as much right taking a look at Matthew's mother on her wedding day, as anyone else. But Kate wouldn't want him there. Not after all the trouble he had caused her. Not after he had tried to take Matthew away from her.

'For the Lord's sake, Daniel, 'ave done with the photos and let's throw the confetti!' Miriam called out, voicing her own, and everyone else's, impatience.

With difficulty, Charlie and Harriet returned their attention to the bride and groom. Carrie's daughter, Rose, presented Kate with a lucky horseshoe. Billy Lomax attempted to present her with a handful of coal so sooty that his hands and face were already as streaked as a miner's, and he was only prevented from doing so by being speedily hauled away by his grandmother.

'Yer stupid little bugger!' Miriam said irately as his cargo scattered far and wide. 'Yer supposed to give the bride a small piece of coal for luck, not half drown 'er in a ton of nutty slack!'

At last, to everyone's satisfaction, the bride and groom prepared to make a run for it through a traditional shower of confetti.

'But first the bouquet!' Pru Sharkey called out, much to her mother's consternation and her father's visible displeasure.

'Throw it this way, luv,' Nellie Miller shouted gamely. 'I could do with anuvver 'usband, just as long as 'e's an improvement on the last one!'

Amid shouts of encouragement and laughter, Kate tossed her bouquet high and in Pru's direction. With pink-cheeked eagerness Pru jumped high, catching it adroitly.

There was a storm of cheers, and Daniel could be heard demanding cheekily, 'So who's the lucky man going to be, Pru?'

'I don't suppose she knows,' Miriam said in an undertone to Hettie, 'just as long as it ain't the insurance man!'

Kate's fingers intertwined tightly with Leon's. Their reception was going to take place in the church hall, and for every step of the way they would be bombarded with confetti and flower petals. It was a moment so perfect, so joyous, she felt as if her heart would burst.

'Ready?' Leon asked, his smile of happiness nearly splitting his face.

'Yes,' she said and then, as their friends and neighbours lined the church path, she looked over their milling heads and saw the car and the figure beside it.

Her face froze. The car was a Bentley, and only one Bentley had ever nosed into Magnolia Square. When it had done so, four years ago, it had been because its owner wished to remove Matthew from her care. He had succeeded in doing so, but only temporarily. And now he was back, standing pugnaciously beside his chauffeured car, exuding wealth and power and menace.

'What's the matter, sweetheart?' Leon asked, immediately sensing the change in her.

'Nothing.' She flashed him a brilliant smile, refusing to let Joss Harvey spoil the most magical day of her life. When he had done his damnedest to permanently remove Matthew from her care, Leon had been a prisoner of war, and it had been a battle she had had to fight alone. She was alone no longer, and any future battles would be battles they would fight together.

She laughed up at her handsome, caring husband. 'There's nothing wrong at all, my darling,' she said, her voice thick with joy and love. 'Shall we make a run for it now? I think we've kept everyone waiting long enough, don't you?'

As they plunged into what, within seconds, was a maelstrom of confetti and flower petals, the silver-haired, bull-necked figure standing by the Bentley yanked open a rear door and barked an order at his uniformed chauffeur.

Seconds later, when a laughing, breathless Kate snatched a glance at where it had been parked, there was no sign of it. She knew, however, that it would return. And she knew that when it did return, she and Leon would need all their strength in order to keep their family intact and inviolate.

Chapter Five

'Tell me what happened between you and Mr Harvey,' Leon said grimly. 'Tell me everything that went on between the two of you during the years I was away.'

They were lying in the blissful comfort and privacy of their big, creaky double bed. It was an hour or so before dawn, and the curtains were pulled back, allowing moonlight to spill milkily into the room. From the next bedroom Carl Voigt's snores could be heard faintly and rhythmically. In the room across the landing, Luke and Matthew were cosily tucked into the same downy bed, a nightlight offering comfort in case they should wake. In the room at the far end of the landing, Daisy was asleep, a battered teddy bear in her arms.

Kate lay, her cheek resting against the naked warmth of Leon's chest, as his arm circled round her. 'Things came to a head between us the same week your ship was torpedoed and you were reported missing,' she said, her voice husky with remembered grief and pain. 'Matthew was still with his grandfather . . . yes, I know he's really Matthew's *great*-grandfather, but he's still only in his late sixties and he's so aggressive and forceful, I find it impossible to refer to him as a great-grandfather. Great-grandfathers should be feeble and as old as Father Time.'

Despite his apprehension at whatever it was she was about to tell him, a smile tugged the corners of his mouth.

'And?' he prompted, his arm tightening lovingly around her. 'What happened that week? Matthew was presumbly still with Mr Harvey at his country home in Somerset?'

Kate moved her head in a nod, her unbraided hair brushing silkily against his flesh. 'Yes. Mr Harvey took him to Somerset, with a nursery nurse, during the first few weeks of the Blitz. I didn't want him to go . . . he was only a few months old . . . but I knew he would be safe there, and I had Mr Harvey's promise that the minute London was out of danger he would return Matthew to me.'

Leon remained silent. It hadn't only been servicemen like himself who had suffered during the war. It had been civilians, too, especially civilians living in bomb-blitzed towns such as Plymouth and Coventry and London.

'What happened, sweetheart?' he asked at last, tenderly. Whatever it was, he would make it up to her. From now on, as long as he had breath in his body, he would never let anyone or anything distress or harm her.

She moved slightly against him, splaying a hand against the broad comfort of his chest. 'Hitler began directing all his energies against Russia, and the bombing was over. Or at least it was over for a time. I told Mr Harvey I would be travelling down to Somerset to collect Matthew and to bring him home with me.' She paused, reliving again the nightmarish moment when she had entered the nursery only to find it empty. 'And he wasn't there,' she said simply. 'Mr Harvey had spirited him away, and he vowed he would never return him to me.'

'*Sweet Jesus!*' The words were uttered softly, so as not to wake the sleeping children, but with such fierce intensity that Kate felt a tingle ripple down her spine. If Leon had been home, Joss Harvey would have paid dear for his high-handed, unspeakable behaviour.

'The next few days were a nightmare.' Her voice was unsteady, and though her head was buried on his shoulder he knew there were tears glinting on her eyelashes. 'I didn't know if you were dead or alive. I didn't know where Matthew was. And no-one would help me. Or at least no-one in authority would help me,' she added hurriedly as he made a swift, angry movement of disbelief.

From the next bedroom, her father's snores reached a crescendo and then, as he turned over in sleep, subsided.

'What did you do?' Leon asked quietly, controlling his inner fury with difficulty. He had known, on his last leave at home with her, that Joss Harvey wanted to adopt Matthew. Why, then, hadn't he realized how dangerous Joss Harvey could be? Why hadn't he realized that a man like Joss Harvey was a man who would never take 'no' for an answer?

'I went to the police. I went to a solicitor. Both were unhelpful. As far as they were concerned, Joss Harvey was respectability personified. And I, very obviously, wasn't.' Her gentle voice held a note of bitterness that, because it was so alien to her warm, compassionate nature, shocked him inexpressibly. 'Not only was Matthew illegitimate, but I was expecting another baby outside of wedlock. In their eyes, if Joss Harvey had

81

removed his great-grandson from my care, he had done so for good reasons.'

He said gently, 'And so what did you do when you received no joy from the police or the solicitor you had consulted?'

'I realized that the most obvious thing was to capitalize on my friendship with Matthew's nanny. I'd always got on well with Ruth Fairbairn and I knew that, thanks to Joss Harvey's lies, she wouldn't be aware that I no longer knew where she or Matthew were. So I put a message in the personal column of *The Lady*, which is a magazine all nannies read, and five days later Ruth was on the doorstep, Matthew in her arms.'

'And now she's about to marry the Vicar!' Leon said, humour re-entering his voice again. 'Which is a nice, happy ending.'

Kate smiled to herself in the moonlit darkness. Ruth's visit to Magnolia Square, with Matthew in her arms, had certainly had far-reaching and happy consequences for her. She had met Bob Giles when he was paying a parochial visit to the Jenningses, and the attraction between the two of them had been instant and mutual.

She kissed Leon's dark, velvet-smooth flesh and said, 'The happy ending came when Nellie Miller introduced me to her niece, Ruby. Ruby is a solicitor and she served Joss Harvey with so many writs, he must have thought he was drowning under them! Since then he's left both Matthew and me very much alone.'

'Until yesterday?'

'Until yesterday,' she agreed quietly and he felt her tremble in his arms.

He raised himself up on his elbow and looked down at

her. 'There's nothing to be frightened of, sweetheart,' he said fiercely. 'Matthew is *your* child. Soon, when the adoption goes through, he'll legally be *my* child as well. Joss Harvey is never going to take him from us. Not now. Not ever.'

As he lowered his head to hers, she hoped with all her heart that his words would prove to be prophetic. But she wasn't convinced. She knew Joss Harvey far better than Leon did. He had lost his son in the First World War and his grandson at Dunkirk. And he wanted his illegitimate great-grandson to take the place his son and his grandson would have filled. He wanted Matthew to be raised by him as his heir. And he was ruthless enough to let nothing stand in the way of that ambition.

'Leon is sure he can handle Joss Harvey, but he hasn't experienced Joss Harvey's ruthlessness at first hand,' Kate said to Carrie next morning, when she stopped by the Jennings's market stall in Lewisham High Street to have a few words with her.

Carrie expertly tipped half a stone of potatoes into a carrier bag the customer would be collecting when he came out of the nearby bookies and said, 'The trouble with old man Harvey is that he doesn't only have endless money for legal fees, he has a lifetime's experience of besting people. Harvey's is one of the biggest construction companies in the country, and it didn't get that way without there being a lot of sharp practice at the helm.'

'Don't I know it,' Kate said, not disguising her apprehension. Yesterday had been her wedding day, and she had refused to have it blighted by dwelling on thoughts of what Joss Harvey might or might not do in order to obtain custody of Matthew. Last night, in bed with Leon, she had felt that nothing on earth could harm her family. Now, in the garish brightness of day, she was not so sure. Joss Harvey was an astute businessman, and he had the power that came with wealth and influence.

Seeing the anxiety in her friend's eyes, Carrie tried to be reassuring. 'Just because he came for a look-see yesterday doesn't necessarily mean he's out to cause trouble,' she said, polishing apples to a rosy shine on her apron. 'Though how he got to hear about your wedding beats me.'

'It doesn't beat me,' Kate said darkly. 'It wouldn't surprise me if he'd known about Leon's home-coming even before Leon knew of it!'

Carrie chuckled and gave her attention to a prospective customer. 'Three pahnds of carrots? Better take four, luv,' she said in warm and friendly south-London fashion. 'They're fresh as a daisy which is more'n can be said for the tired-lookin' carrots Black'eath greengrocers are tryin' to off-load. An' what about a couple of apples? They're luvverly and juicy. Just the thing to keep the doctor away!'

Carrots and apples were speedily tipped into a cane shopping basket. Customers were never in short supply at the Jennings's market stall. Weights were always generous and produce was always fresh.

'And anyhow,' Carrie continued as another happy customer went on her way, 'old man Harvey hasn't given you any trouble for a long time now, has he? Why should he start again now?'

Kate transferred her own shopping basket from one hand to the other. Her real fear as to why he should do so was one she hadn't yet expressed, not even to Leon. She bit the corner of her lip – especially to Leon. She said unhappily, 'When Mr Harvey first tried to take Matthew from me, he told me he was doing so because, as I was having a second illegitimate child, I wasn't a fit person to rear his grandson's child.'

Carrie snorted. Kate had repeated that particular conversation to her at the time, and she had thought Joss Harvey was clutching at straws then; she thought he was clutching at straws now. What court would remove a child from its mother on those grounds? Especially when both children had been conceived during war-time and when the father of one of them had died a war hero?

Kate steeled herself to tell Carrie the real crux of why she was so worried. Her hand tightened on the handle of her basket. By her side, Hector whimpered with impatience. 'And he said that, as the father of my second child was black, no court in the land would consider him a suitable stepfather for his great-grandchild.'

Carrie's jaw dropped.

'And so that's why I'm so worried,' Kate said, knowing she had every reason to worry. If she hadn't, if the notion of a court declaring Leon unfit to be Matthew's stepfather because of the colour of his skin had been ludicrous, then Carrie would have burst into derisive laughter.

And Carrie wasn't laughing. She was looking horrified. 'But . . . but Leon is going to *adopt* Matthew, isn't he?' she said at last. 'And if he does, then he'll be Matthew's legal father, won't he? Not just his stepfather?'

Another prospective customer was eyeing Carrie's

display of onions, and it was obvious that their conversation couldn't continue for much longer.

'But what if Leon applying to adopt Matthew is what Joss Harvey has been waiting for?' Kate said, her face pale and strained. 'When there was every chance that Leon might be dead, he couldn't make an issue about his great-grandson being raised by Leon, but he can now. And I think he will do, Carrie. I think that's why he came to Magnolia Square yesterday. He wanted to see for himself that we had married. And now that we are married, he'll try to take Matthew away from us.'

'Four onions, six pahnds of carrots, a bunch of greens and three apples,' Carrie's customer said, snapping her carrier bag open in front of Carrie's weighing scales. 'And pardon me for saying so, but yer'd take much more custom if yer didn't gab so much to yer friend. Are those radishes yer 'iding be'ind the carrots? Beause if they are I'll 'ave two bunches.'

Kate raised a hand to Carrie to signify she was going to be on her way. Staying any longer was pointless. Lewisham High Street was no place to be discussing her very real fears about Joss Harvey's designs on Matthew.

Carrie tipped carrots on to the scales and watched her go, heavy-hearted. It had only been Kate's wedding day yesterday, for goodness sake. In an ideal world she would have been enjoying a honeymoon now, not trailing down to Lewisham High Street to confide her worries about Joss Harvey.

'And I'd cheer up a bit if I was you,' her customer said to her tartly. 'The war in Europe's been won an' the world's a sunnier place, or 'adn't you noticed?'

Carrie grinned, knowing that her customer was right

and knowing that if she didn't at least look cheerful she'd scare further custom away. 'I 'ad, as a matter of fact,' she said breezily. 'And when the war in the Far East is won as well, you can 'ave a basket of apples for free.'

'Bloody Japs,' her father said later that day at supper-time. 'Why can't Hirohito throw the towel in?' He rattled his evening paper in irritation. 'It says here they lost over a thousand men when the Yanks finally took Okinawa. And still it goes on: Yanks dying, Japs dying, prisoners of war dying.'

Miriam sniffed as she sat in a sagging-bottomed easy chair, darning a pile of socks. She didn't mind Albert being heartsore over the Yanks who were dying out in the Pacific, but she didn't given a tinker's curse about the bloody Japanese. Leah didn't very much care about them either. Her thoughts were centred on Christina, not the ongoing war in the Far East.

Albert, uncaring of his audience's lack of interest, mounted another hobby-horse. 'And look at this,' he said, stabbing at the newsprint with his thumb. 'It says here the Tories stand no chance in the comin' election. It says the new Prime Minister's goin' to be Clement Attlee, not Winston Churchill. And after all that Winnie's done for us. Keepin' our spirits up durin' our darkest hours. It's a damned disgrace!'

'I wish you wouldn't take on so, Albert,' Miriam said, tossing a darned sock on to a pile of similarly darned socks and reaching for an undarned one. 'People want a change, that's all. And you can't blame 'em. Not after all they've been through.' She stuffed a darning-tree into the heel of one of his socks and stretched the thinning wool over the top of it. 'I'm goin' to be votin' Labour,' she said, vigorously attacking the thinning area with her needle, 'and I 'spect everyone else in Magnolia Square will be voting the same way, 'cept for 'Arriet Godfrey of course. 'Arriet will be voting Tory. She'll be votin' Tory till the Second Coming!'

Leah fidgeted uneasily in her fireside chair. It was all very well nattering on about the Japanese and the coming general election, but what about problems a little nearer to home? What about Christina's increasing preoccupation? Instead of being happy as a lark at the prospect of soon being reunited with Jack, she was becoming more withdrawn with every day that passed. And Albert and Miriam didn't seem to notice.

'Where's Christina?' she asked before Albert could give vent to yet another of the bees in his bonnet. 'Why for do we hardly see her these days?'

'She'll be in her room, writing to Jack,' Albert said easily, turning over a page to see what else was wrong with the world.

'No, she isn't!' Miriam broke off her woollen darning thread with her teeth. 'She's gorn up to Kate's. Our Carrie says Kate's worryin' about old man 'Arvey 'avin' turned up at 'er weddin'. I 'spect Christina's trying to cheer 'er up a bit.'

Christina wasn't even aware of Kate's anxieties. Carrie had told her that Kate and Leon were taking Daisy, Matthew and Luke swimming that evening and that she, Danny, Rose and Elizabeth were going to go with them. It meant that, with a little luck, Carl Voigt would be at home on his own.

As she walked from the bottom corner of the Square to the more salubrious top right-hand corner, she reflected on the oddness of what she was about to do. All through the early part of the war years she had regarded Carl Voigt as an enemy. He was an Aryan German. She was Jewish. Only over a very long period of time had she begun to accept that he was no different a neighbour than Daniel Collins or Charlie Robson. And now she was going to him for help. Help that she doubted anyone else would know how to go about giving.

'Kate's out,' he said politely as he opened the door to her. 'She and Leon have taken the children swimming.'

Christina pushed a fall of silky dark hair away from her face. 'It wasn't Kate I wanted to see, Mr Voigt,' she said, her inner tension showing in her voice. 'It was yourself.'

Carl suppressed a stab of apprehension. There had been a time in his life when Christina, by drawing attention to his nationality, had caused him a lot of distress. Hoping fiercely that she wasn't about to do so again, he said reluctantly, 'Then you'd better come in, Christina. Would you like a cup of tea? I was just about to make one.'

Half an hour later, as they sat on straight-backed chairs at opposite sides of the kitchen table, there was no sign of apprehension in his eyes, only compassion.

'The Red Cross would be the first organization to approach,' he said, taking off his rimless spectacles and rubbing the bridge of his nose with his thumb and forefinger. 'Even if they can't help you themselves, they will be able to put you in touch with other refugee and aid organizations.' He laid his glasses on the table and clasped his hands, wondering how best to say what must be said. In the end he said simply, 'You mustn't have too much hope, my dear. Millions have died in Germany over the last ten years. And if your grandmother or your mother *had* survived, it would surely have occurred to them that you might have found refuge in England with your grandmother's old friend. And now that war in Europe is over, contacting Mrs Singer would be easy. She and the Jenningses have lived at number eighteen since the 1914–18 war. There could be no question of mail being wrongly redirected.'

Christina remained silent. It was what Kate had said to her. It was what everyone would say to her.

Carl regarded her with an anguished feeling of helplessness. He knew the irrational burden of guilt she was bearing, a guilt that came of knowing that all her family were almost certainly dead. He, too, was bearing a burden of irrational guilt. Though he was a pacifist and hadn't set foot in his homeland for over thirty years, he felt guilt by proxy for the monstrous crimes perpetrated there. And if he could help just one Jewish family to be reunited, it was a guilt that might, in a very small way, be eased.

'Write down the names of your mother and grand-mother,' he said decisively, 'their birth dates, their last known address. I'll start making enquiries tomorrow.'

Christina gave a small gasp, almost crying with relief. If Carl Voigt was prepared to help her, then it meant her quest wasn't entirely without hope. 'Thank you,' she said unsteadily.

Carl smiled. With his thinning hair and rimless spectacles, he wasn't a good-looking man, but his dif-fident manner possessed its own kind of charm, and

Christina was suddenly aware of just why a shy, middle-aged woman like Ellen Pierce was so attracted to him.

'*Nichts zu danken*,' he said, rising to his feet to make a fresh pot of tea. 'Don't mention it.'

For the first time ever she didn't flinch at being so forcibly reminded of his nationality. It was, after all, her nationality also. '*Meine Mutter ist am ersten Mai 1900 in Heidelberg geboren*,' she said, reaching in her handbag for pen and paper, and speaking German for the first time in nearly ten years. '*Und meine Grossmutter am siebten Oktober 1870 in Bermondsey*.'

When Kate and Leon and the children burst into the house an hour or so later, they were brought up short in shock at hearing an animated conversation in German taking place in the kitchen.

'I didn't know your father ever lapsed into German,' Leon said in startled surprise, Luke straddling his shoulders and clutching at his still damp, crinkly hair.

'Grandpa calls me *mein Häschen*,' Matthew said informatively as they hung their coats and jackets up in the hall. 'It means my little rabbit. And he calls Daisy *mein Schätzchen* which means—'

'It means my little treasure,' Daisy said, smiling winningly up at Leon. She, not Matthew, remembered him from a time even before Luke had been born. A time when he had returned to Magnolia Square on leave, bringing her oranges when oranges were a nearly unobtainable treat. At seven years old, she was old enough to realize that Leon was not her real daddy, just as Kate was not her real mummy, but that only made both of them more special to her.

'Can we go swimming next week as well, Daddy-Leon?' Matthew asked, trying to bring the focus of attention back to himself. 'Will you teach me to doggy-paddle and dive and—'

'It must be Christina he's talking to,' Kate said as Leon swung a squealing Luke down to *terra firma*. 'I think it might be as well if you took the children straight up to bed. I'll bring a tray of cocoa and sandwiches up.'

Leon raised his eyebrows slightly. Kate was indicating that whatever conversation was taking place in the kitchen, it was of a private nature and she didn't want the children interrupting it.

'All right,' he said obligingly, wondering what on earth the subject under discussion could be. 'Come on, troops. We're going to make ourselves scarce for a little while. Whose bedroom am I going to tell a bedtime story in?'

'Mine! Mine!' Matthew shouted eagerly, too delighted at the prospect of being told a bedtime story by his new daddy to protest at being taken to bed the minute they had returned home.

'It isn't your bedroom,' Daisy chided, taking hold of Luke's hand to help him up the stairs. 'It's your bedroom and Luke's. You share it.'

If his new daddy hadn't been there, Matthew would have put his tongue out at her. As it was, he said magnanimously, 'I *know* we share it. We share it 'cos we're a family. But I can still call it *mine*. Calling it mine doesn't mean not sharing, does it, Daddy-Leon?'

Kate grinned and left Leon to it. Walking into the kitchen, she put the carrier-bag with their damp towels and wet swimming costumes down by the copper and said cheerily, 'We've had a wonderful time. I'd no idea

Rose was such a good little swimmer. She and Daisy were like a pair of eels.'

'It was Carrie who taught her,' Christina said, pushing her chair away from the table and standing up. 'Danny can't swim. Is Leon going to teach him?'

Kate's eyebrows shot high. 'I didn't realize he couldn't swim!' she said in astonishment. 'I thought that by remaining in the shallow end and playing with Matthew and Luke he was simply being unselfish.'

A smile touched Christina's mouth. It was typical of Danny that he hadn't admitted to an inability to swim. 'Don't let him know that I told you,' she said, slipping her shoulder-bag strap over her arm. 'You know Danny. He's got a lot of pride where things like that are concerned.'

'Then he shouldn't have.' Kate poured milk for the children's cocoa into a pan. 'Leon would be only too happy to teach him. They could go on their own, without the children. And maybe Danny could teach Leon something in return.'

Christina felt a rush of warmth towards both Kate and her father. It was typical of Kate to try and think of a way Leon could help Danny learn to swim without Danny feeling either foolish or beholden. And Carl Voigt's acceptance that her mother and grandmother could very well still be alive, and his commitment to uncovering whatever information he could, had taken an intolerable burden from her shoulders. She no longer felt isolated and alone. Carl Voigt understood her grief and her guilt and her hope. She had someone now she could talk to, someone who understood the sense of alienation that often overwhelmed her. Someone who, after over thirty years of living in Britain, had admitted he, too, often felt similarly alienated.

'I must be going,' she said to them both. 'I didn't tell anyone I was leaving the house, and if they discover I'm not in they'll begin worrying.'

Kate turned the gas flame low beneath the pan of milk. 'I'll see you to the door,' she said as thumps and bumps shaking the ceiling above them indicated that a pillow-fight, not a story-telling session, was taking place.

At the front door, Christina paused for a moment. 'Your father has promised to help me, Kate,' she said confidingly. 'He's going to contact the Red Cross for me.'

Kate slipped her arm through Christina's and gave it an affectionate squeeze. 'I knew he would. And you can tell Jack that Dad will be very, very painstaking and thorough.'

'Jack?' An odd expression flashed through Christina's amethyst eyes.

Kate stared at her, oblivious of Charlie's cheery wave as he took Queenie for a walk in the direction of the Heath. 'You have written and told Jack you think your mother and grandmother could still be alive, haven't you?' she asked, hardly able to believe her sudden suspicion that Christina had done no such thing. 'He does know you're going to search for them, doesn't he?'

Christina hesitated for a second. It was late evening now and in the deepening dusk her skin looked as pale as alabaster. 'No,' she said reluctantly. 'No. I haven't told Jack. Not yet.' And before Kate could make an astonished response she turned on her heel, running lightly down the shallow flight of broad stone steps that led to the front path and the gate.

As she continued to hurry down to the bottom end of the Square, Kate stared after her, her eyes wide. What sort of a relationship did Christina and Jack have when Christina didn't divulge to him her fears and griefs and hopes?

'Cooee!' a familiar voice called out from the opposite direction. 'What are you doin', standin' starin' into space? Waitin' for Christmas?' Mavis was obviously returning from the same kind of expedition Charlie had been embarking on, for her grandmother's whippet was panting breathlessly at her heels.

'I was just having a quiet think,' she replied truthfully, not wanting to draw Mavis's attention to Christina's receding figure. She looked down at the panting dog. 'Where on earth have you been walking Bonzo? He looks all in.'

'Over to the village,' Mavis replied, coming to a halt at Kate's gateway, much to Bonzo's vast relief. ''E's my only excuse for gettin' out of an evenin'. If I go dahn The Swan, that little bleeder Billy lets on to my mum and then there's all 'ell to pay. At least this way I can call in The Princess of Wales for 'alf an hour or so without there bein' a ruckus.'

Kate was quite accustomed to Mavis's colourful way of referring to her eldest child, and didn't even blink. What did make her blink, however, was the realization that Mavis took even the briefest notice of Miriam's disapproval. For a moment she thought Mavis was teasing her and then Mavis said wearily, 'What trouble Mum thinks I can get up to 'avin' a drink in The Swan I can't imagine, but she's got it fixed in 'er 'ead that Ted will go 'aywire when 'e comes 'ome if 'e thinks I've been what she calls gallivantin'.' She gave an unladylike snort of derision. 'As if anyone could gallivant in The Swan! Lord, but life's borin' now there's no more air-raids or rocket attacks! I don't 'alf miss the excitement, don't you?' And with a grin and a friendly wink she continued on her way, her teeteringly-high heels tapping out ringingly on the pavement, her leopard-printed cotton skirt and scarlet chiffon blouse garishly exotic in the blue-spangled dusk.

Kate stepped back into her hallway and shut her front door. All through the height of the Blitz Mavis had been in the ATS, riding Ted's motor bike on life and death errands through shattered and blazing streets. She was now working as a bus conductress, and it was no wonder she found the peace boring. And Jack Robson, who had served in the Commandos all through the war, would no doubt find it boring also.

'Why are you looking so worried, sweetheart?' Leon asked a few minutes later when she put a tray bearing mugs of milky cocoa and Marmite sandwiches down on Matthew and Luke's bedside table, and then sat down next to him and Daisy on the edge of the bed. 'Has Christina got problems?'

'Yes,' Kate said unhappily, slipping her hand into his, 'and I rather think that in the near future she's going to have even more.'

Chapter Six

'You're just in time for a cup of char,' Miriam called out from the kitchen as Christina stepped inside the cluttered hall. 'I'm just puttin' the kettle on.'

'You needn't make a cup for me,' Christina called back, negotiating a lawn-mower that for some inexplicable reason had been left in the hallway, and wondering for the umpteenth time why it was the British couldn't survive so much as an hour without a cup of hot, strong, tea. 'I've already had two cups at the Voigts'.'

'Then you were bloomin' quick about it,' Albert retorted cheerily from the depths of his armchair, 'Carrie's only bin back ten minutes and she an' Kate an' Danny an' the kids all came 'ome from the swimmin' baths together.'

Christina walked into a sitting-room almost as cluttered as the hallway. Albert was reading the paper, the sleeves of his collarless shirt rolled high. Danny was trying to tune the wireless into some light music, his coppery-red hair still wet from the duckings he had received at the swimming baths. Leah was finishing off Miriam's pile of darning.

'Did the children enjoy themselves?' she asked, not wanting to disclose that it had been Kate's father she had been talking to and drinking tea with, not Kate.

'They nearly bloomin' drowned me,' Danny said, successfully tuning the wireless into some dance music. 'That little Daisy swims like a fish.'

'And so does our Rose,' Albert chipped in, not wanting his granddaughter to be put in the shade by her friend. 'Pru Sharkey used to be like greased lightnin' in the water,' he added, dropping his newspaper to the floor where Bonzo immediately sat on it. 'I remember her mother tellin' me 'ow she won medal after medal when she was at school.'

Everyone looked at him in astonishment. 'Pru Sharkey?' Danny said, perched on the arm of a battered sofa and swinging his foot up and down to the strains of Reginald King and his orchestra. 'I wouldn't 'ave thought Pru would 'ave been *allowed* to go swimmin'. I would 'ave thought old man Sharkey would 'ave 'it the roof at the thought of 'er in a swimmin' costume.'

Miriam came into the room, a pint pot of tea in one hand for Albert, a mug of tea in the other for her mother. ''E did,' she said expressively, handing Albert his tea. 'An' if it wasn't for the 'eadmaster, the poor little mare would 'ave 'ad to give it up.'

Even Christina was intrigued. Wilfred Sharkey saw himself as an authority figure who bowed to no-one except, very reluctantly, Bob Giles. 'What did the headmaster do?' she asked moving a half-knitted pullover to one side in order to sit down on the littered sofa.

''E told Wilfred he was out of order,' Miriam said, handing the mug of tea to Leah and plumping herself down next to Christina. ''E said Pru's athletic ability was a God-given talent an' that it would be a sin if she wasn't allowed to express it, an' that if Wilfred was 'alf the Christian he professed to be 'e'd encourage 'er, not put obstacles in 'er path. An' then he said that if Wilfred persisted in refusin' to allow 'er to swim, 'e'd tell the Vicar.'

Danny laughed so hard he nearly fell off the arm of the sofa. Albert chuckled into his pint of tea. Leah said in high admiration, 'That headmaster was a clever man, *bubbeleh*. He knew Wilfred's Achilles' heel, all right.'

'I don't know about Wilfred's Achilles' 'eel,' Miriam said, eyeing the large pile of finished darning. 'I think Albert must 'ave dodgy 'eels the way 'e goes through 'is socks!'

That night, in bed in the room she shared with Rose, Christina lay awake for a long time. It was always the same whenever she stepped over the threshold of the house that had become her home. There would be good-natured bantering. Endless mugs of tea. Lots of gossip and laughter. And when Jack was demobbed she would be packing her bags and moving out, leaving all the noise and clutter and camaraderie behind her in order to build a home of her own.

She lay on her back, her hands clasped behind her head. Where would that home be? Would it be at number twelve, with Charlie? She liked her father-in-law. Despite his dubious criminal past, it was impossible not to like him. But Charlie was engaged to Harriet Godfrey and she couldn't envisage herself sharing a home with Harriet and she certainly couldn't envisage Jack doing so.

In the darkness Rose stirred, murmuring in her sleep.

She looked across at her lovingly. She had already been living at number eighteen when Rose had been born, and she would miss Rose and Rose would miss her. But she would have Jack. Her stomach muscles tightened in a fierce, chaotic tumble of emotions. Why had he still not written to her with news of when he hoped to be home? Was it because, with the war still continuing in the Far East, home leave for Commando units was still not on the cards? And did that mean that Mavis had been imaginatively inventive when she had said Jack had written to her with the news that he hoped to be home soon? Or had she simply mistaken whatever it was he had written to her?

She turned over on her side, trying to control the surge of jealousy that threatened to bring her almost to tears. Why, when she loved Jack so much, did she find it so difficult to confide in him? Why hadn't she told him of the guilt and grief that still wracked her where her family were concerned? Was it because she instinctively felt that a man who lived for the moment, as Jack so spectacularly did, wouldn't understand? That he would think her inability to free herself from the tragedies of her past was morbid and pointless?

She dug her fingers into the soft down of her pillow. 'Come home soon, Jack!' she whispered fiercely, tears scalding her cheeks. 'Come home soon and let everything be all right between us!'

Pru Sharkey sat miserably in the bus-shelter at the corner of the Heath. It was August now, and London was suffering one of its periodic summer thunderstorms. In the distance, lightning flashed over Blackheath Village, searingly illuminating All Saints' Church. A little nearer, the donkey-man had donned a capacious mackintosh and sou'wester and had thrown groundsheets over his animals to keep the worst of the rain off them while he stoically waited for the storm to rumble away.

The donkeys looked exceedingly despondent and Pru sympathized with them. She, too, felt despondent. She had felt despondent for so long she had forgotten what it was like to feel anything else. She looked down at her sensibly shod feet. Brown, low-heeled, thick-soled shoes with a sturdy strap across the ankle. They were unfashionable shoes – old women's shoes – shoes that looked like boat-barges.

'They're serviceable,' her father had said as he towered over her in Jem Porritt's linoleum-floored Repair and Shoe Shop. It had been an adjective impossible to disagree with.

Rain drummed down on the roof of the bus-shelter, and Pru sighed heavily. She was nineteen years old. No-one else she knew of her age had to suffer being taken for a new pair of shoes by their father, especially when the money for the shoes was being paid for out of her own hard-earned money. She sighed again. And she hadn't wanted to shop for shoes in Mr Porritt's musty-smelling shop. She had wanted to shop for them in Lewisham or Catford, and to do so in a shoe shop that sold stylish shoes, not just old women's shoes and working boots and slippers.

Trying to explain to her father was hopeless. It always was. All he cared about was that she didn't look flighty and cheap. 'Kate Emmerson doesn't look flighty or cheap,' she had said frustratedly, 'and Kate doesn't buy

101

her shoes at Jem's. She buys them in Lewisham, at Timpsons.'

Whether Kate had bought her tan leather and white buckskin, cuban-heeled shoes at Timpsons, Prudence didn't truly know. But they *looked* as if they had come from Timpsons. Although they were sensible, they were also classy. Everything about Kate Emmerson was classy.

'You're damned out of your own mouth!' her father had said harshly. 'Katherine Voigt is the mother of two illegitimate children! And one of them is a half-caste child who will never be accepted by either its mother's race, or its father's!'

'Kate's name is Emmerson now, not Voigt,' she had said mutinously. 'And you're wrong about Luke. Everyone adores him!'

'They won't when he's older and eyeing their daughters,' her father had retorted crushingly. 'And now let's get some dubbin to waterproof those shoes.'

A bus trundled into view. Pru remained seated. She wasn't waiting for the bus, she was simply taking shelter and delaying the moment when she would have to return to her joyless home. Malcom Lewis, Mr Giles's young scoutmaster, was standing on the platform, obviously about to jump off even before the bus splashed to a stop. Pru felt a stirring of interest. Malcolm Lewis was extremely personable. He was also very often the subject of Magnolia Square gossip. 'Why he's not in the Forces beats me,' she remembered Hettie Collins once saying to Miriam Jennings, when the Blitz had been at its height and they had all been crammed together in the local air-raid shelter. 'He's young and fit, and for all he's a scoutmaster, he's not a conchie.'

'Mebbe 'e's somethin' 'igh in intelligence,' Miriam had proffered, sucking on a glacier mint. 'Mebbe 'e's 'ighly indispensable to the government.'

Pru eyed Malcom Lewis speculatively as he jumped nimbly off the bus. Was he a secret service agent? And if he was, how was it he'd spent the war in Lewisham and Blackheath? Why hadn't he been in Paris or Tangiers or Cairo?

'You'd better be quick,' he said to her affably as the bus driver looked towards her. 'He won't wait for ever.'

'I'm not going anywhere,' Pru said, flushing and feeling foolish.

The bus driver raised his eyes to heaven and slammed his bus once more into gear. Malcom Lewis grinned. 'It isn't raining so heavily now. Shall we walk over to Magnolia Square together and dodge the raindrops?'

With awkward self-consciousness, she rose to her feet. Whether Malcom Lewis had or hadn't a glamorous war-time past, he was most definitely the most good-looking young man for miles around. Far too good-looking for her to have ever hoped he might take an interest in her. And he wasn't taking an interest now, she reminded herself glumly as they left the pavement and struck out across the sopping wet grass of the Heath. If he'd come across Miss Helliwell or Nellie Miller at the bus stop he would have chatted to them just as companionably. He was that kind of young man.

'Where have you been?' he asked, turning the collar of his jacket down as the raindrops decreased to an occasional spatter and a weak sun speared the clouds.

'Work.'

She sounded so morose that his grin deepened. 'It

can't be that bad, surely? Didn't your father get you a position as a filing clerk with Baileys, the solicitors?'

Pru nodded. He had, and the work bored her to tears. The office was cramped and fusty-smelling. Mr Bailey was older than Methuselah, and Miss Crabtree, his secretary, had been employed by him since before the 1914–18 war. If she had been allowed to choose her employment for herself she would have chosen to work in a dress shop, but she hadn't been allowed to choose her own employment. Her father regarded shop-work as common, and clerical work, albeit lowly clerical work, as being far more respectable.

'OK. It *is* that bad,' he said as he received no answer to his query. 'So why stay? There's plenty of jobs about. You could take your pick.'

'No,' she said briefly, not turning her head to look at him. 'I couldn't.'

He regarded her with a mixture of amusement and perplexity. She was a strange girl. Plain and oddly unforthcoming. He wondered why she didn't make more of herself. His sisters were no older than Pru and they both wore a touch of lipstick and darkened their eyelashes. With a flash of surprise he realized that if Pru Sharkey wore lipstick and darkened her eyelashes she would look quite pretty.

'Have you heard about the Polish girl who's coming to live in the Square?' he asked, changing tack as he quite obviously wasn't getting anywhere with his present subject of conversation. 'She should be arriving any day now.'

Pru's jaw tightened. Had she heard about the Polish girl! For the last few weeks she and her mother had heard of nothing else. 'It's criminal short-sightedness!' her father had ranted time and time again. 'We already have Germans, market-traders, a West Indian and a criminal living in the Square! Any more riff-raff and we might as well be living in Bermondsey or Limehouse!'

'There's only *one* German living in the Square, dear,' her mother had protested bravely, speaking of Christina.

The interruption had been a mistake.

'*And what do you think the Voigts are?*' he had demanded savagely, spinning round on her. '*English landed gentry?*'

Her mother's face had drained of colour and Pru's intention of reminding her father that Leon Emmerson was only *half* West Indian and that Charlie Robson was an *ex*-convict rapidly vanished. If she deliberately antagonized him he would only take his temper out on her mother, turning physically abusive as he had the day before Kate and Leon's wedding.

'Yes,' she said, remembering that, via his church activities, Malcolm Lewis was a kind of colleague of her father's, 'I'd heard.'

Malcolm dug his hands into the pockets of his flannels and gave up. He couldn't make her talk if she didn't want to. He wondered what activity his scout-pack would enjoy that evening. And he wondered if he could persuade Mavis Lomax to encourage young Billy to become a scout. If he did, Billy might, just might, end up a law-abiding young man and not a tearaway, or worse.

'Not perishin' likely!' Billy said with fervour when his mother put the proposition to him. 'Scouts wear short trousers and I ain't stayin' in short trousers a day longer than I 'ave to!'

The fact that he wasn't already in long trousers was an ongoing source of contention between them. 'Jimmie Binns is in long trousers an' 'e's only eleven!' he had pointed out in simmering frustration. 'An as 'e's in my gang it makes me look ridiculous!'

Mavis had been uncaring. 'Jimmie Binns is only in long trousers 'cos they're 'is big brother's 'and-me-downs,' she had said, smoothing Vaseline on her eyebrows to make them glossy. ''Is short trousers 'ad so many 'oles in 'em 'e looked like a colander.'

Jack Robson sprang off the still-moving train as it eased its way into Blackheath Station. He was home again on leave and, judging by the cataclysmic news broadcast that morning by the BBC, in another few months he would be home for good. The Japs couldn't possibly prolong the war now, not after two of their biggest cities had been obliterated by A-bombs. He strode down the platform, his kit-bag slung easily over his shoulder, a tall, loose-limbed, hard-muscled young man. Would he be demobbed by Christmas? It was certainly a possibility.

'Wotcher, Jack!' the aged ticket collector said, his face wreathed in welcoming smiles. 'A forty-eight-hour one, is it? Your missus'll be pleased.'

'She'll be surprised as well,' Jack said with a grin. 'For all she knows I'm still in Greece.'

The ticket collector chuckled. If any other young serviceman had told him he was arriving home after an absence of over a year, without prior warning, he would have told him he was taking a hell of a risk. Many young wives behaved themselves between their husbands' far too infrequent leaves, but a staggering amount didn't. They were off dancing and drinking and having themselves a rare old time. Christina Robson wasn't one of them, though. Jack was as likely to find someone else in his home, his feet under the table, as the Pope was likely to turn Protestant.

Well aware of the ticket collector's thoughts, Jack swung out of the station and into the heart of Blackheath Village. He hadn't written to Christina with the news because he hadn't been a hundred per cent sure his leave would come off and because if it *did* come off, he wanted to see the incredulity and joy on her face when she opened the door to him. And he hadn't written and told her he felt an early demob was on the cards, as he had to Mavis, because until this morning's news it had only been a fierce hope. Now, however, with Japan facing the threat of more A-bombs and virtual extinction unless she speedily surrendered, he felt wide-scale demobilization was a sure-fire certainty, and he whistled exuberantly to himself as he began to stride up Tranquil Vale, towards All Saints' Church and the Heath.

'Hello there, Jack!' Hettie Collins called out to him from the other side of the street as she stood in a long queue outside the butcher's. 'Nice to have you home again! When's it going to be for good, though, that's what I want to know!'

Jack merely grinned, not slackening his pace. However long the interval between leaves home, some things never changed. The queues, for one thing. Housewives had begun queuing when food shortages had first hit in the early days of the war, and they were queuing still. Outside the greengrocer's he spotted little Miss Helliwell, her old-fashioned georgette summer dress reaching almost to her ankles, chiffon scarves and multitudinous necklaces fighting for space around her neck. He suppressed the temptation to stop and chat with her. There would be time for such chats later, after his reunion with Christina.

Desire surged through him. From the first moment he had seen her, he had wanted her. And he had known why he had wanted her. It had been because, with her shiny black hair and delicately-featured face, she was as beautiful as a Madonna. And, like a Madonna, there was a mysterious air of self-containment about her. Unlike the bright and breezy south-east London girls he had grown up with, Christina never chattered for the sheer joy of chattering, or ever indulged in light-hearted banter. Always polite, always pleasant, her thoughts were her own and impossible to guess at. He had found her intriguing and tantalizing, and had pursued her mercilessly.

Easing his kit-bag a little more comfortably on his shoulder, he set out across the Heath, thinking back to the early days of their courtship. Such pursuit had been a novel experience for him. Ever since he had been a toddler, the opposite sex had sought him out remorselessly and, by the time he had been in his late teens, his reputation as a lady-killer had been well established. His mouth quirked in amusement. It had been a reputation Christina had been singularly unimpressed by. How long had it taken him to break down her defences? Four years? Five? The war hadn't helped. He had volunteered for the Commandos, and ever since he had enjoyed only intermittent leaves at home. Soon, however, he would be home for good, and then his and Christina's life together could really start.

'Jack! *Jack!*' An ecstatic female voice shrieked, breaking in on his thoughts.

He shielded his eyes from the sun and saw that it was little Beryl Lomax who was racing towards him, her eyes alight, her face glowing.

'*You're home! You're home! You're home!*' she shouted joyfully, as he dropped his kit-bag to the grass and opened his arms wide.

'I am, but not for long,' he said, his arms closing round her, 'so you'd better make the most of me while you can!'

Laughingly he swung her dizzyingly round and round. When at last he set her totteringly back on her feet, she said admonishingly, 'I'm nine years old now! Only babies get swung round.'

'Oh no, they don't,' Jack said, picking up his kit-bag and slinging it back across his shoulder and taking hold of her hand. 'No young lady is ever too big to be swung around.'

Beryl giggled. With her fine, fair hair worn short and straight she wasn't a spectacularly pretty child, but she was an engaging one. 'Will you swing Ma around?' she asked, skipping along at his side. 'Will you swing Mrs Miller around?'

'I shall probably swing your ma around,' Jack said equably, 'but I'd need the help of a crane to swing Nellie Miller around!'

Beryl giggled some more and then said, 'I suppose you want the news. When people have been away for a long time they always want news.'

'That's very true,' Jack said, knowing she was trying to be grown-up and refraining from teasing her. 'So fire away. What's been happening? Has Kate had news of her fellow yet? Has Nellie heard from her nephew? Has the Vicar re-married?'

They were nearing the edge of the Heath now and Beryl knew that once they entered Magnolia Terrace word of Jack's homecoming would spread like wildfire and her precious time alone with him would come to an abrupt end.

'Leon's home, and he and Kate are married,' she said, eager to impart all important information. 'And the Vicar is engaged to Miss Fairbairn. I don't know anything about Nellie and her nephew, but I do know your dad is going to be married. He's going to marry Miss Godfrey.'

Jack stumbled. Regaining his balance he said with feeling, 'Quit the teasing, Beryl. You nearly gave me a perishing heart attack!'

Beryl tilted her head slightly to one side and regarded him gravely. 'I'm not teasing,' she said, mildly offended. 'I wouldn't tease about people getting *married*. 'Course, they're both ever so *old* to be getting married,' she added, trying to see the news from his point of view and remembering something she had overheard her granddad saying to Mr Collins when they had been discussing the forthcoming wedding, 'but there's many a good tune played on an old fiddle.'

Jack made a choking sound and she said, perplexed, 'Well, that's what Grandad said, but I don't understand it. Your dad doesn't play a fiddle, does he? And Miss Godfrey only plays the piano.'

When Jack could trust himself to speak he said

110

hoarsely, 'And when's this wedding going to take place?'

Beryl shrugged her shoulders. 'I dunno. I 'spect they're waiting for you to come home.' She flashed him a smile that almost split her elfin face in half. 'And you're home now, aren't you? Perhaps it will be this week!'

It was Billy who saved Jack from having to make any kind of a response. He had been languishing high up in a favourite tree in Magnolia Terrace, and the second he saw them he jack-knifed upright, nearly falling out of it.

'Jack! *Jack!*' he yelled, waving madly. 'Have yer got any Commando knives with yer? 'Ave yer got any Jerry 'elmets?'

By the time Beryl and Jack reached the foot of the tree Billy, whooping like a dervish, had shinned down it.

'Wotcher, mate,' Jack said affectionately, rumpling Billy's spiky mop of hair. 'Who were you on the look-out for? A Luftwaffe pilot that doesn't know Germany's surrendered yet?'

'Nah,' Billy said, not wanting his idol to think he was so daft, 'but it ain't 'alf borin' not 'avin' anything to look out for. Mum thinks it's boring too, 'specially as my gran's kicking up a ruckus about 'er goin' out at night. Gran says my dad'll be 'ome soon,' he added confidentially, 'and that as Mum will 'ave to start behavin' 'erself then, she might as well start behaving 'erself now.'

Jack, well accustomed to the plain speaking that took place in the Jennings and Lomax households, merely grinned at the thought of Miriam trying to clip Mavis's wings at this late stage of the game. Inwardly he wasn't grinning at all. He was trying to come to terms with Beryl's shattering news.

Had his father really proposed marriage to Harriet

111

Godfrey? Harriet Godfrey, a woman he and his friends had always referred to, when she had been their junior school headmistress, as a prissy old trout? He'd known, of course, that the two of them had struck up an unlikely friendship. His father had never grasped the difficulties of reading and writing and, inexplicably, Harriet Godfrey had one day taken it into her head to begin teaching him. Even more inexplicably, his father had happily allowed her to do so. From then on the two of them had been regularly seen together, walking Queenie on the Heath or enjoying a drink at The Princess of Wales. And now, according to Beryl, they were going to get married.

As Billy grabbed the lids off two dustbins and began leading the way into Magnolia Square, clanking them together and shouting to the world at large, 'Jack's home! Jack's home!' Jack wondered if there was any hope that Beryl had misheard or misunderstood. Children often did, after all. Or perhaps whoever had told her the news had been teasing her. Or had been just trying to stir up trouble. Or . . .

'Welcome home, Jack!' Daniel Collins cried, pushing his bedroom window up and hanging half out of it, his braces dangling. 'Has Beryl told you Leon Emmerson's come marching home as well? Smashing news, isn't it?'

Other windows were also being opened. Doors were being thrown wide. Despite his consternation as to whether Beryl's news was genuine or not, Jack couldn't help being vastly amused by the shouts of welcome being hurled at him from all sides. There had been a time, before the war, when he and his twin brother had been the local bad boys. Then Jerry had died, fighting the Fascists in Spain, and everyone had immediately

112

forgotten their previous opinion of him and had eu-
logized him instead. Now, it seemed, it was his turn to
come in for a bit of the same treatment.

As Billy noisily led the way past the Voigts' house, the
door was tugged open and Kate burst out of the house, a
dark-skinned, curly-headed toddler at her heels, Hector
charging in front of her.

'Jack! How wonderful!' she cried, running down to
her gate, her eyes shining, her long braid of flaxen hair
swinging like a schoolgirl's.

For Kate, he paused. There had been a time, long ago,
when he had wondered if she might one day become his
sister-in-law. Then news had come of Jerry's death and
he had never known if his assumptions about their
relationship had been correct or not. He kissed her
warmly on the cheek, saying, 'I've heard the news about
Leon,' adding teasingly, 'I'm glad to know he's made an
honest woman of you at last. Wasn't before time though,
was it?'

'It certainly wasn't,' she agreed with full-throated
laughter.

Luke tugged at her skirts. 'Who that man, Mummy?'
he demanded, not liking the disconcerting familiarity
between his mother and the big, dark-haired stranger.

'He's a friend and neighbour, sweetheart.' She bent
down and scooped him up in her arms so that he could
say hello to Jack face to face. 'And his name is Jack.'

As if to corroborate her words, there were cries of
'Jack! Jack!' and half a dozen of Billy's mates came
dashing up the street, eager to give their local hero a royal
welcome.

'You'd best be on your way,' Kate said to him as Luke

put his thumb in his mouth and leaned his head against her shoulder, and Nellie Miller steamed into the Square from the direction of Magnolia Terrace. 'Nellie's a one-man welcoming band. If she gets you in her clutches you won't be reunited with Christina until Christmas!'

Well aware of the truth of her words Jack gave Nellie a cheery wave and then, a growing entourage of children and dogs at his heels, set off at a brisk pace towards the bottom end of the Square.

Swiftly he strode past number six and number eight and then past the Sharkeys' house. Net curtains twitched to one side but whether it was Wilfred Sharkey or his wife taking a surreptitious look-see, he neither knew nor cared. His own house was next, but he didn't even pause by its gate. Christina wouldn't be there. She would be at the Jennings's. Or she would be if she wasn't down the market, helping Albert out at his fruit and veg stall.

Excitement and anticipation knotted his stomach muscles into painful knots. 'Please God,' he prayed inwardly, 'don't let her be down the market. Let her be in the house. Let the waiting be nearly at an end!'

With Billy still leading the way, and clanging his filched dustbin lids together as if they were giant cymbals, he strode past the overgrown bomb-site that had once been the Misses Helliwells' house. The roses of medieval France and Persia that Emily Helliwell had once so lovingly tended ran riot over the rubble. Uncaring of their beauty and scent, he turned the corner on to the bottom end of the Square.

The Lomax's front door was slammed back on its hinges so hard a slate fell off the roof. '*Jack!*' Mavis shrieked, rocketing down her pot-holed pathway at

114

suicidal speed. 'For the love of God! What 'ave you got with you? A bloody brass band?'

Next door, at the Jennings's, an upstairs window was shuttered open and Miriam leaned out, metal hair curlers bristling hedgehog-like all over her head. 'Jack's home!' she shouted over her shoulder to the household at large. 'Someone tell Christina to get to the front door sharpish!'

Leah was already at the door, Carrie was running down the stairs to join her. Danny, in the kitchen mending a pair of working boots on Albert's last, put down his hammer and decided to have a cigarette. In his opinion too much fuss had always been made over the fact that Jack Robson was a Commando. Being a Commando didn't automatically make a man a hero.

Through the open window, he could see Christina pegging washing on the clothes-line. 'Your old man's 'ome,' he shouted to her laconically. 'And at this rate you're goin' to be the last person in the Square to give 'im a welcome!'

Christina stared at him for a moment in disbelief then, as the sound of Billy's clanging dustbin lids impinged on her consciousness, she dropped the towel she had been about to peg on the line, running, running, running. Up the back garden path and into the house, through the kitchen, down the littered hallway to the open front door. And there he was, as devastatingly handsome as ever, swinging a squealing Mavis round and round in his arms.

Chapter Seven

'Nevertheless, I do feel Moshambo has let me down very badly,' Emily Helliwell said to her wheelchair-bound sister and to Nellie Miller, who had called in on them to tell them the news of Jack Robson's homecoming. 'If only he had communicated with me and told me when Jack was coming home, we could have organized a proper welcome party for him.'

Moshambo was Emily's spirit-guide, and both her sister and Nellie were well accustomed to hearing her speak of him as if he were a tangible presence.

'It ain't old Moshambo's fault,' Nellie said fairly. 'Jack's only 'ome on leave after all.'

Though they were in the living-room, she was sitting on a straight-backed kitchen chair as it was the only type of chair she could rise from without the help of three strong men.

Esther Helliwell's wheelchair was stationed near the window. From this viewpoint she could watch all her neighbours' comings and goings and also see the bombsite of what had once been the home she and Emily shared. The church, unfortunately, obliterated her view of the opposite top end of the Square, but its Christmas-card prettiness and its magnolia tree were ample compensations.

She dragged her eyes away from the sight of Doris Sharkey scurrying home from the direction of Lewisham as if her life depended on it, saying helpfully, 'Perhaps you could communicate with Moshambo and ask him when dear Jack will be demobbed?'

'An' if you do communicate with 'im, ask 'im when my Arthur's goin' to be released by the Japs,' Nellie said, not wanting her nephew's plight to be forgotten in the euphoria of Jack Robson's home-coming.

Emily's liver-spotted hands fiddled a little nervously with one of the several bead necklaces draped around her neck. It was all right Esther and Nellie suggesting she communicate with Moshambo, but it wasn't as easy as they seemed to think. Moshambo was an American-Indian spirit-guide and didn't take kindly to being summoned as if he were a civil servant at the Public Information Bureau.

'We could ring the Public Information Bureau,' Daniel was saying to his fellow deputy churchwarden as they met with Bob Giles for their weekly meeting.

'To find out if, and when, local authorities are going to be given the power to requisition empty houses?' Wilfred Sharkey asked deridingly.

Daniel was unabashed. As far as he was concerned, a public information service was empowered to give the public information. And he wanted to know what was going to happen to number seventeen now the Binns family were moving out of it. He wanted to know, because Carrie and Danny were anxious to move into it.

'I'll speak to Housing and find out what I can,' Bob Giles said, uncomfortably aware that if he hadn't agreed to number eight, a church property, being set aside to accommodate a Polish displaced person, the young Collinses could have moved in there and enjoyed a peppercorn rent. 'And now I'd like to ask your opinion on something I intend doing, but which might be a little controversial,' he said, changing the subject.

His two churchwardens, arraigned at the far side of his desk, waited, Daniel trustingly, Wilfred suspiciously. Bob Giles gave himself an extra minute's grace by tamping tobacco into the bowl of his pipe. At last, after lighting it, and sucking it into life, he said, 'Monday's news, about the A-bomb dropped on Hiroshima, was terrible enough, but today's news, that a second A-bomb has been dropped on Nagasaki, is terrible, truly terrible.'

Daniel bit the corner of his lip. It *was* terrible, there was no doubt about that, but it was also bound to result in the Japs surrendering and so, as he saw it, out of a terrible event would come a mercy. Wilfred Sharkey's thin mouth tightened until it virtually disappeared. If the Vicar was going to suggest what he thought he was going to suggest . . .

'I intend offering prayers at tonight's evening service for the victims,' Bob Giles continued, fulfilling Wilfred's expectations. 'I shall also, of course, be offering prayers for the safe return of men still being held prisoner in the Far East and—'

'I protest!' Wilfred's nostrils were pinched and white. 'The Japanese are in league with the devil. The rain of

118

ruin now descending on their cities is just and righteous punishment! The—'

'Hey, steady on, old chap,' Daniel said in consternation as Wilfred's limbs began to jerk like a marionette's. 'There's no need to take on so, you'll make yourself ill.'

Wilfred took no heed of him. He'd had a headache all day and now his head felt as if it were in a vice. The Vicar didn't understand about the Japanese. He didn't understand how all evil was pre-ordained. He didn't understand the cleansing power of fire and blood. '"And I saw the seven angels which stood before God,"' he declaimed suddenly, falling back on to the sturdy rock of *Revelations*, '"and to them were given seven trumpets and the first angel sounded and there followed hail and fire mingled with blood . . ."'

'I think you should sit down for a few minutes, Wilfred,' Bob Giles said, rising to his feet, deeply concerned.

'". . . and they were cast upon the earth, and the third part of trees was burnt up, and all green grass was burnt up . . ."' Wilfred continued, spittle forming at the corners of his mouth, '"and the second angel sounded, and as it were a great mountain burning with fire was cast into the sea, and the third part of the sea became blood . . ."'

'Oh dear, oh dear,' Daniel said unhappily. 'I think you need a dose of salts, Wilfred. A glassful of Epsoms would soon put you to rights.'

'I think we need a pot of hot, strong tea,' Bob Giles said, aware that he had a serious problem on his hands and wondering how best to deal with it. 'And then I think it would be a good idea if you knocked at the Sharkeys', Daniel, and asked Doris to come over here.'

119

'". . . and the four angels were loosed which were prepared for an hour and a day,"' Wilfred continued, eyes glazed and oblivious of the concern he was arousing, '". . . and thus I saw the horses in the vision and the heads of the horses were as the heads of lions, and out of their mouths issued fire and smoke and brimstone . . ."'

Bob took hold of one of Wilfred's twitching arms. 'That's enough, old chap,' he said gently, 'sit down and have a rest—'

'". . . and the same shall drink of the wine of the wrath of God and shall be tormented with fire and brimstone in the presence of holy angels and the smoke of their torment ascendeth for ever and ever . . ."'

Daniel, about to leave the study in order to make the suggested pot of tea, paused at the doorway, his eyes meeting Bob's. 'Oh dear,' he said again, graphically, 'oh dear, oh dear.'

Seconds later Bob heard him enter the kitchen and say to someone, presumably Ruth, 'Poor old Wilfred. I do believe he's finally lost his marbles.'

Though he wouldn't have expressed himself in quite the same way, Bob Giles thought Daniel had summed the situation up pretty accurately. Through the stress and strain of the war years, he had been a witness to many such breakdowns, though why Wilfred should suffer a mental collapse now, when the war in Europe was over and the war in the Far East was all but over, he couldn't quite fathom.

'"And I heard a great voice out of the temple saying to the seven angels, Go your ways,"' Wilfred said, his eyes still glazed and unfocused, but the frenzied passion beginning to drain from his voice, '"and pour out the vials of the wrath of God upon the earth . . ."'

Hopeful that the worst was now over, Bob said to him again, 'Sit down, old chap. Today's news has been too much for you. Doris will be here in a minute, and she'll take you home and put you to bed so that you can have a proper rest.'

It was like setting a match to blue touch-paper. 'Whore!' Wilfred spat, springing back into full throttle with renewed vigour. '"The great whore that sitteth upon many waters, with whom the kings of the earth have committed fornication and the inhabitants of the earth have been made drunk with the wine of her fornication!"'

Aware that, instead of making things better, he had somehow made them worse, Bob glanced towards his wall-clock. It was 11.15 a.m. He wondered if Dr Roberts would still be taking his surgery and, more to the point, if the Sharkeys were his panel patients. If they were, he would suggest to Doris that she allow him to telephone the surgery and ask Roberts to visit Wilfred as soon as possible.

'". . . and I saw the woman sit upon a scarlet-coloured beast, full of names of blasphemy, having seven heads and ten horns . . ."'

Daniel pushed the door open with his elbow. He was carrying a tray bearing a pot of tea, milk-jug, sugar-bowl, three cups and saucers and three teaspoons.

'Ruth's gone to give Doris a knock,' he said, setting the tray down on Bob's cluttered desk. 'She's going to tell Doris that Wilfred's had a bit of a funny turn—'

'Whore!' Wilfred spat again. 'Mother of all harlots!'

'We've moved from fire and brimstone to the great

121

whore of Babylon,' Bob said in answer to Daniel's startled expression.

'Blimey!' Daniel was impressed. Rambling on about whores in front of the Vicar was really going it. He began to pour the tea, wondering what Doris Sharkey would make of it all. Unlike everyone else in Magnolia Square, the Sharkeys didn't mix much with their neighbours. They kept themselves to themselves. Or they had until now. They certainly wouldn't be able to continue doing so with Wilfred spouting at the top of his voice about fire and brimstone and the great whore of Babylon.

Bob frowned, a very unnerving thought suddenly occurring to him. It had been mention of the Japanese that had first set Wilfred off on his fire-and-brimstone diatribe, but what was it that had caused him to change tack to the great whore of Babylon? Surely it couldn't have been mention of Doris? And if it had been . . . There came the sound of the vicarage door being opened in haste.

'Hopefully that's Ruth with Doris,' Daniel said as the door slammed shut and two pairs of hurrying footsteps reached as far as the kitchen and paused.

Bob knew very well why they had paused. In order to spare the Sharkeys embarrassment, Ruth was refusing to accompany Doris any further. That way she wouldn't be another witness to Wilfred's breakdown. It was exactly the sort of sensitivity his late wife, Constance, would have shown. In a moment of overpowering certainty, he knew that Constance would have approved of Ruth; that his marriage to Ruth would have had her whole-hearted blessing. Love and gratitude, both for the wife he had lost and the wife he was soon to gain, roared through him.

It was a moment quickly curtailed as Doris Sharkey knocked apprehensively on his study door and then, even more apprehensively, edged into the room. She had obviously been interrupted by Ruth whilst doing her weekly laundry. Soap suds still clung to her cherry-red pinafore, and the sleeves of her violet wool cardigan were pushed high, her damp hands and forearms flushed and mottled from the heat of the water in her copper.

'Miss Fairbairn said as how Wilfred had been taken badly—' she began nervously.

'*Whore!*' Wilfred roared, bounding to his feet and confirming all Bob Giles's worst suspicions. '"Arrayed in purple and scarlet colour!"'

'Telephone for Dr Roberts!' Bob shouted to Daniel and then, to a terrified Doris, 'And take your apron and cardigan off, for the Lord's sake!'

'What's goin' on at the vicarage?' Mavis said to Kate as they paused for a chat by the Helliwells' bomb-site, Mavis *en route* for the main road flanking the Heath and a bus to central London, Kate heading in the opposite direction, towards Lewisham. 'Ten minutes ago Ruth Fairbairn came runnin' out, sprintin' like a gym mistress for the Sharkeys. Then she 'ared back with Doris in tow. Now Dr Roberts's Morris Ten is parked outside.'

As Matthew, Hector at his heels, ran on ahead of her, Kate looked towards the top left-hand corner of the Square and the vicarage. The car was certainly Dr Roberts's. She frowned. 'I don't know. I hope Mr Giles hasn't been taken ill. I won't call in now, whilst Dr Roberts is there, but I'll call in when I get back from Lewisham. What's happening at number eighteen? Is a welcome-home party for Jack in full flow?'

Mavis shrugged, her magnificent bosom straining against a frilly white organza blouse. 'If there is, I 'aven't been invited. And knowin' Christina, I bet no-one else 'as either.'

Kate tried to hide her amusement. Like almost every other resident of Magnolia Square, she had seen the whole-hearted way Mavis had greeted Jack. That Christina now wanted Jack to herself for a little while would come as no great surprise to anyone. 'I expect he'll be having a knees-up tonight in The Swan,' she said consolingly. 'I'll have to be on my way, Mavis. I don't want Matthew and Hector running loose in Lewisham High Street.'

'No, I don't suppose you do,' Mavis said, for all the world as if, when Billy and Beryl had been under-fives, she had been similarly conscientious. 'Maybe I'll see you in The Swan tonight. Cheery-bye for now.'

'Cheery-bye,' Kate said, wondering if a knees-up in The Swan really was on the cards. It certainly would have been in the days before Jack's marriage to Christina. The Swan had always been Jack's watering-hole. He'd never had any patience with pubs that veered on the pretentious. Christina, however, had never been known to enter any pub, not even the very respectable Princess of Wales.

She turned into Magnolia Hill, her two-toned, cuban-heeled shoes tapping out a smart rat-a-tat on the pavement as she began catching up with Matthew. Luke was with Leon, helping him make a new strawberry bed. Daisy was at school. Her father was visiting Ellen in Greenwich. As she drew abreast of Matthew and tucked his chubby little hand into hers, she wondered if she had enough points in her ration book to buy some dried fruit. She wanted to make a proper Christmas cake this year, not a poor replica made with carrots instead of currants and raisins, but storing up a suitable cache of dried fruit via the points system wasn't easy.

'Can we have honey sandwiches for tea?' Matthew suddenly asked as he skipped along beside her, his thoughts, like hers, on food. 'I like honey sandwiches and Daddy-Leon likes honey sandwiches and . . .'

The Bentley's engine was so quiet, Kate wasn't even aware of its approach. Sleekly it purred to a halt at the kerbside, a few yards in front of them. She came to a far more abrupt halt, her heart racing, her throat so tight she thought she was going to choke.

'What is it, Mummy?' Matthew asked, looking up at her in perplexity. 'Have you got a tummyache?' The sun glinted on his thick shock of fair hair, burnishing it the colour of ripe barley. 'Are you going to grow another baby in your tummy, like you grew Luke in your tummy? Are—'

Hector bounded ahead and round the corner into Lewisham High Street. The Bentley's uniformed chauffeur walked around the car, opening the nearside rear door. Joss Harvey stepped out, his thickening shoulders still impressively broad beneath his Savile Row tailored suit, his silver hair unhatted.

Kate gripped Matthew's hand so tightly he gave a yelp of pain. She wanted to run, but her legs wouldn't move and even if they would have done, there was nowhere to run to. After nearly four years of leaving her in peace, Joss Harvey was quite obviously all set to engage her in

125

battle again. And this time he was doing so confident that he held every advantage.

'You married him then?' he said succinctly, walking towards her and halting a foot or so away.

The force of his barely reined-in aggression was so intense, her every instinct screamed at her to fall back, to retreat as far and as fast as possible.

Defiantly she held her ground. 'I'm married, yes,' she said tersely. As always, whenever she was in confrontation with him, she found it impossible to believe there had ever been any blood link between him and Matthew's father. Toby had been good-humoured and good-natured. And tolerant – above all he had been tolerant. His upper middle-class upbringing and public school education ensured he would have been as staggered as anyone if he had known she would one day marry a half-caste seaman. But he would have trusted her judgement. And if he had ever met Leon, he would have liked him.

'No Black Sambo is going to be stepfather to my great-grandson,' Joss Harvey said bluntly, just as she had known he would. 'We can settle this out of court, or in court. And if you choose to go to court, you'll regret it. The case will be splashed all over the local newspapers, and you and your blackie husband will soon find out what the public thinks to marriages like yours. Especially when there's a white child involved. A white child from a good background, with a great-grandfather well known and well respected and willing to provide a home and education for him.'

Dimly Kate was aware that Hector was trotting back up Magnolia Hill towards them; that a group of workmen had stepped out of The Swan and were looking across at the Bentley with undisguised interest and envy; that Matthew was tugging impatiently on her hand, trying to gain her attention. Joss Harvey had said nothing she hadn't already anticipated him saying, but her reaction was as intense as if she had been totally unprepared for it. Waves of sickness surged over her. This was the man Toby had admired, respected and loved: the man Toby would have wanted his son to grow up admiring, respecting, loving. And he was a man who referred to Leon with ugly racial epithets, a man she wanted her son to have nothing to do with at all.

'There was a time when I was happy for Matthew to spend time with you,' she said tautly as Hector skittered to a halt beside them. 'You were the one who put an end to that situation. You abused my trust in the most dreadful way possible, and I've no intention of allowing you to do so again.'

Hector, sensing hostility, had begun to growl low in his throat. With her free hand Kate took hold of his collar. She didn't want him to bite Joss Harvey. If he did, Joss Harvey would inform the police and would insist on Hector being destroyed.

'Mummy?' Matthew was tugging on her hand in even greater urgency. 'Mummy, who's this man?' He hadn't understood anything that had been said but, like Hector, he sensed her distress and his eyes, so like Toby's eyes, were troubled and perplexed.

She didn't answer him. Instead she gripped his hand even tighter and it was the man who was making her angry and upset who answered his question.

'I'm your great-grandpa, young man,' he said, bewildering Matthew even further, 'and from now on we're going to get to know each other very well. You're going to visit my house, the house your father lived in when he was a little boy. It has a big garden. A garden as big as a park. And you're going to go for rides in my motor car—'

'*Oh no he isn't!*' Panic bubbled high in Kate's throat, almost choking her. She had envisaged Joss Harvey using all kinds of brutal tactics in his attempt to gain guardianship of Matthew, but one thing she hadn't anticipated was his attempting to seduce Matthew away from her. Or that Matthew would allow himself to be seduced.

'In that motor car?' he was now asking, his eyes like saucers. 'With that Army man driving it?'

'He isn't an Army man,' Joss Harvey replied, and to Kate's even greater distress, his voice had lost its habitual harshness and held undeniable tenderness and even amusement. 'He's a chauffeur and his name is Hemmings.'

'His name is *Mr* Hemmings!' Kate hissed, incensed. It was bad enough Joss Harvey trying to bribe Matthew into his clutches without his teaching him upper middle-class high-handedness into the bargain.

Joss Harvey ignored her. 'Would you like to go for a ride now?' he asked Matthew. 'Would you like me to give you and your mummy a lift to wherever you're going?'

'We're going to the market and it's barely fifty yards away,' Kate retorted furiously as Matthew's little face lit up in happy anticipation, 'and I wouldn't accept the offer even if I had two broken legs!' It was a crudity totally alien to her and she felt inner shock at having been goaded so far as to have sunk to it. No-one else seemed remotely concerned. Not even Matthew.

'Please, Mummy!' he begged, the outburst washing

over his head as all the previous angry exchanges had done. '*Please!* I've never been in a motor car.' He looked away from her and towards the powerful-looking figure who, incredibly, claimed he was his great-grandpa. 'Does it go very fast?' he asked. 'Does it have a loud horn that makes people jump out of the way?'

'It has a horn just like the horn on Mr Toad's motor car,' Joss Harvey said with a gruff geniality that sent fresh shock waves through Kate.

It was all very well standing firm against him when he was being coarsely threatening and blatantly hostile, but it was a different matter when he was being caring and gentle with Matthew.

Matthew was looking mystified, and Joss Harvey's bushy silver eyebrows pulled together in a frown. 'Hasn't anyone read *Wind in the Willows* to you, young man?' he asked, concerned. 'Your father used to love the characters in *Wind in the Willows*. Mr Toad and Ratty and Badger . . .'

Kate fought a dizzy sense of disorientation. It was like being confronted with an affable Mr Hyde after tangling with an enraged Dr Jekyll. And it was no wonder that, if this was the only side of his grandfather Toby had ever seen, Toby had loved him. After all, with his parents dead, his grandfather had been Toby's only family. And now Matthew was Joss Harvey's only family. Watching the two of them together – Matthew looking up at Joss Harvey with shining trust on his face, Joss Harvey looking down at Matthew with hungry tenderness – Kate's throat tightened. It was a devil of a situation, and always had been.

Right from the beginning, when Toby had been killed

and she had known she was carrying his child, she had tried to ensure that the day would come when a loving relationship would exist between Joss Harvey and his great-grandchild. She had done so because she had believed it was what Toby would have wanted, and because she felt it was morally right that, despite Matthew's illegitimacy, the two of them should have the opportunity to forge loving links with each other. And Joss Harvey had scuppered her every attempt. He had abused her for her German paternity with the same ugly crudity he had employed over Leon. When Matthew, as a small baby, had been evacuated to his country home for the duration of the Blitz, he had refused to hand him back to her and had sent Matthew and his nanny into hiding.

Kate's jaw clenched, old anger flooding through her. It had been a ploy that had failed, for the nanny in question had been Ruth Fairbairn, and Ruth had returned Matthew to her. After that, instead of trying to encourage contact between Joss Harvey and Matthew, she had done her utmost to ensure there was no contact whatsoever. And there hadn't been – until now.

'Mole is a very fine chap,' Joss Harvey was saying to an entranced Matthew. 'But he's timid. Mr Toad, however, is far from timid. Mr Toad is a noisy, swashbuckling fellow who lives in a very grand house called Toad Hall and . . .'

Hector had long since given up growling and, sensing that the halt to his walk was going to be a long one, was now lying flat on the pavement, his head resting morosely on his paws. On the far side of the road the workmen, having gazed their fill at the Bentley, were noisily dispersing in the direction of Lewisham High Street. Kate wished fiercely that she and Matthew were hurrying in their wake, her decision about what line to take with Joss Harvey now safely reached. What *was* she to do? Unless she deflected him, he would most certainly begin a legal fight for guardianship of Matthew, and the fight would be long and ugly. He would accuse her of being an unfit mother and was unscrupulous enough to both fabricate evidence and bribe so-called witnesses. And he would make as much mileage as possible out of Leon's and Matthew's racial differences.

The very thought of the ways in which he might do so filled her with sick apprehension. Whatever the outcome, it would almost certainly put an end to Leon's hopes of adopting Matthew, and it might also put an end to their neighbours' easy acceptance of their mixed marriage. The nerves in her stomach tightened into knots. She had had too much experience of the way latent prejudices could be whipped into life to ever be complacent about acceptance and tolerance. Before the war, her father had lived for twenty years in Magnolia Square without his German nationality ever being an issue and then, when war broke out, he had found himself ostracized and vilified and spat upon.

'. . . and so Toad bought himself a large and very expensive motor car . . .'

'Like your motor car, Great-Grandpa?'

Listening and watching, Kate found it almost impossible to believe that, until a few minutes ago, Matthew hadn't even known he had a great-grandfather and that, as a baby, he had spent months in his care. With an ease that both deeply disturbed her and yet left her reluctantly

131

admiring him, Joss Harvey had forged the kind of rapport with Matthew she had once fervently hoped for. Was it a rapport that, with forbearance on her part, could be maintained? A rapport which Joss Harvey could be made to realize would be lost if he embarked on an ugly legal fight?

She thought of the alternative, and of what she and Leon might lose, and cleared her throat. 'I take back what I said earlier,' she said crisply. 'I will accept a lift to the market. But only on the understanding that we have a civilized discussion together. A discussion with no name-calling, no threats, and no attempts at blackmail.'

Joss Harvey's pugnacious jaw tightened for a moment and then he said tersely, 'Get in the car. And if we have to take that apology for a dog with us, make sure it stays on the car floor and doesn't clamber on to the seats.'

Praying to God her decision was not one she would live to regret, Kate roused Hector from his torpor and walked towards the Bentley. As she did so her heart began to beat in swift, erratic strokes. In front of her Matthew and Joss Harvey were walking companionably together, Matthew's chubby hand tucked trustingly in Joss Harvey's large, powerful paw.

Chapter Eight

'What sort of home-coming is this, for Christ's sake?' Jack Robson was demanding in angry and disappointed frustration, dark hair tumbling low over his brow. 'I got more of a welcome from the dog!'

Christina stood facing him across the narrow width of her pristinely made single bed. Why, why, why had she not been able to control her crushing jealousy when she had seen him whirling Mavis around in his arms? Why, instead of running joyfully to greet him, had she allowed the presence of so many onlookers freeze her into immobility? Why had she allowed *anything* to mar such a long-awaited, precious moment?

A sea of conflicting emotions churned inside her and she could give expression to none of them. Instead of doing what she longed to do, rounding the bed, hugging him tight, explaining that she found it hard to display private feelings in front of an audience, she heard herself saying stiffly, 'I'm sorry, Jack. I *am* glad to see you. Truly I am.'

There was a brief moment when she feared it wasn't going to be enough and that he was going to turn on his heel and leave the room. She wouldn't have blamed him if he had. They had spent only one night together since their wedding and that, too, had been ruined because of her inability to reveal to him her troubled thoughts and feelings. Ever since then he had been fighting in Europe, undergoing God only knew what kind of horrors, and he had come marching home in happy anticipation of a south-east London welcome from his wife. And, as she well knew, a south-London welcome was anything but restrained. How could it be, when the women were breezy and boisterous and the men were as unlike archetypal Englishmen, all repression and stiff upper lip, as it was possible to imagine? Jack would have been expecting her to run joyously to greet him, no matter how many onlookers there were. And she hadn't done so. Instead she had stood in the Jennings's doorway, to all outward appearances as unmoved and unemotional as Hans Andersen's Ice Queen.

Silence spun out between them, so taut it was almost a physical presence. A pulse had begun to beat at the corner of his jaw. None of the scenarios he had envisaged on his long journey home had included being greeted by his wife as if they were casual acquaintances and nothing more. His savage disappointment was exacerbated by hurt pride. Half the Square had been a witness to Christina's coolness and restraint, and he knew the kind of gossip that would soon be going the rounds in The Swan. The question was, did he care? The instant the question entered his head he shrugged it impatiently away. Of course he didn't care. He'd never given a damn what people said or thought about him and he certainly wasn't about to start now. What the hell did it matter if she hadn't given him the kind of public welcome Mavis had so enthusiastically given him? Christina wasn't

Mavis. She was quieter, classier, far more reserved.

A smile crooked the corner of his well-shaped mouth, his anger ebbing as speedily as it had erupted. It was Christina's reserve that had first intrigued and attracted him and, if one of the consequences of it was behaviour that would have their neighbours gossiping to kingdom come, so what? It didn't matter. All that mattered was what took place in private between them, not what took place in public.

He said in a voice raw with emotion, 'I'm sorry for reacting like a kid.' It was the first apology he had ever made, but it was worth it to see the misery lift from her eyes.

Her relief that he wasn't going to walk away from her, out of the room, was so intense her knees buckled slightly against the edge of the bed. 'And I'm sorry for being so . . . so unsouth-London.'

Through the open window came the sound of an approaching horse and cart and the unmistakable street cry of a rag-and-bone man. Three gardens away, Queenie began barking, outraged by the intrusion. Nellie Miller shouted out that she had an old wash-tub she wouldn't mind a few coppers for. Billy, hopeful of earning one of them as a middleman, eagerly announced his willingness to dig it out of her scullery and bowl it up on to the back of the cart.

Oblivious of the intruding noise, Jack's eyes held Christina's, the heat in them hot and urgent. 'I love you,' he said, and she knew that in another second he would have rounded the bed and she would be in his arms. And then they would make love. With the hurly-burly taking place in the Square infiltrating the room; with Leah and

135

Miriam and Carrie and Danny in the house; with Rose possibly in the house also; and Bonzo; and God only knew how many nosey visiting neighbours.

Panic beat its way up into her throat. Desperately as she loved him, how could she possibly respond uninhibitedly to him with half the Square within earshot? And if they didn't make love now, in the crowded bedroom she shared with Rose, where could they make love? Charlie would be *in situ* at number twelve, and certainly wouldn't have the sensitivity to remove himself from the house. They didn't possess the kind of money that would make booking into a hotel a feasible option, and even if they did and she made such a suggestion, Jack would be mystified by it. For working-class south-Londoners, hotels were for special, one-off occasions, such as wedding nights, and then only for the fortunate few. She knew that Carrie had never set foot in a hotel and she doubted if Kate had either.

Jack was rounding the bed towards her in swift brief strides. For a split second she had a vision of the Heidelberg of her childhood. Of eating *Schokoladenkuchen* with her parents in the chandelier-hung splendour of the Hotel Ernst.

'A tanner?' Nellie Miller's voice roared out indignantly. 'A *tanner*? That wash-tub's worth more than a tanner, mate! Melted down it'd go 'alf-way to making a battleship!'

His arms were around her, his body hard against hers. 'Forget Nellie,' he said urgently, 'forget everyone.' It was the first time he had ever read her thoughts with such sensitive accuracy.

She pressed against the roughness of his uniform with

136

a sob of gratitude and relief, answering desire roaring through her like a rip-tide. This time everything was going to be all right. This time she wasn't going to let him down. This time she was going to think of nothing and no-one but him. 'I love you!' she whispered hoarsely. 'I love you with all my heart, Jack. Now and for ever.'

His mouth came down on hers, hot and sweet, and then he was pressing her back on the yielding, creaking bed and the world spiralled down until all that existed was the passion uniting them.

'Can I have a little garden of my own, Daddy?' Luke asked, trotting at Leon's heels as, with the back garden tended to his satisfaction, Leon led the way through the house towards the much smaller front garden.

Leon stood on the top step and surveyed what had once been a handkerchief-sized lawn surrounded by flowers, enhanced by an aged magnolia tree. At the outbreak of war the Government had exhorted Britons to 'dig for victory' and to turn over their gardens to the growing of fruit and vegetables in order that they could be as self-supportive as possible. Kate had certainly followed the directive to the letter. Raspberry and gooseberry and blackcurrant bushes fought for space with lettuces and tomatoes and onions. Edging the broad, shallow stone steps leading down to the pathway were pots crammed with herbs: mint and parsley, basil and thyme, rosemary and tarragon.

'You can, if we can find room for it,' Leon said, the tender tone of his deep, rich voice leaving Luke in no doubt that room would be found. He walked musingly down the sun-dappled steps, helping Luke off the last one. 'What about right here?' he asked him. 'At the foot of the steps? We'll have to dig out this gooseberry bush and sacrifice a few lettuces, but there'll be space here for you to grow whatever you want.'

'Want to grow pretty flowers,' Luke said confidingly. 'Want to grow *orangie* flowers.'

Leon nodded, in complete agreement with the beguiling little person who was his son. Orange flowers would certainly put the zip back into the garden. It was too late, though, to grow anything from seed, and a three-year-old couldn't be expected to wait until next spring to see his garden in flower. What was needed was to transplant some established late-flowering marigolds and nasturtiums. He wondered if Daniel had any lurking in his garden. If he hadn't, there was always the Helliwells' bomb-site. There were more flowers rampaging over that than there were in Kew Gardens.

Hettie interrupted his thoughts. She was on her way home from a lengthy shopping expedition in Blackheath Village. It had been lengthy, not because she had been happily browsing but because she had had to queue at the butcher's, queue at the baker's, queue at the greengrocer's. 'I didn't mind queuing because of food shortages when old Hitler was making our lives a misery,' she had said to Emily Helliwell, a black straw hat crammed on her iron-grey curls, 'but it's a bit of a liberty now the old bugger's rotting in hell. When's life going to get back to normal, that's what I want to know? When are we going to be able to burn our ration books and put decent meals on the table?'

She said now to Leon, 'I suppose you're not familiar

with gooseberries. I suppose they don't have them where you come from.'

The words were guileless, without any intended offence, and Leon didn't take any. Abandoning his study of the gooseberry bush, he said equably, 'I come from Chatham, Hettie. There's plenty of gooseberry bushes in Chatham.'

Hettie pursed her lips. Leon might well have lived in Chatham before the war, but he didn't *come* from Chatham, not in the way she came from south-east London. Her parents had been born in south-east London, as had her parents' parents and her parents' *parents'* parents, and Lord alone knew how many generations before them. Leon came from Africa. All black people came from Africa. She wasn't educated the way Harriet Godfrey and Ruth Fairbairn were, but she did at least know that. And she knew they ate funny food there because she'd seen pictures of an African market in the *National Geographic* when she'd been in Dr Roberts's surgery.

Two bright spots of colour burned her cheeks as she remembered something else. A lot of people in Africa didn't wear many clothes, which was probably why Leon preferred her to think he came from Chatham. 'Do you know Jack Robson's home?' she asked, not blaming him for his evasiveness and diplomatically changing the subject. 'He'll only have a weekend pass, I expect, but it won't be long till he's home for good. Not now the Yanks have put the kibosh on the Japanese.'

'Kate told me.'

Leon kept the conversation to local matters, not wanting to think of the significance of the atomic bombing of Japan, or the fact that for the first time in history Man had the power to put the kibosh on the entire planet. 'I don't know Jack myself,' he said, wondering what Bob Giles thought of it all. 'When I first came to Magnolia Square he was fighting in France, and we've never been home on leave at the same time. Nellie Miller tells me he's the nearest thing to Clark Gable south-east London possesses.'

Hettie sniffed, and the artificial rose on her hat wobbled. 'I don't know about Clark Gable,' she said, safely assuming that Nellie wasn't in the habit of saying the same thing about Danny, 'but he is all damn-your-eyes and swagger. His brother was just the same. Went off to fight Franco and died in a Spanish bullring. If that isn't exhibitionism, I don't know what is.'

Leon was saved from the difficulty of replying by Billy Lomax. After spending a happy couple of hours riding shot-gun with the rag-and-bone man, he was returning home for his tea, waving his arms like propellers as he did so and dive-bombing anyone and anything in his path.

As the Misses Helliwell's cat sprang to safety, Hettie said suddenly, 'If Billy's heading home it must be tea-time. Rose is coming to me for her tea today so I'd best be getting a move on.' She squared her shoulders, preparing herself for the last lap home with her heavy shopping, adding confidingly, 'You'd never hear me say a word wrong about her other gran, but Miriam isn't a cook. It's Leah does all the cooking in that house, and when all's said and done, if it's Jewish it must be foreign. Stands to reason, doesn't it? Cheerio for now. And you should try some gooseberries some time. They're a rare treat with custard.' Stepping off the kerb, she headed diagonally across the Square to number three, intent on making Rose a proper London tea of boiled bacon and pease pudding.

Leon sat down on one of the sun-warmed steps, feeling quite exhausted. How on earth did Daniel Collins Senior cope? Presumably he just turned a deaf ear. Whatever he did, it was no wonder he put so much zest into being a churchwarden. Meetings with Bob Giles and Wilfred Sharkey must be havens of rest after long hours in Hettie's company.

''Ello, Mr Emmerson!' Billy shouted breezily from the far side of the Square. 'Do you know Jack's home? I'm goin' to ask 'im to teach me to fight like a Commando! Did you know Commandos are taught to kill with their bare 'ands? I'm goin' to ask 'im 'ow it's done!'

The very thought was enough to make a strong man quail, but Leon merely grinned. 'I'll teach you how to box, if you like!' he shouted back. 'Boxing might just be a little more useful.'

'I'd rather kill with my bare 'ands,' Billy responded sunnily and, arms going like windmills, he continued careening down the far side of the Square, a Spitfire intent on winning the Battle of Britain all over again.

Leon once again surveyed the tiny patch of ground that he had promised Luke would be his, and his alone. With the war in Europe over, food shortages would surely soon become a thing of the past, and when they did, even more of the garden could be Luke's own. It didn't have to be too big an area, just enough for him to be able to plant and sow, dig holes, puddle in, water, pull, pick and poke about, and tramp up and down in wellington boots, firming the earth.

141

At the thought of all the time that stretched ahead of him – time with Kate and Daisy and Matthew, time with his little son – happiness coursed through him, bone-deep. Only short weeks ago, he had been in a German prison camp. Now he was home in Magnolia Square and he would never, ever, voluntarily leave it. There would be no more Navy for him. He was going to go back to his previous profession of Thames lighterman. He had been born by the river and he loved it far more than he loved any sea.

As Luke scrambled on to his knee, one of the straps of his home-made dungarees slipped off a shoulder. Leon settled him comfortably and looked towards Magnolia Terrace and the great, open vistas of the Heath. Then, adjusting the straying strap, he looked in the opposite direction towards Magnolia Hill, as content as a king surveying his kingdom.

This little area, bounded by the Thames and historical Greenwich to the north, genteel Blackheath Village to the east, and market-orientated Lewisham to the south, was where he belonged. It was where he and Kate were going to raise their children. It was where they were going to live, love, laugh and grow old together.

'Did Great-Grandad really mean it when he said I could visit him?' Matthew asked eagerly, skipping along at Kate's side as they rounded the bottom corner of Magnolia Hill on their journey home. 'Will Mr Hem-mings come for me in Great-Grandad's big car? Does Great-Grandad know the King and Queen? Why does he never visit us? Why does—'

'No more questions, sweetheart,' Kate said, struggling

hard to keep anxiety from her voice. 'I'm tired and I just want to get home and have a nice cup of tea.'

Matthew looked up at her, bewildered. How could Mummy be tired when they had just had a lovely afternoon sitting with Great-Grandad in the café in Chiesemans department store? A café they only usually went into when it was for a special treat, such as his birthday, or because it was Christmas and they had been to visit Father Christmas in his grotto? And how could Mummy possibly be looking forward to another cup of tea when Great-Grandad had ordered a second pot of tea for her at the same time he had ordered the unbelievably wonderful ice-cream sundae? Sensing that she really was tired and that she wasn't going to merrily chat with him as she usually did, he let go of her hand and began running up the hill in a vain effort to catch up with Hector.

Kate watched him, her heart feeling as if it were being squeezed within her breast. Had she done the right thing in agreeing to talk with Joss Harvey? Had she compromised herself utterly by stepping into his ostentatious Bentley and having afternoon tea with him in Chiesemans? And what of the agreement she had come to with him? What was Leon going to think of it? Was he going to be hurt that she hadn't consulted him first? And had she been wrong in not doing so?

''Ello there, petal!' Charlie shouted amenably from the far side of the street as he ambled in the direction of The Swan. 'Yer know it's party-time tonight, don't yer? Jack wants everyone in The Swan by seven o'clock, an' 'e says the drinks are on 'im. I just 'ope the pub 'as a big enough barrel on tap.'

Kate waved in acknowledgement. It would be nice to have a knees-up in The Swan. At one time, when Magnolia Square's men had all been at home, knees-ups at The Swan had taken place every Saturday night. Boozy, noisy evenings had still continued all through the war, of course, but they had been different in character. Soldiers and sailors foreign to the district had squeezed shoulder-to-shoulder into both the saloon bar and the public, and the strictly neighbourly, cosy atmosphere had been lost.

Ahead of her, Matthew and Hector disappeared around the top right-hand corner of Magnolia Hill, into the Square. Kate was unworried. Neither of them would come to any harm. Very little motorized traffic, apart from Dr Roberts's Morris and Ted Lomax's motor bike and side-car which, in Ted's absence Mavis had appropriated, ever trundled through the Square. Far more common were horse-drawn vehicles. The milkman's cart, the rag-and-bone man's cart, the coalman's cart, the old hearse Albert Jennings used for ferrying his fruit and vegetables from Covent Garden.

Her full-lipped mouth tightened. It was no wonder that, on the rare occurrences when Joss Harvey's Bentley entered Magnolia Square, it always caused such a stir. She wondered if anyone had seen the Bentley draw up beside her earlier on, and if they had seen her stepping into it. If so, Leon would most certainly already know whom she and Matthew had been with for the last hour or so. For the umpteenth time, she wondered what his reaction would be. She rounded the corner in the wake of Matthew and Hector, her clear blue eyes darkening unhappily. And how would he react when he learnt the vicious extent of Joss Harvey's racial prejudice? So far, their life together had been untouched by such ignorant nastiness. It was going to be so no longer, for Joss Harvey was not a stranger whose existence could be ignored.

Bob Giles walked out of the Sharkeys' house and hurried across to the church. As she watched him, a biblical image sprang to her mind and a shiver ran down her spine. It was as if she and Leon and the children had been living in their own, very private Garden of Eden, and Joss Harvey's racial viciousness was the serpent about to eject them from it into the brutal harshness of the real world. She drew in a deep, steadying breath. Letting her imagination run away with her in such a manner would neither do her, nor Leon, nor the children, any good whatsoever. What was needed was a little common sense, and surely, in her dealings with Joss Harvey that afternoon, she had shown a great deal of common sense?

She fervently hoped so. She was abreast of the scented luxuriance of the Helliwells' bomb-site now, and the riot of roses, running wild and intermingling with foxgloves and rose-bay willow-herb, cheered her as they always did. What on earth was she being so glum about? She had talked Joss Harvey out of taking court action in order to try and obtain guardianship of Matthew. A compromise, however uneasy, had been agreed between them. That evening there was going to be a welcome home knees-up for Jack in The Swan, and her dad, never a great party-going man, would baby-sit for her and Leon. Whatever Dr Roberts's reason for visiting the vicarage, it hadn't been occasioned by sickness, for Bob Giles had looked as fit as always as he had walked from the Sharkeys' house across to the church.

145

The bomb-site was behind her now and she walked past the Robsons' house, wondering if Christina would move in there now that Jack was home. Way ahead of her, Matthew and Hector bundled through the gateway into the garden of number four. A smile touched her mouth. With a little luck, as well as laying a new strawberry bed, Leon and Luke would also have been picking strawberries, and they would be able to have them for tea with milk and a little sugar. With her earlier anxiety now firmly under control, she walked past the Sharkeys, wondering how long it would be before the church-owned, empty house next door to them would be occupied. As she did so, she looked towards the Sharkeys' windows, half expecting to see Doris or Pru and giving them a cheery wave.

Her eyes widened, shock stabbing through her. Though there were hours to go yet before dusk, every curtain was tightly drawn, as if there had been a death.

Chapter Nine

'We've picked stwabewwies for tea,' Luke said, running to greet Kate with shining eyes. 'An' Daddy says we can have our tea in the back garden an' that he'll take us to the park afterwards!'

'*We've* had ice-creams in Chiesemans,' Matthew began importantly in brotherly one-upmanship. '*We've* been in a big, big car . . . a car *so* big.' He held his arms as far apart as possible.

Leon stopped what he was doing, which was rinsing strawberries, and looked across at Kate in bemused curiosity. Matthew loved to exaggerate, as all kiddies did, but he never told out and out fibs. '*Have* you been in a big car?' he asked, trying to think, if she had, who on earth it could have belonged to. The only person they knew with a car was Dr Roberts, and his little Morris couldn't be called big, even by Matthew's standards.

'So big it had a horn like the Last Trump,' she said wryly.

'It was Great-Gra . . .' Matthew began, about to tell his Daddy-Leon who the car had belonged to.

Kate clapped her hand over his mouth. 'That's quite enough chatter from you for the moment. Off you go into the garden and when you've found a nice place for us to have our picnic tea, I want you to sit on it and count to a hundred.'

The request didn't seem too unreasonable to Matthew. He was always counting to a hundred when he played Blindman's Buff or Tag with Rose and Daisy. With Luke toddling at his heels, he set off to find a picnic place, pretending he was doing so in the middle of a big, dangerous jungle.

'Well, love?' Leon asked, a frown beginning to crease his forehead. 'Who did you run into while you were out shopping?'

Kate crossed the kitchen and slid her arms around his waist, resting her head on his broad and comforting chest. 'Our own personal Demon-King,' she said with a heavy heart.

His frown deepened as his arms closed round her. 'Joss Harvey?'

She nodded. The whole relationship between herself and Joss Harvey was so convoluted and fraught with so many contradictions that, even to Leon, she didn't truly know how best to explain it.

'And?' he prompted. Though the word was said gently enough, she could sense his sudden inner tension.

She pressed the palms of her hands against his chest, looking up into his dark, handsome, caring face. 'He said some ugly things, Leon – about you – about you not being a suitable person to be his great-grandson's adoptive father.'

A pulse began to throb at the corner of Leon's strong jawline. He didn't have to ask her what kind of things had been said, he already had a very good idea. Joss Harvey's insults would have had nothing to do with his ability to be a kind and loving father to Matthew, or to his ability to provide for him; they would have been racial slurs, the kind of slurs he had suffered all his life.

Kate's eyes held his steadily. 'He said that we could settle the matter either in court or out of it, but that if we chose to go to court, he would make sure that his viewpoint was splashed all across the local papers.'

From outside they could hear the voices of Matthew and Luke raised in argument as they disputed over the best place in the garden for their picnic tea. A lawn-mower was being trundled in a nearby garden. Distantly, the sound of a long tug whistle carried up from the river.

'His viewpoint being?' Leon prompted tautly.

Reluctantly, not wanting to hurt him yet knowing that he had to know just what depths Joss Harvey would sink to if he was ever to understand the agreement she and he had reached, she said, 'That Matthew is his flesh and blood. That he is a white child whose father came from a middle-class background and that he, Joss Harvey, a wealthy pillar of the local community, is far more suited to have custody of Matthew than . . . than—'

'Than a Black Sambo seaman,' Leon finished bitterly.

'I'm sorry, love,' she said, hating Joss Harvey's ignorance with all her heart, 'but you were the one who warned me of the kinds of things that some people would say and—'

'And was this said to you before you got in the car with him, or afterwards?' There was an edge to his voice she had never heard before, an edge that warned her that for the first time in their entire relationship they were on the verge of gravely misunderstanding each other.

'It was before I got in the car,' she said quietly, 'and I

149

got in the car because I knew that unless I reached some sort of an accommodation with him, he would begin a long, vicious fight with us for guardianship of Matthew.' Her voice broke slightly and she could feel tears beginning to burn the backs of her eyes. 'And that one of his ways of doing so would be to bring to everyone's attention the fact that you and Matthew are racially different. At the moment, no-one thinks it at all odd that you should become his legal father, and I don't want them to start thinking differently. I don't want us to have to go through all the hideousness that would bring in its wake, or to have the children go through it . . .'

Her voice cracked completely and his arms tightened around her. 'I don't want that either, sweetheart,' he said thickly, pulling her close again, his lips brushing her hair. 'And so what "accommodation" did you and he come to?'

She took a deep, steadying breath. 'That he could begin building up a relationship with Matthew. That he could take Matthew out once a week—'

'And you'd trust him? After all that happened when Matthew was a baby, you'd trust him?'

Once again she looked into his dearly loved face, her eyes holding his. 'We have to, Leon. Only this way will your adoption application go through unopposed.'

Anger and frustration chased across his face. None of this would be happening if it wasn't for his skin colour, and yet he was as British as Joss Harvey! He had been *born* in Britain. His mother could probably have traced her Kentish ancestry further back than Joss Harvey could trace his.

'Let's go to bed,' he said urgently, needing to love her;

needing to reassure himself that none of the difficulties they were going to meet as a married couple would ever take her away from him.

Her own need for comfort was just as great as his. It flamed through her eyes as she said despairingly, 'We can't – the children . . .'

'The children can picnic on their own,' he said, releasing his hold of her and picking up the bowl of strawberries. 'You go up to our bedroom. I'll be with you just as soon as I've taken these out to Matthew and Luke.'

'Hey up, there! Let the dog see the rabbit,' Daniel Collins said genially that evening as he tried to reach the bar through the crush. 'A pint of mild, barman, when you have a mo. Goodness, gracious me, if it's going to be like this in here every night now Jack Robson's home, I'll have to start drinking in Blackheath!'

The elderly barman grinned. 'If all Jack's mates keep coming here to drink once Jack's home for good, your custom won't even be missed,' he said affably, pushing a frothing pint across the bar-top in Daniel's direction. 'Try not to spin it out till the end of the night. If I had to rely on your custom, my right hand would think my right arm was broke.'

It was well known that Daniel was practically a teetotaller, and there were gusts of laughter from the throng hemming him in. Daniel was happily uncaring. He'd only come down the pub in order to welcome Jack back. He looked around, trying to find a quiet place to sit.

'Yer won't find one!' Miriam called out from the table

she was sitting at with her mother and Christina. 'All Jack's mates from Lewisham and Catford 'ave come to see 'im.' She moved over a little on the shabby banquette that served as seating on the wall side of the table, to make room for him, saying, 'An' 'e's got a lot of mates, 'e always did 'ave.'

'It's nice to see Jack home,' Daniel agreed wholeheartedly, 'but dear, oh dear, his mates make it as crowded as the Yanks did last summer. A pub should be where a man can come for a bit of peace and quiet and a game of cribbage, not somewhere he can't hear himself talk.'

'Why for do you want peace and quiet when you go out?' Leah asked. 'Peace and quiet you can get at home.'

'Not in our 'ouse, you can't!' Albert boomed, squeezing through the crush and setting Miriam's and Leah's drinks down on the table. 'In our 'ouse peace and quiet is as rare as bananas. Talking of which, I've been told we'll soon be seein' a banana boat cruisin' up the Thames again. Now, that'll be a grand sight, won't it?'

'It will be if we all get the chance of some and there's not too much black-marketeering,' Daniel said cautiously.

Nellie Miller was seated three tables away, but she had ears like the proverbial elephant. 'Black-marketeering?' she thundered in a voice that could have been heard in Greenwich. 'If there's any black-marketeering about, count me in! My last little windfall was parachute silk. It made wonderful knickers.' She twanged an elasticised ruche just above a mammoth-sized knee. 'I'm safe as 'ouses in these, an' if I should fall from a great 'eight I'll 'ave an easy landin'!'

'The poor bugger you fall on won't!' some wag rejoined, and the pub rocked with ribald laughter.

'Hey, Nellie!' Danny Collins pitched in from his favourite spot near the end of the bar. 'Is it true you don't get undressed any more, you just strike camp?'

As the laughter reached deafening proportions, Christina smiled so that she wouldn't look as if she were being a killjoy, and tried to catch Jack's eye. He had gone to the bar ten minutes ago to buy a round for all the mates who had heard he was home and had popped in to The Swan to see him. From where she was sitting she could see him easily, tall and broad-shouldered and the centre of attention.

Her stomach muscles tightened in a mixture of desire and love and apprehension. This was the way it always was with Jack, and she had the common sense to know that it was the way it always would be. People gravitated to him like moths to a flame, attracted by a magnetism impossible to analyse. He had been the leader of every gang he had ever been a member of. Leadership was his style, but only a very particular kind of leadership: a leadership with a hint of lawlessness about it. She clasped her hands tightly in her lap. Her father would not have approved of Jack. Nor would her mother. They had been very middle-class, very respectable, very law-abiding. And her middle-class, respectable, law-abiding father had been shot in the street and her very correct, very conventional mother had been forced to scramble at rifle-point into a truck no better than a meat truck *en route* to a slaughterhouse.

Fresh laughter was rocking the room. Was it something else Nellie had said? Something Charlie had said?

153

She didn't know. She was impaled again on the pain of her past, a past no-one else in The Swan had shared or could even begin to understand.

'Come on, pet. Drink up your lemonade and 'ave another,' Albert was saying to her as he rose from the table to get another round in. 'Why don't you have some whisky in it this time?'

'You don't know why the Socialists won the election?' Malcolm Lewis was saying to the barman. 'I'll tell you why! It's because this country has just fought a war, and if we'd lost, all the landowners in Great Britain would have lost all their land. It would have gone to Germany. Now here you've got millions of young men coming home out of the forces . . .'

'I've nothing against cats,' a mate of Jack's was saying to a gullible Miss Helliwell, 'but when I've eaten one of 'em I've 'ad enough.'

'. . . they'll all be getting married and wanting homes,' Malcolm Lewis was continuing heatedly, 'and when they get a house, that house will be costing them extra money because somewhere along the line someone had to pay for the land it's built on. Now that land is land that British men have fought and died for and it's land that should now be theirs by right . . .'

'Stop screaming, Emily, for the Lord's sake,' Nellie was saying to a distraught Miss Helliwell. ''E was only kiddin' yer about the cat. No-one eats cats in Britain, they don't even make muffs out of 'em!'

'Do you think the Vicar knows young Malcolm Lewis's politics?' Daniel asked the table at large, a troubled frown creasing his brows. 'Because they seem a bit on the Red side for a scoutmaster—'

'To hell with politics, let's have a sing-song.' The speaker was Mavis. Her almost white, peroxided blonde hair was piled high, tumbling in curls over her forehead. Her mouth, fingernails and toenails were all painted a fiery red. Her chiffon blouse was purple, her tight shiny skirt emerald. She looked as gaudy as a South Sea parrot and as life-enhancing as a roaring fire.

'Wot about "Cruising Dahn the River"?' her mother suggested, moving empty glasses out of the way in order to make room for the second round of drinks which Albert was depositing on the table.

'What about "We'll Gather Lilacs in the Spring"?' Daniel, a romantic at heart, suggested as two of Jack's mates gave Mavis a lift up on to the bar.

Christina reached for her half-drunk glass of lemonade, her sense of disorientation growing. Didn't anyone realize what a foreigner she really was? Didn't anyone realize how *alien* she felt among them all? Albert pushed another lemonade, this time with whisky in it, towards her. Jack turned away from the bar and at last caught her eye, flashing her a wide, heart-stopping smile. For a brief, joyous moment she thought he was going to join her and then someone shouted across to him, demanding his attention, and the moment was lost.

Her hand tightened around her glass. This noisy, laughter-filled, often bawdy, free-and-easy get-together was the kind of evening everyone else in The Swan had been brought up on. When they had been youngsters they would have sat on the pub's doorstep whilst their parents enjoyed a knees-up. Billy and Beryl, and possibly Rose and Daisy, would most likely be sitting on the doorstep this very moment, enjoying crisps and lemonade and

155

anything else their parents, or parents' friends, might take out to them. Her childhood evenings had been very different. Friday evenings, for instance, had meant Shabbas and a special meal to celebrate it. It had meant her grandmother picking up the bread in the light of the candles and breaking it, dipping a piece in the salt and passing it across the table to her. It had meant dignity and tranquillity and a sense of tight-knit family security.

Unsteadily, she set her glass back on the table. For years and years she had kept the past firmly buried, no longer the Christina Frank who was German and Jewish, but Christina Frank who lived in south-east London and worked in a south-east London market. The Christina Frank who had fallen in love with a south-east London boy and married him in a south-east London, Anglican church. Her throat tightened. If she continued secretly allowing her past to encroach on her present in this way, she would lose her reason. She had to share her anxieties and her anguish with Jack. She had to tell him of the guilt she felt for having turned her back on her religion and her culture; of the even more crushing guilt she felt at having escaped from Germany when so many hundreds of thousands had failed to do so. She had to tell him of her growing hope that her mother and grandmother had somehow survived and were waiting for her to trace them.

Mavis, ignoring both Miriam's and Daniel's requests, had launched into a rip-roaring version of 'Chatanooga Choo-Choo'. Even Harriet Godfrey, standing contentedly next to a euphoric Charlie, was singing along. Jack was laughing, motioning her to join him. Out of

Army uniform and in a short-sleeved cotton shirt and flannels, he looked like a very useful, middle-weight boxer, his chest well-muscled, his biceps bulging, his hips narrow. She forced a smile, shaking her head, dark wings of hair falling forward and brushing her cheeks. If she joined him now, standing beside him as Harriet was standing beside Charlie, and Carrie was standing beside Danny, her inner turmoil would be blatantly obvious. She didn't want to be with Jack in full view of all their friends and neighbours. She wanted to be on her own with him. She wanted to be able to share her thoughts and emotions with him and, when she had done so, to have the reassurance that he understood and sympathized.

It had been impossible to reach such mental and emotional union after their love-making. As they had lain in a sweat-sheened tangle of sheets and pillows, Rose had knocked on the door to announce that her gran had just made a fresh pot of tea and that it was waiting on the table for them in the kitchen and that Charlie was also in the kitchen, impatient to welcome Jack home. Though she had hastily dressed and slipped her shoes on and brushed her hair, Jack had only bothered to pull his trousers on before walking downstairs with her to the crowded kitchen. She had wanted to die with embarrassment, certain she and Jack smelled of sex, positive that everyone present knew they had been making love.

Miriam had poured out mugs of tea, Leah had handed round oven-hot bagels, Charlie had informed Jack that Harriet Godfrey was going to be his stepmother and was miffed to discover that he already knew. Jack, barefooted and bare-chested, his hair tumbled, had made all

157

the proper noises of congratulation and Charlie had then
told them that he and Harriet intended making their
marital home at number two and that when Jack was
demobbed they would have number twelve to themselves. More tea had been drunk. More bagels eaten.
Nellie Miller had steamed in, wanting to know if Jack
had brought any black-market goodies home with him.
Later, Jack's mates from Catford and Lewisham had
begun arriving, and the noise and laughter had grown
even louder.

Christina wasn't sure, but she thought that Carrie
knew exactly how she was feeling, and that she thoroughly
sympathized with her. Carrie's marital bedroom was
squeezed between Albert's and Miriam's bedroom and
Leah's bedroom and, looking across to where Carrie was
leaning against Danny, singing the last notes of 'Boogie
Woogie Bugle Boy', she wondered how on earth they
managed *their* love-life.

The door burst open, and Kate and Leon entered to a
storm of greetings.

'Where've you bin, the two of you?' Charlie demanded, ambling forward to give Kate an avuncular and
beery kiss on the cheek. 'It's nearly winkle time an' yer
'aven't 'ad a drink yet.'

'Whose goin' for the winkles?' Nellie demanded, not
missing a trick. ''Cos if it's young Billy, he didn't put
enough vinegar on 'em last time. Winkles need lots o'
vinegar if they're to put 'airs on yer chest.'

Kate was wearing a full-skirted, candy-pink-and-white
striped dress, her waist cinched by a broad white belt. A
white ribbon was twined in her long, thick braid of hair,
making her look positively bridal, and Albert called out

158

jovially, 'Could you plait my 'orse's tail like you've plaited your 'air, Kate? 'E wouldnt 'alf look a bobby-dazzler trottin' dahn the Old Kent Road with ribbons in 'is tail!'

Kate's smile was instant. 'I probably could, Albert,' she responded, well used to being teased about her childish yet oddly elegant hairstyle, 'but you'd have to keep him still while I was doing it.'

''E can't keep 'imself still, let alone his blinkin' 'orse,' Miriam said as Albert charged off to give Billy the orders for the winkles. 'Sit down 'ere, Kate. I think 'Ettie and Daniel are goin' to do a "Knees up Mother Brown" in a minute.'

Kate squeezed along the banquette next to Christina. 'Dad's got some news for you,' she said in a low voice so that no-one else should hear. 'A response from the Red Cross. No real information in it of course, but . . .'

'Let's 'ave one of the old songs now, Mavis!' Daniel demanded. 'There's no Yanks boogie-woogie-ing here any more—'

'More's the pity,' aged Esther Helliwell interrupted from her wheelchair, her sunken cheeks pink with daring.

'. . . so let's have "Maybe it's because I'm a Londoner" or "My Old Man",' Daniel persisted doggedly.

'Is your father in on his own? Would he mind if I had a word with him now?' Christina's eyes were bright with urgency.

'Yes he is, and no, of course he wouldn't. But there's really no hurry, Christina. It's little more than an acknowledgement and—'

Christina was already on her feet. She looked in Jack's

direction, trying to catch his eye, but he was leaning over the bar, ordering another round of drinks.

Mavis, having suitably warmed up with 'Chatanooga Choo-Choo', spectacularly ignored Daniel's request for an old favourite and launched into another newly popular song. Only later, as she hurried up Magnolia Hill towards the Square, did Christina realize that its title, 'My Guy's Come Back', was, with Jack standing only feet away from her, brazenly provocative.

Behind her, in The Swan, Miriam's eyebrows rose nearly into her tightly curled, netted hair. 'Where's Christina 'ared off to?' she demanded. 'Billy'll be back with the winkles in a minute.'

'She's gone to have a word with my dad about something,' Kate said, knowing that if she didn't suitably satisfy Miriam's curiosity, Miriam would publicize Christina's departure to all and sundry by asking the pub at large if they knew where she had disappeared to. 'Is that Malcolm Lewis over there, earwigging Daniel? It's not often he comes down to The Swan, is it? I always thought scoutmasters were teetotal.'

With his latest order of drinks generously distributed far and wide, Jack turned to catch Christina's eye. Why she was sitting in the corner like an old biddy, he didn't for the life of him know. He wanted her next to him, in the centre of the throng, so that he could stand with his arm proprietorially around her waist, showing her off to all his mates. When he saw her empty place on the banquette he frowned slightly. Where the devil had she gone? If she'd gone to the Ladies she'd have had to walk right past him and he would have seen her.

Seeing his perplexity, Kate rose hastily to her feet,

160

about to go across and quietly tell him that Christina had slipped out for a few minutes. Miriam saved her the trouble.

'If you're looking for your trouble and strife, Jack, she's gorn to 'ave a word with Kate's dad,' she informed him loudly, 'an' while I've got yer attention, that last round you bought might 'ave reached everyone else but it didn't reach this little corner and mine's a port an' lemon.'

Carrie, standing with Danny in Jack's extended circle, groaned with embarrassment. Her mother was always the same when she'd had a couple of drinks. Louder than usual and playfully aggressive with it. 'You'll have to excuse her,' she said to Jack, more for the benefit of his mates than himself, 'she thinks she's still down the market.'

Jack barely heard her. All he was aware of was that Christina had walked out of the pub without even bothering to tell him where she was going, or why.

Kate, seeing his frown deepen, carried out her initial intention and squeezed from behind the corner table, shouldering her way through the crush towards him. 'It's all right, Jack,' she said a trifle breathlessly as she reached his side. 'Christina tried to get your attention to let you know she was slipping out for a minute or two, but you were busy ordering drinks. It's a grand party, isn't it? There's faces here I haven't seen since I was at school. Is that Archie Cummings with the moustache? I'd heard he'd been invalided out of the paras. And is—'

'Why on earth has Christina gone to have a word with your dad?' Jack asked, not as easily side-tracked as

Miriam. 'It's not that long since she wouldn't even wish him the time of day!'

'It may not seem a long time to you, Jack, because you've been away from home for so long,' Kate said, understanding why it would seem so incomprehensible to him, 'but Christina and my dad have been on speaking terms for ages now.'

'But what have they got to talk about that's so urgent?' Jack persisted, keeping his voice low so that his mates wouldn't know he was even remotely put out by his wife's disappearing act.

His real question, and Kate knew it, was why would Christina go up the Voigt home to speak to Carl Voigt in such peculiar privacy? If they had anything to talk about, why couldn't it be talked about in daylight, in the Square or over the Voigts' garden gate? Kate hesitated, in a dilemma. If Christina had told Jack about her growing certainty that her mother and grandmother were still alive, and of her decision to try and find them, he would have known why she wanted to talk in private with the only other German resident in Magnolia Square. That he didn't, indicated that she hadn't yet told him, and it was a subject too personal and too close to Christina's heart for her to be the one to break the news.

Awkwardly, she said, 'I'm not sure, Jack. I think it's something she thinks Dad can help her with, him being German.'

Jack's perplexity turned to downright incredulity. Christina couldn't bear to even hear the word 'Germany', and he didn't blame her. If there was one thing there was no room for in their lives, it was reminders of the hell she had left behind her when she had escaped to England. 'I think someone's been spinning you a line, Kate,' he said, his hazel eyes dark, his thumbs tucked into his belt loops, his body tense. 'With all due respect, Christina wants no reminders, in any way shape or form, of Germans or Germany.'

Kate's unhappiness increased. She could hardly tell Jack he was wrong, without also telling him *why* he was wrong.

'Come on, Jack!' Mavis exhorted, reaching out and ruffling his hair from her vantage position perched on the bar. 'Stop lookin' as if you've lost a tanner and found a penny! Get up 'ere with me and let's get a proper sing-song goin'.'

'Who's the blackie?' one of Jack's mates asked him as, with athletic ease, he did as she suggested. 'Is he a Yank?'

'No,' Jack responded swiftly before Kate could draw breath, adding as he settled himself comfortably on the bar top. 'He's home-grown and this is his local.'

'Well, if it's all right by you, it's all right by me,' the speaker, a sallow-complexioned young man with a tic near his eye, said grudgingly, reading aright the infer-ence to back off, 'but Yank blackies usually keep to their own kind. Makes things simpler, if you know what I mean.'

Kate felt almost unbearable pressure building up behind her eyes. This was the second time in a day that Leon's skin colour had been derogatorily remarked upon. Right from the beginning of their relationship Leon had warned her that it would happen and, until now, she had felt confident of being able to handle whatever ignorant abuse was handed out. What she hadn't expected, however, was that she would have to cope with that kind of abuse from her son's great-grandfather, or that she would meet with it in The Swan.

The urge to tug on Jack's mate's arm and give him a piece of her mind, died. It would only result in an ugly scene and she didn't want to spoil Jack's party. Nor did she want to remain at the party any longer. She wanted to be at home with Leon. She looked down the crowded bar to where he was deep in conversation with Charlie and Harriet, his dear, dark face looking tired and strained. She knew the reason why. It was because of their long discussion about how best to handle Joss Harvey's re-emergence in their lives.

'He's a mate,' Kate heard Jack say to his friend as she turned away from them, 'so give it a rest.'

As she squeezed past Malcolm Lewis, Kate felt a spasm of gratitude. Jack's statement was a lie, for he barely knew Leon, but he was obviously taking the line that any husband of hers was a friend of his. Word would now spread among his cronies that derogatory remarks about Leon were off-limits, and there wouldn't be any – at least not in his hearing.

As she reached his side he slid an arm lovingly around her waist. 'Hello, sweetheart. I thought you'd deserted me.' Despite his inner dejection at the problems now facing them, he smiled down at her, his eyes crinkling at the corners. 'Harriet and Charlie have set the date for their wedding. They're planning to have it on a weekday so that Billy won't be able to present Harriet with half a hundred weight of nutty slack for good luck!'

'It's going to be a quiet wedding,' Harriet Godfrey said, striving to make herself heard over Mavis and

Jack's spirited rendering of 'There'll Always be an England'.

Charlie shook his head in disbelief. For an intelligent woman, his Harriet could be incredibly naïve at times. 'Don't be daft, pet,' he said reasonably, 'this is Magnolia Square. 'Ow the 'eck could anythin' possibly take place quietly?'

It was a question even Harriet couldn't answer.

'*Winkles!*' Albert shouted over the now communal singing. 'If you want 'em, come and get 'em!'

'I think I want to go home,' Kate said to Leon as everyone began to make a bee-line towards Albert and his precious cargo. 'Do you mind, darling?'

He shook his head, his arm tightening around her. 'No,' he said tenderly, 'let's slip away now. I don't think we'll be missed.'

'If you ain't got yer own winkle-pin, I'm not lendin' yer mine,' Miriam was saying crossly to her son-in-law. 'Lor' 'elp me, Danny, don't you ever get yourself organized?'

'I ain't 'ad a winkle since I can't remember when,' Mavis was saying with saucy sexual innuendo to Jack as he swung her down from the bar. 'But if you think it's time I 'ad one . . .'

'Never mind 'is winkle, I've got a winkle goin' spare!' Archie Cummings shouted.

There was a roar of bawdy laughter and then, as Kate and Leon stepped out of the pub and on to the street they heard Mavis saying tartly, 'An' you can keep it, Archie Cummings, 'cos from what I've 'eard, you'd need a pin to bloomin' find it!'

The laughter reached gale-force proportions and then

the pub door swung shut behind them and Leon said, amusement thick in his voice, 'And Harriet's hoping for a quiet wedding! She doesn't stand a cat in hell's chance!'

Despite her inner weariness, Kate gave a throaty chuckle. 'I think Charlie's made her realize that.'

His arm went around her shoulders, and she slid an arm around his waist. 'They're an odd couple, aren't they?' she said, her weariness easing in the comfort of his nearness. 'Harriet was always such a prim spinster. Hair in a bun, no lipstick, always very authoritarian and proper. No-one *ever* called her by her Christian name. It would have been unthinkable. And then, after she retired as a headmistress, she took it upon herself to teach Charlie to read, and suddenly the entire Square was on Christian-name terms with her and now she's not only drinking in The Swan, she's joining in the singing too!'

'Lots of happy, perfectly suited couples seem, on the surface, to be oddities,' Leon said as, shoulder to shoulder, hip to hip, they turned the corner into the Square. 'Take you and me, for instance. I'm sure most people must shake their heads when they see us together, and wonder what a half-German south-east London girl and a half-Bajan sailor could possibly have in common. And then there's Christina and Jack. Christina's German and Jewish and, though she never talks about it, she obviously comes from an extremely refined, middle-class background. Jack is a south-east London tearaway. Lord only knows how he's going to settle down to Civvie Street when he's demobbed from the Commandos.'

Kate didn't answer him. She was wondering a lot of other things about Jack. She was wondering how long it would be before Christina began confiding in him as a wife should confide in her husband. And she was wondering what Jack's reaction would be when she finally did so.

Chapter Ten

With an unsteady hand, Christina knocked on number four's front door. The primrose paintwork gleamed palely in the moonlight, and as she waited for Carl Voigt to answer her knock, Christina was aware of the heavy, pungent perfume of roses and night-scented stocks.

He opened the door to her, blinking slightly. As usual when left to baby-sit, he had taken advantage of the relative privacy to sit and enjoy one of his classical music records and had fallen asleep whilst doing so. 'Come in, my dear,' he said, gathering his wits, ushering her through into the sitting-room as the sound of Bach's *Brandenburg Concerto Number One* played melodically to a close. 'Kate's told you about the letter, has she? I was going to leave it to the morning to tell you about it.' He smiled his reticent, oddly charming, smile. 'I knew it was Jack's party tonight and I thought perhaps you wouldn't want to be troubled.'

'It's no trouble.' Her voice was nearly as unsteady as her hands had been. 'What did the letter say? Are the Red Cross going to be able to help us? Do they have lists of names of Displaced Persons? Lists of names of people who were released from, or who survived, the concentration camps?'

'It's not quite so simple and straightforward,' Carl said, wanting to put her out of her suspense, yet wanting to let her down gently. 'Here.' He patted an armchair. 'Sit down and let me get my glasses and I'll show the letter to you.'

In a fever of impatience, she sat down whilst he lifted the arm of the record-player from the record and set it back on its rest, and then fumbled for his glasses and the letter on a nearby cluttered table. When at last he put the letter, with its distinctive letter-heading, into her hand, she was so nervous that her eyes would barely focus properly.

Dear Mr Voigt, she read with a beating heart, *Thank you for your communication regarding your efforts to trace Jacoba Berger née Levy born London, 7.10.1870, and Eva Frank, née Berger, born 1.5.1901, Heidelberg. At the moment of writing, these names do not show up on any of the Displaced Persons files presently held in Great Britain. These files are, however, constantly being updated and it does not mean to say that the names you enquired after will not appear eventually. Our advice would be to write again with your query in three months' time.*

As to your query regarding the availability of concentration camp records; some camp records are in our possession, but not for the years 1936/7.

It is known, however, that a significant number of people imprisoned during this period of time were later released.

If there is any chance at all that Jacoba Berger and Eva Frank were among them, and that they subsequently became refugees, the newly established Headquarters of the United

Nations High Commission for Refugees in Geneva may be able to help you.

In a rush of conflicting emotions, Christina put the letter down and looked across to where Carl Voigt was sitting. 'Is it hopeful news?' Somehow, even though there was no real information about her mother or grandmother in the letter, just seeing their names typed on Red Cross headed notepaper seemed to make the hope that they were still alive more feasible.

'I think it is, yes,' Carl said cautiously. 'It's certainly hopeful to have corroboration from such a source that German Jews imprisoned in 1936 stood a slight chance of subsequent release. That certainly wouldn't be the case if we were talking about a later date.'

'And the United Nations Commission for Refugees? You will write to them for me?'

At the fraught urgency in her voice, Carl felt a wave of compassion for her, wishing he had warned Kate not to tell her about the letter so soon. Tomorrow would have been early enough. As it was, her husband's welcome-home party had been spoiled for her, and all to no real avail. There was still nothing she could do but wait and hope, certainly for weeks, possibly for months.

'I've already done so,' he said gently. 'Would you like a cup of cocoa, or are you impatient to get back to The Swan?'

'I'd like a cup of cocoa, please,' Christina said, in no hurry at all to return to the noisy, raucous pub.

As she watched Danny struggling, tipsily, to undress, Carrie lay back against the pillows on their big, brass-headed bed, her thoughts on Jack and Christina. Compared to her and Danny, they were lucky. Very lucky. When Jack was demobbed and home for good, they would have number twelve all to themselves.

Danny, his right leg safely extricated from his trousers, tried to extricate his left leg and, in doing so, stood on his right trouser leg, half-falling against the bed. 'Oops,' he said, grinning blearily at her from beneath his thatch of spiky, mahogany-red hair. 'Someone's moved the bloomin' bed again.'

Despite her exasperation with him, Carrie grinned. He was an absolute idiot at times, trying to keep up with Jack's hard-drinking mates when he knew very well that more than five pints would see him half-seas over, but he was *her* idiot and she loved him dearly.

He sat down on the edge of the bed, embarking on the difficult task of pulling his pyjama bottoms on without putting both legs down the same pyjama leg. Carrie moved over slightly, making more room for him, her thoughts once again on Jack and Christina. Number twelve was a large, roomy house. One day it would, presumably, be full of children, but for the moment Jack and Christina would be able to enjoy it in absolute privacy. At the thought of such privacy Carrie felt weak with envy. She and Danny had never spent as much as one night together without being aware of the close proximity, through the paper-thin walls, of her mum and dad and gran.

As if on cue, Miriam banged on the bedroom wall. 'Yer dad's flaked out without bringin' any water up for durin' the night, Carrie! Can yer bring 'im a pint mug in? I'd do it, but me legs ain't 'alf givin' me gyp!'

Carrie rolled her eyes to heaven and heaved herself from the bed. After a few jars at The Swan, her dad always woke in the middle of the night with a thirst, and usually had the foresight to arm himself accordingly. And she doubted very much that her mum's legs were paining her. She was tight, that was all, and it was no wonder, considering the number of port and lemons she'd downed!

'Blimey, it ain't mornin' already, is it?' Danny asked as, giving up the battle with his pyjama-cord, he sank back heavily against the pillows.

As she walked towards their bedroom door, her high-necked, white cotton nightdress brushing her ankles, she resisted the temptation to fib and cause even more confusion to his addled brain. 'No,' she said, opening the door. 'I'm just going to get some water for Dad. Do you want me to get some for you as well?'

He didn't answer and she paused in the doorway, looking towards him. He was dead to the world, his arms and legs spread-eagled, his eyes closed, his mouth sagging open. With rising exasperation, she went downstairs to the kitchen. Men! If they knew how *unappetizing* they looked when drunk, they surely wouldn't *get* drunk. As she slammed a cupboard door open, taking her father's pint mug down from a shelf, she wondered if Jack Robson and Leon Emmerson were equally comatose, and doubted it. Jack had an awesome reputation for being able to hold his drink, and Leon had taken Kate home while the evening was still young.

She took the mug over to the sink and turned on the tap. When it came to housing, Kate and Leon were nearly as lucky as Christina and Jack. Apart from the children, who didn't count, they only had to share number four with Kate's father, and in the near future he would be marrying Ellen Pierce. She brushed her unruly, near-black hair away from her face with her free hand. And when Carl Voigt and Ellen Pierce married, Carl would most likely move into Ellen's home in Greenwich, and Kate and Leon and their children would have number four to themselves.

There came the sound of heavy knocking again, this time from the direction of the kitchen ceiling.

'*Where the 'ell 'ave yer got to, Carrie!*' Miriam's market-trading voice carried downstairs magnificently. She thumped the bedroom floor again with her shoe. '*Yer dad'll be wanting that pint of water tonight, not next Christmas!*'

Carrie sighed heavily and turned the tap off. She loved her mother dearly, but there were times when she found her a sore trial. She began to make her way upstairs again, thankful that, as Rose had been moved into the roomy attic bedroom for the duration of Jack's visit, she was unlikely to be woken by all the commotion.

'It's on its way!' she shouted before her mother could really get her knickers in a twist.

From behind her grandmother's bedroom door Bonzo growled, bad-tempered at having his sleep disturbed. Carrie's lips tightened. Bonzo would have his sleep disturbed even more frequently when the baby was born. And so would everyone else. Her grandmother, of course, wouldn't mind in the slightest, but her mum and dad had to be up before the crack of dawn to be at Covent Garden, buying in fruit and veg, and broken nights would be hard for them. And what about Danny? She pushed open her parents' bedroom door. She hadn't told him about the baby yet. She hadn't told anyone, not even Kate. And she didn't intend telling anyone until she heard whether she and Danny were going to be able to move into number seventeen now that the Binns family were moving out of it.

'That's the gel,' Miriam said, her pink slumber-net crammed on her head back to front. 'Put it dahn by your dad's side of the bed, but not too close. I don't want 'im goin' for a paddle in the middle of the night, as well as a piddle.'

'It's looking hopeful, Carrie,' Bob Giles said to her next morning as she faced him across the desk in his cluttered study. 'Housing don't have any immediate plans for number seventeen, and it's just possible we could pull a fast one and have you and Danny in there before the house is even officially listed as being empty. The landlord is the Harvey Construction Company.'

Carrie's sea-green eyes flew wide. 'Blimey!' she said expressively. 'I didn't know old man Harvey owned property in Magnolia Square, and I bet Kate doesn't know either!'

'Joss Harvey owns a lot of property in Blackheath and Lewisham,' Bob Giles said, well aware of the fraught relationship that existed between Kate and Mr Harvey, 'but I think number seventeen is the only house in Magnolia Square owned by him.'

'And wouldn't you know it has to be the only house me and Danny have a chance of moving into!' Carrie said, not at all sure how she felt about having Joss Harvey as her landlord.

174

Bob Giles, well aware that church property in the Square was still standing spectacularly empty, adjusted his clerical collar a little uncomfortably. 'If I'd realized earlier how very much you and Danny wanted a place of your own, I would never have agreed to house a refugee in number eight. As it is, Miss Radcynska is due to arrive any day now and . . .'

The unthinkable happened. Without so much as a knock or a by-your-leave, his study door flew open. '*It's over!*' Hettie announced euphorically, her wraparound, floral-patterned pinafore tied tightly around her ample waist, her hat crammed on her head at an almost jaunty angle, a feather-duster clutched in one hand. 'The bloody Japs have given in! We're not at war any more! Not with anyone!'

'*Praise God!*' Bob Giles bounded from his chair, oblivious of Hettie's colourful language, Miss Radcynska forgotten. 'Is Daniel at work, Hettie? Can he help me ring the bells?'

'He should be at work but he's got a bad back,' Hettie answered, not wanting to admit to the fact that Daniel had woken with an almighty hangover. 'It won't stop him ringing the bells though! He knew it's what you'd be doing and he's gone straight to the church!'

'Is it official, Hettie?' Carrie asked as they hurtled out of the vicarage in Bob Giles's wake. 'Was it announced on the wireless by the Prime Minister?'

'It was announced on the wireless, but not by Mr Attlee,' Hettie panted, eager to share the moment with as many Magnolia Square residents as possible. 'He'll be announcing it official-like, later on. But it's in the bag, Carrie! The man on the wireless said it was!'

175

Carrie's sudden doubt that Hettie might be wrongfully anticipating things was dispelled the minute they burst out of the vicarage and into the Square.

Harriet Godfrey was running down her garden path, tears of thankfulness streaking her face. Kate was dancing a joyful 'Ring-of-Roses' with Matthew and Luke. Charlie was standing at his open doorway, throwing the sheets of his morning newspaper into the air as if they were giant pieces of confetti. Emily Helliwell was hanging a Union Jack out of her bedroom window. Nellie Miller was struggling down her garden path on elephantine legs shouting, *'An' now my 'Arold'll be 'ome just like every other bugger!'* Mavis was standing by Ted's motor bike, sounding its klaxon so hard, it was a wonder anyone could be heard shouting anything. Jack was hanging out of an upstairs window at number eighteen, his chest bare, his hair tousled, his grin so wide it was like the Cheshire Cat's.

'Then it's really over?' Carrie said incredulously beneath her breath as Bob Giles sprinted in the direction of his church and Hettie set off in his wake at a fair old trot, intent on dragging Leah out of number eighteen for a public knees-up. 'No more killing? No more waiting in dread for military telegrams? No more enemies to beat?'

There was no-one nearby to hear, nor answer, her queries and it didn't matter because she already knew the answers. She lifted her face to the sun, joy and relief and pride surging through her. Dear old Britain had done it! She had vanquished Germany and now, with America's help, she had put paid to Japan as well! As St Mark's bells joyfully began to peal, she gave a whoop of exultation and exuberantly kicked off a shoe, sending it spinning as high and as far as she possibly could.

Doris Sharkey had opened the door of number ten and was standing uncertainly on the doorstep, looking as if she hadn't yet heard the news and didn't know what all the commotion was about.

'It's peace!' Harriet Godfrey called out to her as she hurried down the Square to number twelve in order to share the moment with Charlie. 'The Japanese have given in! Isn't it wonderful news, Doris? Peace at last after all these years!'

If Doris also thought it wonderful news she didn't say so, instead, like a frightened rabbit, she ducked back inside number ten, closing the door behind her.

'Well?' Wilfred demanded of her querulously. 'What's all the ruckus about? Have the Americans dropped another A-bomb? Is the Pope dead? Has that damn-fool Helliwell woman made spiritual contact with Hitler?'

'It's peace, dear,' Doris said nervously, wishing Pru was home, wishing Bob Giles would visit, wishing her present domestic nightmare would end. 'The Japanese have surrendered. The war's over.'

Her husband glared at her. He was standing full-square in front of the fireplace, two home-made notice-boards slung around his neck so that they covered him, front and back, from his neck almost to his feet.

'And so, dear,' she continued even more nervously, 'as the war's over there's really no need for you to go out in the street like that and for—'

'A spiritual war is still raging!' Wilfred thundered, slamming a fist on the notice-board covering his chest. REPENT FOR THE END OF THE WORLD IS NIGH was emblazoned on it in large, scarlet letters. '"If *any man hath an ear, let him hear! Babylon the great is fallen, and is become the habitation of devils . . .'''*

He began to stride purposefully towards the hallway and the front door, and Doris pressed her hands to her face, saying in a cracked voice. 'Please don't go outside wearing those placards, Wilfred. Mr Giles won't like it. He may ask you not to be a churchwarden any more—'

'I am a prophet of the Divine Jehovah! The Anglican Church is a man-made abomination! Mr Giles is a disciple of the devil!'

Silently and hopelessly Doris began to weep, the tears trickling through her fingers. It had been like this ever since Daniel and Bob Giles had brought Wilfred home from the churchwardens' meeting. No-one, not even Dr Roberts, had been able to get a word of sense out of him. And now he wanted to go outside wearing his placards, and what would happen then? Small boys would laugh at him and perhaps throw stones at him. Right-minded people would cross the street to get out of his way. People might even be scared of him. Tears dripped from the end of her nose. *She* was scared of him. He had called her a whore of abomination, a harlot and a scarlet woman. Mr Giles and Dr Roberts had said he needed rest and quiet and that he'd probably be his old self in next to no time. Though Mr Giles and Dr Roberts had been unaware of it, they had been offering very little comfort.

'Please don't go outside, Wilfred,' she said again, wondering how she would live with the shame if he did so. 'Everyone's happy and celebrating and—'

'Get thee behind me Satan!' her husband roared, steadfastly walking out of the room into the hallway, his

placards swaying cumbersomely. '"For thou savourest not the things that be of God, but the things that be of men!"' A placard caught on the hatstand, delaying his progress slightly. Wilfred turned sideways on, the better to navigate his passage towards the front door. '"And fire came down from God out of heaven",' he announced, reverting once again to the Old Testament, '"and the end of the world is nigh!"'

Doris's hands were no longer pressed to her tear-stained face. She was wringing them, beside herself with distress and apprehension and despair. Fire and harlots – it was all Wilfred seemed capable of thinking about. Dr Roberts had said that Wilfred's obsession with fire had been triggered off by the atomic bombing of Hiroshima and Nagasaki, and that what he described as 'Wilfred's temporary nervous collapse' was merely delayed reaction to the strain and stress of the last five years. Doris wasn't so sure. Wilfred had always been strange about the Bible, quoting disjointed passages from it whenever he wanted to prove a point, which was often. And though Dr Roberts's explanation would account for Wilfred's obsession with fire, it hardly accounted for his unnerving obsession with harlots.

'Harlots!' Wilfred said vehemently, as if reading her mind. 'Whores and sinners!' He was at the door now, his fingers on the latch.

Distantly Doris could hear some of her neighbours discordantly singing 'There'll Always be an England'. A klaxon was sounding. Harriet Godfrey would no doubt still be out in the Square, as would Leah Singer and Hettie Collins and Mavis Lomax and goodness knew who else. At the thought of what Mavis would make of

179

Wilfred's exhortations against harlots and whores, Doris felt quite faint. Wilfred *couldn't* go outside and make himself such a laughing-stock. Somehow, some way, she had to prevent him. As the door opened she made a lunge for him, grabbing at his rear placard. The front placard shot upwards in response, nearly cutting his windpipe in half. As he staggered, half-throttled, Pru came running into view around the corner of Magnolia Terrace and Doris fell against the door-jamb, nearly senseless with relief.

''Ave they let you 'ave the rest of the day off work?' the landlady of The Swan, a Northerner, shouted out as Pru ran grim-faced past the bottom of Harriet Godfrey's garden. 'Do you think the shops'll be shut tomorrer and we'll all be laking?'

Pru didn't answer her. Whether there was a national holiday tomorrow, she neither knew nor cared. All she knew was that her father was on the verge of stepping out into the Square, his ridiculous placards clanking about his person, and that her long-suffering mother would probably die with the shame of it if he did so. Breathlessly she raced past number eight and flung the gate of number ten back on its hinges.

Her father, yanking hard on his front placard in order to ease the pressure on his windpipe, stared at her in mental confusion. 'What are you doing home?' he demanded, fire and harlots temporarily forgotten. 'You should be at work.'

'I've been given the rest of the day off,' Pru panted, grateful that the unexpectedness of her arrival had induced a flash of lucidity. 'Now go back in the house, Dad. You haven't got the right shoes on.'

'Haven't got the . . .' Wilfred began bewilderedly, straining to look over the top of his placard and down towards his feet.

Before he could realize she was talking almost as much nonsense as he'd been talking, Pru seized him by the shoulders, whipped him smartly around and thrust him back into the hallway.

As the door slammed mercifully shut behind them Wilfred said again, 'What do you mean, I haven't got the right shoes on? I always have the right shoes on. Brown for weekdays and black for Sundays—'

'Let me help you take your placards off, Dad,' Pru continued, aware that she just might have found a way of successfully handling the religious lunatic she and her mother were now obliged to live with. 'It's Tuesday today. You can't wear placards on a Tuesday. Placards are for weekends.'

'Placards are for . . .' Wilfred began, his sense of disorientation growing.

Seizing advantage of it, Pru began lifting his front placard up and over his head. '"To every thing there is a season",' she began, hoping a biblical quotation would settle the matter utterly, '"and a time to every purpose under heaven".' The front placard fell hard against the back one. 'And the time for placards is Saturday,' she finished firmly as the offending four-foot by two-foot constructions slithered to the floor.

'Oh, Pru! How do you do it?' her mother asked in heartfelt admiration. 'I couldn't do anything with him. He wouldn't listen to me and—'

The door knocker tapped lightly against the front door.

'"*And the Lord God shall come amidst thunder and Holy angels!*"' Wilfred declaimed, once more picking up steam.

Doris and Pru looked at each other fearfully. What if it was one of their neighbours wanting them to come out and join in the general celebrations? What if, when the door was opened, the person or persons calling on them barged right in the house and Wilfred began regaling them with hell and damnation? The door knocker tapped against the door again, this time with a hint of impatience.

'It might be Mr Giles,' Doris said, her voice fraught with hope, 'or Dr Roberts.'

'"*Knock, and it shall be opened unto you,*"' Wilfred moved with intent towards the sitting-room door and the hallway beyond.

Pru moved like greased lightning, dodging in front of him, saying adroitly, 'Let me go, Dad. I'll see if whoever is there is fit for you to meet.'

Wilfred halted in his tracks. Pru was quite perceptive at time. Prophets of Jehovah couldn't hob-nob with any Tom, Dick or Harry.

Praying that her mother was right about the possible identity of their visitor, Pru opened the door, but only a cautious couple of inches.

It wasn't Mr Giles or Dr Roberts. It was Malcolm Lewis. 'Hello,' he grinned cheerily, his white shirt open at the throat, his hands laconically in his trouser pockets. 'Are you coming out to join in the fun? Jack Robson has suggested going up town. The King and Queen are bound to be making an appearance on the balcony at Buckingham Palace and—'

'"*Cast not your pearls before swine!*"' Though he couldn't be seen, there was no mistaking Wilfred's stentorian tones.

Malcolm blinked.

Pru flinched.

'. . . and there'll be singing and dancing until the early hours in Piccadilly Circus and Trafalgar Square,' Malcolm continued, refusing to let the interruption deflect him from his purpose.

It had been Mavis who had suggested Pru might like to join them all on a jaunt up town. 'Poor little devil gets little enough pleasure, 'avin' old sourpuss for a dad,' she had said, showing a great deal of leg as she had sat astride her absent husband's motor bike. 'Why don't you go and ask 'er if she wants to come with us while I take Emily for a victory spin over the 'Eath? You're a scoutmaster and old man Sharkey isn't likely to pitch into you the way 'e would if me or Carrie or Jack did the asking.'

Without Mavis's prompting, it would never have occurred to him to have asked Pru to go anywhere, no matter how big the group. He was twenty-seven and she was only sixteen or seventeen and, in his eyes, little more than a child, but as he had strolled towards number ten he had been aware of a very pleasant sense of anticipation. There was a blunt straightforwardness about Pru that he found both endearing and amusing, and, despite her curiously frumpish dress-sense, she was really quite pretty.

Mavis had roared past him on her husband's motor bike, eighty-year-old Emily Helliwell on the pillion, her scrawny, chiffon-clad arms around Mavis's waist as she clung on for dear life. He had grinned and shaken his head in disbelief, reflecting that such a sight could only take place in Magnolia Square, which was why he liked the Square and its inhabitants so much. As he had dropped the Sharkeys' highly polished door knocker on to pristinely painted wood, he had been thinking of how he would like to live in the Square and, when he had heard Pru's footsteps walking down the hallway to open the door, he had been looking forward to her surprise and pleasure when he announced the reason for his visit.

'No,' she said now to him tautly. 'I'm not coming out. I don't want to celebrate.'

He stared at her in disbelief. 'But it's the end of the war, Pru! *Everyone's* celebrating. And everyone's going up town. Jack Robson and his wife. Mavis and Carrie. Kate and her husband . . .'

'"*Let the sinners be consumed out of the earth, and let the wicked be no more!*"'

'Well, I'm not,' Pru said abruptly, and slammed the door in his face.

Malcolm stared at the reverberating wood in incredulity. What on earth had he said to her to have occasioned such a reaction? And who on earth had Wilfred Sharkey been in conversation with? He shrugged, aware he would probably never have the answer to either question. Turning away from the door, he walked back down the path, towards the gate. If Pru didn't want to join in the celebration of the century, it was her loss, not his. All the same, it was a pity. He rather suspected that, when she was in a good mood, Pru would be exceedingly jolly company.

As he reached the gate a faint but unmistakable sound

impinged on his consciousness. He paused, looking back towards the house, his eyebrows contracting in a deep frown. Someone in number ten was crying. Someone female. Someone sixteen or seventeen years old.

Chapter Eleven

Ellen Pierce plumped and rearranged the cushions on her sofa, hurriedly removed a small dog-basket from the side of the hearth and re-located it in a discreet position in the corner of the kitchen, checked her appearance in the mirror hanging over the fireplace, and then plumped and rearranged the sofa cushions yet again. Why did she get so agitated when Carl was about to visit her? Why couldn't she simply relax and enjoy his company and cease fretting about whether the house was suitably tidy and whether or not the dogs were going to be annoying and if he was ever going to ask her to marry him? She knew Harriet didn't behave in a similar manner where Charlie was concerned, but then Harriet was the most sensible woman imaginable and Charlie had already asked her to marry him and, in any case, Charlie wasn't a complicated personality in the way Carl was complicated.

'Down, Hotspur,' she said, flustered, as a Welsh Terrier jumped up at her, eager to gain her attention. 'Your basket is in the kitchen for the rest of today. And *please* don't jump on the sofa! I'm sure Carl doesn't like it when you jump on the sofa. And where are Macbeth and Coriolanus? Are they sulking because I've taken their baskets upstairs?'

Hotspur yapped in an excited frenzy, certain he was about to be taken for a walk. Ellen did her best to ignore him. Was it because of her dogs that Carl still hadn't suggested they formally spend the rest of their lives together? She knew that, before Kate had given a home to Hector, the Voigts had never owned a dog. And though Carl had never said a single word to indicate he wasn't happy at Hector's presence in his home, she couldn't really *tell* whether he was unhappy about it or not.

It was never possible to tell *what* Carl was thinking. He was such a quiet, introspective, *complex* man that his private thoughts were a complete mystery to her. And that was the source of all her anxiety. How could she relax and be happy in their relationship when she didn't know how Carl viewed that relationship? Though he was affectionate towards her, they weren't lovers in the accepted sense of the word. They had never gone to bed together. But then, they weren't married, and Carl was a very moral man. She couldn't imagine him even considering going to bed with someone to whom he wasn't married. And it wasn't as if she were an experienced sex-siren! She was a forty-year-old virgin, for goodness sake!

A large, ungainly mongrel lolloped into the room and clambered on to the sofa. Ellen was too distracted by the route her thoughts had taken to even notice. Was her unwanted virginity one of the reasons their relationship never achieved real mental and emotional intimacy? Or was it because he couldn't imagine being married to a woman who, though capable of holding down a responsible position at Harvey's, was not his intellectual equal?

A woman who very foolishly shared her small Greenwich terraced house with three bombed-out dogs?

As Coriolanus nuzzled contentedly deeper into the cushions on the sofa, she looked despairingly into the mirror. She'd had her mouse-brown hair permed shortly after VE Day, and now VJ Day had come and gone and the perm still hadn't settled down! She'd been a fool, of course, to have ever had it cut. At one time she had worn it in a sensible bun, as Harriet wore her hair. Only her bun had never looked as elegant as Harriet's, and she had thought that a cut and perm might make her look a little more fashionable. It didn't, of course. She looked the same as always. A middle-aged Plain Jane.

There came the sound of his familiar knock on the door and her heart jarred against her ribs. He was here! They would spend the rest of the day together and she knew that she was lucky, lucky, lucky! If he wanted, Carl could have his pick of middle-aged, unmarried lady companions, yet he continued to seek only her company and she was deeply, unspeakably grateful. If only she could be sure he would *continue* to seek only her companionship, she would be the happiest woman in the world. She hurried to open the door to him, wondering if she had put enough lipstick on, or too much; wondering if he would be impressed by the sponge cake she had made for their tea, or if he would think it a poor thing compared to the sponge cakes his late wife had no doubt once made for him; wondering if she should chatter on about the celebrations of VJ Day, or if he would like a little peace and quiet now that the boisterous celebrations were over.

Carl, happily ignorant of being the cause of such

tormented indecision, was wondering if the suggestion he intended putting to Ellen that afternoon was, perhaps, offensively cavalier. Her house wasn't very big. Not when Hotspur, Macbeth and Coriolanus were taken into account. And even if her home was twice the size, it still wouldn't alter the fact that it was a man's responsibility to provide a marital home for his wife. Moving into a woman's home was, after all, little different from living off her money.

As he heard Ellen's dearly familiar footsteps hurrying towards the door, he knew it was a problem he had to face up to. Though his own home was a spacious, Edwardian family house, it wasn't spacious enough to accommodate another three dogs. Or at least not to do so in comfort. And besides, much as he loved his daughter and her children, he didn't have a temperament suited to boisterous family life. He liked to read and listen to music, and he liked to do so in peace and quiet. Ellen, too, was accustomed to living quietly, or as quietly as her dogs allowed. To start off their married life sharing number four Magnolia Square with Kate and Leon and the children, would be a sure-fire recipe for disaster. And as he had no capital with which to buy a second house, the only other alternative was for him to move in with Ellen.

The door opened and Hotspur shot past him like a bullet from a gun.

'Hotspur! Hotspur!' Ellen shouted ineffectually, having no choice but to hurry straight past Carl in an attempt to call Hotspur to heel before he should reach the main road.

Hotspur, dimly aware that things were not quite as

they should be, had the sense to come to a halt when he reached the street corner.

'Naughty, *naughty* dog!' Ellen chastised, gulping for air, realizing too late that she didn't have a dog lead with her.

Twenty yards away, Carl was still standing at the doorway, waiting patiently for her return.

Hotspur was not the best trained of dogs. Ellen knew that if she once let go of his collar, he would immediately dart off in the wrong direction in the happy expectation of again being chased. Resignedly she hooked a finger under his collar and, stooping lop-sidedly like the Hunchback of Notre Dame, awkwardly began to drag him back to the house.

Carl continued to wait for them patiently. Who but Ellen would nearly break her back in dragging a recalcitrant Welsh Terrier home? If necessary, he knew she would be quite capable of laying down her life for one of her dogs; or for anyone she loved. The sensation of warmth he always felt when in her company eased through him. Loyal and loving, totally incapable of a harsh thought or word, she had brought romantic companionship back into his life at a time when he had been bereft of companionship of any sort. As memories of the internment camp he had been imprisoned in during the war flooded into his mind, he thrust them firmly back. Those days were over, just as the war was now over. The neighbours he had lived amongst for over twenty years and who, when war had broken out, had ostracized him because of his nationality, had long since sheepishly befriended him again. One memory he would never try to suppress, however, was the memory of how a middle-aged lady he had never even met had, when she had heard of his internment, shyly begun a pen-pal relationship with him in order to ease his loneliness and isolation. It had been an act of Christian charity, and utterly typical of her. His heart swelled with love. Dear Ellen. Sometimes he wondered if she had even the remotest idea of how much her letters had meant to him, how they had renewed his faith in human nature.

'Hotspur's not usually such a naughty dog,' she said now, dragging Hotspur off the pavement and on to her short garden path, still bending at an almost impossible angle as she did so. 'It's just that he does so love a walk.'

Carl closed the garden gate so that Hotspur shouldn't make yet another bid for freedom. 'We'll take all three dogs to the park, if you like,' he said amenably, 'but first I want to have a chat with you, Ellen. I'm afraid it's all a little difficult and I shall quite understand if you think my suggestion unacceptable . . .'

Ellen released her hold of Hotspur and, not without a little difficulty, straightened her spine, fear flooding through her. What on earth could he be about to suggest that might be unacceptable to her? Was he going to suggest they didn't see each other quite so often? Was he about to try to end their relationship? She led the way into her tiny, linoleum-floored hallway. Macbeth, her aged Scottie, barked in greeting. In the sitting-room Coriolanus raised his head from the cushions and, on hearing more than one set of footsteps, prudently abandoned the sofa and did his best to make himself comfortable on the floor.

'I'll put the kettle on for a cup of tea,' Ellen said a few

seconds later as Carl sat down in the place Coriolanus had vacated.

'No,' he said gently, trying to ignore the suspicious warmth emanating from the sofa cushions, 'don't make a pot of tea yet, Ellen. Let me tell you what's been preying on my mind.'

She sat on the edge of an easy chair, her hands clasped on her knees, as apprehensive as a little girl about to receive a catechism.

'I don't quite know how to go about this,' Carl began awkwardly, hoping the warmth Coriolanus had so obviously left behind him, wouldn't prove to be damp warmth. 'But with Kate and Leon now married . . .'

Ellen's knuckles showed white. He was going to leave the house in Magnolia Square to Kate and Leon and the children. He was going to leave London. Maybe, now Hitler and Nazism had been ground into the dust, he was even contemplating a return to Germany? She clenched her knuckles even tighter. She wouldn't cry when he told her – she wouldn't. But she would cry afterwards, when he had gone. She would cry and cry and she doubted if she would ever stop. For the moment, though, she had to listen to whatever it was he was trying to tell her. She had to try and concentrate.

'. . . and so if I moved in here—'

'In here?' she blinked. What did he mean? Was he asking her if he could become her lodger? And if he did so, what would her neighbours say? They all knew that he was her gentleman-friend and they would come to some very incorrect and salacious conclusions! Or would their conclusions be incorrect? Scarlet spots of colour stained her cheeks.

Carl, mistaking the emotion that had occasioned them, said with even greater awkwardness, 'I'm sorry, Ellen. I shouldn't have even put the suggestion to you. It's just that I think it will be years before German is reinstated on grammar school syllabuses and until it is, my income won't cover the cost of buying a second property. We could probably rent somewhere, of course, though finding a landlord or landlady willing to accept Hector and Macbeth and Coriolanus won't be easy and, as you're so comfortable here, I didn't think you'd like the idea of starting married life in rented accommodation.'

'Married life?' The blood had begun to beat in her ears so loudly that she couldn't be sure she had heard correctly. 'Did you say "married", Carl?'

He looked at her shiningly beautiful face, naked of powder, naked of guile. Had she been wool-gathering again? Had her thoughts been on Hotspur, still yearning for his walk, and not on what he had been saying to her? Tenderly he said, 'Of course I said married, Ellen. You can't imagine I would have suggested my moving in here *before* we were married!'

Tears had begun streaming down her face. 'Oh, Carl! Oh, of *course* we can live here after we're married! It's just that I hardly dared hope . . . I thought perhaps you were going to go away . . . I thought . . . I thought . . .'

There was no way she could possibly tell him all the foolish things she had thought. And it didn't matter that she couldn't do so. All that mattered was that he wasn't going away. He wasn't going to end their relationship. He was going to marry her. And he was going to marry her because he loved her; because she was just as necessary and dear to him as he was to her.

193

Her legs were too weak with joy and relief to be able to support her unaided and Carl crossed the room towards her, taking her hands in his, drawing her to her feet. 'I love you, Ellen,' he said simply. 'I love you with all my heart.'

'And I love you, Carl.' Her voice was unsteady, tremulous with joy.

Behind them Coriolanus cocked a speculative eye towards the sofa.

'There's no sense in our having a long, formal engagement, is there?' Carl said, the light glinting on his spectacle lenses. 'If you're happy for me to do so, Ellen, I'd like to ask Mr Giles to announce the banns this coming Sunday.'

His arms were around her and she could feel his heart beating next to hers. 'Oh, yes!' she said, happier than she had ever been in her entire life. 'I'm *very* happy for you to do so, Carl!'

Behind them Coriolanus made his move, heaving himself back on to cushioned comfort.

Carl lowered his head to Ellen's in loving commitment. Ellen's hands slid up and around his neck.

Coriolanus closed his eyes, intuitively knowing that no-one was going to disturb him for quite some time.

Jack Robson and Mavis Lomax sat on the grass by the Princess of Wales pond. Mavis had her knees hugged to her chest, her arms circling them. Jack was sitting with his legs slightly apart, his arms resting on his knees, his hands clasped loosely. It had been an accidental meeting, though Mavis doubted that any busybody seeing them would think it so. Jack had left number eighteen in order to buy a packet of cigarettes. She had been taking Bonzo for a walk on the Heath. Bonzo now lay a few feet away from them, his head on his paws, snoring soundly.

'If I knew what was wrong, I could put it right,' Jack was saying bluntly. 'But the hell of it is, I don't *know* what's wrong!' He ran a hand through his hair dishevelling it and, unwittingly, making himself look even more attractive. 'We haven't had a row over anything. Nothing has been *said*, but this leave home hasn't been anything like I anticipated it would be.'

'In my experience, things never are,' Mavis said dryly, unclasping her hands and plucking a blade of grass. She began to shred it with a scarlet-lacquered nail. 'Christina probably finds it 'ard 'aving a reunion with you while she's living at number eighteen,' she said, showing a perspicacity that would have surprised a great many people. 'I know *I* wouldn't 'ave wanted to 'ave been living there when I 'ad my reunions with Ted.' She chuckled throatily. 'It was bad enough 'aving to cope with our Billy and Beryl charging in and out of the bedroom at inconvenient moments, without 'aving Mum and Dad and Gran doing it as well!'

Despite his despondency, Jack grinned. 'Maybe,' he said, not totally convinced. His grin faded. 'The thing I *really* don't understand,' he said, frowning slightly and disclosing a perplexity he wouldn't have disclosed to one of his mates in a million years, 'is why Christina is now so friendly with Carl Voigt. I mean, the man's a *German* for Christ's sake! You'd think he'd be the last person in London she'd want to hob-nob with! Yet the first night I was home she slipped away from the knees-up at The Swan, just to have a natter with him. And she did the same thing again yesterday morning.'

Mavis plucked another blade of grass. 'I don't 'ave an answer for that one,' she said frankly. 'Leaving out 'is being German, Carl isn't exactly the kind of fella to 'ave a laugh and giggle with, is 'e? 'E's far too quiet and serious.'

Jack remained silent. Christina never laughed and giggled in the way Mavis and Carrie and their friends did. It was one of the many things about her that had first caught his attention. And as it was quite obvious Christina wasn't merely having a laugh and giggle with Carl Voigt, as Mavis did with Daniel for instance, it only made the puzzle of why Christina was chin-wagging with him so often even more perplexing.

Some twenty yards or so away from them, on the far side of the pond, Leon Emmerson was squatting down on his haunches at the edge of the water, Matthew beside him. Slowly, and very carefully, he was launching a magnificent-looking sailing ship.

'They're an odd couple, aren't they?' Mavis said, intuitively realizing that Jack had said as much as he wanted to say where his wife was concerned.

'Kate and her bloke?'

Mavis nodded. 'And 'im and the kiddie. I mean, 'owever much Leon loves and cares for Matthew, no-one's ever going to believe 'e's Matthew's *real* dad, are they?'

Jack's mouth twitched in amusement. 'No,' he agreed, as Matthew clapped his hands in delight at the sight of the sailing ship forging its way across the pond, his hair the colour of pale wheat in the bright afternoon sunshine, 'it would beggar belief a bit, wouldn't it?'

They remained in companionable silence for a little

while, watching Leon's dark figure as, time and again, he retrieved his handiwork, making adjustments to the sails and then floating it again, Matthew eagerly helping him and chatting to him non-stop.

'I can't wait for me and Christina to have kids,' Jack said suddenly, with surprising passion. 'You know Dad's moving out of number twelve when he marries, don't you? There'll be room in that house for me and Christina to bring a large family up.'

'You won't want so many blinkin' kids if the first one's anything like my Billy,' Mavis said wryly, swatting a bee away. 'You know what 'is last trick's been, don't you? Tryin' to make a bomb in the back garden out of an empty shell casing and sugar and sodium chloride!'

Jack gave a crack of laughter. There was nothing he'd like better than to have a son as lively as Billy. They could go to football matches together and he'd teach him to box and how to play a mean hand at cards and . . .

'We've been spotted,' Mavis said, indifferent to the fact. 'There's a black straw 'at bobbing along over there,' she nodded peroxide-blonde curls in the direction of the nearest of the three narrow roads that traversed the Heath, 'and unless I'm very much mistaken, the body bobbing along beneath it, is 'Ettie Collins.'

Jack turned his head in the direction she was indicating, squinting his eyes against the sun. She was right. It was Hettie. And if the indignant set of her shoulders was anything to go by, she'd seen them and drawn a predictable, and very erroneous, conclusion. He gave a sigh. Under normal circumstances he wouldn't give a fig what conclusion Hettie had come to, only the present moment, with Christina behaving so oddly and his leave about to come to an end, was not normal circumstances. He didn't want Hettie filling Christina's head with ridiculous suspicions hours before he and Christina were going to be parted. An early demob was, after all, something he only hoped for, not something that was a foregone conclusion. It could very well be months before he was back home for good. It might not even be until next year.

'Bloomin' old tabby,' he said, disgruntled. 'Why she should be so ready to stir up trouble beats me.'

Mavis stretched out her legs and rolled on to her side a little. 'She's a bit of a stick-in-the-mud is old 'Ettie,' she said sagely, resting her weight on her elbow. 'She thinks you should 'ave married a south-London girl.'

Jack grinned, recovering his good humour. 'How could I? The best ones were all taken.'

Incredibly, under her carefully applied make-up, Mavis blushed. Not wanting Jack to see her reaction she turned her head swiftly, looking again in the direction of the pond and Leon and Matthew. 'Odd that neither of us worried what conclusion Leon might come to, seein' us sittin' on the grass together.'

His grin deepened. 'You're not sitting on it any longer. You're lying on it. And no, it would never occur to me to think Kate's bloke might come to a wrong conclusion and broadcast that conclusion far and wide. For all Carl Voigt's a German, he's the most non-judgemental person I know. Kate's the same. And she'd never have married a judgemental man. Not in a million years.'

'Unlike poor old Doris Sharkey,' Mavis said, remembering Magnolia Square's latest piece of titillating gossip. 'Did you know Wilfred was seen in Lewisham 'Igh Street

198

yesterday afternoon, paradin' up and down with placards slung about 'is neck announcin' that the end of the world was nigh? 'Ow Doris and Pru put up with 'im, I can't begin to imagine. It must be like livin' with Moses on a bad day!'

'Why can't *I* go with Matthew tomorrow to see Great-Grandad?' Luke asked, tugging at Kate's skirt as she rolled pastry for a strawberry tart. 'Why can't *I* go for a ride in a big motor car?'

Kate paused in her task, brushing a stray strand of hair away from her face. The problems she had known would come when she had agreed to Joss Harvey renewing contact with Matthew, were already beginning. How did she explain to a three-year-old that, though Joss Harvey was Matthew's great-grandad, he wasn't *his* great-grandad? And that Matthew would now quite often be enjoying the kind of treats that he and Daisy would never be able to enjoy?

She bent down to him, taking hold of his chubby hands, saying gently, 'Though we're all one family, you and Daisy and Matthew all had different daddies, and so your grandads and your great-grandads on your daddy's side of the family, are all different. That's one of the things that makes all three of you so wonderfully special. And though it's sad that only Matthew's great-grandad is still alive and able to visit him and take him out for treats, we mustn't be jealous of that, must we? Instead we must be very pleased for him. Nothing in life is ever the same for *everyone*, darling. And while Matthew is out with his great-grandad, you will be able to go somewhere nice with Daddy.'

Beneath his mop of silky dark curls, Luke frowned, struggling to understand the complicated talk of different daddies and grandfathers and great-grandfathers. 'But, though my daddy wasn't *always* Matthew and Daisy's daddy, he is their daddy now, isn't he?'

'He's going to be their *adopted* daddy,' Kate said, drawing him into the circle of her arms, 'and he loves them just as he loves you.'

Luke's frown deepened, his toffee-brown eyes bewildered. 'But if *I* share Daddy with Matthew and Daisy, why can't Matthew share his great-grandad with me?' His bottom lip began to tremble. 'Want to go out with Great-Grandad Harvey,' he said, his eyes brimming with uncomprehending tears. 'Want to go for a ride in a motor car.'

With an aching heart, Kate lifted him up in her arms. Perhaps Leon would be able to explain to Luke in a way he could more easily understand. Perhaps, in time, Luke wouldn't mind the expensive treats Matthew enjoyed when out with Joss Harvey.

Cold shivers of apprehension slid down her spine. What if things went the other way? What if Luke began to mind more, not less? What if Joss Harvey's re-emergence into Matthew's life resulted in the relationship between Luke and Matthew being permanently marred? What would she do then? How would she ever forgive herself? As Luke's arms slid around her neck, she knew that she never would be able to forgive herself; that the entire responsibility would be hers, and hers alone. Luke's tears trickled damply on to her neck and she hugged him close, wishing Leon would come home. She needed him to comfort her just as she was now comforting Luke. Once in the shelter of his arms, nothing would seem quite so daunting.

'Come along, sweetheart,' she said tenderly. 'No more tears. Are you going to help me fill this pastry-case with strawberries? Would you like to make a strawberry tart all of your very own?'

Chapter Twelve

Christina lay beside Jack in their bedroom. He was sleeping soundly, his breathing heavy and deep, and she lay very still in order not to wake him. It was very early, faint slivers of light just beginning to ease the curtained darkness. He spoke indistinctly in his sleep. She wasn't sure, but she thought he was saying her name. She stared up at the ceiling. In another few hours he would be leaving her. And when he returned, he would be doing so for good. Carefully, she slid her legs from beneath the sheets and stood up. It had been a hot night and the linoleum beneath her feet was welcomingly cool. With her cotton nightdress skimming her ankles, she padded across to the window and drew back a corner of the curtain.

Pure and piercing, the first fingers of the dawn stabbed the sky. Number eighteen was at the bottom right-hand side of Magnolia Square, and from her bedroom window Christina had a magnificent view of St Mark's Church, standing proudly on its island of grass, and of all the even numbered houses, from number fourteen all the way to number two.

In the Lomaxes' bedraggled front garden, a disused pram had joined Billy's scrap-metal collection. Presumably he was going to strip it down and use the base and wheels for a trolley or go-kart of some kind. Next door to the Lomaxes', the Helliwells' flower-strewn bomb-site added a touch of exoticism to the Square. In the now golden light, roses of medieval France and Persia rampaged in what had always been an unorthodox garden. Left untended, the rose bushes had grown jungle-thick, reaching head-high in some places, white and crimson and heart-achingly beautiful.

Next door to the bomb-site's botanical splendour was number twelve. One lot of banns had already been called for Charlie and Harriet's wedding, and in another three weeks they would be man and wife, and living in Harriet's house at the Blackheath end of the Square.

'So you'll 'ave plenty of time to fix number twelve up to yer own fancy before Jack comes 'ome,' Charlie had said to her affably. 'The only things I'm leavin' behind that I care about are my pigeons. 'Arriet says there's no room for 'em in 'er back garden. Wot she really means is, she don't want a pigeon shed bang against 'er kitchen winder and pigeon droppings all over 'er lawn, and I don't suppose you can blame 'er.'

Beyond number twelve were the heavily curtained windows of the Sharkeys' house, windows that, as often as not, were now curtained throughout the day. What was going on there, Christina didn't know, though there were rumours in plenty. Albert had told his clan that he had it on good authority from Daniel Collins that Wilfred Sharkey had completely lost his marbles. Miriam had given it as her opinion that Wilfred was a secret wife-beater, reminding everyone of the way Doris Sharkey had worn her hat halfway over her face at Kate and Leon's wedding.

'The nasty brute 'ad given her a shiner, I said so to 'Ettie at the time. Bible-bashers are all alike. All spare the rod and spoil the child, and I 'spect they're just the same with their wives. Poor Doris never passes the time of day with anyone now. She scurries in and out of that 'ouse like a frightened rabbit, and word is Pru's 'ad to give up 'er job at the solicitors in order to 'elp 'er mother keep Wilfred in 'and.'

Next door to the Sharkeys', number eight stood starkly empty. The Tillotsons still hadn't returned to the upper part of the house, and no-one knew when the Polish refugee destined to move in to the lower half of the house was going to put in an appearance, though it surely couldn't be much longer before she did so. Then there was the Voigts' house, soon, no doubt, to become known as the Emmersons' house, and Harriet Godfrey's house. When Harriet married Charlie she would become Jack's stepmother and her stepmother-in-law. It was an odd thought, but so many of her thoughts were odd now that one more was of no importance whatsoever. What *was* important, though, was that she still hadn't shared her innermost thoughts with Jack. She still hadn't told him of her fierce hope that her mother and grandmother had survived the war, or of the efforts Carl Voigt was making, on her behalf, to find them. She leaned closer to the window, her cheek pressed to the cool glass. Why hadn't she unburdened herself to him? Was it because the celebratory atmosphere of VJ Day, and days that had followed it, had been so ill-suited to such a discussion? Goose-bumps came up on her bare arms, but not from cold. The trip up town on VJ Day, with Jack, Kate, Leon, Danny, Carrie, Mavis, Malcolm Lewis and goodness only knew who else, had been a nightmare for her.

Relieved though Christina was that the war in the Far East was finally over, she hadn't wanted to celebrate it by whooping and singing and making an exhibition of herself in Piccadilly Circus and Trafalgar Square. The others had, though. And they hadn't been alone. Londoners had been out in full throng, and not just Londoners. There had been servicemen in Dutch, Polish and Czechoslovakian uniforms. There had been so many Americans and so many Stars and Stripes vying for prominence with Union Jacks that it would have been quite easy to imagine they were in an American city.

When people had begun dancing in the streets, the Magnolia Square contingent had joined in wholeheartedly, dragging her in their wake. In Trafalgar Square, Mavis, Carrie and Kate had scrambled up on to the back of one of Landseer's bronze lions, and Jack had laughingly insisted on her joining them. Outside Buckingham Palace they had sung the National Anthem and cheered King George and Queen Elizabeth until they were hoarse. Then, when it was evening, they had forged a way through the crowds to Piccadilly Circus. At midnight, Big Ben's chimes had boomed out resonantly, signalling the official end of the Japanese War, and what had seemed to be every motor horn in London had begun to blare.

Klaxons had sounded. Policemen had blown whistles. From the direction of the Thames, tug horns had hooted. The cheering had become deafening, and it had been then, at the apex of exuberant joy, that some GIs standing near them had stretched out a stout blanket to serve as a trampoline and Mavis had recklessly and willingly allowed herself to be flung by them, time and time again, high into the air, her legs and arms all over the place, her skirts flying. She rubbed the goose-flesh on her arms. Jack had roared out his approval along with every other red-blooded male massing the Circus, and she had felt, terrifyingly, mentally and emotionally distant from him. It had been a sense of distance that had escalated into an all too familiar sense of dizzy disorientation. Trapped in a sea of celebrants, her heart and mind obsessed with the probable whereabouts of her mother and grandmother, it was a disorientation she was powerless to suppress.

Round and round her thoughts had gone, wondering if and where her mother and grandmother were celebrating the end of the war in the Far East. Were they in a hospital? A refugee-camp? Were they perhaps picking up scraps from gutters in order to survive, as cinema newsreel films had showed thousands of European homeless doing? No-one around her, with the possible exception of Kate, was sparing her mother and grandmother a thought, and in such an atmosphere it had been impossible for her to have spoken their names to Jack. And so nothing had been said; not then; not afterwards. And now, in only a few short hours, he would be returning to his Commando unit, and unless she took very speedy action, the mental and emotional gulf yawning between them was going to remain unbridged.

He stirred, beginning to wake, stretching a naked, well-muscled arm across to her side of the bed. As his hand failed to come into contact with her warm flesh his eyes opened abruptly, sleep vanishing. 'Christina?' He pushed himself up against the pillows. 'What are you doing out of bed at this unearthly hour, love? What is it? Five o'clock? Six?'

'It's just after five.' She began to walk back towards the bed and he threw the sheets aside for her, suppressing a surge of impatience. If she'd woken early on this, the last morning of his leave, why on earth hadn't she woken him also, in order that they could make love? Why, instead, had she been standing staring out of the window?

As she lay down beside him, he pulled her lovingly into his arms, his desire and need of her blatantly obvious. Answering response flared through her, to be immediately checked at the thought of the occupants of the adjoining rooms.

'It's Saturday,' he said reassuringly, reading the expression in her eyes with unerring accuracy. 'Miriam will have gone up to Covent Garden with Albert. She always does on Saturdays.' He reached down, lifting the hem of her nightdress, sliding his hand up the satin smooth softness of her flesh. 'And Leah's snoring like an old porker,' he said, cupping her left breast and gently brushing her nipple with his thumb, 'and Carrie and Danny and the kids are still fast asleep.'

She trembled at the warmth of his touch, once again strung on exquisite cords of need that reached deep within her.

He sensed the instantaneity of her response and relief roared through him. She wasn't regretting their marriage. She wasn't beginning to fall in love elsewhere. She was still in love with him. And, dear God, he was going to make sure she stayed in love with him! He lowered his head to hers, kissing her temples and then the corners of her mouth, his eyes dark with passionate need.

She moaned softly in submission, her hands sliding up into the thick tumble of his hair. This time, when they had made love and were still lying conjoined, she would confide in him all her hopes and fears where her mother and grandmother were concerned. This time she wouldn't waste the opportunity; she would breach the mental and emotional chasm dividing them and they would be united utterly, just as they should have been from the very first moment he had arrived home.

His hand uncupped the pleasing weight of her breast and slid downwards to the coarse, springy-dark triangle of her pubic hair. 'This will be the last for a long time, sweetheart,' he said huskily as he felt her warm, velvet-soft dampness, 'let's make it memorable, shall we?'

'Oh, yes,' she whispered with fierce urgency, for once oblivious of Leah asleep in the room next door, and of the presence of others elsewhere in the house. 'Oh, yes, Jack! Love me! Please love me!'

Only too happy to oblige, he eased his hard, superbly fit body over hers and silenced her pleas with hot, sweet lips.

Later, as they lay naked and sheened with sweat in a tangle of bed-linen, listening to the house beginning to creak to life, she said at long last, 'There's something I want to talk to you about, Jack. Something that's been troubling me.'

He had been lying, one arm around her shoulders, a cigarette in his free hand. He took one last drag on the Craven 'A' and then stubbed it out in the saucer by the bed that served as an ash-tray. He'd known ever since he had returned home that there was something troubling her. Now, not before time, she was going to tell him what it was. He felt a spasm of apprehension. Christina was a highly intelligent young woman. Whatever was troubling her would not be trivial. He just hoped to God Carl Voigt wasn't part and parcel of it. In another time and place, Carl Voigt was exactly the kind of well-educated, middle-class gent Christina's family might well have been happy for her to have married. Or would have, if he had been Jewish. Even taking that little difficulty into account, he knew there were many people who would have found the idea of Christina marrying a widower of Carl Voigt's standing a great deal less surprising than her having married a south-east London roughneck like himself.

Stalling for time, not knowing quite how to continue, Christina pushed herself up into a sitting position against the tumbled pillows. She didn't only want to tell Jack about the search she and Carl Voigt had embarked on, she wanted to try and make him understand the burden of guilt and grief she felt at having survived the war in the cosy security of Magnolia Square, when so many millions of fellow Jews had perished in concentration-camp ovens – of the guilt she felt at having turned her back on her religion and culture. She pulled a sheet over her knees and drew them towards her chin, circling them with her arms.

Jack lay, his weight propped on an elbow, his eyes on her face. She was sitting in exactly the same position Mavis had adopted when he had been on the Heath with her. There, however, the similarity ended. There was no blowsy, happy-go-luckiness in Christina's demeanour. Framed by a halo of soot-dark hair, her delicately boned face was intent and pale.

'Yes,' he prompted. 'What is it, Tina? Is living with the Jenningses beginning to get you down?'

The very idea was so ridiculous and, even if it hadn't been, was so trifling an issue that her eyes flew wide with shock. 'No, of course not! I love them all far too much for them ever to get me down! It's something else . . . something that isn't easy for me to talk about.'

From the attic room above them came the reverberation of footsteps and the muffled sound of childish voices. Soon Rose would be on her way downstairs to the kitchen and breakfast. There were already familiar sounds emanating from that direction. The rattle of a frying pan being slapped on top of the stove. Water filling a kettle. Cutlery being clattered. It would be Carrie who was up and doing, for there had been no movement from Leah's bedroom. Saturday, the Jewish Sabbath, was a day when Leah often stayed in bed for an extra half hour or so, and on both Saturday and Sunday mornings Danny *always* stayed in bed for as long as Carrie's patience would allow.

'What is it then?' he asked again, beginning to wish he hadn't stubbed his cigarette out. Whatever the problem troubling her, it was obvious it wasn't going to be aired and over with quickly.

She said at last, her voice resolute, her dark-lashed eyes holding his, 'Ever since the war with Germany came to an end, I've been thinking more and more about *meine Mutti* and *Grossmutter* . . .'

He felt the tension in his stomach relax. Christ! Was that all this was about? Was it nothing to do with their personal relationship at all? He sat up, his strong back muscles rippling.

'That's only to be expected, love,' he said understandingly, covering her clasped hands with one of his. 'But that nightmare's over now. You need never, ever, give the bastard Germans or Germany another thought.' He grinned, his teeth dazzlingly white against a skin that had been weathered by fighting in Italy as well as Greece. 'You're a south-east London girl now. And south-east London girls don't brood. It isn't in their nature.'

He had meant to jolly her out of her sombre mood but instead of returning his smile her eyes darkened. 'I'm not a south-east London girl,' she said tautly, 'I don't have a south-east London girl's history or temperament. I'm a German – a German Jew.'

If she'd said she was a creature from another planet, he couldn't have been more pole-axed. How on earth, after all that the Germans had done to her family, could she possibly think of herself as being German? *He* certainly didn't think of her as being so. He ran his free hand through his thick shock of hair. Christ Almighty! He'd just spent six years fighting the bastards. He certainly didn't think of himself as being married to one of them. And if Christina thought he was labouring under such a misapprehension, it was no wonder she was troubled!

He slid an arm around her shoulders, pulling her close against him, saying reassuringly, 'You're wrong about your not being a south-east London girl, sweetheart. This is your home now. It's been your home for nearly ten years, and it's going to be your home for life. We need neither of us ever speak about what you suffered before you came here. It's in the past and the past is dead and buried.'

She tried to shake her head but he was holding her too

close against him. 'You don't understand,' she said, an edge of panic entering her voice. 'The past isn't dead and buried for me, Jack. It isn't dead and buried for *any* Jew that has survived . . .'

Rose's footsteps hurried past their bedroom door. A smell of fish was beginning to permeate the house – kippers, perhaps, or maybe smoked haddock.

'It is for Jews who married in an Anglican church,' he said wryly, interrupting her and trying to get her to see things in perspective. Hell, her Jewishness had never been an issue between them. If it wasn't that it had been the cause of her having to flee Germany, he would no more have thought of her as Jewish than he thought of her as German!

'Nationality and religion are never going to be an issue for us, sweetheart. No-one in Magnolia Square thinks of you as being German, and, despite the reason for you having come here in the first place, I doubt if many people think of you as being Jewish, just as no-one thinks of Miriam as being Jewish, or of Carrie having Jewish blood. You're a south-east Londoner now, just like the rest of us, and—'

Rose burst into the room, fizzing with energy. 'We're having kippers for breakfast!' she announced, her eyes sparkling in happy anticipation. 'Mum's serving them up now, so you'd better hurry!'

'Don't go waking Jack and Christina, Rosie!' Carrie shouted up from the bottom of the stairs. 'I can keep their breakfast warm for them!'

'Too late came the cry,' Jack said dryly, ensuring that the sheet was covering him to the waist. 'Off you go, young Rose. Tell your mum we're on our way.'

212

'Good,' said Rose, who had had no intention of eating breakfast with no-one for company. ''Cos kippers aren't very nice warmed up, are they? An' you should 'ave told Dad you didn't 'ave any pyjamas. 'E'd 'ave lent you a pair of 'is. Mum says if you don't wear pyjamas in bed you get chills on your chest.'

Jack cracked with laughter. 'I don't have chills on *my* chest, young Rose! When my luck's in I have something far more interesting! Now scarper so's we can get dressed.'

As he threw a pillow in the general direction of her unruly curls, she dodged adroitly, running out of the room, shouting down to her mother, 'Jack and Christina don't want to stay in bed! They're getting up and going to have their kippers now!'

Jack swung his legs from the bed, still laughing. Rose was a little minx and no mistake. A chill on his chest indeed! And him a Commando! He reached for his trousers, grateful for the way she had burst in on them. If she hadn't, Christina's conversation would no doubt have turned to the subject of concentration camps, and he had determined never to allow her to brood on such horrors. The war was over and they need never think of it again. What mattered now was the future. The minute he was back in Civvie Street he was going to set about making a tidy fortune, and if he had to cut a few corners and skirt the law in order to do so, what did it matter? Risk-taking had always been second nature to him, and six years in the Commandos had turned it into a way of life, a way of life he thrived on. He wanted to be able to give Christina, and the kids they would have together, lots of creature comforts.

He grinned across at her, buckling the leather belt sitting low on his waist. 'In a year or so, perhaps even less, we'll have a little madam of our own, just like young Rose. Perhaps we could give her a name just as pretty. Holly or Poppy or Primrose.'

She was fastening her skirt, her head turned away from him. 'Don't you think it would be a flower name too many?' she said, struggling to keep the despair she felt from showing in her voice. 'There's already a Daisy in the Square. And besides,' a new note had entered her voice, one he had never heard before, 'I would like any daughter I have to be named after my mother and grandmother.'

He was standing by the door, waiting for her, his naked chest broad and bronzed. 'That's fine by me,' he said easily, 'remind me what your ma and grandma were called?'

Her hands shook as she fastened the buttons on her blouse. 'My mother's name is Eva and my grandmother's name is Jacoba.' He'd forgotten their names! How could he have forgotten their names? And how could he be so insensitive not to notice that where he had used the past tense in talking about her mother and grandmother, she had used the present tense?

'You'd better go down to the kitchen or your kippers will be cold,' she said, knowing that unless she had a little time to herself she would break down completely. 'I'll be with you in a minute, when I've put my stockings on.'

When he had left the room she sank down on to the edge of the bed, her stockings in her hands. How was it possible to love someone so much, and to communicate

214

with them so badly? How could she and Jack ever enjoy the kind of relationship Kate and Leon, and Carrie and Danny, enjoyed together, when her hopes and fears were a closed book to him?

'Your kippers are going cold, Christina!' It was Rose, intending to be helpful.

With an aching heart, she began to put on her stockings, knowing that if she didn't speedily put in an appearance at the breakfast table Rose, or perhaps even Jack, would be coming upstairs to see what it was that was delaying her.

The cotton skirt she was wearing was toffee-coloured, her blouse pale buttermilk. She cinched her waist with a cream belt and slipped her stockinged feet into cream-coloured, wedge-heeled sandals. In an hour or two, when Jack had left for the station, she would go up to the Voigts and see if Carl had any further news for her. There might be letters she could write, a fresh line of enquiry to follow.

As she entered the kitchen, Carrie gave her a strained smile. She was beginning to suffer from morning sickness, and kippers were the last thing she had wanted to cook. They were, however, Jack's favourite breakfast and, as this was the last breakfast of his leave, she had made a special effort. She bit into a piece of dry toast. Christina was looking under the weather as well, though that would be because of Jack's approaching departure. She sighed. Christina certainly had nothing else to be despondent about. In another few months Jack would be home for good, and they would be setting up home in number twelve. If only she and Danny could look forward to setting up home in a house of their own, she wouldn't let anything get her down, not even morning sickness.

She looked up at the kitchen clock. It was nearly half past nine, and Danny was still in bed. With a surge of rare irritation, she pushed her chair away from the table, carrying her plate over to the sink, saying to a startled Rose, 'Will you tell your dad that if he doesn't show his face within the next five minutes I won't be serving him his kipper on a plate, I'll be slapping him around the face with it!'

Chapter Thirteen

'It's time you got yourself a steady girl-friend,' Mavis said to Malcolm Lewis.

It was a week after Jack had returned to his unit, and she was leaning against Ted's motor bike, clad in the serviceable slacks and jacket of her bus-conductress's uniform, her blonde hair scooped into a scarlet headscarf, the ends fastened in a knot on top of her head.

Malcolm grinned. 'If you're offering, I might,' he said, knowing he stood no chance at all and not too seriously upset by the fact. He was a scoutmaster and an active Christian, and adultery wasn't on his agenda. If Mavis had been single though . . . His grin deepened as he thought of what his mother's reaction would be if he brought a sex-siren like Mavis home as a girl-friend. Common. Tarty. Fly-by-night. Those would be the kind of words his mother would use to describe Mavis.

Even now, dressed in a far from glamorous clippie's uniform, Mavis still exuded earthy glamour, impossibly blonde curls escaping from her confining headscarf, tumbling *à la* Betty Grable over her forehead, her lips and fingernails painted the same searing scarlet as her turban. 'Don't be so cheeky,' she said, without the least trace of censure in her voice. 'I'm a respectable married woman, Malcolm Lewis, and well you know it.'

Malcolm eyed her in genuine perplexity. Was she? She certainly wasn't if the rumours about her relationship with Jack Robson were anything to go by. Their chat was being conducted on the kerb of the pavement, outside number sixteen. Next door, on the bomb-site, Emily Helliwell's giant-sized cat had returned to his erstwhile home and was stalking some poor unsuspecting creature through thick undergrowth. On the corner across from number sixteen, Nellie Miller was seated in state on a dining chair placed full-square in her open doorway. From this admirable vantage-point, she was keeping tabs on her neighbours' comings and goings, and was taking enjoyable interest in Mavis's and Malcolm's *tête-á-tête*.

Well aware of Nellie's affable scrutiny, Malcolm said, changing the subject slightly, 'When will your husband be demobbed? Have you heard from him?'

Mavis's thoughts, too, had flicked to Ted. It was all very well harmlessly flirting with Malcolm and teasing him as to whether or not she was all that she should be, but when Ted came home she would no longer be able to flirt with anyone, harmlessly or otherwise. 'I had a telephone message from him via Mr Giles. He said he'd definitely be demobbed by Christmas, and with luck he'd be home for our wedding anniversary in October.'

Any telephone message for Magnolia Square residents came via the vicarage as no-one else in the Square possessed the luxury of a telephone. It meant messages by phone could be delivered but that conversations between message-giver and eventual message-receiver rarely took place. Mavis wished she'd been able to have a few words with Ted. They'd been separated for so long

that the unthinkable was happening to her; she was growing nervous at the thought of a reunion that wouldn't
only be for the length of a leave, but would be for good.

'That'll be nice for you,' Malcolm said, vaguely
surprised that the Lomaxes gave thought to such conventional niceties as wedding anniversaries. 'I expect that
will mean another good old celebratory knees-up in The
Swan.'

'It might not,' Mavis said, seeing no reason why
Malcolm should live in happy anticipation of an event
unlikely to take place. 'Ted isn't Jack. He's a quiet
bloke, and I doubt if he'll want a rowdy get-together.'

Malcolm tried to suppress the surprise he felt. True,
he barely knew Ted Lomax, for Ted had volunteered for
duty at the outbreak of the war long before he, Malcolm,
had become St Mark's scoutmaster, but it was inconceiv-
able to imagine Mavis married to a man who didn't enjoy
a rowdy night out amongst friends.

Mavis, aware of his surprise, said wryly, 'It does take a
lot of believing, doesn't it? Me, married to a non-
partygoer.'

Malcolm coloured slightly, wondering if Mavis always
read his thoughts with such embarrassing accuracy.

Mavis adjusted her stance a little more comfortably
against the motor bike. 'The attraction of opposites,
that's me and Ted,' she said with typical frankness. 'We
haven't a single thing in common, except the kids,
whereas—'

She broke off abruptly. She'd been about to say,
'Whereas me and Jack have everything in common.' It
was no use allowing her thoughts to go down *that*
particular road.

'. . . whereas Carrie and Danny are alike as two peas in a pod.'

Malcolm, who didn't know either Carrie or Danny very well, accepted her statement without demur. 'I suppose it comes of them having known each other since they were nippers,' he said easily. 'I don't think I'd fancy it myself. There can't be many surprises in store when you know someone so well, and I rather like surprises, they make life interesting.'

Mavis, too, liked surprises, but not the kind of surprise Jack had sprung on her when he had become so obsessed by Christina. What on *earth* was the attraction there? Jack was flamboyant and extrovert and dangerously reckless, and Christina was prissy and unemotional and agonizingly uptight. And, as if that weren't enough, Jack was as south-London as jellied eels, while Christina was utterly and quite unmistakably foreign. She chewed the corner of her lip. It was a foreignness no-one else, not even Jack, seemed aware of, probably because of Christina's nearly flawless spoken English. And it was a foreignness that wouldn't have mattered a jot if only Christina had been more . . . more . . . . She sought vainly for a suitable word and failed to find it. Approachable, perhaps? Outgoing?

'I'm going up the open-air swimming pool this evening with the Emmersons and their kids,' Malcolm said, breaking in on her thoughts. 'Do you fancy coming? It might be a last chance now we're into September.'

Mavis shook her head, no longer in her usual happy-go-lucky mood. 'No thanks, Malc. I've things to do.' She stepped away from the motor bike. 'You could do worse than ask Pru Sharkey if she wants to go with you, though,' she said as an afterthought. 'She's been holed up in number ten like a latter-day Rapunzel for days now. A couple of hours of fun is just what she needs.' She walked across the pavement towards the munitions dump that was her front garden, her coarse-woven clippie's trousers not diminishing her sexiness an iota, no longer a Betty Grable look-alike but a Marlene Dietrich look-alike.

Malcolm remained on the pavement, watching her sashaying hips in flagrant admiration. Rapunzel? Where on earth had Mavis heard, or read, the story of the incarcerated Rapunzel? And how come in all the time they had been speaking together she hadn't dropped an aitch once? As the front door of number ten closed behind her, he shook his head in bemusement. There was far, far more to Mavis than met the eye.

'Givin' you the run-around, is she?' a vastly amused Nellie shouted across to him. 'I could've told you she would if you'd bothered to ask.' She wheezed with laughter. 'Yer need a bit o' Commando panache to succeed with Mavis. A scout's whistle and a lanyard just ain't enough!'

Malcolm grinned, not taking umbrage. If Nellie wanted to entertain herself at his expense she was more than welcome to do so. Whether he should knock on the door of number ten, risking having it slammed in his face again and thereby giving her even more entertainment was, however, a moot point. He plunged his hands into his flannels pockets, debating it for a minute or two. Did he want a graceless young woman, little more than a child, giving him the brush-off again? The answer was, of course, that he didn't. He began walking in the

221

opposite direction to number ten, towards Magnolia Hill, pondering on the kind of activity his scouts would most enjoy at their next meeting.

Unseen by anyone but Nellie, Pru Sharkey let the corner of an upstairs window curtain fall back into place. Why couldn't *she* be the one Malcolm Lewis was interested in? Why couldn't *she* be more like Mavis, not giving a fig what people thought of her, dressing as outrageously as she pleased, having respectable single young men as well as dangerously attractive married men, falling besottedly in love with her?

'Pru?' her mother called out nervously from the foot of the stairs. 'Pru? I think your dad's sedative is wearing off. He'll be wanting to go out with his placards. Come down and help me with him for the Lord's sake!'

Carrie rounded the corner of Magnolia Terrace into the Square, easing her basket of groceries from one hand to the other. It was mid afternoon and she still felt queasy. Had she felt queasy all day when she'd fallen for Rose? She couldn't remember. Those days, when the war was a new and frightening experience, seemed so far in the past as to be ancient history.

She walked desultorily along the top end of the Square, past St Mark's vicarage. The war had been exciting, as well as frightening, what with cramming into public bomb shelters with babies and dogs and knitting and thermos flasks of tea, and having a good old sing-song to try and drown out the noise of the German bombers, and doing war work down the ammunitions factory at Woolwich, and having a bit of freedom in life for once.

She turned the corner, walking past Harriet Godfrey's

spick-and-span front garden. The war had certainly changed Harriet's staid way of life. Although well in her sixties when war had broken out, she had become a volunteer ambulance-driver, racketing through burning, bomb-shattered streets, a tin hat on her neatly coiffured hair, a rope of pearls incongruously around her throat. And she had reclaimed the Square's local villain, teaching him to read and write, and falling in love with him in the process.

Carrie shook her head in wonderment. Did people as old as Harriet Godfrey and Charlie really fall in love? And make love? Would she and Danny still be making love when they were in their sixties and seventies? She just couldn't imagine it. She certainly couldn't imagine her mum and dad making love. Miriam never went to bed without an armoury of steel curlers in her hair, and Albert's snores could be heard throughout the house the instant his head touched the pillow.

She lifted the latch on Kate's gate. The way she and Danny were going on, love-making would be a thing of the past long before they were thirty, let alone sixty. They'd had another row that morning. She couldn't remember now what it had been over, but it had been over something trivial, just like all their recent rows. She gave a cursory knock on the front door to announce her arrival and then opened the door, bracing herself for Hector's boisterous welcome. As he half-knocked her off her feet she remembered why Danny had erupted so bad-temperedly before leaving for work. It had been because she had made cheese and tomato sandwiches two days running for his packed lunch.

'You should be so lucky, Danny Collins!' she had

flared back at him, weary of morning sickness that stretched throughout the entire day; taut with tension at the prospect of telling him about the baby when their living conditions were so stressfully cramped; apprehensive as to whether they would, or would not, be able to move into the house the Binnses had now vacated. 'Plenty of other men only have jam to look forward to!'

'Well, I ain't one of 'em and I ain't goin' to become one of 'em!' he had shouted back. 'My ma never dished up jam sandwiches! We always 'ad a proper meal on the table! Pig's trotters and peas! Steak an' kidney puddin'! Tripe an' onions!'

It had been useless to point out that it was his packed lunch they were at odds about, not the hot meal she cooked for him every evening. The row had gone on, common sense lost to the winds, ending only when he had slammed out of the house, too late to be able to clock in at work on time. And there, Carrie thought wearily as she fondled Hector's ears, lay the true root of all their domestic difficulties. He hated clocking in at the factory. He hated the mind-deadening work he did there. He hated the lack of respect and deference that were accorded him.

'I'm in the kitchen!' Kate called out from the depth of the house, guessing correctly her visitor's identity. 'Don't let Hector be a nuisance! And don't let him get his nose into your shopping basket! He's developed a craving for dried fruit and sugar!'

Lifting her basket firmly out of the way of Hector's nose, Carrie walked down the passageway towards the multi-coloured stained-glass panels decorating the kitchen door.

How could she have been expected to know, when she had encouraged Danny to leave the Army, how much he would hate Civvie Street? To her, Danny being in Civvie Street had meant that, after years of living apart, they would at last be sharing a home together, even if that home was her parents' home. It had meant she would be able to see him off every morning with a packed lunch and greet him home every evening with a hot dinner on the table. It had meant they would be able to go to the cinema together every week, take Rosie for walks in Greenwich Park, enjoy a drink together of an evening in The Swan. The prospect had seemed idyllic. The reality had been a slow decline into querulous disillusionment.

'I'm making a treacle tart,' Kate said in greeting, rolling pastry out on the floured surface of her kitchen table. 'There's enough pastry here for an extra one. Are you going to be here long enough to take it home with you, or shall I pop down with it later this afternoon?'

'If it's all the same with you I'll stay till it's ready,' Carrie said, dumping her shopping basket down on the nearest available surface. 'I need a cup of tea, probably several cups of tea, and a long, long chat.'

Kate paused in her task, her hands still on her rolling-pin, a smudge of flour on her cheek. She and Carrie had been friends ever since they had been toddlers, and she knew her as well, if not better, than she knew herself. 'Is it as bad as all that?' she asked, reading aright the depth of feeling behind Carrie's bland words.

Carrie pulled a chair out from under the far side of the table. 'Yes,' she said, sitting down heavily. 'Me and

Danny are falling out over the least little thing. This morning it was over his sandwiches. Yesterday it was over the way I iron his shirts. Tomorrow it will probably be over something even more trivial. And I'm pregnant. And I haven't told him yet. And Mr Giles hasn't come back with any news over number seventeen.'

'Pregnant?' Kate seized on the only really important item in Carrie's weary litany. 'But that's not bad news, Carrie, it's *wonderful* news!'

Carrie smiled sheepishly, pushing a thick fall of dark hair away from her face. 'Yes, it is,' she said, ashamed of having lumped the news of the baby in with grumbles about Danny and anxiety about number seventeen. 'And if only Danny wasn't so *difficult* these days, and if only we were living in a house of our own, I'd be over the moon about it.'

Kate put down her rolling-pin. It wouldn't do her pastry any harm to rest for a little while. 'I'll put the kettle on,' she said, resorting to the oldest panacea she knew. 'If you're only a few weeks pregnant I expect you're feeling queasy all the time, and *that* won't be helping you see things in perspective.'

She began to fill a kettle at the sink. 'And there's no need yet to get despondent about number seventeen. It isn't as if anyone else has already moved in. And until they do there's still hope.' She set the kettle on to the gas ring. 'As for Danny, there must be some underlying reason he's so grouchy. It could be that he's beginning to feel cramped, living with your mum and dad and gran, and that when you do get a place of your own, he'll be his usual equable self again.'

Carrie grinned, beginning to feel better already. It was

an effect Kate always had on her. There was a sunny, inner serenity about her childhood friend that complemented her own, more turbulent nature perfectly. 'Danny equable?' she said wryly. 'Who's been pulling your leg? He's about as equable as a rumbling volcano.' Her grin faded. 'And no, it isn't because he's feeling cramped, living with Mum and Dad and Gran. It's something more serious. Something I don't know how can be put right.'

Kate's long braid of hair had fallen forwards over her shoulder while she had been making pastry and she flicked it back again, her eyes holding Carrie's. 'Tell me,' she said simply.

Carrie rested her clasped hands on the scrubbed deal table. 'Danny hates Civvie Street. He hates not being Sergeant Collins any more. He hates not being in a position of authority and not being respected, and being only a name and a number on a clocking-in card. He's unhappy and miserable, and the worst thing of all is that it's my fault he's unhappy and miserable. His health wasn't so bad that he couldn't have stayed on in the Army if he'd chosen to do so. It was just dodgy enough to allow him to make a choice. And because I wanted him out of uniform and at home, I talked him into the wrong choice.'

The kettle had begun to steam and Kate poured a small amount into a teapot, swirling it round and then emptying it down the sink. 'But that's understandable, Carrie,' she said gently. 'It isn't as if, before the war, you and Danny were living in married quarters, is it? He was always at Catterick Camp or somewhere equally far away, and you were living with your mum and dad and gran.

227

After all these years of his never being at home, it's only natural you wanted him to opt for an early discharge.' She tipped three caddy spoonfuls of tea into the warmed pot. 'And so the first thing you can do is to stop feeling guilty,' she said firmly. 'Feeling guilty solves no problems whatsoever.'

'And do you think it's a problem that can be solved?' Carrie asked hopefully, unclasping her hands as her tension began to ease.

Kate emptied the boiling contents of the kettle into the teapot. 'We can certainly try. There must be another job Danny could do, a job he would enjoy.' She carried the teapot across to the table. 'All we have to do is to think what it could be.'

Through the open kitchen window came the sounds of childish shouts and squeals.

'Leon dug out our Anderson shelter and built a sand-pit on its site,' Kate said as Carrie's eyebrows rose queryingly. 'Matthew and Luke love it. Their favourite game is trying to bury Hector.'

Carrie grinned. It was typical of Leon that, instead of leaving a gaping hole where the air-raid shelter had been, he had utilized it to give pleasure to his children. It was also typical of Leon that he had made no wrong decision when he was discharged from the Navy. Before the war he had been a Thames lighterman, and it was a profession he had happily returned to.

'I can't imagine when Dad and Danny are going to get around to digging ours out,' she said, pouring milk into the two mugs which Kate had set on the table. 'Emily Helliwell asked Daniel to dismantle her indoor Morrison and reassemble it in the garden so that she can keep

228

rabbits in it. It's about all those mesh-sided contraptions are good for. I only climbed into one once, when an air-raid caught me short at a friend's, and I felt like an animal in a zoo.'

The minute Kate had sat down, Hector had laid his head in her lap and she stroked the top of his silk-soft head lovingly, saying, 'Well, you'll never have to do it again, thank God. No more air-raid sirens. No more panic-stricken shouts that a V2 is heading our way, no more—'

Heavy, urgent knocking at the door broke her off short.

'Were you about to say no more emergencies?' Carrie said dryly as Kate jumped to her feet. 'Because if you were, I think you might have been speaking a bit too soon.'

The knocking came again, harder and even more insistent. With Hector bounding at her heels, Kate hurried out of the kitchen and down the long hallway leading to her front door. Through half-panes of frosted stained glass, an authoritative, dark-suited, masculine figure was discernible. She broke into a run. Had Daisy had an accident at school? Had Leon had an accident down on the river? With her heart racing, she yanked open the door and saw that the dark suit was offset by a pristinely white clerical collar.

'Thank God!' Bob Giles said with heartfelt relief. 'I was beginning to think you were out. Could you give me some help, Kate? Miss Radcynska has arrived and I've got a problem. A very awkward, distressing problem.'

'Yes, of course.' Kate's reaction was instant. 'But I'll have to ask Carrie if she'll keep an eye on Matthew and

Luke for me. They're playing in the back garden at the moment and—'

'And with a bit of luck they'll remain in the back garden while I enjoy a mug of tea in peace,' Carrie said, joining her at the open doorway.

Bob Giles shot Carrie a look of gratitude and turned swiftly on his heel, taking the shallow flight of broad steps leading to the pathway two at a time. Kate exchanged a quick, perplexed look with Carrie and hurried after him. Carrie remained on the doorstep, one hand restrainingly on Hector's collar, curious to see whether Mr Giles would head towards the vicarage or the church. He did neither. Instead he made a bee-line for the house two doors down, the house that had long been awaiting its new Polish tenant.

'I haven't time to prepare you properly for this encounter,' Bob Giles said as Kate caught up with him. 'Suffice to say that Miss Radcynska suffered obscenely in Ravensbrueck and her body, and perhaps her mind, has been permanently damaged.' He ran a hand distractedly through his still thick hair. 'I've known all along, of course, just what her history was,' he continued, harrow-faced, 'and I knew, or thought I knew, the kind of problems she would meet with.' He pushed open the unlatched gate of number eight. 'I hadn't, however, anticipated lack of co-operation on her part, even though it is a reaction she can't, perhaps, be held responsible for.'

As they hurried up a pathway rank with weeds, Kate shot him a mystified glance. What on earth was he trying to tell her? And why should Miss Radcynska, after being hospitalized by the Red Cross and settled in England, be unco-operative with the clergyman trying to settle her in her new home? It didn't make sense.

Bob Giles didn't respond to her glance. Rage and revulsion, almost disabling in intensity, were again roaring through him, just as they had roared through him when he had first heard details of Anna Radcynska's suffering. 'How,' he had asked the Red Cross official thickly, 'how in the name of all that is holy, could human beings descend to such depths of cruelty and evil?'

'You're a minister of God,' the official had said, sending a thin folder skimming across his desk-top in Bob's direction. 'You tell me.'

Bob had been unable to do so. He had certainly been unable to speak specifically of Anna's suffering to his churchwardens when he had first broken the news to them of who was to tenant number eight. He had talked to Ruth, however, sitting with her in the blessed comfort and familiarity of his fire-lit study. 'Along with countless other non-Aryan women and children, Anna was medically experimented on in Ravensbrueck,' he had said, one arm around Ruth's shoulders, the other clenching his pipe, the knuckles white. 'What genetic conundrum the monsters were trying to unravel, God only knows, but she will never look, or sound, feminine again.'

'Dear God in heaven,' Ruth had whispered, her face draining of blood. 'The poor, poor girl. What will happen to her now? Will she ever be able to live a normal life again, Bob? Will she really be able to feel at home in England?'

'Yes,' he had said firmly, 'everyone in Magnolia Square is going to make quite sure of that.'

Three hours ago, when he had come face to face with

Anna at last, he had wondered with sick anxiety if he had been over-optimistic in believing such a grievously damaged woman could ever live an uninstitutionalized life. He had known she was in her late thirties, and had imagined her being slightly built and heartbreakingly vulnerable. Instead, she was tall and raw-boned, a woman who must have been masculine-looking even before being subjected to medical experimentation. Her hair stuck out as if it had been cropped with a knife and fork. Her teeth were bad and many of them were missing. There was badly shaved stubble around her mouth and on her chin and cheeks. The cotton dress she had been given was far too short and far too tight for her, the body beneath it a parody of femininity. Her laced-up shoes were heavy enough for a navvy and worn without socks or stockings.

'Hello,' he had said, aware since reading her file that before the war she had taught English at Kraków University. 'I'm Bob Giles and I've come to take you to your new home.'

It had been a nightmare journey. Anna didn't walk, she lurched, and people had stopped in the street, staring after them. On the Underground, fellow passengers had whispered and sniggered. On the train from Charing Cross to Lewisham, a group of youths had shouted ribald comments, uncaring of his clerical collar. A child in Lewisham High Street had thrown a tomato at Anna. Another group of giggling, cat-calling children had followed them all the way up Magnolia Hill. Nor had matters improved when they had entered the Square.

Leah Singer, on her hands and knees white-stoning number eighteen's front steps, had taken one look at

Anna and had abandoned her task immediately, gathering her bucket and scrubbing brush and barrelling into number eighteen's hallway before he could even make an attempt to introduce her.

Billy Lomax, who should have been at school but was instead in his front garden stock-taking his arsenal of discarded Home Guard weaponry, had shouted out in genuine enquiry, '''Ello, Vicar. Who's your funny friend? She looks like she's a mate of Desperate Dan's.'

At the Robsons', Queenie had charged down the pathway, barking furiously. At the Sharkeys', Doris had paused in her task of shaking crumbs from a tablecloth out on to her front pathway, her mouth hanging open wide enough to garage a double-decker bus. As he shepherded his ungainly charge up the pathway of number eight, he had known that integrating her into Magnolia Square's little community was going to be a far harder task than he had at first envisaged. And then, when he had escorted her across the threshold of her new home, had come the *coup de grâce*.

'Go vay,' she had said brusquely in her gutturally accented voice. 'I don't like English children. I don't like English dogs. Go vay and leave Anna alone.'

In vain he had protested that he hadn't yet shown her over the house; that there was milk and tea and sugar in the kitchen and that he had intended making a cup of tea for the two of them; that he had hoped he would be able to answer any queries she might have, and give her any reassurance she might need.

'Go vay,' she had said again and then, to his stunned disbelief, she had manhandled him, Amazon-like, back over the doorstep and slammed the door on him, ramming the top and bottom bolts firmly home.

As he and Kate climbed the five broad, shallow stone steps leading to the still-closed door he said, 'I'm afraid Miss Radcynska has locked herself in, Kate. It's an understandable enough reaction in the circumstances. There were a few . . . incidents . . . on our journey from central London to Lewisham and it's only to be expected that she is feeling uncertain and insecure.' They came to a halt on the top step. 'It is, however, an embarrassing reaction,' he said, his kindly face deeply troubled. 'Anna needs to be introduced into our community in a sympathetic manner, and if she sends out the wrong signals so early on . . .'

If she sent out the wrong signals so early on, it would be impossible to win people's understanding. She would simply be regarded as a freakish curiosity, best avoided, and her life would be even lonelier than if she had been sent to a displaced person's camp.

Apprehensively he knocked on the door in what he hoped was an unintimidating manner.

'*Go vay!*' Anna roared. '*I vant to be alone!*'

It was such a parody of Greta Garbo's often-quoted request that, in other circumstances, he would have been vastly amused. Instead, he raised his voice loud enough for her to hear but not, he hoped, loud enough to attract public attention.

'I have a young woman with me, Anna. Her name is Kate. She's one of your new neighbours and she'd like to say hello and make friends.'

There came the sound of long, low muttering in Polish and then a heavy object was thrown at the door. Bob slipped a finger inside his dog collar to loosen it and give

234

himself a little more air. In retrospect he realized he should have taken Ruth, or Kate, with him when he had gone to collect Anna. That way she might have been a little more trusting. As it was . . .

'Miss Radcynska?' Kate's voice was gently calming. 'I live two doors away. Would you like to share a cup of tea with me? I have a dog, and I know you don't like dogs very much, but Hector is very friendly.'

No sound came from behind the closed door. Bob Giles held his breath. He had known the minute he had found himself on the wrong side of the barred door that if anyone could gain Anna Radcynska's confidence, it would be Kate Emmerson.

'I'm in the middle of baking a treacle tart for tea,' Kate continued, just as if she had received vocal encouragement. 'I'm doing a second one for a friend and I could quite easily make some more pastry and do a third one, so that you have something in for tea. I know that Reverend Giles will have stocked your kitchen cupboards with essential groceries, but I doubt if he's thought to leave anything freshly made.'

Again there was no reply. Nellie Miller who, from the chair in her front doorway, had seen Anna's lurching arrival, was stumping with equal lack of grace up the far side of the Square towards the Collins's house, her eyes fixed avidly on number eight as she did so.

Bob Giles again loosened his clerical collar, knowing that in another few minutes Nellie would be sharing her news with Hettie, and that when she had done so, Hettie would shoot straight out of the house in order not to miss a second of the bizarre scene now taking place.

'Miss Radcynska?' Kate said again, not allowing the

235

faintest sign of anxiety to show in her voice. 'Mr Giles tells me you are Polish. During the war lots of young Polish airmen were posted at Biggin Hill Aerodrome, which isn't too far from here. They were very handsome and brave and popular.'

Bob Giles quelled a spasm of near-hysterical mirth. The Poles' good looks had certainly made them popular with the women of the area. It had been rumoured that Mavis had enjoyed the attentions of a Polish boy-friend, and certainly Eileen Dundas, in nearby Dartmouth Hill, had had a Polish boy-friend. Her little boy's Slavically high cheekbones were clear enough proof of that.

'Go vay,' Anna said again, though this time without the same vehemence. 'No like dogs. No like children. No like men.'

Kate's eyes held Bob's. Hettie and Nellie were now out on number three's doorstep, enjoying a grandstand view. Leah was standing at the Robsons' gateway, quite obviously imparting news of Anna's arrival to Charlie. Another group, who had trailed them up Magnolia Hill from Lewisham, were congregated beneath the shade of St Mark's magnolia tree.

'I think you'd better go,' she said to him apologetically. 'I don't think Miss Radcynska is going to open the door knowing you're still here.'

Bob didn't think she was going to either. 'All right,' he said reluctantly, aware that their audience was growing larger by the minute. 'But I have to warn you that—'

'There's no need,' Kate said swiftly, knowing what he was about to say. 'I've already guessed.'

Still Bob hesitated. Anna Radcynska had manhandled him out of her new home with all the strength of a

236

Samson. If she should turn that strength, in fear and anger, on to Kate . . .

''Ere, Vicar! Is it true you're collecting people from funny farms to live in Magnolia Square?' A lout he had never seen before in his life shouted from the vantage point of St Mark's grassy island. 'Do you 'ave to be bonkers to get an 'ome round 'ere?'

Bob's face tightened. If he didn't abandon his stand-off on number eight's doorstep, there was every chance of an ugly public incident erupting. 'I'm going,' he said to Kate tersely. 'Give it five minutes and if Anna still won't open the door to you, abandon the attempt. Meanwhile, I'll try and disperse this growing crowd of onlookers.' He turned away from her, trusting her sensitivity and judgement utterly. 'I don't know where you're from, young man,' he said seconds later to the lounging youth. 'But your remarks show a great lack of Christian charity.'

'I ain't from round 'ere,' the youth smirked, enjoying the high feeling he was creating. 'An' I'm glad of it. I wouldn't live 'ere. Not with all these barmies. It ain't safe.'

'There are no "barmies", as you so ignorantly put it, living in Magnolia Square,' Bob began stiffly and was broken off by the sound of a door being flung hard back on its hinges. He swung his head round, certain he was about to be met with the sight of a violently agitated Anna. Instead he saw that it was the Sharkeys' front door that was swinging open, and that the person cumbersomely propelling himself down the front steps was Wilfred, placards swinging. Never in his life had Bob Giles blasphemed, but the present temptation was nearly overpowering.

237

'See!' the youth shouted, pointing triumphantly towards Wilfred. ''E's a barmy! See wot's written on 'is placard! "THE END OF THE WORLD IS NIGH"! An' the war only just over. If that ain't barmy, I don't know wot is!'

Chapter Fourteen

It was Charlie who saved Bob Giles the extremely awkward task of shepherding Wilfred on his attention-getting procession down Magnolia Hill and into Lewisham. 'I'll take care of 'im,' he had said, aware that the Vicar's dog collar would only draw more attention to Wilfred's bizarre behaviour. ''E likes to stand outside Lewisham clock-tower when 'e's in this kind of a mood. I dunno why. No-one takes a ha'porth of notice of 'im.'

Bob wasn't at all convinced that Charlie's summing up of the situation was accurate. Lewisham clock-tower, standing on what had become a traffic-island at the confluence of three major roads, was the best-known landmark for miles around. Every autumn a gypsy woman appropriated the site, selling lavender from it at sixpence a bunch. To local people, she was as much an indication of the passing of summer and the drawing-in of winter as the change in weather, and Bob couldn't help feeling that Wilfred might very speedily become another such fixture.

Dragging his thoughts away from his mentally troubled churchwarden, deeply thankful that neither Doris nor Prudence were adding to the free show by trailing into Lewisham in their patriarch's wake, he concentrated

239

once more on the tragic problem of Anna Radcynska. Why on earth hadn't he realized just how deeply disturbed she would be? How was he to integrate her into the community? What plan of action could he possibly take that would have a happy outcome? With a relief so intense, he groaned aloud in thankfulness, he saw that Kate was no longer standing on number eight's doorstep. At some moment when his, and everyone else's attention, had been focused on Wilfred, she had obviously been invited inside, no matter how reluctantly. And once inside, Kate would do a magnificent job of winning Anna's confidence, of that he didn't have a second's doubt. He began to breathe a little more easily. He would go back to the vicarage and wait for Kate there, and he would call in at her house on the way in order to let Carrie know that Joss Harvey had agreed to her and Danny tenanting number seventeen.

'Did you ever visit England before the war?' Kate asked Anna as she filled a kettle of water for a pot of tea.

'Many times,' Anna responded gruffly, sitting full-square on a kitchen chair that the Binnses had conveniently left behind. 'My mother was English. She came from Vandsworth.'

'Wandsworth?' Kate flashed her a wide, sunny smile. 'Wandsworth is only seven or eight miles away. Do you still have relatives there?'

'No.' A closed, shuttered look came down over Anna's large-boned features. 'No relatives. No children. No dogs. No men.'

Kate searched for cups or mugs and found them in a

cupboard above the sink. Bob Giles, or most likely Ruth, had done a good job of scratch furnishing number eight, though there was still room for vast improvement. She had already mentally ticked off lots of things she could spare from her own home which would make number eight cosier and more comfortable. She poured milk into two mugs, reflecting that the mug of tea she had made for herself a little earlier was still standing on her kitchen table.

'The fact that your English is so good will make it easier for you to feel at home here,' she said, her slightly husky voice full of warmth and sincere friendliness. 'And people *are* friendly here, Anna.'

Anna shook her head vehemently. 'Not to Anna. People are afraid of Anna. People shout and laugh.'

Kate hesitated. She didn't know just how self-aware Anna was of her own condition, yet it had to be spoken of. Only by frankly accepting that it was her appearance and manner that caused the name-calling and cruel laughter, could steps be taken to mitigate it.

In her own mind, Kate had already decided what those first steps should be. Top of the list was suitable clothing. As far as Kate was concerned, the person responsible for dressing Anna so unsuitably from a rag-bag of charitable cast-offs, deserved to be shot. The obscenely skimpy dress only emphasized her masculine physique and ungainliness. Her lack of stockings, or even socks, was a cruel oversight when her legs were as muscular and hairy as a navvy's. As for the monstrosity of her gaping boots . . . Kate intended burning them and replacing them with a pair of light brogues, or sandals, at her first opportunity. The dress would be added to the flames also, replaced by a tie-neck blouse and a skirt that reached well below the knees.

Taking the bull by the horns, she said gently, 'People are often unkind about what they don't understand, Anna. What happened to you during the war shouldn't be kept a secret. Your neighbours in Magnolia Square should be told, not in order to pity you, but so that they can understand and come to terms with you as you are, as *you* are going to have to come to terms with the person you now are.'

There was a long, long silence. Kate waited, taut with nervous tension. The expected violent outburst didn't come. Instead, tears glinted on Anna's sparse eyelashes and slowly began to trickle down her ravaged face. In vast relief, Kate closed the couple of feet separating them and, while Anna remained sitting on the chair, put her arms around her. Anna leaned her head against Kate, who cradled her as if she were a distressed child.

'It's going to be all right, Anna,' she said soothingly, her voice cracking with emotion. 'Just trust me and you'll see. You'll be happy here. You'll make friends. You'll belong.'

An hour later she was saying fiercely to Bob Giles, 'I don't care what advice the Red Cross gave. People *have* to know what Anna suffered in order to be able to understand why she looks and behaves as she does. And they have to be told quickly, before they form judgements they'll be reluctant to abandon.'

'But the Red Cross thought it would awaken an interest entirely prurient—'

'Not here,' Kate said, her eyes ablaze with conviction. 'Not in Magnolia Square.'

His eyes held hers, and then he nodded his head in agreement. 'And what else?' he asked, knowing she was burning to say far, far more.

'We have to treat Anna as if there was nothing odd about her. And the less outwardly odd she looks the better. She shouldn't step over the doorstep of number eight in that monstrosity of a frock! Nothing I have will fit her, but Harriet is Junoesquely built. I'm sure Harriet will be only too happy to give Anna some blouses and skirts. I think Anna's feet will be far bigger than Harriet's, but a pair of men's sandals will be a million times better than the boots some oaf thought fit for her to wear! And then there is her hair . . .'

Bob sent a silent prayer of gratitude heavenwards. With Kate as her champion, Anna was as good as integrated already.

'. . . Carrie is quite a good amateur hairdresser. A trim and a home perm will transform Anna just as it transforms any woman. And Anna must have stockings. The kind of lisle stockings Miriam and Hettie wear. And she needs far more creature comforts in her house. If everyone in the Square made a search of their attics for things in good condition that they have no further use for, we could have her comfy and cosy in no time.'

Feeling like a new man, Bob rose to his feet. 'I'll take the left-hand side of the Square,' he said, picking up his pipe, 'you take the right. We'll knock at every door and state Anna's case to everyone we find at home.'

As they walked out of the vicarage, it occurred to him that he could do worse than to ask Kate's advice where Wilfred was concerned. Once put in the picture about the situation at number ten, her compassionate nature

243

would be invaluable in giving Doris and Prudence the kind of support they so desperately needed.

'. . . and so if you have any spare suitable clothes, Anna is in great need of them,' Kate finished saying to Harriet Godfrey.

Harriet, who had listened to Kate's explanation of Anna Radcynska's history in grim-faced silence, said, 'I have two dirndl cotton skirts I bought when going for a holiday in Eastbourne last year. They're elastic-waisted, so there'll be no problem about fit. And I have several blouses going spare, both long-sleeved and short-sleeved. And a cardigan. And a capacious raincoat.'

Fifteen minutes later Kate staggered through her own front doorway hardly able to see where she was going for the mound of clothing she was carrying.

'What's this? Jumble sale time?' Carrie asked equably.

'They're Harriet Godfrey's cast-offs,' Kate said, dropping her cargo on to the nearest available chair, 'so "jumble" is certainly not the right word. The skirts have Harrods labels on them, and at least one of the blouses is silk.'

'They're going to be a little on the large size for you, aren't they?' Carrie asked teasingly, knowing full well that Kate hadn't purloined them for herself. 'Or are you thinking of growing?'

'They're for our new neighbour, Anna Radcynska.' With gratitude Kate saw that Carrie had not only finished baking the treacle tarts but had made a batch of scones as well. 'When I've told you a little about her, I'll take you round to meet her. I'll take my treacle tart and the scones around as well. And this afternoon, when you go and collect Rose from school, could you stop off at the shops and buy a home perm kit?'

'I think I could do that,' Carrie said incuriously, bursting with her good news. 'In fact, I think I could pop in for a home perm kit just as soon as I've picked up the keys for number seventeen!'

Though Kate urgently wanted to tell Carrie Anna's story, in order that she could continue with her task of telling Anna's other neighbours, she shared in Carrie's relief and joy first and then, her eyes darkening, said, 'I've something to tell you, Carrie. Something almost beyond words.'

Carrie's reaction was just as intense as Kate had known it would be. She had been sick, and hadn't blamed her physical reaction on her pregnancy. Next she had been furiously, ragingly angry. Then she had said, 'Let's take these clothes round to her now, then I'll stay with her while you finish calling in at the rest of the houses on this side of the Square. And make sure Mavis knows to have a word with Billy. She won't be able to explain fully to him, but if she tells him Anna is ill, it'll be enough to make him mind his manners.'

Leaving Carrie cheerily displaying Harriet Godfrey's largesse to a bewildered Anna, Kate continued on her errand. Outside the Sharkeys' house she paused. Doris would undoubtedly be at home as, if rumour was correct, would Prudence. The front room curtains were, however, forbiddingly closed. The charitable said this new habit of Doris's was occasioned by Wilfred's illness; that he had a virus infection, that he hadn't been able to work since just before VJ Day and that his eyes were susceptible to light. The less charitable said it was

245

because Doris didn't want anyone seeing the kind of shenanigans now taking place in her home.

'I've seen 'im myself dahn Lewisham High Street,' Albert had said, shaking his head in disbelief, 'wearing "THE END OF THE WORLD IS NIGH" placards and shouting at people to repent.'

Kate hadn't seen Wilfred wearing his placards, but she did know that something was very, very wrong in the Sharkey house, and that the inmates might very well not want anyone calling on them. Instead, she called on Charlie, leaving a quarter of an hour later with a pair of nearly new sandals that he vowed he'd never wear, ''Cos 'Arriet don't like to see me in 'em. She says they make me look like a spiv.'

As Harriet would never disapprove of any article of clothing that would improve Charlie's shambolic appearance, and as the word 'spiv' was not a word she could imagine Harriet using, she hadn't believed his statement for a moment. He was being generous and was trying to cover up the fact, as he always was and he always did.

At number sixteen, Mavis, conveniently caught before leaving home for her afternoon bus shift, stared at Kate and said, 'They did *wot* to her? The bloody, bleeding bastards did *wot*?'

Later, when Mavis had calmed down, she had said, 'I know quite a few words of Polish myself. I'll pop in on my way 'ome from work and say hello to her. An' from the sound of it, wot she needs is someone 'andy with the Veet.'

'Veet?' Kate had asked, hoping the words Mavis had culled from her Polish airforce friends would be suitable words, and wondering if 'Veet' was one of them.

246

'Depilatory cream,' Mavis had said, 'you know . . . for under the arms. Only with Anna, we could use it on her face an' she'd be no more whiskery than you or me.'

Vastly relieved that Mavis hadn't thought to proffer any items of her own clothing to stock Anna's sparse wardrobe, Kate walked up the familiar pathway of number eighteen.

'I'm in the kitchen, *bubbeleh*,' Leah called out from the rear of the house, anticipating quite correctly that her visitor would be a female member of her family, or Kate or Christina. 'Be careful of the step! I've just white-stoned it.'

Kate negotiated her way down the long, cluttered passageway, edging her way round Rose's tricycle and stubbing her toe on a pile of dog-racing magazines.

As she entered the kitchen, Leah looked up from the shirt she was ironing and said with a beaming smile, 'You're a treat to see. There's freshly made bagels on the oven-top, but if it's Carrie you're after, she's out doing I don't know what.' She lifted the flat of the iron upwards, spat on it, and then slammed it down hard on one of her *goy* son-in-law's recalcitrant collars.

Kate helped herself to a rich, golden brown confection with a hole in its centre. 'It's you and Miriam I want to see, Leah,' she said, sitting down with her treat.

'Miriam's down the market,' Leah said, setting the iron back on its stand. 'But I'm here, Dolly, and I'm all ears.'

Kate wiped a bagel crumb from the corner of her mouth. 'Number eight's new tenant arrived today and—'

'*Oy vey!*' Leah raised her hands to heaven. 'I knew that house should have gone to Carrie and Danny! I knew it was bad luck to give it to a stranger, and now see what has happened and how we are! I saw the arrival with my own eyes and now we have to live with a freak of nature in the Square, as well as a religious lunatic!'

Kate said steadily, 'Anna Radcynska isn't a freak of nature, Leah. She's suffered terribly and when I tell you how, and at whose hands, I know you'll feel differently about her moving into number eight.'

It had been a long, hard battle to convince Leah. 'But why for isn't she in a special hospital?' she had asked, time and time again. 'Why for isn't she being cared for in her own country?'

'Because her mother was English,' Kate had said patiently. 'Because displaced people are being settled in the countries best able to offer such assistance, countries such as Britain and America.'

'She'll frighten Bonzo,' Leah had said intransigently.

'She won't frighten anyone,' Kate had retorted firmly, 'not now we know why she is as she is.' She had risen to her feet, so disappointed in Leah that her voice was unsteady. 'And you might remember, Leah, that what happened to Anna could have happened to Christina. It could have happened to any woman taken into a concentration camp.'

Leah's wrinkled face had crumpled. '*Oy vey*,' she had said, thinking of her old friend Jacoba. '*Oy vey, oy vey*.' She had hugged her arms, beginning to rock herself, and Kate hadn't been at all sorry that she had had to cause such distress in order to bring understanding.

'I've arranged for a welcoming social for Anna to be held in the church hall this evening,' Bob Giles said to Kate when all their visits were finally completed. 'Hettie and Daniel are going to trundle their piano across so that we can have a sing-song. Nellie is making jellies and assures me that if they're put in her cellar to set, they'll be in perfect condition for this evening. Miriam is all set to give a public recitation of "Albert and the Lion". Emily Helliwell is gearing herself up to sing "Jerusalem". It's going to be a grand evening. One of Magnolia Square's best.'

When Kate returned to number eight, it was to find Anna seated on the same hardback kitchen chair, a Paisley cotton dirndl skirt decorously covering stock-inged legs, a toning blouse tie-fastened at her throat, a mass of Miriam's steel curlers in her hair.

'The stockings came care of Nellie,' Carrie said with a grin, 'as has a pile of towels, an eiderdown, two casserole dishes and a chamber-pot.'

'There's going to be a get-together tonight at the church hall so that you can meet all your other new neighbours,' Kate said to Anna as the latter doubtfully fingered the curlers in her hair.

Alarm flared across Anna's face. 'No children!' she stated violently. 'No dogs! No men!'

Carrie suppressed a grin. Kate was going to have her work cut out introducing Anna to Charlie, Leon and Danny, Albert and Daniel and all the other male residents of Magnolia Square, not to mention Billy, Beryl and Daisy, Rose, Matthew and Luke.

Kate said unflappably, 'You're going to have to overcome your aversion to children, Anna. There are lots of children in Magnolia Square, and many of them will be at the party this evening. And there'll be men there, too. Nice men. Men like Charlie Robson, who gave you the sandals you're now wearing. Men like my dad and Carrie's dad. Men like Reverend Giles.'

'No men,' Anna said again, mutinously. 'Maybe children, but no men.'

'And no dogs,' Carrie whispered naughtily to Kate under her breath. 'How are you going to solve *that* little problem?'

It was Ellen who, in her clumsy, naïve manner, solved the problem that evening. Loving dogs herself, unable to think of life without one at her side, she had been unable to bear the thought of Anna living without the benefit of such comfort.

'Her name is Ophelia,' she said, depositing a bedraggled-looking mongrel on to Anna's vast lap. 'Two small boys rescued her from the Thames a week ago. She'd been thrown in with a stone tied to her neck and she's *such* a lovely doggie.'

Anna shot to her feet, sending Ophelia sprawling. 'No dogs!' she roared. 'No children! No men!'

A score of appalled eyes turned in her direction. Ellen flushed an ugly, agonized red. Luke, hoisted high on Leon's shoulder, began to cry. Miriam and Hettie began to murmur their shocked disapproval. Aware that the evening was plummeting towards disaster, Bob Giles began to hastily explain that Anna had an aversion to dogs and that, though he knew Ellen's gesture had been well-meant, it had unfortunately been inappropriate.

Not waiting for him to finish his awkward explanation, Kate caught hold of Ophelia and, tucking her under one arm, walked resolutely across to Anna. 'Ophelia is a *gift*, Anna,' she said, speaking in the same tone of voice she

250

would a rude and impolite child. 'She's a creature who has been badly treated, just as you have been, and who is in need of a home, just as you have been in need of one and now have one.'

The implication was obvious, and Bob Giles held his breath. If Anna spurned Ellen's gift a second time he doubted if even the intervention of holy angels would be enough to integrate her among her new neighbours. Kate held Ophelia out towards Anna. Ophelia wagged a stubby tail.

'She's yours, Anna,' Kate said quietly. 'She needs someone to love, someone who will love her in return.'

Someone cleared their throat. Luke's sobs hiccupped into silence.

Very stiffly Anna's arms moved from her sides and she took awkward hold of her gift. 'No men,' she said, gruffly capitulating. 'Maybe children and dogs, but no men.'

'We can promise you that, dearie!' Nellie shouted out from the far end of the hall. 'There ain't enough of 'em to go around as it is!'

The laughter that followed dissipated any lingering awkwardness. Ellen, assured by Bob Giles that she hadn't acted crassly at all, but had instead acted with great sensitivity, recovered her composure and happily showed off the engagement ring sparkling on the fourth finger of her left hand. Hettie voiced it as her opinion that Anna had probably been terrorized in the past by Gestapo-owned German Shepherd dogs, and that it was no wonder she was cautious where the canine world was concerned. Charlie declared that a dog as young as Ophelia would be in need of training, and that he would be happy to help Anna train her. Miriam changed the subject by announcing that Albert had brought home a hearse-load of condemned tinned food and that with a little luck they'd be able to live on it for the next twelve months.

'But how can you do that if it's condemned?' Emily Helliwell asked, perturbed. 'Won't it give you food-poisoning? I don't like the thought of you giving Albert food-poisoning, Miriam.'

'Lord love me! It ain't the *food* that's condemned,' Miriam had said impatiently. 'It's the tins! They ain't got no labels on, so 'ow can anyone sell 'em?'

'An' 'ow can anyone know what the 'ell they're goin' to be eatin' when they open one of 'em?' Danny Collins had said in an aggrieved aside to Charlie. 'I've 'ad spam mornin', noon and night this last week, all in the 'ope of openin' a tin of salmon!'

'I think it's time for party-pieces!' Bob Giles announced, vastly relieved that yet another crisis had been surmounted. 'First, Miriam is going to recite "Albert and the Lion", then Emily is going to sing "Jerusalem", and then Charlie is going to give us a tune on his accordion.'

'And where's Christina?' Hettie asked Miriam as they sat down to enjoy the show. 'I never see her anywhere these days.'

'I've no idea,' Miriam retorted archly, uncomfortably aware that though Carl Voigt's lady-friend was radiantly showing off her engagement ring to all and sundry, Carl himself was nowhere in evidence. 'She's a grown woman, 'Ettie. She doesn't 'ave to report all 'er comings and goings to me or to anyone else.'

252

'I think we're beginning to make encouraging headway,' Carl Voigt said to Christina as they sat companionably side by side at a table on which was spread a sheaf of letters. 'I've had a response from the Headquarters of the United Nations High Commission for Refugees in Geneva.' He picked up a letter dominated by an impressive crest and handed it to her. 'Don't be disheartened by the first paragraph where it is explained that, despite the impressive title, they don't have anything to do with actual refugees, only policy! The second paragraph is the one that is of interest.

'. . . *the Registry for Refugees, also housed in the Palace of Nations, Geneva, may be of help to you,*' Christina read, her heart beginning to slam, as it always did when she felt a step forward, however slight, had been taken.

'At least now we are collecting the addresses of organizations that are in the know.' Carl took off his rimless spectacles and polished them on his handkerchief. 'And one thing is becoming obvious.' He put his spectacles back on again. 'The Gestapo were meticulous record-keepers. They kept a log of nearly everyone they arrested and imprisoned, and many of those logs are now in departmental archives in Geneva or New York.'

'Not London?' Christina's heart plummeted. 'If there are no copies of such records in London, how can we possibly search through them? It would mean having to go to Switzerland or America!'

Carl nodded. 'It might,' he said, not as pole-axed as she was by the thought. It was one that had occurred to him from the moment they had embarked on their search, and he had long since decided that if such

253

trips were necessary, he would take them. 'This letter here,' he sifted through the paperwork in front of him and withdrew a letter just as officious-looking as the letter from the United Nations Commission for Refugees, 'is from the International Refugee Organization. They have been very helpful. They say our best bet is to contact the newly set-up International Tracing Centre in New York. It's a brainchild of General Eisenhower's, and its sole purpose is to help in the reuniting of displaced children with parents.'

'But I'm not a displaced child . . .' Christina began doubtfully, too dazed by the monumental difficulties that still lay ahead to appreciate just how valuable a piece of information this last address might prove to be.

Carl's voice was gentle. 'You may not be a child in the accepted sense, but you are seeking information about a parent and a grandparent, and if the Tracing Centre holds copies of Nazi records it will be of invaluable help to us.'

'And you will write to the Centre?'

Christina clasped her hands tightly, the knuckles white. Ever since Carrie had told her of how Anna Radcynska had been medically experimented on in Ravensbrueck, she had suffered mental horrors so terrible she had thought she was going to lose her mind. Ravensbrueck was one of the few women's camps that had been in existence when her mother and grandmother were taken prisoner. If they, too, had been taken to Ravensbrueck then they, too, could well have suffered similar abominations.

'Yes.' Carl gathered up the letters and put them neatly into a folder. 'And if we have to, Christina, we will go to

254

New York to continue the search. We will go wherever is necessary.'

'Even to Germany?' she asked, her throat so tight, she could barely force out the words.

Carl's studious-looking face was grave. 'Yes,' he said sombrely. 'If needs be, even to Germany.'

Chapter Fifteen

'I'm sorry, Doris,' Dr Roberts said compassionately, 'but there is no "tonic", as you call it, that I can prescribe for Wilfred that will put his mental health back on an even keel again. And while he isn't a physical danger to himself or to anyone else, it's impossible for me to recommend he be detained in a mental home. Religious mania isn't a mental illness as such, not unless the person in question is seeing visions and hearing voices, and to the best of my knowledge Wilfred is doing neither.'

'But what about the great whore he keeps on and on about?' Doris said piteously, wringing her hands in her aproned lap. 'He must be able to see her, mustn't he?'

Bob Giles put his hand gently on her shoulder. He'd tried many times to explain to Doris that the Great Whore of Babylon was a biblical city, not a woman, but whenever he did so Doris's confusion only grew worse. 'What Dr Roberts is saying, Doris, is that Wilfred is deluded, but that he isn't certifiably insane.'

It was all too much for Doris. How could they say Wilfred wasn't insane when he was as mad as a March hare? And how did they expect her to live with him when he frightened her so? 'There must be *something* you can do,' she pleaded desperately, looking from Dr Roberts to Bob Giles.

Dr Roberts shook his head unhappily. Bob Giles looked anguished.

Doris twisted round in her chair to where Pru was protectively standing and seized hold of her hands. 'Tell them they have to do something, Pru! Tell them if your father isn't insane enough to be put away, I soon shall be!'

Pru had every intention of telling them, and of telling them a great deal more, but not in her mother's hearing.

Dr Roberts cleared his throat, well aware of Pru's silent, burning disappointment in him. 'Your mother needs a sedative and an iron tonic to strengthen her nerves,' he said, fully aware that he was on the verge of having not just one mentally disturbed patient at number ten, but two. He took out his prescription pad, writing in a heavy scrawl. 'Here,' he handed Pru the flimsy piece of paper. 'Take this to the chemist and I'll call in again towards the end of the week.'

'And I'll call by again this evening,' Bob said, aware that he, too, had to be on his way. His next meeting was with his archdeacon and they had a lot to discuss, not least how most tactfully to relieve Wilfred of his position as churchwarden.

Doris made no effort to rise from her chair and accompany them from the room. She had begun crying again, rubbing at her arms, her thoughts whirling and spiralling down to a dark, terrible, inescapable conclusion.

Immediately Pru was alone with Dr Roberts and Bob Giles in the narrow hallway she said tautly, 'My mother needs a lot more help than a sedative and a nerve tonic!

Unless my dad's sorted out soon, she's going to have a complete breakdown.'

Dr Roberts cleared his throat uncomfortably. He, too, knew that Doris was heading for a nervous collapse, but with the best will in the world he could see no obvious and easy solution to her problem. 'Perhaps if your mother could be made to understand that she isn't the only person having to cope with a mentally disturbed partner, it might help her,' he said, edging towards the door. 'Thanks to the stress and strain of the war, and especially as a result of last year's V1 and V2 rocket attacks, I have several other patients on my panel list suffering mental breakdowns similar to your father's.'

Pru wasn't interested in other people. 'How long are you going to be able to keep issuing Dad with sick notes for work?' she asked bluntly. 'How long is it going to be before he loses his job? And what will happen when he does? I've had to give up work because Mum can't manage Dad on her own. If I go back to work, Mum's going to give way altogether, and even if I do, I'll only be on a junior's wage and that isn't going to be enough for the three of us, is it?'

Dr Roberts sighed heavily. He certainly couldn't keep on supplying Wilfred's employers with sick notes stating he was suffering from a virus infection, nor could he be expected to saddle himself with all the consequent problems of his patient's illness.

Bob Giles looked down into her pale, pinched face, and his heart felt as if it were being squeezed within his breast. She was far too young to be bearing her present burdens. 'Don't worry about possible financial problems just now, Pru,' he said quietly. 'Leave that to me.'

With Dr Roberts's silence thundering in her ears, knowing she had guessed right about the imminent cessation of the sick notes, Pru opened the door. As she did so, Doris stepped into the hallway behind them.

'Goodbye, Dr Roberts,' she said waveringly, remembering her manners. 'Goodbye, Vicar.'

'Cooee there, Pru!' a neighbour from Magnolia Terrace called out as she hurried home with a basket full of groceries. 'Your dad's just caused ever such a ruckus in Lewisham High Street! The Lady Mayoress was paying a visit to Chiesemans and he called her a whore and a harlot! Ever so entertaining it was. Best fun I've had in years!'

Doris gave a low cry, like an animal in pain. Pru didn't speak. Instead, tight-lipped and ashen-faced, she slammed the door behind her, pushing past Dr Roberts and Bob Giles, running, running, in the direction of Lewisham High Street.

Kate was in the middle of doing her weekly wash when Doris disturbed her, knocking on the front door and stepping into the house, saying in a fraught voice, 'Can you lend me sixpence for the gas meter, Kate? I'm out of change and Pru isn't in and—'

'Of course I can.' Kate flashed her a sunny smile, putting down the wooden tongs she had been using to transfer steaming clothes from her copper to her dolly-tub. 'Are you all set for the wedding tomorrow?' With wet hands, she took a purse out of a kitchen drawer and unclasped it.

'Wedding?' Doris looked blank, her eyes red-rimmed from weeping.

'Harriet and Charlie's wedding,' Kate said, finding a

259

sixpence and handing it across. 'Harriet hasn't sent out individual invitations, but she's hoping everyone in the Square will be there.'

Doris clutched hold of the sixpence with childlike intensity. 'Yes . . . no . . . I don't know . . .'

'Why don't you stay and have a cup of tea?' Kate continued, aware that Doris was distressed and hoping that over a cup of tea she might be able to offer her some comfort. 'I'm just about to make one and—'

'No!' This time there was nothing indecisive in Doris's voice. 'No. I mustn't. I can't.' Agitatedly she backed out of the kitchen, turning around in the passageway and almost running for the still-open front door.

Kate stood for a moment, staring after her, wondering what to do for the best. Doris was an intensely private person. Unlike every other house in the Square, neighbours had never been encouraged to drop in at number ten. Forcing her own presence on Doris now might do more harm than good.

'*Mummmmy!*' Luke shouted plaintively from the back garden where he was digging a hole in the hope of reaching Australia. '*Mummmmy!* There's a nasty wriggly thing and it's fwightening me!'

Kate dried her hands on a tea-towel and stepped out into the garden to rescue him. She would speak to Bob Giles about Doris. He would advise her on the right action to take. And she would speak to him today, just as soon as she had her weekly wash out on the line.

'Come home, Dad,' Pru was saying urgently, agonizingly aware of the small groups of people gathering on the pavements at either side of the road.

'Get thee behind me Satan!' her father roared at her. *'I am a prophet of Jehovah bearing record of the word of God, and of the testimony of Jesus Christ!'*

A number twenty-one bus slowed down on its way past the clock-tower's triangular-shaped traffic-island, and a group of youths standing on its platform cat-called derisively.

'Take 'im 'ome, luv!' a woman shouted, watching the show from outside the Midland Bank on the corner of Lewisham High Street and Lee High Road. ''E'll be gettin' 'imself in trouble with the police if he carries on much longer!'

On the opposite corner, outside the entrance to Chiesemans department store, another well-intentioned bystander called out, 'Let 'im alone, why don't yer? 'E ain't causin' anyone any 'urt, is 'e?'

Pru resisted the urge to shout back that he was causing his wife plenty of hurt. Instead she tugged yet again on his arm. 'Come on, Dad. You're not supposed to be down here today. It's Friday today, not Saturday.'

As often happened when she tried to confuse or divert him by such statements, she attracted and held his attention.

'Friday?' he frowned. 'What's wrong with Fridays?'

Pru desperately tried to think of what could be so wrong that it would persuade him to return home. Before she could do so, a young man leaning out of one of the Midland Bank's upper windows, cried out in sudden recognition, 'Hey! That's Wilfred Sharkey! He's a churchwarden at St Mark's! What's happening to St Mark's then? Is it going all Evangelical?'

Something very like hysteria began to bubble up in

261

Pru's throat. Now a connection had been made between the clock-tower's Bible-basher and St Mark's, the situation could only get worse.

'What's wrong with Fridays?' her father demanded again, oblivious of the interest he was arousing. 'The time is at hand to read and listen to the words of the prophets. He that hath an ear let him hear what the Spirit saith! And the Spirit saith repent, for the end of the world is nigh!'

'If he's a churchwarden someone should write to the papers about him,' a smartly dressed woman announced to those standing nearby her. 'He's an affront to public order!'

Pru's self-control snapped. '*Shut up!*' she shouted, still holding tightly on to her father's arm. 'Shut up, you silly woman! Why don't you go home and mind your own business instead of making things worse?'

There were 'tut-tutts' from many of the bystanders, but whether their sympathy was directed at herself or the woman on the pavement, was unclear.

Pru tugged violently on her father's arm. 'Come on, Dad,' she said again, her voice cracking. 'Please don't do this! Please come home!' As her father remained obdurately unresponsive, she became aware of a slim-hipped figure sprinting towards them from the direction of the number twenty-one bus stop. 'Oh no!' she whispered, her cheeks flooding scarlet with mortification. 'Oh *no!*'

Malcolm Lewis dodged a number thirty-six bus on its way to Catford, avoided a cyclist and breathlessly made the comparatively safe haven of the clock-tower's tiny island. 'What on earth's going on?' he demanded, concerned. 'I saw you both from the top of the number twenty-one. Is your father ill?' He turned towards Wilfred. 'Are you ill, Mr Sharkey? Are you not feeling quite yourself?'

Wilfred glared at him, still troubled by Pru's insistence that if it were Friday he shouldn't be in Lewisham High Street. 'Of course I'm not ill!' he said querulously, wondering if he should be in Woolwich or Greenwich instead. 'I'm full of the spirit of the Lord and the gift of prophecy!'

'Then if that's the case, you're not likely to come to any harm,' Malcolm said, much to the prophet's satisfaction. He turned towards Pru, now knowing why her neighbours had been seeing so little of her, and why the Sharkeys' front-room curtains were almost permanently drawn. 'Let me take you home,' he said compassionately. 'You can't protect your father from the kind of attention he's attracting, all your presence is doing is making the situation worse.'

'What do you know about it?' Pru was on the brink of hysteria. 'It isn't your dad who's making a public spectacle of himself, is it? It isn't your dad who's about to get himself arrested and whose name will be in all the papers!'

'Not today it isn't, no,' Malcolm agreed matter-of-factly. 'But my father was a flat-earther, and he's spent a very large part of his life haranguing anyone and everyone about his belief, just as your dad is haranguing people now.'

Pru stared at him. 'In the street?' she asked, the hysteria she was about to give vent to held in precarious check. 'He marched up and down in the street? Just like Dad's doing?'

'Speakers' Corner was my father's favourite spot,' Malcolm said, taking her gently by the arm and leading her a few feet away from where the prophet of God was adjusting his placards. 'So you see, I *do* know how you're feeling. I also know the best way of handling such a situation, and it isn't by having public confrontations. At the present moment, the most sensible thing you can do is to let me take you home and leave your father to come home under his own steam and in his own good time.'

Pru's eyes held his, her hysteria beginning to ebb. 'What's a flat-earther?' she asked, as she unresistingly allowed him to lead her off the clock-tower's traffic-island and into the busy main road. 'Is it a kind of Jehovah's Witness?'

Despite the awfulness of the situation a glimmer of a smile tugged at Malcolm's mouth. 'No,' he said, as he guided her through the traffic. 'It's someone who believes that the earth is flat, and that it's possible to topple over the edge of it.'

As they stepped up on to the pavement outside Chiesemans, Pru said incredulously, 'He couldn't possibly have believed that! Not when ships sail right round the world!'

Malcolm looked down at her. Her hand was still where he had tucked it, in the crook of his arm. He rather hoped she would keep it there. It felt as if it belonged there.

Behind them, on the clock-tower's traffic-island, Wilfred's voice rose stentorously. '*Repent! For the end is nigh! The world will be destroyed with fire and brimstone!*'

Neither of them turned their heads.

'That's *exactly* what my father believed,' Malcolm said, wondering what was on at the local flicks that evening; wondering if Pru would go with him to see whatever was showing. 'He thought ships were simply going round and round on a flat surface.'

They rounded the corner on which Chiesemans stood, continuing down the bottom end of the High Street into Lewisham Road, heading towards the turn-off for Magnolia Hill.

'Did he believe in dragons as well?' Pru asked, no longer acutely aware of their nine-year age difference, and no longer painfully self-conscious in his company. 'On maps that were made when *everyone* thought the earth was flat there are drawings of monsters in the corners, warning that "Here be dragons!"'

'I never thought to ask him,' Malcolm said, happily aware that Pru was going to keep her hand tucked in the crook of his arm, 'but he probably did. Would you like to go to the flicks tonight? I don't know what's on, but if there isn't anything worth seeing on in Lewisham, we can always go to Greenwich.'

Kate carried a basket of wet laundry out into her back garden and began pegging it on the line. It was a sunny day with a refreshing breeze, and everything would be dry by tea-time.

'Can I peg out?' Luke asked toddling over to her, as grimy as a coal-miner from his digging activities.

'Not on this clothes-line, it's too high for you, and not with hands that colour you can't!' Kate said, dropping the shirt she had been holding back into the basket and scooping him up, tucking him under her arm.

Her long braid had fallen forward over her shoulder when she had bent down towards him and she flicked it back with her free hand, saying in mock severity, 'A soapy flannel on your hands and face is what you need, young man. And stop wriggling. You're worse than that worm you were frightened of!'

He shrieked and giggled as she carried him into the kitchen and sat him on the draining-board, next to the sink.

'There's enough dirt under your fingernails to grow potatoes in,' she said, making him giggle harder than ever. She turned on the tap and reached for the flannel. Then a distant scream froze her into immobility.

It was followed by another scream. And another. They weren't the screams of children at play, or even adult screams of pretend terror. They were terrified. Horror-riven. Desperate. And they ran one into another, on and on.

She whipped a startled Luke off the sink-top. 'Stay here! Don't leave the house! Do you understand?'

Uncertain and alarmed, he nodded, putting his thumb in his mouth for comfort as she raced out of the house and into the Square.

Bob Giles was running down the vicarage's short front path in his shirt-sleeves. Leah was running up from the bottom end of the Square, moving at a speed Kate could scarcely believe. Charlie was charging out of his garden gate. Emily Helliwell was hurrying across from the far side of the Square. All were making a bee-line for the open front door of number ten. Charlie reached the Sharkeys' gate first, Kate hard on his heels.

'*Run for the vicar!*' Malcolm Lewis could be heard shouting from inside the house. 'Tell him to ring for an ambulance!'

'Ring for an ambulance!' Charlie shouted over his shoulder to Bob Giles, who was fast approaching the Sharkeys' gate.

'Ruth's already ringing for one!' Bob panted, racing into the house in Charlie and Kate's wake.

The smell of gas was overpowering. They ran down the long hallway leading to the kitchen, bursting into it, seeing instantly the open oven door, the cushion Doris had placed inside it for her head, the heavy ornamental tablecloth she had draped over the oven and her shoulders so that no fumes would escape. Malcolm Lewis had carried Doris's comatose body out into the back garden and, as Pru continued to scream, was trying to revive her, pressing down hard on her shoulder-blades, lifting her chest free of the ground by her shoulders in order to draw air into her lungs, pressing down again, lifting, pressing down, lifting.

'Is all the gas turned off?' Bob Giles demanded urgently, dropping down on his knees beside Doris, feeling for her pulse.

Malcolm nodded, still pressing down and lifting, pressing down and lifting. 'Yes . . . but all the windows in the house need opening, and for the love of God tell no-one to strike a match!'

'Charlie's seeing to the windows,' Kate said as Pru's screams subsided into terrified sobs.

'Our Father which art in Heaven,' Emily Helliwell was saying quietly, standing several yards away so that she wouldn't impede the resuscitation attempts of Bob Giles and Maclom Lewis, 'Hallowed be thy Name . . .'

'It's Dad's fault! It's all Dad's fault!' Pru sobbed, hugging her arms, rocking herself to and fro. 'And now Mum's killed herself and I'll never be able to forgive him! Never!'

There was a hoarse, wheezing sound as Malcolm Lewis lifted Doris's shoulders clear off the ground yet again.

'She's alive, my life!' Leah's voice was fervent. If Doris had succeeded in killing herself, it would have been a terrible thing; a criminal action.

'Don't stop what you're doing till she regains consciousness or the ambulance-men arrive,' Bob Giles said tautly to Malcolm, his fingers still on Doris's frighteningly weak pulse beat.

Malcolm nodded, beads of sweat standing out on his brow, his face fierce with concentration.

'I fink I'll just remove that cushion and 'eavy tablecloth from the oven, Vicar,' Charlie said ruminatively from behind them. 'We don't want the ambulance-men gettin' any funny ideas about wot 'appened, do we? They might go reportin' it to the police.'

After only the slightest of pauses, Bob Giles said, 'No, Charlie. We don't. I rather think Doris left the gas on by accident when she made her lunch-time cup of tea, and then fell asleep and was overcome by the fumes. Make sure the oven door's closed, there's a good chap.'

Doris gave another, barely audible, rasping sound of life.

Pru's knees buckled and she sank down on them, saying through her tears, 'Come on, Mum! Please come back to me! Please!'

Miss Helliwell said in a voice rendered quavery by shock, 'I can hear an ambulance bell ringing, Vicar. It's going to be all right, I know it is. If Doris had been going to die, Moshambo would have told me.'

Seconds later, they could hear Charlie shouting informatively to the ambulance-men as they ran into the house, 'The lady's out the back! She's 'ad a bit of a nasty accident with 'er gas!'

'And then what happened, sweetheart?' Leon asked, concerned. He was sitting at the kitchen table and she was forking a generous wedge of toad-in-the-hole from a baking tin, on to his dinner plate.

'One of the ambulance-men confirmed she was alive and praised Malcolm Lewis for the way he had acted.' She handed him the plate, her face pale with distress. 'Then they rolled her on to a stretcher and put her in the ambulance and took her to Lewisham Hospital.'

'And Pru went with her?'

She nodded, making no attempt to put anything on her own plate. 'Malcolm Lewis went as well,' she said, her voice unsteady. 'I think he and Pru must be very fond of each other. He had his arm around her shoulders and she was leaning against him as if he was all the comfort she needed.'

Leon made no move to pick up his knife and fork. He knew his Kate, and he knew there was something else distressing her, something she hadn't told him yet. 'What is it, love?' he asked gently. 'What are you fretting about?'

Her eyes held his, the expression in them agonized. 'That it was partly my fault,' she said hoarsely.

269

He stared at her in utter bewilderment, 'But how on earth . . .' he began, his dinner forgotten.

'I was the one who lent her the money for the gas!' Tears began streaming down her face. 'Oh, Leon! I didn't know what she was going to do when she asked me for it, but I did know she was troubled, and I didn't do anything about it. I simply went on with my laundry! And all the time she was . . . she was . . .'

He was out of his chair, his arms around her, drawing her to her feet, holding her close against him. 'How could you possibly know what was going to happen?' he said, his voice full of loving reason. 'If you hadn't lent her the money, she would only have borrowed it off someone else. Leah, perhaps. Or Nellie.'

'But I feel so guilty!' Her words were muffled against the comforting warmth and strength of his chest. 'I feel so responsible!'

'Then you're taking far too much on yourself.' He put a finger beneath her chin, tipping her face up to his. 'The only thing that should be concerning you is how Doris can best be helped. Do you know if she has any family she could go and stay with for a short holiday? If she has, shall we ask Pru if she'd like to stay with us while her mother's away? Daisy's room is plenty big enough for another single bed to be put in there.'

'What about Wilfred?' she asked, her arms around his waist, dinner forgotten. 'Who is going to look after Wilfred?'

'I rather think everyone in Magnolia Square might have to help in looking after Wilfred,' Leon said wryly. 'Mr Giles will have the matter in hand, you can be sure of that.'

★ ★ ★

'The dear Vicar sorted things out very speedily,' Emily Helliwell said confidingly to Nellie Miller. 'Doris has gone to stay with her sister. She lives in Essex, and Ruth Fairbairn drove her over there this morning.'

Nellie, her swollen feet encased in brand-new carpet slippers bought in honour of Harriet and Charlie's nuptials, said doubtfully, 'It's all very well you thinkin' everythin' is nicely sorted, Emily, but what about Wilfred? Word is, Doris's little accident with the gas 'asn't been enough to bring 'im to 'is senses, and if *that* won't, what will?'

Miriam bustled down the aisle, intent on securing herself a place in one of the front pews. Albert followed her at a more leisurely pace, nodding cheerily to friends and neighbours, his beefy neck uncomfortably constrained by a rarely worn collar and a tie.

Unable to answer Nellie's question, Emily changed the subject. 'I do hope Ruth is going to be back in time to play "The Wedding March" for Harriet,' she said, casting her eyes over the growing congregation. 'It would be such a shame if, after being a spinster for over sixty years, Harriet should end up getting married without walking down the aisle to "The Wedding March" . . .'

'After sixty years of being a spinster, I imagine she'll 'ave more on 'er mind than wedding marches,' Nellie said dryly. 'Lord love me, but what the woman's thinking of, I don't know. Before I was widowed I 'ad my fair share of bein' married, and I'll tell you this for nothing – it ain't all it's cracked up to be, not by a long chalk. Given a choice between marital obligations and a cup o'

271

tea, I'll 'ave a cup o' tea any time! Especially if it 'as sugar in it!'

'Do I look bridal enough, Katherine?' Harriet Godfrey was asking Kate anxiously as she and Kate and Leon stood in her sunlit hallway. 'Perhaps I should have chosen something a little more summery than navy blue and white, but with rationing being what it is, I just had to take what was on offer.'

'It looks like something bought before the war,' Kate said truthfully, surveying Harriet's trim, white-revered suit. 'And your hat looks wonderful. That little posy of fresh marguerites you've pinned to the brim is *very* bridal.'

Harriet's net-gloved hands tightened around her white leather prayer book. 'I never ever thought I would get married,' she said suddenly. 'Not even when I was a young girl. I was always so plain. My father told me that, as no man was ever likely to provide for me, I should concentrate on getting myself a good education and then a good job. And that's what I did.' She fell silent, thinking of the far and distant, lonely past. In the days before the First World War, when she had been at teacher training college, she had had no boy-friends, and she had certainly had none afterwards, when the fields of France and Belgium had been stained red with blood and single, able-bodied young men had been at a premium. 'I'm very lucky,' she said, checking her reflection in her hall mirror for the last time. 'Not only lucky to be marrying a man as kind as Charlie, but lucky in my friends, too.' She turned her head, looking across at Leon. He was standing a little behind Kate, impeccably

272

dressed in a much-brushed, much-pressed dark grey suit, a grey-and-red striped tie emphasizing the pristine snowiness of his starched white shirt. 'Thank you for agreeing to give me away, Leon,' she said gratefully. 'And now I think it's time we walked across to the church, don't you? I've never kept Charlie waiting, and I'm not going to start doing so today.'

From his look-out at the church door, Danny Collins signalled to Bob Giles and to a rather breathless Ruth Fairbairn, that the bride was on her way. Ruth, still wearing the coat she had worn to drive Doris Sharkey to her sister's house in Essex, settled herself a little more comfortably at the organ.

In one of the front left-hand pews, Ellen Pierce slipped her hand into Carl's. Luke and Matthew were sitting with them, patiently waiting for their mother to join them. Daisy was in the pew behind with the Collins family. As Carl's fingers tightened lovingly over hers, Ellen realized with a deep rush of pleasure that very soon all three children would be regarding her as their step-granny.

In the pew behind, Mavis thought about the letter lying in her fake lizard-skin handbag and wished that Luke and Matthew would stop fidgeting. What did it matter if Ted was demobbed before Jack? What earthly difference was it going to make to anything? There was the sound of activity at the church entrance. Kate hurried down the aisle towards the front left-hand pew, pretty as a picture in a pastel-blue dress she had skilfully renovated with crystal, pre-war buttons and a spanking new white belt. The stately strains of 'Here Comes the Bride' filled the church. Charlie stood facing the altar,

273

his best man, Daniel Collins, at his side. No-one present had ever seen Charlie wearing a suit before, and all of them found it a strange experience.

'Are you sure it's 'im?' Nellie Miller asked Emily Helliwell doubtfully. 'It don't look like 'im.'

As if to reassure everybody, Charlie turned slightly, looking down the aisle to where his beloved was approaching on Leon Emmerson's arm, her navy picture-hat dipping with French chic over one eye, the marguerites on its brim delightfully girlish. A beam of pure happiness split his crumpled face. She was a smasher, was his Harriet. She was a diamond, an absolute diamond.

'Course they're not goin' away on a 'oneymoon,' the landlady of The Swan said knowledgeably to a nosy enquirer at what was, for Magnolia Square, a remarkably restrained wedding reception in the church hall. 'They're both in their seventies, for heaven's sake! They got married for a bit o' companionship, not for a bit of 'ow's your farver!'

'I like this companionship lark, don't you 'Arriet?' Charlie asked with a cheeky chuckle as, much, much later on in the evening, they lay in each other's arms in the vast double bed that had once belonged to Harriet's parents. 'It don't 'alf make the mattress springs creak though, don't it?'

Harriet flushed rosily and then, as Charlie began to chortle and then to laugh so hard that the bed began to shake, she clung to him, laughing as she had never laughed before in her life.

Outside in the Square, a man walking his dog heard the unrestrained, bellying, full-throated gales of laughter and shook his head in bemusement. Whatever the joke that had occasioned it, it must have been a good one. He whistled his dog to heel, wondering what it could have been.

Chapter Sixteen

Jack Robson lay on his back in his upper bunk. It was midday, and there was no-one else in the Nissen hut. He took a deep draw on his cigarette, propped it on an upturned Marmite lid, and began to re-read Mavis's letter.

. . . it was a shame you couldn't be home for the wedding. Your dad was a sight for sore eyes. He and Daniel had white carnations in their lapels and their hair (or what they have left!), was so slicked with brilliantine they looked like a couple of old spivs! Harriet Godfrey looked the bee's knees. It's the first time in my life I've ever seen her not wearing tweeds and brogues. She wore a navy suit with white revers, navy court shoes and a hat that must have come from Harrods. Do you remember when she was you and Jerry's headmistress at Junior School and the two of you used to call her an old trout? Bet you never thought she'd one day marry your dad!

As for other news, Leon and Danny are now good mates. They take their kids swimming together on Sunday mornings and the two of them go to the Baths without the kids every Friday evening. I have a sneaking suspicion that my pain-in-the-neck brother-in-law can't swim and that Leon is teaching him. He and Carrie have moved into number 17, much to Mum's relief. It means she can now listen to the news without having to listen to Danny's know-all comments on each and every news item. According to him, he could do a much better job of running the country than Mr Attlee. He wasn't amused when I asked him if it was only his job at the biscuit factory that was stopping him from giving the Prime Minister a hand!

Jack grinned. He and Danny had been mates since their schooldays, and he knew very well what a cocky, self-opinionated little bleeder he could be. He picked up his cigarette and inhaled deeply. Working in a factory instead of strutting about with sergeant's stripes decorating his arm must have been a pretty painful come-down for a bloke of Danny's temperament. He rested his cigarette back on the edge of the Marmite lid. What Danny needed was a job with a bit of action. And once he was back home in Magnolia Square he, Jack Robson, would be just the person to be able to put such a job Danny's way.

. . . the other main bit of news is that number eight's new tenant is beginning to settle in. She still looks decidedly odd, but thanks to me and Carrie and Kate, not as odd as when she first moved in! She talks to herself in the loudest, gruffest voice you've ever heard when she's out in the street, but no-one in the Square takes any notice any more, not even the kids. Compared to Wilfred Sharkey, Anna is practikly normal! Poor Doris Sharkey is still hiding away at her sister's. Pru has moved in with the Emmersons (and is on public hand-holding terms with Malc Lewis??!!), and Wilfred is now a semi-permanent fixture at Lewisham clock-tower preaching hell and damnation to anyone dozy enough to listen to him!

Jack's grin deepened. A lot could be said about the

residents of Magnolia Square, but no-one could ever accuse them of being dull or boring.

What else? Now that Gran's tin helmet is obsolete she's put it to use as a soup tureen. Nellie's using hers as a rose bowl and Emily Helliwell has transformed hers into a bird bath. Lord alone knows what Billy is going to do with all the junk he's hoarded in our front garden. Wilfred Sharkey told me yesterday morning he thought the outside of my house was a public health hassard and that I should be reported to the council. According to Pru it's the only rashional comment he's made since VJ Day. When he made it, he was on his way to his pitch at the clock-tower wearing a placard that read HER HOUSE IS THE WAY TO HELL! PROVERBS CHAPTER 7 VERSE 8. As for Kate . . .

Jack turned another vivid pink page of Mavis's satisfyingly long and chatty letter.

. . . she's her usual wonderful self. Billy and Beryl call in at number four nearly every day after school for a piece of home-made gingerbread or shortcake or whatever else she's made for her kids teas. She's taken Anna under her wing just as she once took Nellie under it (you might not remember, but there was a time when if she hadn't bathed and bandaged Nellie's ulcerated leg for her every week, Nellie would have been bedridden). Her dad's married his mousy, middle-aged lady-friend and has moved in with her. Joss Harvey's chauffeured Bentley cruises into the Square once a week and parks outside number two waiting for Matthew to climb into the back of it. How Kate feels about it I don't know. Nor does anyone else. Not even Carrie. I only wish I was the one enjoying such luxury! A ride in the back of a Bentley would go down very well, thank you very much!

And that's about it, except to say that now I'm no longer in the ATS but on the buses life isn't half the fun it used to be. I don't miss poor buggers being killed and maimed by bombs and V1s and V2s, but I'd got used to the danger of the war and the excitement and the sense of urgency and being part of it all. Being a clippie isn't half as exciting, though I expect it's better than working for my dad down the market.

    Ta-ra for now,

              Love Mavis.

PS. *Harold Miller's on his way home at long last. Nellie got word yesterday.*

PPS. *Ted's on his way home too. Looks like you're going to be the last of the Magnolia Square lot to be back in civvies. What's keeping you? Are you scared you'll slip up and call your new stepmother by her old nickname?'*

Jack's grin deepened as he ground his cigarette stub out. Though he hoped to God he would never be so drunk as to call Harriet an old trout to her face, he knew it was the way he would always privately think of her. He wondered what Jerry would have thought of their father's second marriage. His grin faded. Jerry. How many years was it now since Jerry had been killed in Spain? Eight? Nine? As clear as if it were yesterday, he remembered one of the last days they had ever spent together. It had been a glorious summer day, and every resident in Magnolia Square had been up on the Heath celebrating St Mark's annual church fête. There had been side-shows and stalls, a Bonny Baby Competition for the proud mums of the parish, a cricket match for the men, donkey rides for the kids. Jerry had spent most of the day laughing and talking with Kate. And he, Jack, had first set eyes on Christina.

He reached under his pillow for his packet of Craven 'A'. It had been love at first sight as far as he had been concerned. In all the years since, he had never felt for any other woman what he had felt, and continued to feel, for Christina. He tapped a cigarette out of the packet. The question was, though, did she love him as fiercely and urgently as he loved her? He rolled over slightly, fumbling in the pocket of the Army jacket hooked on to the corner of his bunk. The letter he withdrew consisted of only two, neatly penned sheets. He scanned the half-dozen unsatisfactory paragraphs.

. . . the wedding was lovely. Queenie wore a white satin bow around her neck and Daniel Collins took photographs . . . Carrie and Danny have moved in to number 17 and Carrie is expecting another baby . . . The weather has been very mild for October, Albert says it means we will have a hard winter . . . I hope you are well and that you'll be demobbed soon . . .

There was nothing in it that could be described as intimate or personal. Nothing about what she was doing with her time when she wasn't working. Nothing about how much she was missing him. There wasn't even any mention of whether she had moved into number twelve now that Charlie was living with Harriet. Nor was there any mention of Carl Voigt's wedding. He lit his cigarette, blowing a thin filter of smoke towards the Nissen hut's ceiling, wondering if much could be read into that particular omission. Mavis had written that Carl Voigt was no longer living in Magnolia Square, which meant

280

that Christina was presumably no longer having her long, mysterious chats with him. He chewed the corner of his lip. What on earth had those chats been about? No matter how much he pondered over them he couldn't come up with any likely answers – apart from one. He sat up abruptly, swinging his legs over the side of his bunk. Christina and Carl Voigt? Was it really a possibility? The man was old enough to be her father. And he was an Aryan German. It didn't make sense. It didn't make any sense at all.

He gave his well-muscled shoulders an angry shrug and jumped to the floor. Whatever was wrong with his marriage, it couldn't be sorted by lying on a bunk, brooding about it. In another month or so he would be demobbed and home and *then* he would sort it. He would sort it if it was the last thing he ever did.

'Two pahnds o' carrots and an 'andful of greens,' Christina's customer said to her, holding her canvas shopping-bag open wide, 'an' throw in a couple of onions while you're abaht it, there's a dear.'

Christina, wearing cotton gloves so that her hands didn't get as rough and red as Carrie's, burrowed into the giant pile of carrots fronting Albert's market stall. Her customer sniffed. She preferred it when Carrie was serving. Carrie was always ready with a friendly word and a bit of banter. Christina, with her fancy name and dark, almost foreign looks, was polite enough, but it was the kind of politeness assistants in posh stores doled out. And when people shopped down the market they didn't want to be treated as if they were in Fortnum & Mason or Harrods, they wanted a bit of heartwarming, friendly cheek.

281

Christina weighed the carrots, well aware of her deficiencies as a market-seller. She had no chat, no repartee, and she could no more shout her wares than fly to the moon. She tipped the carrots into her customer's bag and reached for a couple of onions. It was she who had suggested, when the Jenningses had first taken her into their home, that she should contribute to the family's finances by working on Albert's fruit and vegetable stall. Albert had been delighted. It meant he could branch out and run two stalls instead of just one. The second stall, the one Christina and Carrie alternated on, was at the opposite end of the High Street to his original stall near the clock-tower, neatly capturing the custom of shoppers coming into the market from the Catford and Ladywell areas.

'One and threepence, please,' she said, packing the greens neatly in on top of the onions and carrots.

Her customer sniffed again, but not in dissatisfaction. Prices on a Jennings market stall were always fair. As Christina rummaged in the leather pouch at her waist for change of the florin she was being proffered, she knew she only had herself to blame if she found her work uncongenial. Albert wouldn't have minded in the slightest if, at any time over the last few years, she had found herself a job elsewhere. For much of the war, when she and Carrie had been seconded to do war work at an ammunition factory in Woolwich, he had had to manage without her, and he would certainly be able to manage without her again.

Perhaps she would give up working on the stall when Jack came home. Perhaps she would have other demands on her time by then. Perhaps she would be looking after her mother and grandmother.

'Ta, dearie.' Her customer slipped the sixpence and threepenny bit Christina had given her into a battered purse and, meeting with no response, sniffed again and took her leave.

Christina barely noticed. Apart from Charlie's racing pigeons in their hut in the garden, number twelve was standing empty, waiting for her and Jack to move into it. It was a roomy, family house. Roomy enough to accommodate not only any family she and Jack might have, but her mother and grandmother as well. She knitted her hands together tightly. If her mother and grandmother were alive. If they could be found.

'You don't think you're perhaps building your hopes up too high?' Kate had asked her doubtfully the previous evening as they had sat in the kitchen at number four, enjoying mugs of milky Ovaltine.

'No,' she had said shortly, closing herself off as she had closed herself off from everybody, apart from Carl. He alone understood how nothing else in her life mattered apart from the search they had embarked on. He understood how impossible it was for her to even think of anything else. And the letters he had received from organizations such as the United Nations High Commission for Refugees, the United Nations Relief and Rehabilitation Administration and the International Tracing Center, were proof that their search wasn't without hope. People *were* being traced and found. Families *were* being reunited. The International Tracing Centre in New York had confirmed that they had both Bergers and Franks on their files, but there had been no Jacoba Berger, no Eva Frank.

'We must try and trace anyone on the International Tracing Center lists who was arrested at the same time as your mother and grandmother, and who were living in the same area at the time of their arrest,' Carl had said, refusing to be deterred. 'They may very well have all been taken to the same camp. They may have known your mother and grandmother. They may be the perfect short-cut to our finding them.'

Christina stared unseeingly down the High Street and its seemingly endless row of market stalls. No-one else talked so positively. No-one else talked of her mother and grandmother as if they were still alive.

'For how can they be, *bubbeleh*?' Leah had said, bewildered, time and time again. 'They were arrested and taken off in a truck, and no-one has seen or spoken to them since.'

'We don't *know* that!' she always responded fiercely. 'They *may* have been released! And if they had been, how would they have been able to find me if I was already on my way to Switzerland, or even, perhaps, on my way to England? They may be looking for me just as I am looking for them!'

'Then why for hasn't your grandmother written to me, her old friend?' Leah always asked unhappily. 'Why has there been no letter enquiring if you are here?'

It was a question never answered. A question it was impossible to answer.

'I'll 'ave 'alf a stone of potatoes, four pounds of onions and three pounds of apples,' a regular customer said, breaking in on her reverie. 'And if that's dew on those lettuces I'll take two of 'em.'

Christina shovelled up a weighing scale scoop of

284

potatoes. An idea had been growing in her mind for days now, an idea she hadn't voiced to anyone, not even to Carl. She rattled the potatoes into her customer's large wicker basket. What if she were to go back to Heidelberg? What if she were to make enquiries about her mother and grandmother in the town that had been their home; in the town where they had been arrested?

'You've weighed me three pounds of onions, not four,' her customer pointed out, not very kindly. 'And have you heard the news about Harold Miller? Nellie says he'll be home by the end of the month.'

Christina added an onion to the weighing scoop. 'Yes,' she said, wondering if she would be allowed back into Germany. 'I'd heard. It's wonderful news.' And if she did go back, how would she manage for money? She doubted if Albert would be able to lend her any, and she knew that Carrie and Danny wouldn't be able to. And there were other considerations as well. How, for instance, would she be able to endure all the terrible emotions that being in Germany again would arouse in her?

'You might look a bit happier about it,' her customer said tartly. 'Some people suffered more than others in the war. And Harold Miller's one of them.'

'Heidelberg?' Kate put down the potato she had been peeling. '*Heidelberg?* You can't mean it, Christina! You can't mean it in a million years!'

Christina removed a toy train from a kitchen chair and sat down. 'I do mean it,' she said steadily. 'If you think about it, Kate, it's the most logical next step to take. Heidelberg was our home. If my mother and

285

grandmother are alive and looking for me, it's where they would begin their search. And it was in Heidelberg that they were arrested. If all surviving Nazi files and records are now in the hands of the Allies, there may well be files in Heidelberg which could tell me where my mother and grandmother were taken.'

Slowly Kate wiped her hands on her apron. Initially, when Christina had first embarked on her search for information as to where her mother and grandmother had been taken and what had happened to them, she had been utterly sympathetic. She, too, would have wanted to know. She would have wanted to know in order that she could grieve for them without the added mental torment of wondering and wondering how, and where, they had died.

Christina, however, was no longer searching only for information. The wild hope that her mother and grand-mother might have survived had turned into the obsessive conviction that they *had* survived, and that, with enough effort on her part, she would find them and be reunited with them. Kate bit the corner of her lip. Such a con-viction could, surely, only lead to crushing, annihilating disappointment, and it would be a disappointment which, because of the sympathy and encouragement she had given, she would be partially responsible for. With growing apprehension, she wondered how Christina would bear the blow when it came. She had always possessed an air of Dresden-china fragility, but now she was beginning to look positively unwell. There were blue shadows beneath her eyes, and her delicately-boned face was taut and pale.

She said, choosing her words carefully, 'Dad is making

all the enquiries anyone could possibly make. If there are any authorities in and around Heidelberg that can be helpful, then he will contact them. It's best to leave it to him, Christina. Truly it is.'

Christina shook her head, her silk-dark hair falling forwards, framing her face. 'No,' she said fiercely. 'I must go back. Until I spoke about it, I wasn't sure. Now I am. I must search for them myself, Kate. And I will find them! I know I will find them!'

Kate glanced at her wall clock. It was only five-thirty. Leon wouldn't be home for nearly another hour, and even when he did come home, she doubted if anything he might say would change Christina's mind. The only person likely to do that was Carl. 'How about a walk?' she said, knowing that if Christina agreed, she would have to substitute spam and chips for the cottage-pie she had been going to give Leon for his dinner. 'We could go over the Heath and down into Greenwich and call on Dad. He may have some more news for you, and even if he hasn't, you can talk over the pros and cons of going to Heidelberg with him.'

She took off her apron. 'Daisy is out playing with the other two Graces. She and Rose and Beryl are inseparable these days. We'll have to take Matthew and Luke with us, though. I'll put Luke in his push-chair. He doesn't like it too much, now that he's three, but it serves a purpose when there's no time for dawdling.'

She opened the back door, taking Christina's silence as acquiescence. 'Matthew! Luke! Come in and wash your hands. We're going to visit Grandad.'

'You're hoping your father will change my mind for me, aren't you?' Christina said as they walked out of

287

Magnolia Terrace and began to cross the main road flanking the Heath.

'Yes.' The traffic was busier than usual, with office-workers beginning to make the homeward trek out of the City into the suburbs, and it was with relief that she trundled the push-chair off the tarmacadamed surface and on to springy grass, Matthew trotting along by her side, Hector obediently at their heels. 'Of course I am. I think it's a terrible idea. You're going to be face to face with hideous memories—'

'I'm always going to have hideous memories,' Christina said abruptly, pushing a wing of jaw-length hair away from her face.

'You don't know what people's reaction to you will be,' Kate said, equally abruptly. 'How can you voluntarily return to a country that tried to annihilate your entire race?'

'Because I may still have family living there.'

They had reached the part of the Heath known as Point Hill. Down below them lay a view of London stretching from the bomb-damaged docks in the east to Alexandra Palace in the north, and the City and Westminster in the west. It was a view that always made Kate catch her breath. A view that always filled her with a rush of fierce pride and love for the city that was her home.

'And I can't come to any harm,' Christina continued as they came to a mutual halt, staring out over the vast panorama that was London. 'Hitler's dead, remember? Germany is occupied by Allied troops.'

'Can we go through Greenwich Park, Mummy?' Matthew tugged at Kate's skirt as Luke grizzled and

288

grumbled at being confined in the push-chair. 'Can we visit the deer?'

'We can go through the park, but we can't visit the deer. We haven't time.'

With luck, her father would be as appalled by Christina's decision to return to Germany as she was. Even if he wasn't, even if he encouraged her, how could Christina carry out her intention? She was a civilian. Civilians couldn't travel to Germany, not unless they were on government business or had a special permit.

'Daddy-Leon comes home through the park, doesn't he?' Matthew said, unhappy at his mother's introspection and trying to gain her attention again. 'Might we see him? Might Daddy-Leon come with us to Grandad's?'

'If we see him, he will.' She and Christina turned away from the view and began to walk in the direction of Greenwich Park's southern side entrance. 'Why don't you have a game with Luke to see who sees him first?'

'And then I can run to meet him, can't I?' Matthew said, recovering from his disappointment over the deer. 'Luke can't run to meet him, 'cos he's in a push-chair.' He skipped along at her side, holding on to the push-chair as he did so. 'Only babies ride in push-chairs, don't they?' he said in happy self-importance. 'Luke's still a baby, isn't he? He isn't a big boy, is he? He isn't a big boy who has a great-grandad and . . .'

'I'se *not* a baby! I'se *not*!' Luke yelled, drumming his heels against the push-chair's footrest in impotent fury.

Two well-dressed middle-aged women, about to enter the park gates, paused. 'Dear, dear, dear,' one of them said in mock chastisement, beaming down at Luke,

289

'what a little tantrum! The Bogyman will come and get you if you don't mind your temper.'

Luke stopped yelling and stared up at her, his attention caught. What was a Bogyman? It didn't sound very nice.

'Mummy . . .' he began doubtfully, 'what's a . . . ?'

'And what lovely curls he's got,' the woman said, this time directing her beaming smile at Kate. 'More like a little girl than a little boy, isn't he? 'Course, darkie children always are bonny. Is he from Barnardo's? Are you just taking the little chap out for a walk?'

Kate's polite, answering smile, died. 'No,' she said, a note in her voice Christina had never heard before. 'He's not from Barnardo's. He's—'

'He's just like a little gollywog,' the woman's companion said indulgently, ruffling Luke's tight, silky curls. She bent down over the push-chair, saying in a baby voice, 'Golly, Golly, Golly. Who's a lovely Golly then? Golly, Golly, Goll—'

Kate removed the woman's hand from Luke's hair, her eyes ablaze with the force of her anger. 'His name isn't Golly. It's Luke. And he isn't from Barnardo's! He's my son!'

Furiously she bumped the push-chair over the park gate's shallow step, striding down the footpath at such a pace that Matthew and Christina had to run to catch her up.

'What's the matter, Mummy?' Matthew panted, bewildered and distressed. 'Why did that lady call Luke a Gollywog? Why are you so angry? Why . . .'

Kate came to an abrupt halt. Putting the push-chair's brake on she bent down and put her arms reassuringly around him. 'That lady was being rude and ignorant and patronizing,' she said, speaking very slowly and quietly so that he would understand how very serious she was. 'She didn't mean to be, but she was. And whenever people call Luke by anything other than his proper name, even if they do so thinking they're being friendly or funny, you must be very fierce about it. Because if you aren't, people might never know how rude and hurtful and . . . and *belittling* they are being. Luke's name is Luke. It isn't anything else. It isn't Golly or Sambo. It's Luke.'

Her voice was unsteady and Matthew's arms tightened around her. 'I'll remember,' he said, not understanding why she was so upset, but not wanting her to be upset any longer. 'I won't let anyone call Luke names. I promise.'

She hugged him, painfully aware that there would be times when it would be impossible for him to stop people calling Luke names and aware too that, because the incident had taken her by surprise, it had resulted in her putting far too much on Matthew's shoulders, far too soon.

'Does that happen often?' Christina asked quietly as Matthew ran on ahead of them and they resumed their walk.

'Often enough. It's something Leon warned me to expect, but it's something I'm never going to docilely accept, not ever.'

The late afternoon, a short while ago so crisply golden, suddenly seemed to have lost its radiance. She looked down the steeply sloping pathway towards the distant gate leading out into Nelson Road, Greenwich. A dark, muscular figure had just turned into the park; a figure that made her pulse beat faster and her heart race.

'*It's Daddy!*' Matthew shrieked joyously. 'I've won the game! It's Daddy! It's Daddy!' With all the speed of a little tornado he began hurtling down the tree-lined pathway, Hector bounding ahead of him, barking furiously.

'Out! Out!' Luke demanded frantically, wriggling to free himself from the push-chair reins. 'Want to meet Daddy! Want to run to Daddy!'

With joy bubbling up in her throat, Kate bent down and released him, lifting him clear of the push-chair and setting him down on his feet. The day was beautiful again. Beautiful and infinitely special. For the first time ever, Leon was no longer 'Daddy-Leon' to Matthew. He was simply 'Daddy'. 'Don't run too fast or you'll fall,' she said to Luke as, with eyes bright with tears of happiness, she watched Matthew run into Leon's arms; saw Leon swing him round and round; heard their happy, loving, joy-filled laughter as if merged with the sound of Hector's excited barking and the sound of tug whistles rising from the nearby river.

Chapter Seventeen

Bowler-hatted and gloved, and wearing a vicuña over-coat, Joss Harvey stomped up the polished wood stairs of his City solicitors. Kate Emmerson, *née* Voigt, no doubt thought she'd been deviously clever in allowing him access to Matthew. She no doubt thought such contact would satisfy him and preclude him from trying to obtain custody of Matthew. He snorted in derision as a female minion hurried out of Cyril Habgood's plushly furnished sanctum to greet him. She hadn't been clever at all, by God. She'd been an absolute ninny. The contact he had since had with his great-grandson had merely served to reinforce his determination to remove the boy perma-nently from her care and to rear him himself. And thanks to the offensive environment in which Matthew was living, such a task was going to be exceedingly easy to achieve.

He snorted to himself again as he was ushered into Cyril Habgood's holy of holies. Despite every appearance to the contrary, he had known his former employee was a slut from the moment she had told him she was pregnant with his grandson's child. How could she be anything else? Respectable young women did not have babies out of wedlock. No doubt if Toby had lived, he would have married her, but the girl would still have been a slut. How could a girl who had happily embroiled herself with a black West Indian seaman be anything else?

''Morning, Joss!' his solicitor said sunnily, rising from behind his massive mahogany desk to greet him. 'Wonderful weather we're having for late October! Or is it news of the income tax cuts that's making me feel so equable? A reduction from ten shillings to nine shillings in the pound isn't to be sneezed at, is it?'

'I'm not here to chat about the Budget,' Joss said abruptly, shaking Cyril's hand and then seating himself heavily in the leather chair facing the desk. 'I'm here to find out how you're going to block a Black Sambo's application to adopt my great-grandchild.'

Leon shipped oars and reached for the hand-rolled gasper tucked behind his ear. It was good to be back on the dear old Thames. Compared to a lot of other recently demobbed men, he was exceedingly lucky. Not only, as a Thames lighterman, had he been able to return immediately to a job he knew and loved, but he was even sailing the very same barge he'd been sailing before the war had broken out. The last six years had left the *Tansy* a little bit the worse for wear, but she was still a solid craft. As she rocked and bobbed safely out of the main shipping line, he took his mid-morning toke, watching the build-up of shipping heading up-river towards London's wharves and warehouses. There were oilers and tugs gunnel-deep with coal and tea and ballast. A boat from Norway surged up-stream, its decks piled high with planed timber. Another boat was from Sweden. Another from Denmark. He watched them without envy. The

Thames would do for him, thank you very much. He'd had enough of foreign seas to last him a lifetime.

He took a last drag at his cigarette before tossing the butt into the eddying water. He was bound for Greenland Dock and he still had quite a bit of river to cover. He set the *Tansy* to hug the south shore off Woolwich Arsenal, wishing he had Matthew with him. Perhaps this coming Saturday, if he had overtime, he would suggest to Kate that Matthew spend the day aboard the *Tansy*. Luke would want to come too, of course, but he wouldn't be able to keep his eyes on two of them, and it was Matthew who was mustard-keen to sail the river.

He slid by Jetty Roads and began pulling across Hook Ness to Galleon's Point, his Navy duffle coat buttoned against the stiff breeze. Perhaps Matthew, too, would one day proudly wear a Waterman's badge on his breast pocket. He looked across to the yawning entrances of the King George and Albert Docks. Matthew could do far, far worse. It was a grand life, working the river. Especially when a man had a cosy home and a loving family to return to every evening.

The *Tansy* rounded the bend into Woolwich Reach. The Woolwich ferry was ploughing across the river, a spume of white water in its wake. It was a free ferry and a favourite haunt of truanting youngsters. Young Billy Lomax, for instance, often spent all day hanging happily over the ferry's rails as it forged back and forth, offering a magnificent view of passing shipping. There was no sign of Billy today, however, and Leon sailed on, past St Mary's Wharf and Trinity Wharf and the huge Siemans factory. With luck, Matthew and Luke would never play truant from school, and he certainly had no worries on that score where Daisy was concerned. Daisy was as happy as a little lark at school. Every mealtime they shared together, she chattered ten to the dozen about the things she and her friends were doing in class and the things they were going to do.

He began to round the bend that heralded Blackwall Point. He was a lucky man. He had a job that satisfied him to the depths of his being; he had children he would die for; and he had a wife he loved with all his heart and body and soul. Just thinking of Kate made him feel breathless. She possessed an inner radiance and serenity that drew people to her like moths to a flame, and she possessed a passion that was reserved for him, and him alone. At the mere memory of it he felt his throat tighten. Only that morning, she had told him that her period was late.

'Please God let her be pregnant,' he prayed as he brought the *Tansy* round head on tide, off Deadman's Dock. 'And let it be a girl this time. Another little girl will make our family complete.'

He continued up-river, past the giant Tate & Lyle treacle factory on the north bank. The area all around it was known locally as Treacle Town, and he grinned to himself, glad he didn't live there; glad he was a south-Londoner; glad that he lived in a part of London rich in history and with wonderful high, open views of the river. Glad, and grateful, to be alive.

'I'm afraid it's still too early to be sure,' Dr Roberts said to Kate, his stethoscope dangling from his ears like permanent appendages. 'However, if your breasts are tender and you're passing urine more often than usual,

296

and certain foods are making you feel nauseated, then it's highly likely the reason is pregnancy.' It was the third time he had broken such news to her, and the first time she had received the news as a married woman. He sighed. Even now, with a wedding ring gleaming on the fourth finger of her left hand, the situation wasn't ideal. He didn't approve of miscegenation. Black races were black and white races were white and, in his opinion, a mixing-up of the two benefited no-one. Especially not the children of such marriages who, in his view, were unlikely to be accepted by either their father's race or their mother's race.

With perfect professional propriety he kept his thoughts to himself, saying, 'Come and see me in another four weeks. An internal examination should be decisive by then.'

'Thank you, Dr Roberts.' Kate smiled politely, turned and left the room, well aware of his unexpressed opinion. It saddened her, but didn't distress her. There would always be people who disapproved of the unusual, and Dr Roberts was one of them. He wouldn't, however, ever cause her or hers grief by name-calling or by behaving towards them in anything but the same, punctiliously correct manner he displayed to the rest of the world.

She stepped out of the surgery into the chill crispness of autumn, dismissing him from her thoughts, thinking only of the baby she was now sure she was expecting. It would be the first child she had conceived and would carry in conventional circumstances. Instead of being alone, unable to share either the weariness of pregnancy, or the exultation of it, with the father of her child, she would be able to share every step of her pregnancy with him; the confirmation of it; the first time the baby moved in her womb; even, perhaps, the actual birth. With a spring in her step and a heart bursting with joy, she unleashed Hector from the surgery railings and began to walk homewards, making a slight detour so that her route would take her past the Point. It was a glorious morning and she wanted to be able to look out over the river in the faint, fond hope of being able to discern the *Tansy* amongst the maelstrom of shipping heading either up-river to the wharves and docks, or down-river towards the open sea.

'Cooee, there!' a woman she knew only by sight called out to her from the far side of the road. 'Where are the little ones today?'

'Matthew is at nursery school, Luke is helping a neighbour care for his pigeons,' Kate called back, wondering just how Charlie was coping with Luke's 'helping'.

With a cheery wave the woman continued on her way, heading down towards Greenwich. Kate continued in the opposite direction, breasting the hill that led out on to the Heath, unleashing Hector from his lead so that he could have a good run. What would she and Leon call this new baby? Always, before, the choice of a name had been hers and hers alone. This time it would be a joint decision. A joint decision that would be enhanced by a lot of suggestions from Daisy.

She skirted one of the Heath's disused, gorse-thick gravel-pits. She wouldn't even think of boys' names because this time the baby was going to be a girl, she was sure of it. Rebecca was a nice name, and biblical, too, like Matthew and Luke. On the other hand, it would be nice to have a name that married well with Daisy.

Briony, perhaps. Or Pansy, or Primrose. She called Hector to heel and crossed the road that flanked the Heath, separating it from the Point. Rose would have been an ideal name, but Carrie's daughter was called Rose, and two Roses in the Square would be confusing.

She came to a halt, her cherry-red coat buttoned high to her throat against the stiff breeze, looking out over the great loops of the Thames as it curved like a snake around Blackwall Point a little to the east, curving again at Greenwich Reach directly below her, and then coiling yet again at Limehouse Reach to the west, just beyond the Greenland Dock. Was that where Leon was now, at the Greenland entrance, waiting for the outer lock gates to yawn open and swallow the *Tansy* in? Or was he already in the main dock, the *Tansy* nose-to-tail with other lighters and tugs and launches as they jostled for their respective wharves? Wherever he was, he would be content. The river was in his blood and his bones, and she knew that he hoped at least one of his children would follow him on to it.

She frowned slightly, the stiff October breeze ruffling tendrils of hair at her temples, her long rope of braided hair hanging straight as a line down to her waist. Matthew was already showing every sign of being fascinated by the river, but how could Matthew ever become a Thames Waterman? Joss Harvey had already entered his name for the preparatory department of the prestigious public school that Toby had once attended. And a public school education led to many things, but not to obtaining Port of London Authority Waterman's and Lighterman's licences and becoming a Freeman of the River.

Hector was barking impatiently, unhappy at the lack of attention he was receiving. She bent down and picked up a stick, throwing it for him, her frown deepening. For Matthew to enjoy a public school education when Luke and Daisy and the new baby attended local schools, would be to bring class divisiveness right into the heart of their little family. Yet what choice did she have when she knew, without a moment's doubt, that Toby would have wanted his son to be educated as he had been educated?

Hector bounded triumphantly back to her, the stick in his mouth. She gently removed it, throwing it again, wondering what effect such a difference of education would have on the children's relationships with each other. Especially the relationship between Matthew and Luke. Down below her there was a subtle change on the river. Was the tide beginning to ebb? If it were, it was high time she returned to Magnolia Square and relieved Charlie of his baby-sitting duties. She called a reluctant Hector to heel and turned her back on one of the most magnificent vistas London had to offer. When Luke was a little older perhaps he would show signs of having the same Thames-loving fever as his father. If Luke became a Waterman then it wouldn't matter that Matthew didn't do so. And the new baby? Briony or Pansy or Primrose? What would she become when she grew up?

Kate raised her face to the hard grey sky, laughing aloud for pure joy. It wouldn't matter. It wouldn't matter in the slightest, not as long as she grew up happy and healthy and kind-hearted. She stepped once more on to the Heath, working out the months. She must have conceived around the beginning of September, which meant the baby would be born in early June. Her own birthday was in June, and next year she would be twenty-five. What a wonderful twenty-fifth birthday present a new baby would be, especially as Leon's application to adopt Matthew would have been approved and granted by then, and he would be Matthew's legal father. She broke into a run of exhilaration, Hector bounding at her heels. Life was good. Life was so good that if it hadn't been for the baby she was certain she was carrying, she would have performed cartwheels all the way across the Heath and into Magnolia Square.

Mavis didn't feel like performing cartwheels. She was on the run from Trafalgar Square, up the Haymarket to Piccadilly and then on into Oxford Street to Marble Arch. It was one of the busiest bus routes in London, thick with shoppers and shopworkers. ''Old tight!' she shouted as Burt, her driver, lurched away from the Simpson's corner stop and into the maelstrom of traffic surging around Piccadilly's Eros. 'Move dahn a bit, or go up on top. There's plenty of room up there.'

A young man who had been strap-hanging, a shiny briefcase clutched to his chest with his free hand, obligingly accepted her advice, squeezing past her as he made his way towards the stairs. Mavis braced herself against one of the crowded passenger seats, leaning back as far as she could to give him room. Burt braked hard as a black cab shot across his path from Vigo Street. The strap-hangers lurched against each other, one woman giving a little scream. A seated passenger's carrier bag fell off her knees, spilling apples and a bottle of Daddie's Sauce into the aisle. The young man with the briefcase staggered hard against Mavis, standing on her toes as he did so.

'*Ow!*' Mavis protested vehemently as his weight pressed her wooden ticket rack hard against her rib cage. 'Mind what yer doin' with yer plates of meat!'

'Sorry if I stood on your toes, miss.' The young man flushed scarlet as he struggled to regain his balance. 'Are you all right? I haven't really hurt you, have I?'

'You've bloomin' well nearly crushed me to death,' Mavis said, pushing herself away from the passenger seat and upright again, readjusting the leather shoulder satchel that held her takings and change. 'Now 'ave yer paid or 'aven't yer? I don't want to be climbing those stairs again just for you.'

'A three a'penny one, please,' he said, fumbling with his free hand in his trouser pocket for change, blushing harder than ever.

Mavis took compassion on him and grinned. He didn't look a day older than twenty, and there was something about him that reminded her of Malcolm Lewis.

'A three a'penny one it is,' she said, taking his money and punching him a ticket. 'An' if you were 'oping to be a ballet dancer, I'd forget about it. You're as 'eavy on yer feet as an elephant.'

There were appreciative chuckles from the passengers within earshot, and the young man's face deepened to the colour of the headscarf Mavis was wearing, turban-fashion, over her buttercup-blonde curls. He didn't scuttle away up the stairs, though. There was more than teasing amusement in the disconcertingly green eyes so flagrantly meeting his. There was come-hither encouragement as well.

Standing his ground, he said with every inch of courage he possessed, 'Perhaps you'd let me make amends. Would you come out for a drink with me this evening? Or perhaps for a meal . . .'

Mavis sighed, regretting her moment of light-hearted flirtation. She was a lot of things but she wasn't a cradle-snatcher. Even if she had been, this young man, as clean-cut and fresh-faced as a Mormon missionary, was definitely not her type. She liked her men to be danger-ously knowing, and she liked them to be tall and toughly built and to move with the springy precision that indi-cated strength and muscular control. The young man now looking at her with such urgent hope in his eyes was more like a clumsy young colt than a superbly fit Com-mando. And it was a Commando, one very particular Commando, that she was yearning for.

As she thought of Jack, slim and supple in his American blue denims, desolation swept over her. Where had the two of them gone wrong? Why hadn't they married a decade ago, when they were even younger than the young man now standing before her, still waiting for an answer to his request.

'No,' she said, finally answering it and trying to sound regretful and to let him down gently, 'I'm a married woman.' She held up her left hand, waggling her wedding ring finger so that he could see the narrow gold ring encircling it. 'Mind the stairs as you go up. We'll be turning into Oxford Street in a minute and it's a sharp corner.' She turned her attention to the rest of her passengers. 'Hold tight! No standing on the platform, please! Oxford Circus next stop!'

*   *   *

'I've just heard word about Wilfred,' Daniel said at the close of his weekly meeting with Bob Giles. 'What are Doris and Pru going to do, now that Wilfred's been asked to resign from his job?'

Bob took off his reading glasses and pinched the bridge of his nose. Wilfred. How much more bizarre were events going to become where his former churchwarden was concerned? Knowing that Daniel would have to be told some time, he laid his glasses on his desk-top, saying, 'Whilst Doris is with her sister in Essex, Pru has begun working again, so there's no immediate problem there.' He paused. Daniel waited patiently. That there was going to be a problem somewhere else, he could tell by the weary tone of Bob Giles's voice. 'As to Wilfred's loss of earnings . . .' Again Bob Giles paused. If he didn't tell Daniel now, Daniel would only hear from another source. By the time Wilfred's 'disciples' began making visits to number ten, there would be wild and wonderful rumours in plenty. 'Wilfred seems to have attracted what can only be described as a paying congregation,' he said, trying to sound as if it were nothing very uncommon. 'A coterie of middle-aged Blackheath ladies have taken him under their wing and are, I understand, funding him extremely generously.'

Daniel blinked. 'Funding him? You mean they're giving Wilfred *money*?'

Bob sympathized with Daniel's incredulity. 'The payments are being described as tythes,' he said, not knowing whether to abhor Wilfred's business acumen, or admire it.

'Blimey!' Daniel thought of St Mark's collection plates. They never garnered more than a handful of loose change. He wondered if Wilfred was quite as adrift in his brain-box as they all thought.

'And they're going to begin holding Sunday morning meetings at number ten,' Bob said, seeing no reason why Daniel should any longer be spared from knowing the worst.

'Oh dear, oh dear.' Daniel shook his head unhappily. 'Doris isn't going to want to come home to that, is she? I've never known a woman so particular about her carpets.' Another thought occurred to him. 'And are these ladies of Wilfred's married ladies or widowed ladies? Because if they're widowed ladies—'

'Whatever their marital status, there will be unpleasant rumours,' Bob said, knowing he was making a colossal understatement.

'Let's hope he doesn't become a polligammything-ummy, like the Jerry O'Gormans,' Daniel said, wondering how on earth he would break such news to Hettie.

'Mormons don't practise polygamy, if polygamy is against the law of the land they live in,' Bob said, feeling faint at the very thought of polygamous wives, as well as so-called disciples, establishing a bridge-head on St Mark's very doorstep. 'Would you like a cup of tea, Daniel? I could certainly do with one.'

'So could I,' Daniel said with heartfelt feeling, 'but Wilfred won't be able to have any cups of tea, not if he starts behaving like a Jerry O'Gorman. And he won't be able to enjoy a glass of beer either!'

For the rest of her shift, Mavis was far less chirpy than usual. Life just didn't seem to be any *fun* any more. By the time she paid in her takings at the end of the day she

305

was even beginning to wish she'd accepted the fresh-faced young man's offer to take her out for a drink. She grinned ruefully to herself. What the heck was life coming to? There'd been a time not so long ago when she'd been ankle-deep in men, and they had been *real* men, not briefcase-carrying, Malcolm Lewis look-alikes who had barely begun to shave. Yanks, Canadians, Australians, Poles. She'd been able to take her pick and, like a lot of other young women whose husbands were serving overseas for sometimes years on end, she had done so. She had never done so, however, with serious intent. A kiss and a cuddle at the end of a night's dancing had been as far as it had ever gone.

She hopped off the service bus that took her from her bus depot to the corner of the Heath. Where were they now, all those Yanks, Canadians, Australians and Poles that she'd danced night after night with? Already de-mobbed and back home probably, and if not already home, on troopships heading for home. She strode out across the coarse grass, the harsh serge of her clippie's trousers rough against her legs. Ted, too, was now heading home. Her stomach muscles tightened in a mixture of anticipation and apprehension. What was life going to be like for them after six years of separation broken only by a few inadequately short leaves? They were going to be strangers to each other. Her sense of apprehension grew. In some ways, they'd *always* been strangers to each other. Ted was a quiet chap. He'd never been one for gallivanting or dancing the night away. Home and hearth, that was Ted.

A surge of pride eased her apprehension. And home-and-hearth Ted Lomax had won himself a medal for

306

saving the life of a comrade under heavy fire. He was a hero, was her Ted. And he deserved a hero's welcome from his wife, not a welcome marred by doubt as to what the future held for them both or, even worse, tarnished because her thoughts weren't centred on him alone.

She saw Harriet and Charlie some distance away, Queenie running in wide circles around them. They were walking away from her and she didn't call out to attract their attention. Instead she continued to ponder the mystery of just *why* she and Jack had ended up as only friends and not as husband and wife. They'd been inseparable as kids. As they had grown older and Jack had started breaking hearts the length and breadth of south-east London, it was always her he'd returned to, saying she was his best girl and his best mate. And then she'd met Ted and was intrigued by his quiet manner and, next thing she knew, she was pregnant with Billy. 'Which just goes to prove that the quiet ones are the worst,' her mother had said darkly on being told the news. Her father, too, had been remarkably philo-sophical. 'Me and yer mother 'ad to get married a bit sharpish,' he had said, standing with his legs apart, the better to balance his beer belly, 'an' we've bin 'appy enough.' Mavis smiled to herself fondly at the memory. Dear Dad – all he asked of life was a hot meal on the table at the end of each day and the luxury of a steamingly deep bath on a Friday night.

She stepped off the Heath, crossing the road that flanked it, her smile fading. It had been Jack's reaction, though, not her parents' reaction, that had been crucial to her. And Jack's reaction had been appallingly indifferent. 'He seems like a good bloke,' he had said to her when she had told him the news. 'And he's a docker. Dockers always bring home a decent pay packet. You'll be all right there, Mavis, just as long as you don't give him the run-around.'

Even now, after all these years, she didn't know whether or not he had been covering up a hurt and disappointment as deep and monstrous as her own.

She turned into Magnolia Terrace, aware that even if he had been, the arrival of Christina Frank would have swiftly put paid to it. Her jaw tightened. Hitler had a lot of sins to answer for, and in her opinion, one of them was in being responsible for Christina fleeing Germany and seeking refuge with the Jenningses. Within days of moving in there, and without even trying, she had caught Jack's attention and he had fallen for her hook, line and sinker.

Was he still quite so besotted? Musingly she rounded the corner into the Square. He certainly hadn't been a hundred per cent happy on his last leave home. 'I can't work it out,' he had said to her time and time again. 'Something's wrong between me and Christina, but I'm damned if I know what it is. And if I don't know what it is, how the hell can I put it right?'

She had had no answer for him. Christina was a mystery there was no unravelling. Why, for instance, was she the only person in Magnolia Square not to have befriended Anna Radcynska? It didn't make sense. Anna had suffered the torments of hell at the hands of the Nazis, just as Christina's family apparently had, yet to the best of her knowledge Christina had never troubled to call on Anna to introduce herself. It was almost as if she didn't want anyone remembering what her past had been; as if she had blanked from her mind all memory of the family she had lost.

A faint sprinkling of rain dampened her face and she quickened her step. In Harriet's carefully tended garden, late flowering Michaelmas daisies jostled with the bronze pom-pom heads of chrysanthemums. In Anna's garden, a freshly planted japonica indicated that the surrounding nettles and weeds would soon be a thing of the past. She wondered who had planted it for Anna. Carrie, probably. Or Kate. The sky, which had been a hard pale blue when she was crossing the Heath, was now purpling to dusk. She looked down the Square, wondering if Billy and Beryl had let themselves into the house and had made themselves some drip and bread or jam and bread for their tea. If they hadn't, she'd get the chip pan out. She grinned to herself, recovering a bit of her old bounce. Egg and chips, a mug of tea, and *Variety Band-box* on the wireless. It wasn't exactly the way she would have chosen to spend the evening, but it had its compensations. She'd be able to go to bed early for one thing, and as her clocking-on time in the morning was six-thirty, an early night wasn't to be sneezed at.

As she walked past the Sharkeys', she saw that someone was seated on her garden wall. Someone masculine and uniformed and very, very tired-looking. She stopped dead in her tracks, terrified that her eyes were playing tricks on her. It couldn't be Ted. It couldn't. There would have been a telegram telling her when to expect him. A phone call via Mr Giles. The seated figure was probably an irate householder waiting to complain to her about Billy's apple scrumping or bicycle-chain filching.

The man raised his head, looked directly at her, and rose to his feet.

'Oh my God!' she whispered, and then, forgetting all her ambivalent feelings of a few moments ago, she began running towards him, shouting joyfully, 'Ted! *Ted!* Why didn't you let me know you'd be 'ome tonight? All I've got for yer tea is egg and chips!'

A grin cracked his tired face as he rose to his feet to meet her. 'So what's new, Mavis love? The last time you cooked a decent tea, 'Itler was just a strugglin' painter and decorator an' the Duke of Windsor was the Prince of Wales an' in short trousers!'

With a shout of laughter she hurtled into his arms, hugging him with all the strength she had. At last, nearly unsteady on his feet with tiredness, he held her away from him a little in order that he could kiss her. His had been a long war and a hard war. He'd fought what had seemed to be the length and breadth of Europe, and he never wanted to see Europe again. England would do for him, thank you very much. Home – that was all he wanted. And rest. Above all, he wanted rest.

'Let's stop givin' the Square a public display,' he said, raising his head from hers. 'Yer might 'ave only eggs an' chips fer tea, Mavis, but I'm ready for 'em. I 'aven't eaten fer so long, me stomach finks me froat's bin cut.'

Mavis blinked up at him. His kiss, for a reunion kiss, had left an awful lot to be desired. Her disappointment vanished as she saw the utter exhaustion in his face. 'What you need, Ted Lomax,' she said perceptively, 'is a scalding 'ot pint of tea with lashings of condensed milk in it. Come on, I'll put the kettle on and yer can get out of uniform. Yer can get out of it and never put the blinkin' thing on ever again!'

With a lop-sided grin, he picked up his kit-bag. No matter that he hadn't been home for anything other than short, and far too infrequent, leaves over the last six years, some things never changed. Apart from the bomb-site where the Helliwells' house had been, Magnolia Square hadn't changed. The houses in the northern half of the Square, nearest to the Heath, were still almost grandiosely Edwardian, the steps leading down from their front doors to their garden pathways, scrubbed and white-stoned. In the southern half of the Square – his half of the Square – there was the same air of cosy ramshackle shabbiness. And Mavis hadn't changed. She was still as fizzingly full of life as ever. He slid his free arm around her shoulders as they walked up their cracked front path together, hoping fervently that some of her irrepressible zest for life would rub off on him and make him feel halfway to human again.

'So where's our Billy and Beryl?' he asked half an hour later as he sat near the kitchen boiler, a pint mug of tea in his hands.

Mavis, who had stoically risen above the disappoint-ment of finding herself not in bed, but at the kitchen sink peeling potatoes for chips, said cheerily, 'Gawd knows. 'E comes an' goes when 'e likes. Beryl will be with Rose somewhere, or maybe with Daisy, the kiddie Kate took in. The three of them are always together.' She began slicing the peeled potatoes into chips. 'Harriet Godfrey calls them *The Three Graces*. She says it's the name of a painting by a bloke called Botticelli, and that it shows three lovely young women, which is what she says our

Beryl and Rose and Daisy are going to grow up to be.' She chuckled throatily as she began patting the chips dry with a tea-towel. 'Dad couldn't get the 'ang of it all. "Who's Botty-jelly when 'e's at 'ome?" he kept asking Harriet. "An' why don't he jus' paint a picture of our Beryl and Rose and their friend an' 'ave done with it?"'

Ted, who didn't know who the painter bloke was either, said impatiently, 'I fink I'll go out and look for the kids. I was 'opin' they'd be in the house when I walked in. I'd sort of imagined how it would be – the two of 'em runnin' to meet me and everyfink.'

Mavis plunged the chips into boiling fat and turned to face him, perceptively aware that he was suffering from a sense of anti-climax. 'You've bin imagining it all for too long,' she said, aware that his home-coming wasn't going to be without complications. 'Things never are as you imagine they're goin' to be. The kids'll be over the moon to see you, but they've got used to you not bein' 'ere. An' they're not little 'uns any more, like they were when you went away. Billy's thirteen and Beryl's nine. They're 'ardly ever in the 'ouse. Why should they be, when I'm workin' on the buses every hour God sends?'

Ted put his mug of tea down a little unsteadily on the kitchen table. He should have stayed the night in the transit camp, as he and all the others returning home fresh from overseas had been advised to do. That way he would have arrived in Magnolia Square showered and spruce and rested. But he hadn't been able to bear the thought of spending yet another night away from home, when home was so blessedly near, and the result was that he felt dead on his knees.

'Well, that'll soon change now I'm 'ome,' he said

reassuringly. 'I'll get my old job back down at the docks an' we'll soon be back in the old routine.'

Alarm flared through Mavis's eyes. No matter how unexciting her job was in comparison to the danger of her war work, at least it put good money in her pocket and gave her independence and got her out of the house. The 'old routine' hadn't been that hot, if she remembered rightly. Cooking, cleaning, being pregnant . . .

''Ang on a minute, Ted,' she said, deciding it would be best to tell him right from the beginning that things had changed on the home front and were never going to be quite the same again, 'I think you ought to know that—'

She was interrupted by the sound of the front door being flung back on its hinges. '*Mum! Mum!*' Billy shouted, racing through the house to the kitchen, Beryl hard on his heels. 'Are you in? Everyone in the Square is sayin' Dad's 'ome! Is it true? Is it . . .'

He rocketed into the kitchen and then stopped short, the blood draining from his face. 'Dad!' he said with a strangled sob. 'Oh, Dad! You *are* 'ome! You *are*!'

'Daddy!' Beryl squealed, dashing past Billy, throwing herself into his arms.

As they hugged and kissed and laughed, Billy remained immobile in the doorway. His dad was home! Not just for a leave, but home for good. It was wonderful and stupendous – and it was too much to take in. In a way he didn't understand, he felt suddenly frightened.

Over the top of Beryl's fair hair, his dad's eyes met his. 'I've missed yer, son,' Ted said simply, letting go of Beryl, aware of Billy's momentary emotional confusion.

Billy gave a choked gasp and then he was running,

running, running, tears streaming down his face as he threw himself into his dad's outstretched arms.

Mavis felt tears sting her eyes. What she had been about to say to Ted could wait till later. All that mattered for the moment was that his long dreamed-of homecoming was, at last, coming true.

Chapter Eighteen

'Where are we going today, Grandad?' Matthew asked, wriggling in happy anticipation on the Bentley's delicious-smelling, leather-covered rear seat.

Joss Harvey patted his great-grandson's hand and smiled down benevolently at him. He liked the fact that Matthew called him 'Grandad' and not 'Great-Grandad'. To have been called 'Great-Grandad' would have made him feel as old as Methuselah. 'It's too foggy a day for parks or zoos,' he said, glad to see that Matthew's mother had had the sense to wrap him up warmly against the nasty November weather. 'Instead, we're going to have a very special tea out. Tea at the Ritz. I used to take your daddy there on his first day home from school every half term. They do the biggest cream cakes in the world at the Ritz.'

Matthew beamed up at him happily. He loved his days out with his grandad. They were special days. Days full of treats and surprises. 'And toasted teacakes?' he asked eagerly. 'When Mummy takes me to Chiesemans we always have toasted teacakes.'

'I'm not sure about the toasted teacakes,' Joss replied as the Bentley purred down the Old Kent Road. 'Would smoked salmon and cucumber sandwiches do instead?'

Matthew wasn't sure what smoked salmon was. It sounded funny. His daddy smoked when he was doing the gardening or was working on the river, but he didn't smoke in the house. 'Gaspers', he called them. He rolled each one himself, his chocolate-dark fingers moving so fast and so neatly that Matthew never tired of watching. Then he would tuck the gasper behind his ear, where it nestled against hair so wirily tight and curly that it tickled Matthew's palms whenever he touched it, making him giggle.

The gasper was in readiness for when he took his 'toke'. Matthew liked tokes. They were the times when his daddy stopped working for ten minutes or so and made a mug of tea. He didn't make it like Mummy made it, in a teapot. Instead, he shook the tea-leaves into a big pint mug, dowsed them with boiling water, then spooned in condensed milk and a shake of sugar. 'And the next bit,' he had said the first time Matthew had ever watched him, 'is the secret bit. The bit that makes a *proper* mug of tea.' Wide-eyed, Matthew had watched him as he had put the mug back on the stove. 'Just to re-heat it,' his daddy had said. 'We don't want to stew it, we just want to bring out the richness.'

And Daddy's mugs of tea *were* rich. They would sit side by side on the back step, their hands around the steaming mugs of treacly, deep brown liquid, companionably surveying whatever work they had just completed, a newly planted bed of spring cabbages or newly seeded bed of broad beans or winter lettuce. And a toke didn't only mean tea and a cigarette. It meant fried egg or bacon in buttered bread so thickly sliced his mummy laughingly called them 'doorsteps'.

316

The Bentley purred around the Elephant and Castle and headed for Westminster Bridge. A group of children seated on the kerb playing 'Five stones' gazed after it open-mouthed, wondering if it belonged to the King or the Queen or the Prime Minister.

'The Ritz is near to a very good bookshop,' Joss said, Matthew's woollen-gloved hand still tucked in his. 'We'll call in at Hatchard's and see if we can buy you a really nice copy of *Wind in the Willows*. And then we'll pay a visit to Hamleys.'

'What's Hamleys?' Matthew asked, knowing it would be something nice; knowing it would be somewhere no-one else he knew had ever been.

Once again, his grandad's pigskin-gloved hand patted his. 'Hamleys is an Aladdin's Cave,' he said, his gruff voice gentle with love. 'Hamleys was your daddy's favourite place in all the world.'

Matthew liked it when his grandad talked to him of his other daddy, the daddy who had died before he had been born. His mummy kept a silver-framed photograph of him on the mantelpiece, and his new daddy said that his other daddy had been very brave and had died a war hero at a place called Dunkirk.

'Did you and my first daddy ever have tokes together, Grandad?' he asked as the Bentley slid to a halt outside the gracious splendour of the Ritz Hotel, Piccadilly.

'Tokes?' As Hemmings stepped out of the car to open the rear door for them, Joss stared down at Matthew, his brows beetling together in a slight frown. 'What is a toke, Matthew?'

'It's when you smoke a gasper,' Matthew said patiently, climbing out of the Bentley in Joss's wake, 'and drink tea that's been brewed in the mug and re-heated on the stove.'

Hemmings began to cough in a strangled manner. Joss was impervious. He had no intention of shutting Matthew up. He needed to pass on to Cyril Habgood as many details as possible about the undesirable, working-class aspect of Matthew's home life in order that Cyril could build up a watertight argument as to why Emmerson's application to adopt Matthew should be refused.

'And you have egg and bacon doorsteps with it,' Matthew continued blithely, skipping along at Joss's side as they crossed the pavement, and a commissionaire in a uniform even grander than Hemmings's uniform, held a door wide open for them. 'Doorsteps are when the bread is cut so thick you can—'

'Good afternoon, Mr Harvey,' the commissionaire said, touching his cap and wondering if he had heard aright.

Joss strode past him, grim-faced. Tokes indeed! Tea brewed in the mug! Doorstep sandwiches! The sooner Matthew was living with him and acquainted with wafer-thin smoked salmon sandwiches, Earl Grey and the Queen's English, the better!

'Maffew's home! Maffew's home!' Luke cried, scrambling down from his look-out post on the settee in front of the living-room window and running through into the kitchen to tell everyone.

Kate was in the middle of washing up the supper things. Leon was seated at the table, enjoying a mug of tea as he read the evening paper. Pru and Daisy were at the opposite end of the table, sticking pressed flowers into a scrapbook.

'And not before time,' Kate said dryly, reaching for a tea-towel and eyeing the clock.

There was a loud, sharp knock at the door and Leon's eyebrows rose, his eyes meeting Kate's. It was an adult knock. Was Joss Harvey at last paying them a personal call? He pushed his chair away from the table. 'I'll get it,' he said, rising to his feet. 'If Mr Harvey wants a word with anyone, he can have it with me.'

Pru prised a speedwell from blotting paper with a pair of tweezers, unaware of the tension the knock had aroused. As far as she was concerned, Matthew was simply returning from a nice day out with his great-grandad. Daisy, aware that Matthew's days out with his great-grandad weren't like normal outings with grandads, put down the scissors she had been about to cut a piece of sticky paper with, and looked from Kate to Leon. She didn't know *why* Matthew going out with his great-grandad was different to his going out with the grandad who had once lived with them and who now lived in Greenwich, but she knew it was. When Matthew was out with Great-Grandad Harvey, her mummy never laughed and teased quite as much as she usually did. And she always kept looking at the clock, impatient for it to be the time when Matthew would return, almost as if she were afraid that he *wouldn't* return.

She sat very quietly, her eyes on the open kitchen door and the corridor beyond that led through the house to the front door. She saw Leon open the door and Matthew charge into the hall, his cheeks flushed with excitement, a brown paper parcel clasped in his arms. Luke rushed to meet him, noisily demanding to know what the present was. Daisy wasn't interested in his reply. Her eyes were on the man at the door. It wasn't Great-Grandad Harvey. It was the man who drove his big motor car for him. He was carrying a box, a box so enormous his face could scarcely be seen peeping over the top of it.

'I can't help it if you think it inappropriate, mate,' she heard him saying to Leon. 'My job is simply to deliver it.' Awkwardly he thrust the box, which looked to be very heavy, at Leon and turned on his heel, striding back to the motor car.

'I've got a *Wind in the Willows* book *and* a train-set!' Matthew was saying to a round-eyed Luke. 'A big train-set! An *enormous* train-set! It's so big it's going to take up *all* the floor! It's so big even a big boy like Billy will want to play with it!'

With difficulty, Leon lowered the box to the floor. Daisy saw the look he gave her mummy. And she saw the look her mummy gave him back. A tight knot of anxiety began to form in her tummy. They didn't like it that Great-Grandad Harvey had given Matthew the train-set. They didn't want Matthew to have it. They wanted to give it back.

'Open it! Open it!' Luke was demanding, dancing up and down in impatience. 'Isn't jus' Maffew's train-set, Daddy! It's mine as well! Maffew says it's mine as well!'

'*And* the book,' Matthew added, shiny-eyed. 'The book is for *all* of us.'

'Did Great-Grandad Harvey say so?' Leon asked, his voice so neutral Daisy wondered if anyone but herself knew how unhappy Matthew's present had made him.

Matthew hesitated. His grandad certainly hadn't said

the book was for everyone, but he must have meant it for everyone or else it wouldn't have been fair.

'Not *'xactly*,' he said, mindful of the need to be truthful, 'but it *is* for Luke and Daisy as well. Truly.'

Once again Kate and Leon looked at each other, and Daisy was aware that her mummy was just as unhappy about the present as her daddy. Daisy didn't like it when her mummy was unhappy. Her mummy was the most special mummy in all the world. Long, long ago, so long ago that Daisy could barely remember it, she had had another mummy. She hadn't called her Mummy, though. She had called her Ma. And she had been frightened of Ma. Ma had smacked her and hurt her and left her alone in the dark, hungry and cold. Her mummy-Kate never smacked her or hurt her. She hugged her and kissed her and played games with her, and when she put her to bed at night she did so with giggles and tickles and cuddles.

Daisy was aware that, because her family had been killed in an air-raid, many people felt sorry for her. 'Poor little mite,' they said, 'her ma and pa and gran crushed to death when their 'ouse was bombed and only 'er saved.' Daisy had a secret. It was a secret she had never told to a living soul: she was *glad* the nasty Germans had bombed her house. Her pa had had a leather belt with a buckle on the end that he used to strap her with, and her gran had smelled of stale wee-wee and of other things that Daisy hadn't known the name of, and she had never interfered when Pa had strapped her or Ma had locked her in the coal cellar. Even thinking about that long-ago, far-off time made goose-bumps come up on her arms. Being orphaned was the very best thing that had ever happened to her, for if she hadn't been orphaned she wouldn't now have Mummy-Kate and Daddy-Leon to care for her and love her.

Every night, hugging her knees beneath the sheets of her crisply made bed, she promised God she would always, *always* be good, asking Him to never let anyone take her new mummy away from her, never, never, not ever!

'Where are we going to put it, Daddy?' Matthew was asking Leon in a fever of impatience. 'Can we get it out of the box and see how big it really is? Can we fit the tracks together? There are two engines so me and Luke can have an engine each, can't we?'

Leon looked across at Kate. 'We may as well, love,' he said, in a tone of resignation Matthew didn't understand. 'There'll only be another set of fresh problems if we don't.'

She nodded, equally unhappy at the gross extravagance of the present; of the way ownership of it could so easily set Matthew apart from Luke and Daisy; at the knowledge that it wasn't a one-off present, but the forerunner of many, many more.

'Blimey,' Pru said as she joined them, the speedwell safely secured in Daisy's scrapbook with tiny strips of see-through sticky paper. 'What's in the box? The crown jewels?'

Later, when the bare bones of the train set had been set out on the floor of the bedroom that had once been Carl's, and the children had finally been put to bed and Pru had gone out to meet Malcolm, Kate said as she put a pan of milk on the stove to boil, 'I'll speak to him about it, Leon. I'll tell Mr Harvey we don't want him giving Matthew such expensive presents.'

322

Leon's good-natured face was troubled. 'He won't like it,' he said perceptively as he stuffed a change of socks and a rolled-up sou'wester into his tommy-bag ready for the morning. 'He'll say that as Matthew's grandad it's his privilege to give him presents and, as he can afford expensive presents, that those are the kind he's going to give.'

'And Luke and Daisy?' Kate asked, spooning cocoa into two mugs. 'How are they supposed to feel? Matthew made it all right for them this time by saying the train-set and the book were for all of them, but you and I know that they weren't. And what's going to happen when Mr Harvey singles Matthew out in much bigger ways?'

Leon could tell by the tone of Kate's voice that her question wasn't an idle one, and that there was something she was working towards telling him, and that it was something he wasn't going to like one little bit. He crooked an eyebrow and waited.

Kate bit the corner of her lip. She had to tell him about Mr Harvey's plans for Matthew's education some time and it might as well be now. 'School,' she said at last. 'Mr Harvey wants Matthew to go to the same schools Toby went to.'

Leon pulled the drawstring tight around the top of his tommy-bag. Kate hadn't said that the schools in question were fee-paying schools, but she hadn't had to, it went without question. And fee-paying schools were schools for nobs' sons, not for working-class boys. 'It won't work,' he said, his face taut as he pushed the tommy-bag to one side. 'It's bad enough now, when it's only presents one child is getting that the others aren't, but to have one child going off to prep school, all togged up in a nifty uniform and mixing with children whose fathers are bankers and lawyers and doctors and diplomats, while the other two go to Blackheath and Kidbrooke where everyone's dad works on the river or in a factory—' He broke off, seeing in his mind's eye what would happen and not wanting to put what he saw into words.

As Kate poured boiling milk on to the cocoa, her hand was unsteady. 'It *might* work,' she said, willing him to understand, knowing all the problems there would be if, on this all-important issue, they were in disagreement. 'It might *have* to work.' She put down the pan and turned once again to face him. 'It's what Toby would have wanted for Matthew,' she said simply. 'And it's *education*, Leon. How can we refuse Matthew the chance of a first-class education?' She saw the misery in his eyes, and her heart went out to him. She knew all the things he was afraid of, because she was afraid of them too. She was afraid that a public school education would result in Matthew growing away from them as he grew up; that he would begin to become slightly ashamed of them, embarrassed not only by Leon's skin colour but by his occupation as well.

She put her fears behind her, saying starkly, 'Toby was never a snob, Leon. He was the nicest person you could ever wish to meet. And no matter what type of education Matthew receives, he's going to grow up like him. How could he fail to, when he's got you and me to teach him what the real values in life are?' She walked swiftly towards him, slipping her arms up and around his neck, her eyes pleading with him to understand. 'We can say "no" to expensive presents but we can't say "no" to an education that will enable Matthew to go to university

324

and to become whatever he wants to become. It wouldn't be fair.' She remembered Matthew's stout avowal that the presents he had been given were for Luke and Daisy as well. 'And as Matthew is very hot on fairness, we must be as well.'

His arms closed around her. She was right about the fairness bit. It was going to be difficult, though. It was going to be very, very difficult. 'I'll be glad when the adoption is finalized,' he said, the words coming from the bottom of his heart. 'At least then I'll be in a proper position to tell Joss Harvey where we'd like him to draw the line in indulging Matthew.'

He rocked her against him, feeling her heart beating against his, smelling the fragrance of her skin and her hair. The children were in bed asleep. Pru was at the cinema with Malcolm. 'Let's go to bed,' he said, the honey-dark timbre of his voice deepening in passionate need. 'Let me show you how much I love you, sweetheart. Let me show you how much I will always love you.'

'I love living with the Emmersons,' Pru said as, with a royal blue beret crammed down low over her ears and a matching scarf snug around the throat of her buttoned-up coat, she walked with Malcolm up gas-lit Magnolia Hill. It was nearly ten o'clock at night, and it was the first time she had ever been out so late. Her father would never have allowed it, but Kate had pointed out to Leon that the cinema didn't turn out till nine-thirty, and that if Pru and Malcolm were to see the big film through until the end, ten o'clock would be the very soonest Malcolm would be able to bring her home.

'I love it so much, I'm dreading the thought of Mum coming back home,' Pru continued, her hand tucked comfily in the crook of Malcolm's arm. 'Not that she wants to come back. She doesn't. But she can't stay away for ever, can she? And when she does come back, I'll have to move back home. She can't manage Dad on her own. He bullies her, and instead of standing up to him she lets him see that he frightens her and that only makes him worse.'

Malcolm looked down at the slightly-built figure hugging his arm. In the foggy darkness her heart-shaped face was resolute. She, he knew, would never allow herself to be bullied by Wilfred. Or by anyone else either. She was still only seventeen and as he thought of all she had endured, cooped up in number ten day after day in order to shield her mother from her father's unbalanced temper and lunatic ravings, his heart felt as if it were tightening within his chest. He wouldn't allow her to do it again, by God he wouldn't! He would see to it that neither she nor her mother set foot across the threshold of number ten again unless they did so willingly.

They were in Magnolia Square now, nearly at the Emmersons' gate. He stopped walking, drawing her round to face him. 'I think,' he said, looking down into a face that had been prettified by a borrowing of Kate's powder and rose-coloured lipstick, and feeling his heart tighten even further, 'I think it's about time your mum met mine.'

Pru's eyes widened. Malcolm's mum was a cut above her own mother. She was a magistrate and sat on committees and had a woman in to do her cleaning. 'I'm not sure they'd have too much in common . . .' she began doubtfully.

'Of course they would. They both know what it's like to be married to men who are fruit-cakes,' Malcolm said patiently, a plan beginning to form in the back of his mind. A plan that, if it worked, would free Pru and her mother from Wilfred for ever. He tried to concentrate on it, but it was hard. The lipstick Pru had borrowed made her lips look very full and very soft. Her hand was in his. There was no sound other than the hissing of the nearest gas-lamp. She was seventeen. He was twenty-eight. He wasn't old enough to be her father, but he was a substantial number of years her senior. She was far too young for him to play fast and loose with. But what if he wasn't playing fast and loose? What if he was very, very serious?

He felt a tightening of his stomach muscles. If he was, then there was something she had to be told. Something he hadn't voluntarily ever told anyone, ever before. 'Pru?' The tone of his voice had changed, and there was something in it, and something in the way that he was now looking at her, that held every single atom of her attention. 'Have you ever wondered why I was never conscripted?' he asked quietly, letting his hands fall and plunging them deep within his trouser pockets.

Pru blinked. She had, many times, but her anxieties over her father's mental breakdown and her mother's well-being had ensured it was a mystery that had never become all-important.

He chewed the corner of his lip, wondering how best to tell her. He didn't want to frighten her. And he knew now, beyond any shadow of doubt, that he didn't want to lose her.

'Yes?' she prompted, bewildered by the sudden change in him, remembering the many rumours there had been about just why he had never served in the Army or the Navy or the Air Force. She felt a shaft of incredulous anticipation. Perhaps, after all, Miriam Jennings had been right. Perhaps the desk job Malcolm was so quiet about *was* located in Whitehall. Perhaps he *had* been an intelligence officer of some kind! Perhaps he still was!

He said, still making no move towards her, 'Do you know what epilepsy is, Pru?'

Her eyes shot wide. Why on earth had he changed the subject of their conversation yet again? First they had been talking about her mother meeting his, then he had begun to tell her why he had never been conscripted, and now he was talking about epilepsy! 'Only that it's not very nice, and people who suffer with it fall down and have fits and froth at the mouth,' she said, wondering why on earth he wanted to know.

'They don't always,' he said, wondering if she would believe him.

Her eyes met his trustingly as she waited for him to get to the point. Epilepsy didn't interest her. What *did* interest her was why he had never been conscripted. There had been lots and lots of reserved occupations, of course, but most of them had been held by men who were middle-aged. 'Yes?' she prompted.

He lifted his shoulders in a slight, almost helpless shrug. 'I'm epileptic,' he said simply, knowing she would have to accept that stark truth before he could begin reassuring her by explaining to her exactly just what *kind* of an epileptic he was.

She stared at him, not, at first, understanding. When

he didn't qualify his statement, didn't shrug it off as some kind of joke, she said in confusion, 'But how can you be? You're not . . . you're not . . .' Hot, embarrassed colour stained her cheeks.

Malcolm knew exactly what it was she had been about to say. He dug his clenched hands even deeper into his pockets. 'Epileptics aren't freaks, Pru,' he said, keeping control over his voice with difficulty. 'They're not subnormal. They don't dribble at the mouth. They don't look peculiar.'

The colour in her cheeks deepened. Had it been so obvious what she had thought? And how must Malcolm now be feeling, having read her mind so clearly?

'I'm sorry,' she said awkwardly. 'Only it never occurred to me . . . I mean, you look so *fit* . . . I always thought you hadn't served in the services because . . . because . . .'

'Because I was a conscientious objector?' he said, finishing her sentence for her once again, knowing that his church work had led more than her to come to the same puzzled conclusion.

She shook her head. 'No. I thought . . . Miriam Jennings once said . . .' Despite the awfulness of him suffering from something which caused him so much misery, Pru couldn't help seeing the farcical side of the situation. 'We thought you were an intelligence officer,' she said, something very like laughter bubbling up in her throat.

Malcolm stared at her in incredulity. 'An *intelligence* officer? What in God's name would an intelligence officer have been doing in Blackheath and Lewisham for the duration of the war?' Over and above his incredulity was a relief so vast he felt as if it were swamping him. Pru wouldn't be seeing the funny side of the situation if his confession had frightened or disgusted her. She was going to take his epilepsy in her stride, just as she took everything else in her stride. And it wasn't as if he suffered *grand mal* attacks. He never lost consciousness. He never suffered anything more than sick, disorientating giddyness. The Army medical board's fear had been, of course, that the nature of his attacks would change. That his *petit mal*, usually only suffered by children, would develop into *grand mal*, and that he would suffer a disabling attack without warning. Well, he had never done so, and even if he *did* do so, Pru would regard him no differently than she regarded him now.

'Pru?' He took his hands out of his pockets, wondering why the hell he was suddenly so nervous. He was twenty-eight years old. He'd kissed girls before. But not a girl he now knew beyond any shadow of doubt he was in love with; a girl he would love for the rest of his life; a girl he intended making his wife. 'Pru? Would you mind if I kissed you?' he asked hoarsely and then, without waiting for her reply, he drew her gently into the circle of his arms and in the gas-lamp's golden glow, lowered his head to hers.

'What a lovely little bungalow,' Cecily Lewis was saying as she sat in state on a rather shabby sofa in Doris's sister's front room. 'I've always been partial to bungalows. You would have thought that Frank, being a flat-earther, would have been partial to them, too, but I could never get him to move into one. Our house was always too big for us, and now there's only me and

Malcolm rattling around in it, it seems vast.'

Doris sat on the edge of an easy chair in an agony of nervousness. Why had this intimidating woman called on her? Had Pru got into trouble? Why hadn't Pru warned her Mrs Lewis was going to descend on her? What was she supposed to say to her? She'd never had the knack of conversation, never been able to chat blithely about anyone and anything as Leah and Miriam and Hettie and Nellie did. And if she couldn't chat to the likes of Leah and Miriam and Hettie and Nellie, how was she supposed to chat to a woman whose white silk blouse and navy blue suit, worn with matching leather hand-bag and shoes, made her look like a lady mayoress?

Cecily Lewis, well aware of Doris's discomfiture, smiled disarmingly. 'I'm so pleased about Malcolm's friendship with Prudence,' she said sincerely. 'She's such a lovely girl. So bright and cheerful and thoughtful.'

Doris's teaspoon clattered in her saucer. Pru's friend-ship with Malcolm Lewis? What sort of friendship? Whatever sort it was, Wilfred wouldn't like it. If the Emmersons weren't keeping a close enough eye on Pru perhaps it was time she returned home to Magnolia Square. But if she returned home to Magnolia Square she would have to live with Wilfred again, and she didn't want to live with Wilfred again.

'Of course, I do appreciate how young Prudence is and that you are probably concerned about Malcolm's inten-tions,' Cecily continued, attempting to put Doris in the picture as painlessly as possible, 'but he has assured me they are scrupulously honourable.'

Malcolm hadn't, in fact, used the word 'honourable'. What he had said was that he wanted to marry Pru and

331

that he intended giving her an engagement ring on her birthday, which was Christmas Day.

'We're going to have to wait until she's twenty-one before we can get married, as her father certainly won't give his permission,' he had said pragmatically, 'but it will give me time to add to my savings. I'd like to buy a house in Magnolia Square. And it will give Pru time to get a bottom drawer together.'

'And she knows about . . . about your medical condition?' she had asked, avoiding the ugly word as she always avoided it.

'She knows I suffer from a mild form of epilepsy,' he had said cheerfully, 'and she knows my being an epileptic doesn't mean I'm mentally retarded.'

'But is the . . . is your medical condition the reason her father won't give permission for an earlier wedding?' she had asked unhappily.

He had shaken his head. 'It's because Wilfred Sharkey is mad as a hatter,' he had said, as if madness was of no consequence whatsoever. 'He Bible-bashes down at Lewisham clock-tower. All hell and harlots. He's as likely to give Pru permission to marry under-age as fly to the moon.'

While she had been coming to terms with this little gem of information, he had added, 'I thought you could help out where the problem of Wilfred is concerned. Pru's mother is mortified by what she sees as the shame of having a barmy husband. I thought if you told her about how you had coped when Father was at his worst it would help her see she's no need to feel ashamed. I also thought the two of you might get on rather well. It would be nice if you did. Especially as this house is so big and you'll soon be all alone in it, and neither I nor Pru want Doris returning to number two to live.'

'You mean you want me to invite Prudence's mother to come and live with me?' she had asked, in a daze.

'Why not?' He had shot her a cheeky grin, a grin that had been melting her heart and ensuring he got his own way with her ever since he had been a toddler. 'Think how convenient it will be for me and Pru, having only one visit to make when the children want to see their grannies!'

She said now to the fraughtly anxious woman sitting opposite her, 'I do hope we can become friends, Mrs Sharkey. We have so much in common.'

'We do?' There was incredulity in Doris's voice. How could she and this frighteningly self-assured, impeccably dressed woman have anything in common?

'Why, yes.' Cecily set her cup and saucer to one side and settled in for a confidence-sharing, friendship-forming chat. 'Our husbands, for one thing. My dearly loved late husband was *extremely* eccentric. He believed the earth was flat, and felt it his duty to proclaim his belief to all and sundry.'

Doris stared at her. Was this amazing woman saying to her what she thought she was saying to her? 'Even in the street?' she asked, leaning further forward on the edge of her seat.

'Even in the street,' Cecily affirmed. 'It was highly embarrassing at times, especially as he was a Justice of the Peace.'

Doris's jaw dropped open. A Justice of the Peace! And barmy! And she'd thought Wilfred was bad!

'I soon learned to take it in my stride, though,' Cecily

continued amiably. 'I told people, "I may be married to Frank, but I'm not joined to him at the hip. What he believes and does is his own affair. It's no reflection on me."'

Doris continued to gape. Was it really as easy as that to deal with gossip-mongers and sniggerers? Even more amazing, this smartly-dressed woman apparently knew of Wilfred's cracked behaviour and yet still wanted to be friends with her! Not since she had been young and single had she had a friend, and she had *never* had a friend so wonderfully self-assured and capable.

'Would you stay for another cup of tea?' she asked, hope and excitement beginning to burgeon deep in her tummy. 'And will you have a biscuit with it this time? They're home-made. Home-made biscuits are always much nicer, aren't they?'

'I wouldn't mind the recipe for these biscuits, Emily,' Leah said as she enjoyed her elevenses in Emily and Esther's cosy kitchen.

Emily's wrinkled face flushed with pride. Leah was Magnolia Square's acknowledged queen as far as baking was concerned, and to be asked for a recipe by Leah was praise indeed. 'It's six ounces of self-raising flour to two ounces of porridge oats, three ounces of sugar and four ounces of margarine that's been melted with a tablespoon and half of Tate & Lyle's golden syrup,' she said, knowing that she needn't write it down, that as it was a recipe Leah would remember it for life after only one hearing. 'The last thing to add is a half teaspoon of bicarb of soda that's been scalded in a teaspoon of hot water.'

'Well, that's simple enough,' Leah said, determining to make some that afternoon if her cache of sugar would run to it. 'What are you doing for Christmas? Are you and Esther going to spend it with Nellie?'

'With Nellie *and* Harold *and* Anna,' Esther said from her wheelchair. 'It will be Harold's first Christmas at home in six years. Nellie's expecting him any day now. He's sailing from Colombo, in Ceylon, aboard the *Empire Pride*. And perhaps Jack will be home for Christmas as well,' she added hopefully. 'Do you know if Christina's heard anything?'

'If she has, she's keeping it very close to her chest,' Leah said darkly. 'No-one gets anything out of her these days, not even me.'

Emily laid down her knitting. 'It can't be easy for her at the moment,' she said gently, 'not with the papers all full of what is happening at Nuremberg. The evidence being given at those trials is terrible, truly terrible.'

They were silent for a moment, thinking of the monsters standing trial at Nuremberg for crimes against humanity. Goering and Hess and Ribbentrop and Fritz Sauckel, the slave labour overlord, and a score of others.

At last Leah said emotionally, 'Christina thinks her mother and grandmother could be still alive. That's why she's so quiet and strange these days. We've all told her it's impossible, but she won't listen to us. She just keeps saying they could be alive and that if they are, she's going to find them.'

Emily and Esther stared at her aghast, and then Emily said slowly, 'Her grandmother was your childhood friend, wasn't she, Leah? Do you have anything that belonged to her? Anything she had worn?'

335

Leah's eyes widened. 'Moshambo?' she asked. 'Are you thinking your Moshambo might be able to contact them?'

'I'm thinking it's about time I tried to help dear Christina in the only way I know,' Emily said, much on her dignity as she always was when her spiritualist skills were being questioned. 'Moshambo is wise and all-seeing and has never let me down yet, not even when the people seeking his help have not been true believers in him.'

'Well, I ain't a true believer,' Leah said frankly, 'but if he settles the question of whether Jacoba and Eva are alive or dead, I will be. Now, what would be of best use? A necklace of Jacoba's I once swopped one of mine with her for, or a handkerchief?'

'The necklace,' Emily said, her aged face alight at the thought of renewing contact with her indomitable Indian spirit-guide. 'Moshambo has a natural affinity with beads.'

Chapter Nineteen

'It's highly irregular, of course,' Bob Giles was saying grave-faced to Christina and Carl.

They were in Carl and Ellen's tiny Greenwich kitchen, Coriolanus sprawled beneath the table they were seated around, Macbeth curled on a Windsor chair which Ellen had made comfy by means of a tie-on seat cushion, Hector hogging pride of place in front of a well-stoked wood-burning stove.

'Red Cross officials are not travel couriers,' Bob continued, his eyes holding Christina's, 'but under the circumstances—'

'The circumstances being your willingness to co-operate with them when a home was needed for Anna?' Carl interrupted queryingly, wondering just how Bob had managed to pull such powerful strings.

'Partly,' Bob admitted, well aware that if he hadn't put himself, and the Parish, at the disposal of the Red Cross over the question of housing a displaced person, he would have had no contacts to approach over the problem of how best to help Christina enter Germany. 'Miss Marshall, a Red Cross official, leaves for Berlin on the seventh of December,' he continued, hoping fervently that neither he nor Carl would live to regret the plans now being made. 'You'll be able to travel with her as far as Cologne, Christina. After that you will be on your own.'

'She doesn't have to be on her own,' Carl said, as sombre-faced as his friend. 'If Miss Marshall is agreeable, I will accompany Christina and—'

Christina shook her head, the dark silky wings of her hair falling forward to frame her face. 'No,' she said quietly but with utter conviction. 'That wouldn't be fair, Carl – not to you or to Ellen.'

'Ellen is as appalled as we are,' he said, speaking for Bob as well as himself, 'at the thought of you travelling through Germany alone.' His hands were clasped on the table in front of him, and the knuckles whitened as he clasped them even tighter, saying, 'It isn't only the personal trauma you're going to suffer at being back in Germany, surrounded by a people that either supported Hitler's Jewish policy or passively acquiesced to it, that's worrying us, Christina. It's the present situation that exists there. Germany is a defeated country in a state of chaos. According to the Red Cross, the entire population is on the brink of starvation. The roads will be choked with hungry refugees, and in travelling south from Cologne to Heidelberg you won't be travelling through a British-occupied zone, but an American-occupied zone.' Behind his spectacles, his grey-blue eyes were deeply troubled. 'It will be far better if I travel with you and—'

'No.' The word was quietly spoken but was quite unequivocal. 'This is something I must do alone. It's something I *have* to do alone.'

There was a long, heavy silence. At last Bob Giles said,

deeply unhappy, 'The Red Cross have supplied me with names and contact numbers of officials operating in the French zone. If you should be in need of urgent help they will do their best to provide it.'

'And while you are away I'll keep on pursuing the leads we have been given from New York,' Carl said, taking off his spectacles and squeezing the bridge of his nose to relieve the terrible tension that was building up over his eyes. 'There is a Berger on the list of Jewish prisoners who survived Buchenwald. I think it's unlikely your grandmother would have been shunted all the way from Heidelberg to Buchenwald but, as anything is a possibility, I'll write for whatever further information might be available.'

'Thank you.' Tears of gratitude glinted on the thick sweeps of Christina's eyelashes. 'I shall never know how to thank the two of you for all the help you've given me. And when I come back from Germany I'll have my mother and grandmother with me, I know I will.'

Neither man spoke. There was nothing they could say. All they could do was pray she returned safely, and that when she did so, her obsession would have been laid to rest.

'She's really going?' Carrie asked Kate, wide-eyed.

Kate nodded, holding her shopping basket at a convenient angle so that Carrie could shoot potatoes into it straight from her weighing-scale scoop. 'She leaves tomorrow. Dad isn't happy about it. He feels terribly responsible.'

'Why?' Wearing woollen gloves with the fingers cut off, Carrie expertly tipped the potatoes into the basket.

'He wasn't the one who got the Red Cross to lend a hand, was he? That was Mr Giles.'

'He doesn't think Christina would ever have thought of returning to Heidelberg if he hadn't helped and encouraged her to look for her mother and grandmother,' Kate said, keeping an eye on Matthew and Luke who, coated and scarved and gloved against the December cold, were hovering hopefully in front of the nearby bakery stall. 'And he thought if she ever *did* return, she'd allow him to go with her.'

Carrie's eyes widened even further. 'Blimey!' she said, blowing on her red raw fingers to warm them up a little. 'Can you imagine what the gossips would have made of that? Hettie would have a field day!'

'She's been having a field day ever since Ruth moved into the vicarage with a wedding ring on her finger,' Kate said dryly. 'According to Ruth, every time she so much as passes the time of day with Hettie, Hettie pitches in with a remark as to how the first Mrs Giles did things differently, the inference being that Constance also did things very much better.'

'It could be worse,' Carrie said with a grin. 'It could be Nellie who disapproves of her. Then she really *would* have a battle on her hands!'

'And so you see, I had to come and put you in the picture,' Ruby Miller, Nellie's niece and the Emmersons' solicitor, said several hours later as she sat with Leon and Kate in their sitting-room. A coal fire was burning. The children were in bed. Hector was asleep on the hearth-rug, his head resting on his paws. Ruby was seated in the winged-back chair that had been Carl's favourite chair

340

for reading and nodding off in. Kate and Leon were seated side by side on a sofa, its shabbiness disguised by pristinely white, prettily hand-embroidered antimacassars.

'I don't quite understand.' Leon's dark rich voice was taut. His hand tightened on Kate's and she knew that he was lying. He did understand. He understood all too well. 'Are you telling us that Joss Harvey has lodged an objection to my application to adopt Matthew on the grounds of my skin colour?'

Ruby nodded and flicked her cigarette stub into the roaring flames of the fire. With hair dyed a mat, dull black and lips and nails painted a scarlet that would have done credit to Mavis, she looked as unlike a solicitor as it was possible to imagine. ''Fraid so,' she said in her deceptively laconic manner. 'And it's an objection the judge might well be sympathetic to, given Joss Harvey's clout.'

'But Leon is Matthew's stepfather.' Kate protested, a familiar feeling of sick dread beginning to churn deep in the pit of her stomach. 'Nothing can alter that. And if he's Matthew's stepfather, it's only sensible that he should be his legal father as well!'

'Where skin colour's concerned, common sense doesn't have a look-in,' Ruby said, crossing nylon-clad legs. 'Ask any black GI.'

'What must we do?' A pulse had begun to throb at the corner of Leon's strong jawline. 'Whatever it is . . . whatever it takes . . .'

'Leave it to me,' Ruby said succinctly, 'that's all you can do.' She bit the corner of her lip. There was something else they had to be told, something that was going to cause them added anxiety and heartache. Reluctantly, she said, 'If the courts decide Joss Harvey's objection is valid, then I think it's safe to say he'll immediately slap in another custody application. And that isn't all.' Her eyes darkened with compassion for them. 'Your joint application to adopt Daisy is also likely to be refused. Sorry, my loves, but there it is.'

Kate's face drained of blood. She'd lived with the fear that Joss Harvey would again seek to obtain custody of Matthew for a long time, but she had never, ever, considered that she might lose Daisy. And that's what would happen if they were judged unsuitable to be her adoptive parents. They would be judged to be unsuitable as foster parents as well, and Daisy would be taken away from them.

'Oh God!' She pressed her free hand hard to her mouth. 'Oh *dear* God!'

'No-one's going to break my family up!' Leon's rage was white hot. 'No-one's going to take our children away from us! Not Joss Harvey! Not the Council! No-one!'

Ruby cleared her throat. 'Where Matthew's concerned, it's not all doom and gloom,' she said, taking another cigarette out of its packet. 'Joss Harvey's attempted abduction of Matthew when he was a baby will go against him in a custody application. The fact that he is Matthew's *great*-grandfather, not his grandfather, will also count against him. Or it will by the time I've finished with him.' She searched in her jacket pocket for her cigarette lighter. 'And though he's only as old as the average grandfather, and fit as the proverbial bull, I'll milk the age factor for all it's worth.' She paused for a moment, lighting her cigarette. A pulse was hammering at Leon's jaw-line. Kate's now clenched knuckles were

342

white. With a scarlet talon, Ruby removed a fleck of tobacco from her tongue and said, 'However, although I might very well be able to stop Joss Harvey from being allowed legal custody of Matthew, it doesn't mean to say I'm going to be able to stop him preventing Leon from adopting Matthew. And if that happens . . .'

Kate gave a choked sob. If that happened, then Daisy might very well be taken away from them. Leon's arm was comfortingly around her shoulder as she said in a voice so cracked and hoarse it was scarcely recognizable. 'When is the hearing, Ruby?'

Ruby hesitated. It was a hell of a date. 'The twenty-fourth of December,' she said reluctantly, knowing that if it didn't go their way it was going to be a nightmare of a Christmas.

'I don't want a night out on the town,' Ted Lomax said apologetically, sticking a poker into the base of the smouldering fire and lifting it, so that a draught of air fed it and it burst into flames. 'I've been away from home for six years, Mavis. I want to stay in and enjoy my own fireside, not go roaming the West End.'

'It doesn't have to be the West End,' Mavis said, abandoning all hope of Piccadilly's bright lights. 'We could go down to the Social Club in Lewisham. There'll be lots of your old mates down there.'

He sat back in his armchair, a thin-faced man of thirty-four who felt fifty-four. 'Not for me, love – not tonight. I just want to be at home. What about some toast? The fire's going a treat now.'

Mavis was about to suggest that they at least walk the few dozen yards down to The Swan, but then thought better of it. What would be the point, with Ted as sociable as a monk? 'Toast it is then,' she said, giving in with as much good grace as she could muster. It wasn't easy. It wasn't as if his refusal to go out was a one-off. They hadn't been out on the town together once since his return home.

She mooched into the kitchen and took the lid off her enamel bread bin. She'd always joked about Ted being a fire and pipe man, but it was now so literally the truth that it wasn't remotely funny any more. She lifted a loaf out of the bin and put it on the bread board. What did the future hold for the two of them if Ted wouldn't even go out for a friendly drink on a Friday or a Saturday night? Ever since the war had ended she had been bored and now, with her husband safely home she was, God help her, more bored than ever. A feeling of shame washed over her. Ted had had a hard war. There had been no sunning himself in cosy little postings. He had been in the thick of the fighting almost continuously, and however unlikely-looking a hero he was, he *was* a hero and he had a medal to prove it.

She looked at the slices of bread she had carved and realized she had carved far too many. With a shrug she returned two of them to the bread bin. If Billy didn't have them with jam on in the morning for his breakfast she'd make a bread pudding out of them. Depression settled heavily on her shoulders. She wanted more to look forward to than the dubious joys of making bread puddings. She reached for the toasting-fork, remembering the Mormon-missionary-looking young man who had invited her out some time ago, and who now travelled on her bus route every chance he got. Is that what she wanted? The glamour and excitement of being taken out and wined and dined? Even before she had finished asking herself the question, she knew the answer. When it came to men, there was only one who could seriously tempt her off the straight and narrow, and he didn't resemble a Mormon missionary. He resembled Clark Gable at his most masculine. She loaded a tray with the plate of bread, the toasting-fork, a butter-dish and a knife. What would happen when Jack came home? Would he and Christina sort out their differences? And if they didn't?

She stared at her reflection in the darkened glass of the kitchen window. If they didn't, chances were it would have no effect on her own relationship with Jack. She had put the kibosh on that years ago, when she had so impetuously fallen for Ted and found herself pregnant. And her having fallen for Ted hadn't ruined her life in any major way. They were far happier together than many couples she knew. Before he had enlisted he had always brought his pay packet home, putting it unopened on the kitchen table every Friday night. He was never violent in drink and never knocked her around. They had two grand kiddies and they had always been satisfyingly compatible in bed.

She lifted the tray, walking through into the sitting-room with it, her habitual good humour reasserting itself. Where bed was concerned, nothing had changed, thank God. A grin touched the corners of her mouth. When they'd had their toast, she'd suggest an early night. If he wouldn't go out, they could at least make the most of staying in!

*   *   *

'To tell you the truth, I don't feel like going swimming this evening,' Leon said to Danny as they met at their regular Thursday night meeting place on the corner of the Square and Magnolia Hill. 'I feel like something a lot more violent.'

Danny tucked his rolled-up towel and his swimming trunks a little more securely beneath his arm. 'Yer mean boxing?' he said, his eyes lighting up. 'We could nip over to the Enterprise north of the river. It's a top-notch boxing club if yer fancy a proper work-out.'

'I fancy punching the hell out of something,' Leon said grimly. 'Preferably Mr Joss bloody Harvey.'

'You imagine yer punch-bag is old man 'Arvey, I'll imagine mine is my gaffer at the bloody biscuit factory,' Danny said, who knew all about the spokes Joss Harvey was putting in the wheels of Leon's application to adopt Matthew. 'Did yer know I was once an Army boxin' champion? Light-welterweight. There was no-one to touch me. If yer fancyin' a work-out, Leon, yer've come to the right man!'

'Christmas trees!' Albert stared at Miriam in stupefaction. 'Don't yer think I've enough on my mind, Christina jaunting off to Germany in the mornin' as if it was no more than a charabanc trip to Brighton, without yer wantin' me to go out in the dark searching for bloomin' Christmas trees!'

'Yer don't 'ave to search for 'em, I know exactly where they're growin',' Miriam said, refusing to think about Christina's imminent departure in case she broke down and never put herself back together again. 'There's two trim little conifers growing near the Ranger's House on the 'Eath. If yer take a bucket and a spade yer can 'ave 'em back 'ere in two shakes of a donkey's tail. We can 'ave one of 'em for ourselves and our Carrie can 'ave the other. Now, are yer goin', or are you just goin' to stand lookin' stupid all night?'

'Your dad's going to come with me when I go to meet Miss Marshall in the morning,' Christina said, sitting in Kate's cheery kitchen, a mug of milky cocoa on the table in front of her. 'It's kind of you and Carrie to want to come with me as well, but I think the fewer people there are with me, the better Miss Marshall will like it.'

'But you can't just slip away as if you're going on a . . . on a . . .'

'Day trip to Brighton?' Christina finished for her, a rare smile touching her mouth. 'That's what Albert says, but really it's the best way. I don't want a song and dance made out of my leaving. People like Miss Marshall don't have hordes of friends seeing them off, do they?'

Kate wrapped the last of the sandwiches she had been making in grease-proof paper and put them in Leon's tommy-bag, ready for the morning. 'People like Miss Marshall are members of a worldwide, official organization,' she said, her voice a little unsteady. 'You aren't, Christina. How are you going to travel from Cologne to Heidelberg? Where are you going to stay when you get there? How are you going to get back to England?'

'I don't know,' Christina said truthfully. 'But thanks to Mr Giles I have money and I'll manage.' Her eyes were fiercely resolute. 'Germany is going to be full of people doing exactly what I shall be doing, Kate.'

Kate regarded her with rising anxiety. If Christina did

find her mother and grandmother, would they be allowed into England with her? Even if they were, the paperwork might take weeks, months even. Would Christina remain with them in Germany while their paperwork was being processed? And if there was no paperwork to process, if entry was refused, what would Christina do then? Would she feel unable to leave her mother and grandmother? Would she stay with them and never return to Magnolia Square ever again?

Feeling nauseous and not knowing whether it was due to her escalating sense of foreboding where Christina's return to Germany was concerned, or to her now confirmed pregnancy, she pulled a chair away from the table and sat down. There was something she had to ask Christina, and she was terribly afraid that she already knew what her answer was going to be.

'Have you told Jack, Christina? Dad is under the impression that you've been keeping Jack informed all along as to what the two of you have been doing, but you haven't been, have you?'

Christina reached out for her mug of cocoa, her eyes avoiding Kate's. 'No,' she said at last. 'I've tried, but it's so difficult. We've had hardly any time on our own together, and in the time we have had . . .' She lifted her shoulders in a helpless, hopeless gesture. 'In the time we have had, Jack hasn't made it easy for me to talk to him about such things. He doesn't seem to have any idea of how I might be feeling. Not only about *meine Mutter* and *Grossmutter* but about other things also.'

'Other things?' Kate asked, her sense of foreboding soaring off the Richter scale, wondering how her father and Bob Giles were going to react when they knew;

wondering what on earth was going to happen if Jack returned home whilst Christina was still in Germany. 'What other things?'

'How I feel at having married in an Anglican church,' Christina said, her eyes at last meeting Kate's. 'How I feel at having turned my back on my religion and my culture.'

It was so totally unexpected, so terrible in all it implied, that Kate sucked in her breath. 'Oh my dear heaven,' she whispered devoutly, 'and you've been keeping all this from Jack? He has no idea of your feelings? None at all?'

Christina shook her head. 'He thinks of me as being a south-London girl,' she said bleakly, 'but I'm not, Kate. I'm a German Jew, and tomorrow I am going to return to Germany.' Her face was set and pale, her eyes anguished. 'I have to return. Not only to find my mother and grandmother, but to find the person I used to be. The person I want to be again.'

'It's all a bit deep for me, sweetheart,' Leon said later that night as they lay in each other's arms in the cosy comfort of their feather bed. 'Are you trying to say that Christina feels as if she's lost her identity? And that it's living in England for so long that's made her feel that way?'

'That and other things,' Kate said, too disturbed to be able to sleep. 'And I think it's mainly the other things that are so deeply troubling her. She feels she's turned her back on her Jewishness by marrying Jack, especially by having married him in an Anglican church. The worst of it is, Jack has no idea she feels that way.'

'Then perhaps someone should tell him,' Leon said dryly. 'He can't help her come to terms with something he doesn't know about, can he?'

They lay silent for a little while, staring into the darkness, drawing comfort from their closeness.

'Danny's having a hard time of it as well,' Leon said at last, his mouth close to the fragrant-smelling silkiness of her hair. 'He hates his work down at the biscuit factory.'

'I know,' Kate said, remembering everything Carrie had told her, 'but what else can he do? He's never been apprenticed to anything, has he?'

'No, more's the pity.' Leon thought of his own father and of how he had taken him, when he was fourteen, down to Waterman's Hall in Billingsgate and had him indentured as an apprenticed lighterman. A smile touched his full-lipped mouth. He'd had to take oaths of loyalty to his sovereign and the company, promising 'to learn his Art and to Dwell and Serve upon the said River Thames'. It had opened up a grand way of life to him and was an action he'd never regretted.

'Danny's a tough little boxer,' he said musingly. 'He loves the ring the way I love the river. We were over at the Enterprise tonight and the manager asked him if he'd like to earn himself a bit of extra cash by acting as a regular sparring partner for the big boys. If the Enterprise were this side of the river, I think he'd do it.'

'What boxing clubs are there this side of the river?' There was a speculative note in Kate's voice. Boxing wasn't a sport that had ever attracted her, but if it was something Danny felt passionate about, something that would restore his self-esteem . . .

'There's a whole wodge of them down the Elephant

and Castle way,' Leon said, pulling her even closer against him as she lay in the crook of his arm. 'But the best clubs are the Enterprise and the Langham, and they're both in the East End.'

'And there isn't a boxing club locally? In Blackheath or Lewisham or Greenwich?'

'Not worth talking about. Nothing that would attract the big boys.'

'Then perhaps there should be.' Their own terrible problem of the impending adoption hearing was temporarily forgotten. Excitement and certainty gripped her. 'And if it isn't possible for Danny to own it, he could at least manage it!'

Leon pushed himself sharply up on one elbow, looking down at her in the darkness, stunned by the brilliance of her idea. A local boxing club! It would be just the thing for kids like Billy. Malcolm Lewis would be interested in such an idea. He was always complaining of a lack of suitable activity for his scouts. The landlady of The Swan would definitely be interested. A local boxing club would put her pub on the map in a big way.

'There'll be a problem getting suitable financial backing . . .' he said, trying to exercise a little common sense and caution.

'No there wouldn't.' In the velvety darkness her eyes met his, her certainty absolute. 'Jack will back it. Jack's never had a problem finding money. And a boxing club will be just up his street.'

Leon stared down at her, his admiration knowing no bounds. He didn't know Jack very well, but from everything he'd heard about him, he knew she was spot on. 'And if there's a problem finding suitable premises, we

351

can use the back rooms at The Swan,' he said, as utterly sure of co-operation from that quarter as she was of Jack's. A grin split his face. 'Hell, Kate! We may not have solved our own problems, and we can't solve Christina's, but I think we've solved Danny's!'

Her arms slid up and around his neck. 'Then let's celebrate,' she said with husky seductiveness. 'I love you, Mr Emmerson. I love you with all my heart.'

There was adoration in his eyes and in his voice as he eased his weight on to her willing, supple body. 'And I love you, Mrs Emmerson.' His mouth was the merest fraction from hers.

'Always?'

'For ever.'

'I must see Christina!' Emily Helliwell announced agitatedly as she stood on the threshold of number eighteen, a riot of variously coloured wool scarves around her throat, her coat so hastily buttoned not one of the buttons was in the right button-hole.

'Lord 'elp you, Emily, 'ow can you?' Miriam's eyes were red from weeping. 'She left this morning and the Lord only knows when she's going to return!'

'Left?' Emily blinked. 'Left for where? It's most important that I see her, Miriam. I have a message for her from Moshambo. He says that her mother and grandmother are—'

'Germany!' Miriam wailed, a fresh flood of tears streaming down her face. 'She's only gorn back to bloody Germany! I told Albert 'e wasn't to let 'er go! Wot if she never comes back, Emily? Wot then?'

'Germany?' Emily's voice was little more than a croak.

'Oh dear, oh dear. Oh, but that's terrible news. That's the worst news I've heard since Moshambo told me what a mistake Mr Churchill was making in 1942, when he ordered the raid on Dieppe!'

'It ain't the worst news I've ever 'eard,' Miriam said, one hand pressed to her heart, her apronned bosom heaving. 'The worst news I've ever 'eard was five minutes ago when Mr Giles came and told me 'e'd 'ad a telephone call from Jack! 'E said that Jack was at Charing Cross station, Emily! That 'e's goin' to be 'ome in 'alf an hour! Wot's goin' to 'appen then, that's wot I want to know? Who's goin' to tell 'im 'is wife is on 'er way to Germany? The bloody Dieppe raid won't be a patch on this hoo-ha, Emily! It's goin' to be like the bloody Blitz all over again!'

Chapter Twenty

'How was I to know she hadn't told Jack?' Bob Giles was saying in horror-struck tones to Ruth. 'Such a thing never even occurred to me!' He ran his fingers through his still thick hair. 'Carl can't know either. And as Carl is tucked away down in Greenwich, I'm the one who is going to have to break the news to Jack.'

Ruth regarded him gravely. Like Kate, she had long doubted whether the encouragement he and Carl had been giving Christina was wise. And she certainly hadn't thought helping Christina to return to Germany was wise. It had been the act of a couple of middle-aged, naïve romantics. 'Perhaps it isn't too late for him to catch up with her?' she suggested without too much hope.

'It's far too late.' Bob's dishevelled hair stuck out around his head like an untidy halo. 'She and Miss Marshall and the Red Cross supplies will be halfway across the Channel by now, and how could he get travel permits?' For the first time, he realized the enormity of his and Carl's action. What on earth had they been thinking of? More to the point, what had *he* been thinking of? He was a clergyman, for goodness sake! He was supposed to be a man of wisdom and sense.

They were in the kitchen. Ruth had been in the middle of making scones and she dusted the flour off her hands, saying, 'Christina was so determined to return to Germany that she would have found a way of getting there with or without help from you and Carl. At least by arranging she travel out with a Red Cross official, you've guaranteed she'll arrive there safely.' She stepped towards him and kissed him lovingly on his cheek. 'Don't be too hard on yourself, darling. Jack can't blame you for Christina's obsession. He's just going to have to try and understand it . . .'

'Emily wants a word with you, Vicar!' Hettie shouted from the hallway where she was arranging sprigs of winter jasmine in a vase on the hall table. 'Shall I send her through?'

Bob groaned and ran his hand through his hair yet again. He couldn't get involved in a discussion with Emily at the present moment. He had to meet Jack off the train at Blackheath Station. He had to make quite sure that he was the one who broke the news to him about Christina. The thought of what would happen if Jack marched breezily down to number eighteen and was given the news by Miriam, made the hair stand up on the back of his neck.

'No, I'm coming out into the hall!' he shouted back, adding hurriedly to Ruth, 'I'm going to have to go straight out. Unless I get over to the station immediately, I'm going to miss him and then the situation will be even worse. Appease Emily for me. Make her a cup of tea. Give her a scone.' He strode out into the hallway, saying as Emily rushed towards him, 'I'm sorry, Emily. I can't stop and talk. An emergency has cropped up. Ruth will

355

make you some tea and I believe there are some scones—'

'But Mr Giles, you *must* stop and talk to me,' Emily protested, her thin-boned hands fluttering agitatedly. 'Something terrible has happened! Christina has gone to Germany and Moshambo has just told me that her mother and her grandmother are—'

The front door slammed behind him. Hettie's eyes were the size of gob-stoppers. In all the long years she had known Bob Giles, she had never known him display such a common lack of courtesy. What on earth was the emergency? Was Wilf Sharkey making a prune of himself again down in Lewisham? And what did Emily mean by saying Christina had gone to Germany? Surely she meant that Christina had *come from* Germany, which was a fact everyone had known for the last ten years.

'I'll put the kettle on,' she said to Ruth, avid for a gossip that would answer both questions. 'I've finished the flowers and I could do with a cup of tea myself. Now, what was it you were saying about Germany, Emily? You're not beginning to ramble, are you? You do know the war's over?'

'That's Jack Robson coming out of the station,' Doris informed Cecily Lewis.

They were in Cecily's little Austin *en route* to her home in Blackheath Vale. A home that Cecily had insisted was, from now on, Doris's home as well. The hastily packed shabby suitcase she had taken with her when she had gone to stay with her sister in Essex, lay snugly on the back seat. Cecily had suggested that they return to number ten for more of her possessions, but Doris hadn't wanted to do so. Returning to number ten meant running the risk of confronting Wilfred, and she didn't want to confront Wilfred ever again.

'It's strange seeing Jack in civvies,' she said as Cecily slowed down to let a horse-drawn coal-cart turn left, and Jack began striding up Tranquil Vale towards the Heath. 'He was in the Commandos. Wilfred said the Commandos deserved him. He didn't mean it as a compliment though,' she added, in case Cecily should think Wilfred had ever had his reasonable, pleasant moments. 'He thought Jack was wild as sin and that the Commandos were a bunch of hooligans.'

Cecily lifted her eyes briefly from the road ahead and took note of the broad-shouldered young man striding athletically abreast of them on the pavement. He was certainly head-turningly handsome. There was something else about him as well. A careless, very attractive self-assurance. An amused smile touched Cecily's mouth. Unless she was very much mistaken, Jack Robson possessed that almost insolent dare-devil quality her Jewish friends called *chutzpah*. It was no wonder Wilfred Sharkey hadn't had a good word to say about him.

'Wilfred never had anything nice to say about any of our neighbours,' Doris continued, turning her wedding ring round and round on her finger. 'He never had anything nice to say about anyone.'

'It doesn't matter now, Doris.' Cecily returned her attention to the road in front of her. 'You don't have to live with him again. Not if you don't want to.'

Doris shuddered. She didn't want to. Dr Roberts had visited her in Essex and tried to persuade her to return home, saying that over the last few weeks there had been a marked improvement in Wilfred's condition, and that

357

there were now times when he was completely rational. It had been no temptation to her at all. What Dr Roberts and Mr Giles didn't seem to understand was that Wilfred was almost as bad when he was rational as he was when he was potty. She'd lived with him for years and she'd lived without him for weeks and she knew which she preferred.

'I *don't* want to,' she said in answer to Cecily's last remark, adding with a flare of vehemence that sent Cecily's eyebrows flying into her hair, 'I don't want to live with the old sourpuss ever again!'

'Kate! Kate! Are you in?' Emily stepped inside Kate's spick and span hallway. 'Mr Giles won't listen to me and . . .' There were voices coming from the kitchen. A peeved, childish voice and a patient, adult voice.

'I can't explain why, Matthew,' Kate was saying. 'You'll just have to believe me when I say I don't know when Great-Grandad will be coming to take you out again, but that I do know it won't be until after Christmas.'

'But what will happen to my Christmas presents?' Matthew's voice was high and indignant and dangerously wobbly. 'Great-Grandad said he'd take me to Harrods to see Santa Claus in his grotto! Harrods is bigger and better than Chiesemans! Harrods is—'

'I must talk to you, Kate!' Emily announced, tottering arthritically into the kitchen, her scarves swinging around her like the ribbons of a maypole. 'It's so very, very important . . .'

'You don't like Great-Grandad, do you?' Tears were streaming down Matthew's face. 'That's why you never come with me when I go and visit him, isn't it?'

'It's more complicated than that, darling,' Kate said, wondering how she could possibly explain to him.

'Matthew can't continue visiting his great-grandfather,' Ruby had said categorically. 'Joss Harvey's desire to see Matthew is the only real weapon we have. If he realizes that, if his objection to the adoption fails, you may never allow him to see Matthew again, he may think twice about going ahead with it.'

'And what else are we doing to encourage him to think twice about going ahead with it?' Leon had demanded in tortured frustration. 'Why won't you let me speak to him? How much worse could it make things?'

'It could make things a lot worse,' Ruby had said dryly.

But Leon hadn't believed her, and that morning, before leaving for the river, he had said, 'I *have* to talk to Joss Harvey, Kate! I can't just stand by doing nothing!'

'Great-Grandad doesn't understand how happy we are with your new daddy,' she said now, struggling for words that wouldn't confuse Matthew more than ever, worried sick as to what might be happening even at that very moment between Leon and Joss Harvey, 'and so he doesn't want your new daddy to adopt you . . .'

'. . . and as you know, Kate, Moshambo is never wrong,' Emily was saying, swinging an emerald green scarf with scarlet fringing out of the way of an interested Hector. 'If only I had known what poor dear Christina intended—'

'*You're lying! You're lying!*' Matthew twisted away from Kate, charging for the door.

'And now Mr Giles has gone to meet Jack at Blackheath Station and . . .'

359

Kate was halfway across the kitchen after Matthew. She halted in her tracks, spinning round. 'Jack's on his way home? He's on his way home *now*?'

Emily nodded, displacing an orange and yellow hand-crocheted creation more the size of a shawl than a scarf. 'That is what Ruth says, but as Mr Giles told me he was going to deal with an emergency, I don't quite understand . . .'

Kate did. She understood all too well. 'Oh my good Lord!' she said, wondering why everything always happened at once. 'You'll have to excuse me, Emily. I need to make things right with Matthew and then I must have a word with Jack. There are things he has to be told. Things I don't think even Mr Giles knows about.'

She whirled out of the room, leaving Emily saying plaintively to thin air, 'But it's *my* news that is the emergency! Someone has to do something! Someone has to do something quickly!'

Jack knew something was wrong the instant he saw a grim-faced Bob Giles striding purposefully across the Heath to meet him. His heart kicked violently. Christina! Something had happened to Christina! He dropped the clumsy cardboard suitcase the government had given him when it had kitted him out in civvies, and sprinted across the frost-white turf.

'What is it?' he shouted as the gap between them narrowed. 'What's happened?'

'No-one's ill, no-one's hurt!' Bob called back, aware that he was not conducting matters in a very dignified way. He slowed to a halt, bending over and resting his hands on his knees, panting for breath. Now that the moment had come, what on earth was he going to say?

'Why've you come to meet me?' Jack demanded as he came breathlessly to a halt a few feet in front of him. 'You *are* on the Heath to meet me, aren't you?'

Bob nodded. 'I thought it best . . . my responsibility . . .'

The word responsibility, coming from a man wearing a dog-collar, drained the blood from Jack's face.

'*Christina?*' he demanded savagely. '*What's happened? Where is she?*'

Bob sucked in a deep, steadying breath. Jack had been a Commando for six years. He wasn't a child. It would be far better to come out with the news bluntly and to save the explanations for later.

'At the moment she's probably in France,' he said, the words so improbable and melodramatic he felt like a second-rate actor in a third-rate farce. 'She's travelling with a Red Cross official, and she's on her way to Heidelberg to look for her mother and her grandmother.'

Jack's first reaction was that Bob Giles was keeping Wilfred Sharkey company and had lost his marbles. 'And I'm the King of Siam,' he said, wondering whether he should bother trudging back for his suitcase or, as he would certainly never wear anything that was in it, leave it for a lucky scrounger to find.

Bob shook his head. 'No,' he said, his breath puffing white in the frosty air. 'I'm not joking, Jack, and I've not taken leave of my senses. Over the last few months Christina has become convinced that her mother and grandmother are alive. Carl Voigt has written on her behalf to scores of refugee and displaced persons' organizations, in the hope that the names of her mother

361

and grandmother are on their lists of those who survived the camps, so far without any luck. Christina believes that, just as she's looking for them, her mother and grandmother will be looking for her and that they will be doing so in Heidelberg, their home town.'

'Jesus God!' Jack was uncaring of Bob Giles's dog-collar. He was uncaring of everything other than one stark fact. Christina had left him. And he knew she hadn't done so for the reasons Bob Giles had given him. How could she have? In all the years he had known her she had never once talked of her mother and grand-mother as if they were still alive. If she'd begun voicing that belief now, it had only been in order to give her disappearance an air of respectability. His jaw clenched so tightly that the tendons in his neck stood out in ugly bunches. He knew why she'd left. She'd left because their marriage was in difficulties. He'd sensed it every hour of his last leave home. He'd *known* something was wrong!

He didn't want to hear another word. He couldn't *bear* to hear another word. Devastated beyond speech, he swung abruptly away from Bob, heading blindly out across the Heath. Something had always been wrong between himself and Christina. Something he'd never been able to put his finger on. Something he'd never understood. For the first time since he'd been a very small boy, sobs rose up in his throat. What in God's name was he going to do? How could he exist without her? He couldn't bear such pain. He couldn't live with it.

Bob stared after him, utterly appalled. Whatever reaction he had expected, it hadn't been pole-axing grief. Had he explained things badly? Had Jack somehow misunderstood him? He groaned, running his fingers wearily through his hair. He couldn't possibly catch Jack up. He was a middle-aged man, not a super-fit Commando. The only thing he could do was to return to the vicarage and wait for Jack to seek him out when he had recovered from his initial, obviously devastating, shock. With creaking knee joints, he turned once more in the direction of Magnolia Square, devoutly hoping there would be no more crises, at least for a little while.

'I'm not waylaying you!' Leon was protesting fiercely, if not altogether truthfully. He was facing Joss Harvey on the steps of a gentlemen's club in Pall Mall and was excruciatingly aware of the attention his dark skin was attracting. It was always the same whenever he stepped a hair's breadth out of the locations and situations a black working-class man might be expected to inhabit. In places close to the river, places such as Bermondsey and Deptford and Greenwich, which were accustomed to the sight of foreign seamen, he attracted very little attention. In Lewisham and Blackheath, heads turned. Outside a Pall Mall club people's heads didn't just turn. People stood and stared.

'*God damn you for your impudence!*' Joss was shouting, frothing at the mouth with rage. 'How can you ever be my great-grandson's legal father? My grandson was a fighter pilot! A man who fought and died for his country! And his son isn't going to be adopted and brought up by a darkie!' His habitually high colour had deepened to puce, and in sinking despair Leon knew he was never, not in a million years, going to be able to hold a rational conversation with him. By seeking him out and speaking to him in person he had made things worse, not better, just as Ruby had predicted he would do. He had let Kate down and he had let Matthew down.

Sick at heart, he turned away. As he did so, a uniformed doorman, vastly relieved that it now seemed unlikely he would have to tangle with him, approached Joss, saying belatedly. 'Do you need assistance, sir?'

'Do I look as if I need assistance?' Joss snapped, regarding Leon's retreating back in satisfaction. 'Of course I don't need assistance! Where's my chauffeur? Where's my damn car?'

His car was parked, unattended, a mere half-dozen yards away. Hemmings, who had slipped across the road to a tobacconist's for a packet of Craven 'A', was standing on the far pavement, unable to sprint back to his post because of a surge of densely heavy traffic. A double-decker bus slowed prior to negotiating the corner with St James's Street. Hemmings took advantage of its decreasing speed, leaping out in front of it in order to try and get back to the Bentley before he was fired from his job. As he did so, a lorry on the bus's blind side, carrying heavy building machinery, surged forward. There was a screeching of brakes as metal impacted on flesh. Amid screams and shouts, the lorry's heavy load broke free of its moorings, crashing into the road.

Leon saw Hemmings's cap roll free of the settling machinery, but Hemmings didn't roll free with it. What looked to be a giant winch lay solidly across his back.

'He's being crushed! He's being crushed!' bystanders shouted hysterically as the driver and the conductress of the bus raced to the scene. 'Call for an ambulance, someone! Call for the fire brigade!'

Leon was running too. The winch had to be lifted, and it had to be lifted now – immediately. It was no use waiting for the fire brigade. By the time the fire brigade arrived, Hemmings would be dead. That is, he would be dead if he weren't dead already.

'He's alive!' It was Mavis, straight off the bus, wriggling forward on her belly beneath the arm of the winch, she had managed to stretch out far enough to be able to feel Hemmings's pulse.

'He won't be alive for much longer if you don't get that winch off him!' someone shouted. 'And it'll have to be prised up and off him, it can't be lifted off, not without a crane!'

Leon was on his knees beside Mavis. 'You get out,' he said to her tersely, 'I'm going to try and prise the weight up long enough for him to be dragged free.'

'An' 'ow the 'ell are *you* goin' to then get out from under?' Mavis asked, wriggling back out of the shadow of the winch, her face chalk-white. 'Do 'ave a bit o' sense, Leon. The fire brigade will be 'ere in a tick and—'

'Get him out! Get him out! What's everyone standing around for? Why isn't anyone doing anything?'

At the sound of the harsh, authoritative voice Leon's head spun round.

''E can't be got out,' a spectator from the pavement informed Joss Harvey helpfully. 'Anyone tryin' to get 'im out will be crushed as well.'

'Someone's rung for the fire brigade,' someone else proffered, 'but I don't think he'll last. He's bleeding from his mouth. He must be hurt horrid bad inside.'

The winch creaked, seeming to settle even heavier,

and there were fresh screams from the women standing on the pavement.

Leon began to scramble out of his jacket. 'The fire brigade will get me out,' he said in answer to Mavis's question. 'If this chap stays under that weight any longer, injured as he is, he's going to be dead by the time they get here. I won't be.'

'I wouldn't bank on it, mate,' Burt, Mavis's driver said pessimistically. 'Still, if you think you can hold it off him, I'll drag him out. I've had plenty of practice. I was an ARP warden during the war.'

As Leon lay flat on his back on the ground, preparing to ease himself under the winch beside the unconscious Hemmings, Joss Harvey dropped to one knee beside him, his camel-coat trailing in the dust of the road.

'It'll take more than one man,' he said tersely. 'I've still got a lot of power in my arms. Let me try and lift from the other side at the same time.'

Leon blinked, wondering if he was hallucinating. Joss Harvey was a great-grandfather, for the Lord's sake! And even if he wasn't, he was far too heavily built to squeeze into the narrow gap between the monstrous weight of the winch and the road.

'You couldn't do it,' he said tersely. 'What you can do is give a hand hauling Mr Hemmings out when I give the word.'

Before Joss Harvey could protest, or make any more ridiculous suggestions, he carefully manoeuvred himself into a position where he could get the flat of his hands beneath the underside of the winch. And then he pushed with all his might and main. And kept on pushing.

*   *   *

366

It was already getting dark and it was bitingly cold. Kate held her cherry-red coat close to her throat and wished she hadn't left the house in such a hurry that she'd left without putting a scarf on. Where might Jack be? Bob Giles had said he had last seen him striding away across the Heath in the general direction of Greenwich. She thought of all the pubs in Greenwich and felt a surge of despair. Her search could well take her all night and even then might not be successful.

'Perhaps you should wait to talk to him until he comes home,' Harriet had suggested when she had explained the problem and asked her if she would look after the children for her.

Kate had shaken her head. She knew Jack. And she knew from what Bob Giles had told her of his encounter with him that Jack would now be in a pub somewhere. Once he was drunk, talking to him would be an impossibility, and she had to talk to him. She had to tell him all the things Christina had longed to tell him and had never succeeded in telling him. As she reached the foot of Maze Hill, at the bottom right-hand corner of Greenwich Park, she hesitated. Opposite her was Greenwich Park Street, which would take her into the heart of old Greenwich and the cluster of pubs around Greenwich Pier. To her left was Park Vista, a narrow road which faced the bottom wall of the park and which boasted a pub, The Plume and Feathers. It wasn't a pub anyone in Magnolia Square ever patronized in the winter, being a little too far to walk in bad weather, but they did patronize it in the summer, calling in for an early evening drink after a picnic or a cricket match in the park. If Jack were going to drink anywhere in

Greenwich, he would very likely do so in The Plume.

Three minutes later, she was pushing open The Plume's door. The minute she stepped inside the low-beamed saloon bar, relief swamped her. He was sitting alone in an inglenook, a half-drunk glass of brandy on the table before him, tension in every line of his hard-muscled body. He looked up at her approach, surprise flaring in his eyes.

'It's all right, Jack, I'm not out on the loose,' she said, sitting down beside him. 'Mr Giles said you'd headed off in the direction of Greenwich, and I thought you might be here.'

'Don't try and commiserate,' he said abruptly. 'There's nothing you can say that can help make sense of what Tina's done.'

'Oh yes there is,' she unbuttoned her coat, knowing very well all the false assumptions he had come to, 'but it's going to take me quite some time to say it.'

'And is it going to make any difference?' There was sarcasm as well as raw bitterness in his voice.

'Oh yes,' she said with quiet confidence, grateful for the heat of the inglenook's fire, 'it's going to make all the difference in the world.'

'Emily's here again,' Ruth was saying to her harassed husband. 'I know you have a lot on your mind at the moment, darling, but I really do think you should talk to her. She says it's very, very urgent.'

Jack pushed his brandy to the far side of the small table. Christ, what a fool he'd been! Christina *had* tried to tell him all the things Kate had just told him. He remembered her words to him after they had made love on the last morning of his leave; she had said there were things she wanted to say to him, things that wouldn't be easy for her to put into words, and then she had told him how, ever since the war had ended, she had been thinking more and more about her mother and grandmother. And how had he responded? He groaned, running his fingers through his thick shock of curly hair. Crassly, that was how. It had never even occurred to him she was hoping and praying her mother and grandmother were still alive. He had told her that that particular nightmare was over and that she had no need ever to think of it again. And then, whilst she had been struggling to tell him of the guilt and misery she was feeling at having denied her religion and culture, he had breezily told her she was now a south-London girl.

'I'm not,' she had said, 'I'm a German. A German Jew.' And even then he hadn't realized the enormity of what she had been trying to convey to him. Thinking he was reassuring her, unwittingly making the situation far, far worse, he had glibly told her he no more thought of her as being Jewish than he thought of her as being German. He groaned again. Dear God in heaven! It was no wonder she'd given up on the attempt to make him understand, especially as he had then left her alone with her mental torment and had gone downstairs to eat a kipper breakfast!

He looked at his watch, his mind racing. The sooner he set off after her, the better. He'd have to fiddle some travel papers and get hold of some cash. The cash bit was easy enough as he had all his demob money, as to travel papers – he'd fiddled far more than travel papers in his time. Adrenalin began to race through his veins. With luck, he'd be across the Channel by midnight and in Heidelberg even before she was.

'Don't bother walking me back to Magnolia Square,' Kate said, reading his thoughts. 'Christina will probably be in Cologne tonight, with Miss Marshall. After that she'll be on her own. The sooner you meet up with her, the better.'

He rose speedily to his feet, flashing her his down-slanting smile. 'You're an angel, Kate Emmerson. Has anyone ever told you?'

'Not this last half-hour or so,' Kate said with a wry smile, her thoughts already skeetering back to her own problems. Would Leon be waiting for her at home? Would he have succeeded in waylaying Joss Harvey, and what would have been the outcome if he had done so?

Jack leaned forward, kissed her on the cheek and then turned on his heel, striding for the door. Kate reached for his undrunk brandy. How would he get down to Dover? Hitch a lift? Borrow Ted's motor bike? And once there, how would he get across the Channel? She sipped at the brandy. Jack had been in the Commandos for six years. He wouldn't let a little thing like crossing the Channel perturb him. If necessary, he'd steal a boat and sail it across single-handedly.

Wondering what Charlie was going to say when she broke the news to him that his demobbed son was *en route* for Germany, she finished the brandy and buttoned up her coat. By the time she had walked back to Magnolia Square, he and Harriet would no longer be baby-sitting for her. Leon would be home and his news could well be nothing more dire than that Joss Harvey had refused to speak to him. She stepped out of The Plume and Feathers' cosy warmth into the biting December cold, grateful for the warming inner comfort of the brandy. One thing, at least, had gone right, and that had been Jack's reaction when she told him of all the feelings Christina had been keeping from him.

'I can't help being a *goy*, but if I'd known how Christina was going to feel about marrying in an Anglican church, I'd have happily settled for Lewisham Registry Office,' he had said passionately, 'and if she'd wanted to celebrate Friday nights like the Jews in Whitechapel and Stepney do, having a special meal and candles and all that, then that would have been fine by me!'

Kate increased her speed as she turned out of Park Vista and into Maze Hill. She didn't want Leon to begin worrying about her, and she certainly didn't want him to set off looking for her. If it had been daylight she could have cut through the park. As it was, it was going to take her a good twenty minutes to get back home, even walking quickly.

By the time she was on home turf, walking briskly down Magnolia Terrace into the Square, she felt quite out of breath. How far on in her pregnancy was she now? Fourteen weeks? Fifteen? The baby hadn't started moving yet, but it would be doing so any day now. She loved those first, fluttery movements and the inexpressible feelings of tenderness they aroused in her. She turned the corner leading into the Square and immediately, in the yellow light of the gas-lamps, saw the black taxi cab parked outside her house and the looming overcoated figure standing beside it.

'What on earth . . .' she whispered, her heart beginning to slam in hard, heavy strokes.

'Kate?' It was a long, long time since he had called her Kate; not since the early days of the war when she had agreed to Matthew being evacuated to his Somerset home and a semblance of friendly politeness had existed between them. Why was he doing so now? Why was he outside her home, and why had he travelled by taxi? Where was his Bentley? She broke into a run, engulfed by fear. Something had happened to Matthew! Why else would Joss Harvey be waiting for her with a face as sombre as that of an Old Testament prophet?

'What is it?' she demanded, distress cracking her voice as she ran towards him. 'Why are you here? What's happened to Matthew?'

'Nothing's happen to Matthew,' Joss said bluntly. 'He's tucked up in bed and being baby-sat by the most efficient-looking woman it's ever been my privilege to meet.'

'Then what . . .' She came to a halt before him, the light of a hissing gas-lamp gleaming on the wheat-gold braid of her hair, her breath coming in harsh rasps, her bewilderment and fear increasing.

'It's your husband,' Joss said, taking her by the elbow and steering her towards the taxi cab. 'He's in Guy's Hospital. He's not seriously hurt. A broken wrist, crushed ribs. But I knew you'd want to see him.'

'Leon? But how . . ? Why . . ?' She stumbled as he bundled her into the cab.

'How?' Joss said as he stepped into it after her, slamming the door behind him. 'He saved Hemmings's life by lifting what must have been a ten ton weight off him, that's how. As for why I'm here . . .'

The cab was already speeding past St Mark's Church. From the adjoining church hall came the sound of Malcolm Lewis's scouts practising carols ready for the Christmas Carol Service.

'. . . I'm here because I'm a man who respects courage, that's why. Your husband may be a darkie, but he's a brave man. Without him, I'd be looking for another chauffeur.'

'And he isn't seriously hurt?' Her voice was urgent, her heart hammering painfully.

'No.' Something suspiciously like a chuckle entered Joss Harvey's gravel-rough voice. 'He was fit enough to be able to ask me if I'd light a gasper for him!'

As Kate sank back against the cracked leather of the taxi's rear seat, weak with relief, a chorus of 'Hark, the Herald Angels Sing' echoed out of the lamp-lit Square and followed them all the way down Magnolia Hill and into Lewisham.

Chapter Twenty-one

The train rolled relentlessly on, through a plundered countryside crawling with the hungry and the homeless, bypassing ravaged, near-obliterated towns. Christina sat on a musty-smelling seat, wedged between Miss Marshall and an over-friendly American GI.

'Wanna smoke?' the GI proffered, shaking open a packet of cigarettes.

Christina shook her head. In the rest of the railway carriage a dozen pairs of eyes, naked with longing, watched as he slipped the packet back into the top pocket of his Army jacket. Her head ached. She had known her journey was going to be traumatic, but already, even before they had reached Cologne, it was painful almost beyond bearing. Everywhere she looked there was not only devastation, there was hunger. On crowded railway platforms, weary women with skinny arms and gaunt faces clutched hold of hollow-cheeked children and pathetic bundles of belongings. London and Londoners had suffered in the war but, heavily rationed though they had been, they had not suffered the kind of hunger the people now crammed into the railway carriage with her were suffering. Slim and petite as she was, in contrast to them Christina felt overweight and indecently overfed.

'*Köln!*' a railway guard shouted through the carriages. '*Bitte aussteigen!*'

Köln not Cologne. *Bitte*, not please. *Aussteigen*, not 'Please prepare to leave the train.' The familiar language reverberated against her ears like waves on a beach. Because it was the language of Nazis, she had, for all the years she had lived in London, barely even thought in it, much less spoken it. Yet the language was her language as well. It was part of her heritage, just as Yiddish was part of it; just as the English her Bermondsey-born grandmother had taught her from her cradle, was part of it.

As all around her people gathered pathetically shabby suitcases and shawl-wrapped bundles, Christina stared out of the grimy windows at a city so destroyed by bombing it seemed impossible that train tracks should still be running into it.

'We're here,' Miss Marshall said unnecessarily. 'Are you quite sure you're going to be all right, travelling down to Heidelberg unaccompanied?'

Christina nodded, uncomfortably aware that the GI had registered with interest Miss Marshall's words. As Heidelberg was under American occupation it was quite possible he was also *en route* there. If he were, once she was no longer in Miss Marshall's brisk and no-nonsense company, he might make a serious nuisance of himself. Not for the first time, her heart lurched as she thought of Jack. Where was he now? She couldn't possibly write to him whilst she was still in Germany. What would he think when her letters stopped arriving? Someone would write to him, telling him of where she was – Charlie or Mavis, or maybe even Bob Giles.

375

'*Köln!*' Someone shouted again, as if there could possibly be any mistake about which ravaged, carpet-bomb-blitzed city they had just entered.

'Can I help you, ma'am?' It was the GI. His smile revealed perfect dentistry. He was young, fit, well fed and hopeful.

'No thank you,' she said firmly. '*Nein danke. Es geht schon.*'

His eyebrows rose. The conversation he had overheard between her and her Red Cross uniformed companion had been in English. And in accentless English as far as he could tell. The easy, familiar way she spoke the German words was a give-away, though. They hadn't been learned parrot-fashion as his smattering of German had been learned. She wasn't English. She was a Kraut and, if the blue-black darkness of her shoulder-length hair and the hint of olive in her skin was anything to go by, she was a Jewish Kraut.

She picked up a canvas travelling-bag and followed her companion off the train. He followed a little distance behind her, still watching her. Christ, she was pretty. Her softly swinging hair had a sheen to it, as if it had been polished. He wondered where she had spent the war years. Certainly not in Germany. There was scarcely a living Jew left in the whole damned country, and those that were, were skin and bone, the expression in their sunken eyes revealing a brutalization which words couldn't even begin to describe. Perhaps she wasn't German but Swiss, and travelling south via Heidelberg to Basle or Berne. He wondered who was awaiting her arrival. Whoever he was, he was a lucky guy.

Christina stepped down on to the platform, the cold so

376

intense she sucked in her breath, reaching hurriedly into the pocket of her navy coat for her beret.

'If you think this is bad, can you imagine what it's going to be like further east, in Berlin?' Miss Marshall asked, grateful for her bulky hand-knitted woollen socks and thickly soled English brogues. Brogues that, in Germany, would have brought her a fortune on the black market.

'Now this is where we'd better say goodbye,' she said practically as they were jostled on all sides by civilians and French and American soldiers. 'Amidst all this chaos there just might be a train heading in the direction you want. You've got all your identity papers and travel permits with you? Good. Then all that remains is for me to wish you good luck and God Bless.' Seconds later she was gone, swallowed up in the throng, far more important matters on her mind.

Christina put her bag down for a moment and pulled her vibrant kingfisher-blue beret low over her ears to protect them from the stinging cold, then, picking up the bag, she set off alone on the next stage of her journey.

It took her three days to travel the near one hundred miles between Cologne and Heidelberg. The bridges that had spanned the Rhine had all been bombed. Hastily erected pontoon bridges rocked in their place. There were American soldiers and American jeeps everywhere. Trains were derailed; were commandeered by occupying troops; didn't run. Breezily confident GIs, accustomed to carrying all before them, attempted to pick her up at every turn. At night, she slept in freezing cold station waiting-rooms. By day, she inched her way nearer and nearer to her destination.

Were her mother and grandmother enduring the rigours of the winter in a similar manner? And if they were, how were they managing to survive? Her mother would now be in her early fifties; her grandmother nearly eighty. Time and again she tried to blot out her last memories of them. The Storm Troopers herding them on to the back of the open truck as if they were cattle. Her grandmother stumbling and falling, her mother sobbing. One of the Storm Troopers had grabbed at her grandmother's hair, dragging her to her feet. No-one who was a witness believed Jacoba Berger and Eva Frank would be seen alive again. And she hadn't believed it – not for a long, long time.

In the corner of yet another rank-smelling railway carriage, as the last few miles separating her from Heidelberg disappeared beneath its wheels, Christina stared unseeingly out at a landscape now familiar and wondered what it was that had so changed her mind. Had it been the sight of Leon Emmerson, striding into Magnolia Square when, for three long years, there had been not a word or a line to indicate he was still alive? She didn't know, but she did know that once the belief had been born, it had refused to die.

Heidelberg's ruined castle came into view. Standing high on its wooded hill, it looked unnervingly unchanged. Had it really been ten years since she had lived beneath its shadow? Her breath caught in her throat. Then, it had signalled home. It did so no longer, for never, as long as she lived, would she think of an inch of German soil as being home. She wasn't home then, but she was back in her past, and her mother and grandmother would surely be there as well, waiting

378

and praying for their reunion with her.

'*Heidelberg! Bitte aussteigen!*'

With savage, urgent hope, she heaved her canvas bag from the luggage-rack. She had reached her destination. All she had to do now was to search.

She began in a narrow twisting street in the old part of the town. The road was cobbled, the houses on either side high and decoratively gabled. Her chest was tight, so tight she could hardly breathe. This was the street of her childhood. It was the street she had played in as a toddler. It was the street she had run down when she had gone to school, her satchel banging against her legs. There, on the right, had been Levy's bakery. It was still a bakery, but the name Levy had long gone from above its door and there were no *bagels* or *bialys* on the half-empty trays in its window. On the left was the room facing the street where Emmanuel Cohen had sat at his shoe-last, nails held between his teeth as he hammered and cobbled, his leather apron reaching almost to his ankles.

Not all the shops had been Jewish. Heidelberg had never possessed a particularly large Jewish population. Wurtz's bookshop was still there. Wilhelm Wurtz had been a friend of her father's. Where had he been, though, when her father had been dragged with Heini out on to the street and shot? Where had any of the people they had lived amongst been? She forced herself to keep on walking, knowing the answer. They had been hiding behind shuttered windows, refusing to see; refusing to be held accountable.

She remembered Nuremberg, and her wool-gloved fists tightened. Some of the main perpetrators were, at

379

least, now standing trial for the millions and millions of lives they had destroyed, but what of the millions who had given them their support? And what of the others? Germans who had never belonged to the Nazi party? Germans who had been appalled by Hitler way back in the thirties and, as he brought their country to destruction and defeat, had continued to be appalled by him?

She walked past Wilhelm Wurtz's bookshop knowing that he, and those like him, were also accountable. That their very passivity made them accountable. Her footsteps slowed, stopped. There was the shop which had once been an *Apotheke* – her father's *Apotheke*. The window was empty now, a handful of overturned display stands showing that it had last traded as a milliner's. Hardly able to breathe, she looked up to the windows above. There, behind the now closed shutters of the third floor bedroom window, she had been born. The room next to it had been her grandmother's room. The room below it had been their sitting-room. Nothing looked as it had once looked. The exterior, once so spick and span, was now shabby and uncared for. Paint peeled off the window frames; the wrought iron of the balconies, once a sunny yellow, were now a patched and dirty grey. A sitting-room window shutter hung by only one hinge. The creeper that had once clothed the upper storey had long since withered and died.

But someone was still living there. Through one of the windows she could glimpse washing drying. With her heart slamming and the blood beating a crescendo in her ears, she walked across to the doorstep and knocked on the door that led up to the rooms above the shop. For a long, long time there was no response and then, at last, she heard sounds of movement. Someone was shuffling along the corridor from the kitchen at the back. Someone elderly and infirm.

'Please God let it be *Grossmutter*!' Christina whispered, her mouth dry, the ground unsteady beneath her feet. '*Please*, God! *Please!*'

'*Ja? Kann ich Ihnen helfen?*' The woman was not, after all, that old. She was simply bone weary and stiff with cold. '*Kann ich Ihnen helfen?*' she asked again, curiosity sharpening her eyes.

'Is . . . Are . . .' Her disappointment was so overpowering she was almost incapable of speech. 'Are Frau Berger and Frau Frank living here?' she managed at last, in German. 'This used to be their home—'

The woman's look of curiosity vanished. 'No-one of the names of Berger or Frank has ever lived here,' she said stolidly. 'Go away, please. I don't talk at my door. My husband is dead – butchered in Normandy. My children are dead. Go away, please.'

'They *did* live here,' Christina said passionately, putting the flat of her hand hard against the door, refusing to let the woman close it on her. '*I* lived here! Have my mother and grandmother been back, asking after me? Has anyone—'

'*Nein! Es tut mir leid!*' This time the woman succeeded in slamming shut the door.

Outside the bookshop, a skinny cat yowled. An American jeep sped past the top of the street, heading in the direction of the Kornmarkt. A snowflake fell on to her cheek. Numbly she wiped it away. They weren't here. She fought a disappointment so monumentally crushing, she could scarcely breathe. Had she really expected them to be in the house that had once been their home? Would there be a Jew in the whole of Germany living back in the homes from which they had been evicted?

With leaden footsteps, she began to walk back down the narrow street, away from the Kornmarkt. Just because she had not found them immediately did not mean that they weren't in Heidelberg. And Heidelberg wasn't London. It wasn't a city so big that people could search for each other in it for a lifetime without achieving success. Mist was creeping up from the nearby river Neckar, snaking over the cobbles. She would have to find somewhere to sleep; somewhere to stay. And she would have to start knocking on doors, showing people photographs of her mother and grandmother; asking questions. Perhaps the American Headquarters might be the best place to begin her search. Perhaps they had a list of people returning to the city to look for lost relatives.

She was again walking past the bookshop and she paused. If Wilhelm Wurtz had seen her mother and grandmother in the city, he would have recognized them. And even if he hadn't seen them since the end of the war, he might have news of where they had been taken to, what had happened to them.

With snowflakes clinging to her beret and the shoulders of her coat, she turned the handle of the door and stepped inside the small, dim, musty-smelling shop. Wilhelm Wurtz was on a step-ladder, dusting the books on one of his top shelves with a feather duster. As his door chimed open, he stopped what he was doing, peering downwards towards her over the top of rimless spectacles.

'*Kann ich Ihnen helfen?*' he asked, beginning to clamber back down his step-ladder.

Christina waited until he had safely descended and then said in German, 'It's Christina Frank, Herr Wurtz. Do you remember me? I lived with my brother and parents and grandmother at number nine.'

Wilhelm Wurtz tottered heavily against a bookshelf. Mother of God! Did he remember her! Her brother and father shot to death in the street! Her mother and grandmother arrested like dogs! How could he ever have forgotten? How would he ever forget?

'*Du lieber Himmel!*' he said hoarsely, crossing himself. 'Where have you come from, child? I thought you were dead. I thought you were all dead.'

'All?' For a dizzying sick moment Christina was tempted to ask if he meant all Jews, and then she saw the distress on his face and knew he had meant her family. 'Heini and Papa are dead, but I don't believe my mother and grandmother are dead. That's why I'm here, Herr Wurtz. That's why I've come back. To find them.'

Wilhelm Wurtz forced himself away from the support of the bookshelves and stepped unsteadily towards her. 'But they're dead, child. Surely they are dead? No-one taken away as your mother and grandmother were taken away, ever returned to their homes. Such terrible years they have been – terrible years.' He reached out for her hands, grasping hold of them, tears of shame and guilt misting his spectacle lenses. 'The Levys were taken away, too, then the Cohens, and others – so many others. What could Germans like myself do? There was talk of people like your family being resettled in the far east of the country. For a long time we believed it. We believed it because we wanted to believe it. But now . . . Nuremberg . . . the newsreels of the camps . . .'

Though tears were now rolling down his face, Christina said nothing. What did he expect her to say? That she understood why he, and others like him, had put their own safety first, not speaking out as their Jewish neighbours were hounded or dragged from their homes? Why they had pretended those taken away were being 'resettled', when anyone with their wits about them would have known they were being rail-roaded across the country into death camps.

He turned his head away, unable to look her in the eyes. For a long moment silence stretched between them and then Christina said, 'You said that you thought all my family were dead, Herr Wurtz. Does that mean you haven't seen my mother or grandmother since their arrest? They haven't been back here, looking for me?'

He shook his head. '*Nein*,' he said thickly. 'No-one has been looking for you, child. And if they do, where shall I tell them to find you? Where are you living now? How did you survive?'

'I live in London.' The words seemed strange, alien, almost unbelievable. 'I live at number twelve Magnolia Square. And I'm married. My married name is Robson.'

Wilhelm Wurtz stared at her. 'An Englishman?'

Christina thought of Cologne, bombed into rubble by the RAF. 'Yes,' she said unapologetically, thinking of other things. Of Dachau and Belsen and Sachsenhausen, of Buchenwald and Ravensbrueck and Maidenek. Of

384

horrors and nightmares beyond speech or imagining.

Wisely, Wilhelm Wurtz kept his thoughts to himself and took a stubby pencil from behind his ear. He would write the address down, just in case anyone should come searching for her. But he wouldn't tell his wife about it. He wouldn't tell anyone. 'The woman now living in your family home is a slut,' he said as he walked her to the door. 'She never cleans. The street is becoming a slum. It was different in the old days, before the war, before Hitler.'

Christina turned her coat collar up against the cold. '*Auf Wiedersehen,*' she said, not wanting to talk about the woman now living in the house; not wanting to know what kind of a housewife she was. Once out in the street, she took one last look towards the house of her birth. A yellow smudge was still faintly discernible on the brickwork, near the door. It was where Storm Troopers had painted a yellow Star of David.

With her jaw clenched tight, she turned away, walking quickly down the street in the direction of the Marktplatz. Once she had found her mother and grandmother, she would take them away from Heidelberg and out of Germany, and none of them would ever return. As she thought of how her friends and neighbours in Magnolia Square would greet and cherish them, homesickness swept over her in swamping waves. Everyone would immediately befriend them, just as they had befriended her. Kate and Carrie, Miriam and Leah, Ruth and Pru, Emily and Esther, Harriet and Nellie, even Hettie and Anna. And the men, too. Mr Giles would see that they were housed. Albert would tend their garden for them, and give them the pick of the produce from his fruit and vegetable stall. Charlie would amble across the Heath with them. Leon would make sure all their odd jobs were done. Daniel Collins would amiably pass the time of day with them. Carl Voigt would give them back their faith in human nature.

She came to a halt at the junction of the Marktplatz and the picturesque alleyway leading to the river, blinded by tears, overcome by love for all the people who now made up her world. Her heart seemed to lurch within her breast as she thought of the person she loved the most. She had to be able to complete her search and return with her mother and grandmother to England before he was demobbed, for if he were demobbed and returned home in her absence, he would never understand, not in a million years.

She turned right, walking down Steingasse to the Alte Brücke, as she had done so many hundreds of times in her other life – the life before the rise of Adolf Hitler. Despite being shrapnel-blasted and battered, the old town bridge still stood. River mist swirled around the base of its turrets, clothing it in a semblance of its pre-war picturesqueness. She walked under the portcullis that led on to it and then stood, her hands deep in her pockets, staring down into the slow-moving waters of the Neckar. What would Jack say when he knew what she had done? Would he see her action as being some kind of a betrayal? He thought of her as a south-London girl, little different from Kate and Carrie and Mavis and Pru. He would have to think differently now. And he might not want to do so.

She shivered, feeling suddenly violently unwell. There was pain behind her eyes and a sickly queasiness in her stomach. Abruptly she turned away from the sight of the grey-green water. She had to find somewhere to sleep; somewhere to stay. And tomorrow she had to begin a search of the city, a search that would leave not a single stone unturned.

The room she found was on Augustinerstrasse. It was meanly furnished and, in a city and a country where coal was as rare as gold-dust, freezingly cold. It was, however, still in the old part of the city, and she slept in her clothes, her coat spread over the worn blankets for extra warmth.

After less than an hour, she knew that her feeling of sickness was nothing to do with fear of what the future held for her and Jack. She was shivering and shaking, not with mere cold, but with a raging temperature.

Morning brought no relief. Deeply grateful for the English tea and biscuits she had brought with her, she forced herself out on to the icy streets to begin her search. However bad she was feeling, her mother and grandmother were probably feeling much worse. In Cologne there had been what had seemed to be armies of middle-aged and elderly women, toiling amid the ruins of their city, extracting with their bare hands bricks that could be used for the rebuilding of houses. It wasn't beyond the realms of possibility that her mother and grandmother were also *Trummerfrauen*, 'rubble women'. Every city she had passed through on her way to Heidelberg had had them. In Heidelberg, they were picking clean a bomb site behind the *Rathaus*. With fear and hope, Christina searched every weary, defeated face. None were familiar and, when she clambered to join them and showed them her photographs of her mother

387

and grandmother, none of them recognized Eva or Jacoba.

None of the residents living in the shadow of the *Heiliggeistkirche* recognized them either, nor any of the residents of Hauptstrasse nor Ingrimstrasse nor Schlosstrasse.

At the American Headquarters, she was eyed appreciatively, leered at and wolf-whistled at, but given no help or hope. There were no lists of people who had returned to the city, trying to trace family or friends. The names Berger and Frank meant nothing. However, if she wanted a decent meal that evening . . . a night out on the town . . ?

Hot and cold, alternately sweating and shivering, the pain behind her eyes almost crippling her, she had declined all hopeful invitations and forced herself to continue with her house-to-house search. It wasn't an easy task. 'Berger? Frank?' Person after person shook their heads. 'No,' they said when she showed them the photographs. 'I don't recognize them. Don't know them. Haven't seen them.'

By the end of the second day she felt so ill, she could scarcely stand. A doctor was out of the question. She hadn't enough money on her for a doctor. And she had to finish her search. She had been so sure her mother and grandmother were in Heidelberg. They *had* to be in Heidelberg, for if they weren't in Heidelberg, where were they?

'No.'

'Don't know them.'

'Don't recognize them.'

Dizzyingly, Christina wondered how many people

were lying to her. Her grandmother had lived in the city for forty years, her mother had been born there. Some of the people whose doors she had knocked on must have recognized them, even if they hadn't seen them since their arrest in 1936. And they must have recognized her, too. Why, then, didn't *she* recognize anyone? Face after face seemed indistinguishable and blurred. The cobbles she was walking on seemed to shelve away at her feet. In the bitter cold, sweat sheened her face and beaded her eyelashes.

Her mother and grandmother weren't here. They weren't looking for her. They were never going to be reunited. The knowledge was like an avalanche of ice, piercing her to her very soul. They weren't here, and she was going to have to return home without them. Home. *Home!* Sobs rose in her throat at the thought of Magnolia Square; at the thought of the green, gorse-flecked expanse of the Heath; of the Thames as it coiled its stately way past Greenwich, thick with tugs and ships.

She wanted to be home, back in that little triangle of south-east London she had come to love with all her heart. She wanted to hear the cry of rag-and-bone men; the clop and rattle of Albert's horse-drawn hearse-cum-vegetable cart; the rattle of Rose's tricycle wheels as she veered into the pathway of number eighteen; Nellie's cackling laughter; Carrie's throaty chuckles. She wanted to smell fish and chips; pie, mash and eels; tripe and onions done in milk; steak and kidney pudding. She wanted to be home and, above all, she wanted to be with Jack.

She was once again at the bottom of Augustinerstrasse, and she leaned against a house wall for support. Jack. In not taking him into her confidence, in excluding him from the obsession that had taken over her life, had she ruined her relationship with him for ever? If she had, she would never be able to forgive herself, not even if she lived to be an old, old lady. She knew that she had to push herself away from the wall, that she had somehow to make her way back to the room she had rented, but she couldn't move. If she moved, her legs would give way. How was she going to begin her journey back to England when she didn't have the strength to walk even a few yards? What if she never saw England again – never saw Jack again?

She wanted to be with him again so much she ached for him down to her fingertips. She wanted to be with him so much that, far down the street she could practically see him, talking to a woman on a doorstep, broad-shouldered and lean-hipped, his thick shock of unruly dark hair tumbling low over his brows. The door closed and the broad-shouldered, lean-hipped figure turned away and looked down Augustinerstrasse. Hazel eyes met hers.

As her legs buckled beneath her she heard him shout, '*Tina!* TINA!' and then he was sprinting towards her, terror and relief fighting for supremacy on his hard-boned face.

'Tina! Oh my God!' His arms were round her, cradling her to him. 'I thought I was never going to find you, Tina! I thought I was going to be searching this Goddamned country for ever!'

'You've come for me?' She stared dazedly up into his dearly loved face, hardly daring to believe that he wasn't a hallucination. 'You're going to take me home?'

He rocked her against him, tears of relief and

thankfulness streaming down his face. 'Yes,' he said, his voice raw with the depth of his love. 'I'm going to take you home, Tina – back to England, back to London, back to Magnolia Square.'

Chapter Twenty-two

And a terrible time they 'ad of it,' Nellie said to Hettie as hey sat squarely in two armchairs in the Emmersons' iving-room, supervising Billy and Beryl and Rose and Daisy as they put up coloured paper-chains ready for he Christmas Eve party that was about to start. 'On the edge of pneumonia, she was. Gawd knows wot would ave 'appened to 'er if Jack 'adn't gorn and found 'er. She'd 'ave died, I reckon. She still don't look too good, all blue shadows round 'er eyes and no roses in 'er cheeks.'

Christina had never been one of Hettie's favourite people, but it was Christmas, the season of goodwill, and the poor girl had certainly had a rough time of it.

'She'll pick up now she's 'ome,' she said comfortably, 'especially now she's sorted things out with Mr Giles.'

'Mr Giles?' Nellie snapped to attention, or she did as far as her twenty stone would allow. Hettie's flower arranging at St Mark's meant she often picked up bits and pieces of vicarage gossip that no-one else stood a cat in hell's chance of overhearing. 'Wot's bin wrong between Christina and the Vicar?'

Hettie looked around to make sure no-one was listening in on them and then, satisfied they weren't, leaned towards Nellie, lowering her voice, saying ominously, 'Religion!'

Nellie blinked. It wasn't quite what she had expected, and it was a bit of a let-down. 'Well, 'e is a vicar when all's said and done, 'Ettie,' she said reasonably. 'I suppose if 'e wants to talk about religion 'e 'as more right than most—'

'Not *his* religion,' Hettie said exasperatedly, '*hers.*' Mindful that the house was full of friends and neighbours, she lowered her voice even further. 'It seems as if Mr Giles should never have married her and Jack in St Mark's, only at the time she said it was what she wanted, and what with it being the war and everything, and Mr Giles always being so obliging—'

'Are you trying to tell me Christina and Jack ain't legally married?' Nellie's eyes were as round as saucers. 'Snakes alive but that'll be a rum do, won't it? She was very nicely brought up, was Christina. Leah says 'er father was a professional man, a chemist. She won't be 'appy livin' over the brush—'

'They aren't living over the brush!' There were times when Hettie wanted to give Nellie a good shake, but Nellie's mountainous bulk made such expressions of exasperation impossible. 'Being married in church is a civil ceremony as well as a religious ceremony. That's why the happy couple have to sign the register, just as they do in a Register Office wedding.'

'Then wot's the kerfuffle?' Nellie asked, bewildered.

'By marrying at St Mark's she was turning her back on her religion,' Hettie said, having overheard enough of Christina's many conversations with Bob Giles to know that this was the central issue. 'And though she once ried to shut everything about her past out of her mind, her religion included, she doesn't want to do so any onger. And Jack doesn't want her to do so, either. He's been with her to see the Rabbi, and he's taking instruction. He says if they're going to have something Christina calls a Shabbas and special candles on the table and eat bread with salt on it, he wants to know what it's all in aid of.'

'Yer mean Jack's thinking of convertin'?' Nellie asked with incredulity. 'Blimey! If 'e does, 'e'll 'ave to 'ave the end of his Jimmy Riddler cut orf! I can't imagine Jack likin' the thought of that very much, can you? Circumspection I think it's called, and it don't sound very comfy.'

'Can I just move you two ladies and your chairs back a bit?' Daniel asked, striding up to them, a beaming smile on his good-natured face as he unwittingly put an end to their gossip. 'Then I can fit a few more spare chairs in around the edges. There's going to be quite a throng tonight. The first Magnolia Square Christmas Eve party of the peace! Even Anna's got her best bib and tucker on, though I don't think pastel pink is really her colour.'

'She bought it herself down Lewisham Market,' Carrie was saying as she and Kate made chicken paste sandwiches. 'I tried to talk her into wearing one of the dresses Harriet gave her, but she wouldn't have any of it. She just kept saying "pink is vunderful", and that it reminded her of candy-floss and summer.'

'And she's quite right,' Mavis said, tipping a packet of hundreds and thousands lavishly across the top of the trifle she had brought with her. 'When it comes to clothes you 'ave to wear wot you feel 'appiest in.'

Carrie eyed the plunging cleavage of Mavis's scarlet chiffon flounced blouse, saying tartly, 'Which in your case appears to be as little as possible.'

Mavis grinned. 'We wouldn't be just a little on the jealous side, would we?' she asked, knowing how bored Carrie was with wearing frumpish maternity tops. 'Yer should lash out on a bit of parachute silk, our Carrie. Yer could 'ide a battalion under parachute silk and still look like Rita 'Ayworth in *Tonight and Every Night*.'

''Eave-ho and up she rises!' Danny shouted as he heaved Hettie's piano over the front doorstep and into the house. 'Thank Gawd it ain't snowing! If there'd bin snow underfoot I'd be at the bottom of Magnolia 'Ill by now with the joanna on top of me!'

'When the boxing club opens, p'raps you should organize a bit of piano moving in amongst the weight-training.'

Leon, relegated to a supervisory capacity on account of the plaster-cast on his left wrist and the heavy strapping beneath his shirt which was holding his broken ribs in a firm position, wasn't altogether joking. Piano moving was tough exercise on the muscles as everyone who had ever shifted Hettie's joanna well knew.

'Can I play "Away in a Manger", Granny, please?' Rose asked Hettie as the piano was finally manoeuvred into the front room.

'Do any of you three lads know how to spell Constantinople?' Daniel, engrossed with compiling pen-and-paper games for later in the evening, asked, 'because if you do, it means it'll be too simple a question for Daisy and Beryl and Rose.'

'We'll be open by the New Year,' Danny said to Leon,

ignoring his father's attempts to be funny. 'Jack says there's no sense in 'anging around, not when Elisha's 'appy for us to set up at the back of The Swan.' He wiped a bead of perspiration from his forehead, his mahogany-red hair standing up in unquenchable spikes despite a liberal application of Brylcreem. ''E's goin' to be payin' me a proper wage, no nonsense about waitin' to see how things go,' he said, a happy grin nearly splitting his freckled, snub-nosed face. 'I give up work at the factory on the thirty-first, and from then on, Jack will be my guv'nor. This boxin' club ain't going to be just any old boxin' club, Leon. With Jack's contacts and my expertise, it's going to be the best there is.'

'Is this party going to get under way, or isn't it?' Mavis asked, entering the room with panache, a plate of hot mince pies held high. 'Dad's serving up the punch, but 'e's 'avin to do it from the kitchen 'cos the bowl's too heavy to carry.'

'Someone's singing carols at the door,' Daniel said, helping himself to a mince pie and having to juggle it from one hand to the other, it was so hot.

'It sounds like Anna and my 'Arriet,' Charlie said, abandoning his efforts at Christmas decorations and lumbering happily out into the hallway.

'Where's Emily and Esther?' Nellie hollered. 'We can't start a party without Emily and Esther!'

Harriet stepped into the house, saying as she received a loving kiss on her cheek from her husband, 'She's being wheeled up the Square now by Malcolm Lewis. His mother is with him and so is Doris.'

'Merry Christ-es-mas!' Anna shouted gutturally, lurching into Kate's hall, resplendent in the ruched pastel pink creation she had been wearing ever since lunch-time, Ophelia tucked like a Christmas parcel in the crook of her arm. '*Prosze! Witaj!* Gut tidings! Great joy!'

'Even to children and to men?' Daniel asked, taking his life in his hands.

Anna guffawed. 'Zum men, my Mr Collins. Zum children. But not all! Never not all! *Dziekuje!* Vere are the mince-pies? Vere is the punch?'

'Merry Christmas, everyone!' Esther's cheeks were rosy with cold from her brief, brisk outing as Malcolm adroitly steered her wheelchair into the living-room. 'Oh, my goodness! Aren't the decorations pretty? Pink and gold chains, and holly—'

'And mistletoe,' Nellie said, a sprig clutched in one hand so that she'd be at the ready if anyone likely came within kissing distance. 'Where's Emily? And where's Mr Giles? He said he'd be popping in before evening service.'

'I have an announcement to make,' Malcolm said as Pru darted in the room to join him, her eyes sparkling, her smile radiant. 'But I want everyone to have a drink in their hands before I make it.'

'Then you'd better wait till everyone comes in from out of the kitchen,' Harriet said practically, looking like Queen Elizabeth in her best dove-grey silk dress. 'I'll go and herd them all up.'

'An announcement?' Carrie whipped off her pinny and fluffed her hair. If an announcement was going to be made then the party had well and truly started. 'Do you know about this, Kate? Has Malcolm popped the question to Pru?'

'If 'e 'as, 'er father won't be too pleased about it.'

Mavis licked a streak of trifle cream from her finger. 'I saw 'im late this afternoon dahn at the clock-tower when I was gettin' the last of my Christmas shoppin' in.' She gave one of her irrepressible chuckles. 'I wished 'im a merry Christmas and 'e told me to prepare to meet my doom!'

Carrie frowned slightly. 'It's all very well laughing at him, Mavis, but what's he going to do for Christmas? Old misery though he is, it's not nice to think of him spending it alone.'

'He isn't spending it alone.' Kate lifted Luke up in her arms in order that he wouldn't be crushed when they went into the crowded sitting-room. 'I asked him if he'd like to come to the party tonight,' she said as her son's chubby legs straddled her hip, 'and if he'd like to have Christmas dinner with us tomorrow. He said he wasn't celebrating an event that had been paganized beyond recognition, but that instead he'd be spending it with like-minded people.' A smile twitched the corner of her mouth. What Wilfred had actually said was that he was spending it with his disciples, but that piece of information would save for later. She didn't want Pru's engagement announcement to be marred by fresh speculation as to her father's mental condition.

'So yer can celebrate Christmas with a clear conscience, Carrie,' Mavis said as Ted took her by the arm and steered her out of the kitchen and into the paper-chain-decorated passageway leading to the sitting-room. 'The only waifs and strays this Christmas will be the four-legged ones Kate's dad's new wife always manages to find.'

'Now that we're all gathered together . . .' Malcolm

398

began, standing on the hearth-rug, one arm around Pru's slender waist.

'We ain't all gathered together!' Nellie interrupted in a voice that would have stopped traffic as far away as Catford. 'The Vicar ain't 'ere and Emily ain't 'ere and Christina and Jack and Kate's dad ain't 'ere!'

'Christina and Jack are coming up the path now!' Daisy volunteered from her look-out position at the front window.

'No, they ain't!' It was Billy, standing behind her shoulder and, in Daisy's opinion, making a nuisance of himself. 'They've stopped to have a kiss and a cuddle!'

'And Grandpa's coming!' Daisy shouted, ignoring Billy's common remark. 'And he's got *lots* of presents with him! Lots and *lots*!'

Ellen, her angular face softened by the happiness that marriage had brought her, wriggled her way through the crush in order to hurry to the door to greet him. This was their first Christmas together as man and wife. Their first Christmas together as a *family*. 'From Grandma and Grandpa' Carl had written on the little cards strung from the children's presents, and *she* was Grandma. Whenever they visited number four, Daisy's face would light up at the sight of her. Matthew would run to greet her. Luke would wind his arms around her legs and beam up at her, chanting, 'Gran! Gran! Gran!' She was loved and she was needed, and she was the happiest woman on God's earth.

'Now that we're all gathered together,' Malcolm said again as Christina and Jack eased their way into the crowded room, and Danny and Leon set about making sure everyone had a full glass of punch in their hand and his mother stood at one side of him and Doris stood at

Pru's side, 'I just want to say how much Magnolia Square means to me. So much so, that I'm going to—'

'Get on with it!' Daniel shouted jovially. 'We ain't got all night, young fellow-me-lad!'

'Where's the Vicar and Emily?' Nellie protested yet again. 'They ain't done a flit together, 'ave they?'

'They'll be here soon.' There was such a look of barely contained excitement on Ruth's face that a temporarily dumbstruck Nellie wondered if the Vicar's young wife was in the same happy condition as Kate and Carrie.

'. . . that I'm going to marry a Magnolia Square girl,' Malcolm finished to a storm of applause.

'Good fer you, Pru!' Nellie called out raucously, recovering her powers of speech. ''E's a better catch than the insurance man!'

'Let's 'ave a look at the ring, *bubee*,' Leah demanded, barrelling forward, all done up to the nines in a toffee-brown dress of shot-silk. 'An engagement ring is the best present in the world, eh, *nu*?'

'Three cheers for the happy couple!' Albert shouted, raising his glass high. 'Hip, hip, hurrah! Hip, hip, hurrah! Hip, hip, hurrah!'

'There's something I want to say to you, luv,' Ted said to Mavis under cover of the cheers that were raising the Emmersons' rafters. His arm was around her waist and Mavis turned to look at him, aware from the expression in his voice that whatever it was he wanted to say, it was going to be something more important than asking her if she wanted her glass refilling. 'I know I've made things difficult for you since I got back home,' he said, acutely aware that for the first time since his demob he was in the same room as Jack Robson, 'my not wanting to go out on the town and all that. It's just that I've needed time to adjust, luv. It's not bin easy for me, away from 'ome, and you an' the kids, for years on end.'

He paused, struggling for words. He'd never been any good at words. Deeds were the things he was best at – showing bravery under fire; being faithful to a wife who was probably not being faithful to him, when the rest of his unit were descending in droves on the nearest whorehouse; doing a hard week's work as a docker and putting his unopened pay packet down on the table every Friday night; loving his family; loving his country; living decently. At the far side of the room he could see Jack, all dark and damn-your-eyes, as he had once heard Hettie so effectively describe him.

His arm tightened around Mavis's waist. 'I don't want to lose yer, luv,' he said fiercely. 'This next year's goin' to be different, I promise. If yer want takin' out on the razzle, that's fine, jus' as long as it's me wot's doin' the takin'. I want us to be 'appy together, Mavis, jus' like we used to be.'

Mavis looked into his eyes, as aware as he of Jack's so-near presence. Around them, for Malcolm's benefit, the room had erupted into a noisy chorus of 'For He's a Jolly Good Fellow!' It was a long moment. She felt as if she would one day look back on it as being one of the longest moments of her life. Was she to go on with her marriage to Ted or, like thousands upon thousands of other women who had, through the war years, discovered a freedom they had never known before, to abandon her marriage and seek a divorce?

And if she abandoned her marriage? She didn't have to turn her head and look towards Jack to know that Jack would never be waiting for her, not in the way she wanted him to be. A wry, realistic smile touched her scarlet-lipped mouth. And if Jack wasn't going to be waiting for her, there was no sense at all in throwing away a good man like Ted Lomax.

'We will be, Ted,' she said, standing on tiptoe in her high, wedge-heeled shoes in order to seal her decision with a wifely Christmassy kiss.

He held back from her a little, his eyes holding hers. 'There's one other thing, luv. Something I'd like you to agree to.'

Mavis suppressed a sigh. Why was it men were only prepared to go out of their way when they wanted something back in return? 'All right,' she said equably, 'if you're prepared to start taking me out on the razzle, I suppose I can't say "no" to whatever it is you want me to agree to.'

'Promise?'

'Promise.'

It wasn't often a grin split Ted's narrow, serious face, but he grinned now. 'I want us to 'ave another baby.'

All around them their family and friends had embarked on a string of favourite carols. As hallelujahs filled the air, Mavis said a swear-word even Ted was barely on familiar terms with. Then glorious throaty laughter spluttered out as she clasped her hands behind his neck, saying, 'All right, Ted Lomax. But see to it yer bring plenty of parachute silk 'ome! If I'm goin' to be wearing maternity tops again, I want to be able to look like Rita 'Ayworth in 'em!'

'Merry Christmas, *Liebling*,' Carl Voigt said tenderly as he kissed Kate on the cheek. 'This is a good

Christmas. A Christmas we've waited a long time for.'

Kate twined her fingers through his, squeezing his hand tight, knowing all the things he was remembering – the Christmases he had spent during the war in an internment camp; the Christmases she had spent alone, and lonely, when anti-German feeling against anyone of German descent had been at its height. Then, after Leon had come into her life, the terrible Christmases when he had been held a prisoner in German-occupied Russia, and she hadn't even known if he were still alive.

She looked around the room, at the throng of friends and neighbours spilling out into the hallway and the kitchen, knowing very well why her German-born father thought the Christmas they were now celebrating was so special. It was because Magnolia Square had chosen to have its collective Christmas Eve party in their family house, eradicating utterly and for ever that almost unbearably painful time when he had been excluded from such community gatherings.

There were other reasons, too, why this Christmas was so special, and not all of them were to do with it being the first peace-time Christmas in six long, traumatic years.

'Leon has something to tell you, Dad,' she said, her eyes shining with a happiness so deep she felt as if it had seeped into her very bones.

Carl looked towards his handsome, muscular, caring and kind black son-in-law. 'The adoption?' he asked, hardly daring to say the words in case he was jumping the gun; in case they hadn't yet heard.

Leon slid his arm around Kate's waist, holding her as close as his injured rib cage allowed. 'Yes,' he said, his relief and joy almost too deep for expression. 'It was granted this morning. Joss Harvey didn't contest it.'

'He said that after being a witness to Leon's bravery he had had second thoughts,' Kate said, well aware that Leon would never speak of the reason. 'There'll be no problem now about our adopting Daisy. We're almost completely legal at last, Dad! We're a family no-one and nothing can separate!'

'Are we going to 'ave carols first? Or charades? Or a knees-up?' they could hear Nellie demanding. 'An' if we're goin' to 'ave carols, can we start off with "Silent Night"?'

'What? With all this rabble?' Daniel retorted equably. 'Chance'd be a fine thing!'

It was when they were on the final chorus of 'Silent Night', Hettie at the piano, everyone crowding around her, that there came the sound of someone knocking on the front door.

'Now who can that be?' Albert said as Hettie continued to play. 'We're all 'ere, ain't we?'

'Emily and the Vicar ain't 'ere!' Nellie proffered, waving her sprig of mistletoe in time to the music.

Ruth, who had been standing next to Esther's wheelchair, rushed for the door as though she had wings on her heels.

'Blimey,' Albert said as everyone else continued to sing, 'I wish Miriam still moved that fast when I knocked on the door!'

On the far side of the piano, Leon and Kate, Christina and Jack, Pru and Malcolm, all swayed to the music as they sang. Or at least, Leon swayed as much as his injuries allowed him to sway, and Christina merely leaned against Jack, looking almost as if she were being

404

physically supported by him, her lips barely moving, her thoughts far, far away, in another time and another place. Mavis and Ted, Carrie and Danny, Miriam and Albert and Leah, were all pressed in around the back of Hettie. Doris and Cecily were by the window, cupping a glass of sherry each. Charlie and Harriet were standing to one side of the fireplace, Carl and Ellen at the other side of it. Daniel was seated in one of the easy chairs, Luke on one knee, Matthew on the other. Nellie was seated in state in the other easy chair. Billy and Beryl and Rose and Daisy were all sitting cross-legged on the floor, singing lustily, Billy cramming a mince pie into his mouth as he did so.

Bob Giles entered the room, Ruth at his side, and there was something so charged about the two of them, such a powerful emotion barely contained, that Hettie's hands faltered on the piano keys and everyone fell silent.

'What on earth is it, Vicar?' Nellie asked, never one to be dumbfounded for long. 'Yer look as though you've just been witness to the Second Coming!'

'I feel as if I have, Nellie,' Bob said unsteadily, his eyes fixed on Christina, his entire attention focused on her. 'Christina, my dear,' he said as if there were only the two of them in the room, 'I've brought another two guests to the party. Two guests you've been looking and looking for . . .'

In the crowded, fire- and gas-lit room a pin could have been heard dropping. Very slowly, with not a vestige of blood in her face, Christina moved away from Jack's supporting arm, walked from behind the piano, crossed the room towards him.

'He can't mean what I think he means!' Leah

whispered to Miriam, pressing a shaking hand to her mouth. 'Ai-yi! He can't mean it! It isn't possible!'

The door behind him, leading into the paper-chain-decorated hallway, was still open. Kate could glimpse Emily, her many scarves reaching almost to her ankles. There were two other people in the hall, standing just out of view of the door. She could glimpse a booted foot, see the wing of a coat hem.

'It wasn't possible to warn you, my dear,' Bob Giles was saying as Christina approached him almost like a sleep-walker. 'We weren't sure, you see. It was impossible to be sure . . .'

Emily moved arthritically forward into the room. Two women, one heavily middle-aged and one looking older than Time itself, moved, dazed and bewildered, into view behind her. Christina sucked in her breath and then gave a broken, animal-like cry that sent every scalp in the room prickling and tingling. The very old woman, her face yellowed and wrinkled, didn't move. Instead, stooped and frail, she looked round at the sea of faces, and at Christina, uncomprehendingly. The other woman gasped and stumbled forward, her arms outstretched like those of a long-drowning woman about, at last, to be saved.

'Mutti!' Christina took one step towards her – two – was in her mother's arms; was clinging to her so tightly, it seemed that nothing on this earth would ever separate them again. 'Oh, Mutti! Mutti! Mutti!'

Leah was on her feet, moving towards Jacoba with all the speed of a young girl. 'Jacoba, my life! Why for don't you say something? Why for do you look as if you don't know me?' She was hugging and hugging her,

406

Jacoba whom she had promised to be kind to long, long ago, when her father had been killed by the nasty Boers, Jacoba who had been her friend for so, so long.

'I don't think she remembers you, Leah,' Ruth said gently. 'She remembers very little . . .'

'*Meine Tochter!*' Eva Frank was murmuring, rocking Christina in her arms. '*Ach, meine schöne, schöne Tochter!*'

'Blimey,' Albert was saying, his eyes over-bright. 'This is a right old Christmas and no mistake.'

'But how . . ? Where . . ?' Harriet was saying bewilderedly.

'Moshambo,' Emily said proudly, looking like a diminutive and ancient pixie in her layers of variegated wool. 'Moshambo told me they were both alive and then, when I asked where, he said to look for them by the Thames.'

'*Grossmutter?*' Still in her mother's arms, Christina was looking towards her blank-eyed, unresponsive grandmother. '*Grossmutter*, it's me, Christina!'

'The *Thames?*' Carl Voigt said disbelievingly, '*Ach, Du lieber Himmel*! How, in the name of God . . .'

'They've been in London ever since 1938,' Bob Giles said, causing everyone to gape at him like stranded fish.

'She doesn't remember you, *Liebling*,' Eva Frank was saying to her daughter, her precious daughter, her daughter who had, by a miracle she still didn't comprehend, been restored to her. 'That was why I couldn't find you! Only she knew her old friend's address. Only she knew where in London her old friend lived!'

'And her mother's been searching for Christina all these years?' Hettie asked, her voice cracking with emotion at the very thought.

'How did they get out of Germany?' Carl was asking Bob.

'Who are those old ladies?' Daisy was asking Kate inquisitively. 'Are they displaced persons, like Anna? Will we have to find clothes for them, like we did for Anna?'

'*Oma?*' It was the name Christina had used for her grandmother when she had been a small child. '*Oma?* It's me, Christina. We've found each other at last, *Oma*.' Tenderly she touched her grandmother's face. 'Please know who I am, *Oma*. Please. Please!'

The tiny wizened figure looked blankly from Christina to Leah and back again. A slight frown puckered the wrinkled brow. 'Christina?' she said at last in a quavering, puzzled voice. 'Christina and Leah?'

Christina took both her grandmother's hands in hers, willing her to understand. 'Yes, *Oma*. Leah lives in Magnolia Square. Do you remember? And I now live in Magnolia Square, too.'

Very slowly Jacoba looked around the room. There were so many faces, so many staring, incredulous faces. The residents of Magnolia Square, even the children, held their breaths.

'Everyone here is a friend, *Oma*,' Christina's voice was breaking with emotion. 'They are all Leah's family and friends. All my friends.'

'It's true, Jacoba.' Leah's face was awash with tears. 'My Miriam is here, and her *goy* husband Albert. And little Carrie is here, only she ain't little any longer, *nu*. When she was little, I used to tell her all about you and me and how we met. Do you remember the schoolroom, *bubbeleh*? Those slates we had to write on, and the smell

408

of chalk and the teacher saying how your pa had died at Majuba and how I was to be kind to you?'

Something stirred in the depths of Jacoba's eyes. Though she was still looking at Leah, her hands tightened on Christina's. 'And you *were* kind to me,' she said to Leah, nodding her head. 'Always kind.' She turned to look at Christina, partial understanding dawning at last. 'And you're here, *bubbeleh*?' Tears began to trickle down her withered cheeks. 'Ai-yi! After all this time, my darling, my dove, at last you're here!'

'No, *Oma*,' Christina said, hardly able to speak for her own tears, '*you* are here. It's *you* have come to *me*!'

'Why is everyone crying, Mr Collins?' Matthew, still on one of Daniel's knees, asked in fascination.

'How did they get out of Germany?' Carl was asking Bob Giles yet again.

'Jacoba has a British passport,' Bob said, knowing exactly how incredulous Carl was feeling. 'They were only imprisoned for a matter of weeks. It was nineteen thirty-six, remember? At that time, Hitler's extermination policy wasn't running at full throttle.'

'And when we couldn't find you, *Liebling*, we knew you had managed to escape, and we knew where you would try and make for,' Eva was saying to Christina. 'But by the time we reached England, *Bubbeleh*'s memory was failing. She couldn't remember her old friend's married name or her address. She only knew it was near Bermondsey, where she and Leah had lived as children. That it was near the Thames.'

Daniel raised his eyes to heaven. Near to Bermondsey, for goodness sake! So it was, in a way, but then so were a thousand streets and terraces and squares.

'I want you to meet my husband,' Christina was saying to her mother and grandmother, her dark beauty ablaze with the joy singing through her veins. Lovingly she led them each by the hand to where Jack was still standing by the piano. 'He isn't Jewish *Mutti*, but he's a *chawchem* all the same.'

'What's a corkem?' Hettie hissed to Miriam.

'A fine man. A man worthy of admiration.'

'Blimey.' Hettie was impressed. 'I've heard people call Jack a lot of things but never that little lot!'

'I'm very pleased to meet you,' Jack was saying inadequately to Christina's mother and grandmother, still pole-axed with shock. Tina's mother and grandmother! And they'd been in London, living near the Thames, ever since 1938! *Where* on the Thames, for God's sake? And how had Bob Giles managed to track them down?

'Where on the Thames?' Doris was asking Ruth. 'They weren't down in Greenwich, were they? They weren't only spitting distance away?'

Ruth shook her head. 'I don't know, Doris. I only know that Emily said Moshambo had told her they were living in London, near the Thames. Since then Bob's visited every synagogue and every Jewish shop and factory south of the river. When he went out tonight it was to make enquiries on nearly the very last place on his list, but he knew a Mrs Berger was at the address he had been given and so we hoped, and prayed . . .'

Eva Frank was still holding Jack's hand, looking at him with unnerving gravity. At last she nodded her head, as if to say that he would do. 'Once it would have mattered,' she said quietly and he knew that she was referring to his non-Jewishness, 'but now . . . now other things matter also. If you love *meine Tochter*, if you are good to her and make her happy, then I am happy, too.'

'What a Christmas!' Charlie was saying, shaking his head in disbelief. 'What a wonderful, wonderful Christmas.'

'Can we have some more carols?' Rose asked, wanting things to get back to normal.

'Can we show your ma and grandma a good old-fashioned knees-up?' Nellie asked Christina, hoping a knees-up wouldn't be thought disrespectful on such a monumentally emotional occasion.

'Can I have another mince pie?' Billy asked Kate, mindful that it was Kate's house they were in. 'They weren't 'alf scrumptious.'

As Daniel and Albert ushered Jacoba Berger towards the comfy easy chair that Daniel had vacated, and Jack told Eva that he hoped she and Jacoba would immediately leave wherever they were living and move into number twelve with him and Christina, so that they would all be living together as a proper Jewish family should live together, there came another sharp rat-a-tat on the front door.

Leon looked down at Kate, his arm around her shoulders. 'Any idea who that can be, sweetheart? You haven't invited anyone else, have you?'

She shook her head. No-one she could possibly think of had yet to arrive.

'I'll get it,' Billy said, darting out of the room and into the hall, eager to make himself useful and to perhaps cadge another mince pie as he did so.

'It looks as if we're going to have two new neighbours,'

Leon said, looking towards Eva and Jacoba and knowing this was a Christmas no-one present would ever forget.

Kate turned to face him, saying lovingly, 'And someone else who is going to be living pretty close to us is making their presence felt.' Gently she took one of his strong dark hands and laid it against her rounded stomach. 'Can you feel those movements, darling? Like a little butterfly fluttering its wings? It's our new son.'

'Or our new daughter,' Leon said, loving her with all his heart, knowing he would love her as long as he lived.

Billy charged back into the room. 'It's a policeman!' he announced at the top of his voice. ''E thought Nellie might like to know there's a young man on 'er doorstep. 'E says 'e's got a kit-bag on his shoulder and that 'e don't 'alf look tired.'

'Oh, my giddy aunt!' Nellie heaved herself exuberantly to her feet. 'Ain't this Christmas just the best ever? Ain't this Christmas the bee's knees? It's my 'Arold! It's my 'Arold, 'ome at last!'

And as Hettie sat herself down at the piano again, Nellie lumbered out of the house faster than anyone had ever seen her move before, intent on ensuring that her nephew would be part and parcel of the best, most memorable Christmas party Magnolia Square had ever had.

THE END

THE LONDONERS
by Margaret Pemberton

Magnolia Square in South London was a friendly and vibrant place to live, not least for Kate Voigt and her father. Carl Voigt had been a prisoner of war during the First World War, had married a cockney girl and never gone back. Now widowed, he and Kate were part of the London life of the square with all its rumbustious and colourful characters. Then came the war.

Suddenly it seemed the Voigts were outcasts because of their German blood. When Carl was interned, Kate's only support was her best friend Carrie, and Toby, the R.A.F. pilot whom she loved. Finally, when Toby was killed, and even Carrie turned against her, she found herself pregnant and totally alone.

Late one Christmas Eve, during the Blitz, she was approached by a wounded sailor asking for lodgings. Leon Emmerson, like Kate, was also a lonely misfit because of his parentage. It was to be the beginning of a new friendship, of startling and dramatic events in Kate's life. And as the war progressed, as the Londoners fought to help each other while their city was bombed and burned, so the rifts in the community were healed, and Kate and those she loved became, once more, part of Magnolia Square.

0 552 14123 2

BLUEBIRDS
by Margaret Mayhew

1939 – And in the back of a three-ton lorry, a strangely assorted group of young women bumped over the road to RAF Colston. They were the first of the Waafs.

Barmaids mixed with secretaries and debutantes. They had appalling living quarters and no uniforms. And, worst of all, the Station Commander, David Palmer, didn't want them. They were a nuisance, unable to do the work of men, and undoubtedly they would collapse and panic if the station was bombed.

Felicity Newman, the officer in charge of the girls, took the scathing criticism with a red face and in angry silence, then began to try and mould the ragtag bunch of girls into a disciplined fighting unit.

There was Anne Cunningham, who knew how to dance and have fun, but found herself peeling vegetables and skinning rabbits in the station kitchens. Winnie Briggs from a Suffolk farm – who longed to work on the aeroplanes themselves but met rigid rejection at every turn. And Virginia Stratton, who saw the Waaf as an escape from a miserable home, wanting to build a new life for herself.

As the war progressed, so the girls showed their worth – behaving heroically under fire, supporting the pilots with their steadfast strength, loyalty, and often their love – a love that was sometimes tragic, sometimes passionate, but always courageous.

0 552 13910 6

THE SECRET YEARS
by Judith Lennox

During that last, shimmeringly hot summer of 1914, four young people played with seeming innocence in the gardens of Drakesden Abbey. Nicholas and Lally were the children of the great house, set in the bleak and magical Fen country and the home of the Blythe family for generations; Thomasine was the unconventional niece of two genteel maiden aunts in the village. And Daniel – Daniel was the son of the local blacksmith, a fiercely independent, ambitious boy who longed to break away from the stifling confines of his East Anglian upbringing. As the drums of war sounded in the distance, the Firedrake, a mysterious and ancient Blythe family heirloom disappeared, setting off a chain of events which they were powerless to control.

The Great War changed everything, and both Nicholas and Daniel returned from the front damaged by their experiences. Thomasine, freed from the narrow disciplines of her childhood, and enjoying the new hedonism which the twenties brought, thought that she could escape from the ties of childhood which bound her to both Nicholas and Daniel. But the passions and enmities of their shared youth had intensified in the passing years, and Nicholas, Thomasine, Lally and Daniel all had to experience tragedy and betrayal before the Firedrake made its reappearance and, with it, a new hope for the future.

0 552 14331 6

A SELECTED LIST OF FINE NOVELS AVAILABLE FROM CORGI BOOKS

13992 0	LIGHT ME THE MOON	Angela Arney	£4.99
12850 3	TOO MUCH TOO SOON	Jacqueline Briskin	£5.99
13552 6	POLO	Jilly Cooper	£5.99
14261 1	INTIMATE	Elizabeth Gage	£4.99
14231 X	ADDICTED	Jill Gascoine	£4.99
14382 0	THE TREACHERY OF TIME	Anna Gilbert	£4.99
13255 1	GARDEN OF LIES	Eileen Goudge	£5.99
14095 3	ARIAN	Iris Gower	£4.99
14140 2	A CROOKED MILE	Ruth Hamilton	£4.99
14299 9	PARSON HARDING'S DAUGHTER	Caroline Harvey	£4.99
14138 0	PROUD HARVEST	Janet Haslam	£4.99
14284 0	DROWNING IN HONEY	Kate Hatfield	£4.99
14220 4	CAPEL BELLS	Joan Hessayon	£4.99
14207 7	DADDY'S GIRL	Janet Inglis	£5.99
14262 X	MARIANA	Susanna Kearsley	£4.99
13709 X	HERE FOR THE SEASON	Tania Kindersley	£4.99
14045 7	THE SUGAR PAVILION	Rosalind Laker	£5.99
14331 6	THE SECRET YEARS	Judith Lennox	£4.99
14002 3	FOOL'S CURTAIN	Claire Lorrimer	£4.99
13737 5	EMERALD	Elisabeth Luard	£5.99
13910 6	BLUEBIRDS	Margaret Mayhew	£5.99
13972 6	LARA'S CHILD	Alexander Mollin	£5.99
10249 0	BRIDE OF TANCRED	Diane Pearson	£2.99
14123 2	THE LONDONERS	Margaret Pemberton	£4.99
14057 0	THE BRIGHT ONE	Elvi Rhodes	£4.99
14298 0	THE LADY OF KYNACHAN	James Irvine Robertson	£5.99
14318 9	WATER UNDER THE BRIDGE	Susan Sallis	£4.99
14245 X	THE GIFT	Danielle Steel	£4.99
14296 4	THE LAND OF NIGHTINGALES	Sally Stewart	£4.99
14263 8	ANNIE	Valerie Wood	£4.99